An

Elusive

Truth

Jerry Timmins

Published by GMT Media Ltd

Print ISBN: 978-1-7393829-0-2

Hardback ISBN: 978-1-7393829-1-9

eBook ISBN: 978-1-7393829-2-6

Cover design and formatting by Let's Get Booked

www.letsgetbooked.com

For Sue, Adam and Clare

This story is partly inspired by real events, but it is a work of fiction with imagined characters. It is set in no specific time because, as Carrick says, time is as elusive as truth. The corruption, drugs, political instability, and violence, which form the backdrop to the story, remain real challenges for Haiti today.

In 1995 its army was disbanded, only to be remobilised in 2017. The National Palace was destroyed by an earthquake in 2010. The geography of Port au Prince has been flexed for the purposes of the story and some place names have been invented.

Somebody who knew Haiti well once berated me at a party because the media does not pay sufficient attention to it.

I had to agree.

CHAPTER 1

Lucas watched, his head barely above the edge of the putrid ditch in which he squatted. He was stock-still, trying to ignore the nauseating stench that rose from the mud beneath his feet. He focused on what was in front of him. On the other side of the earthen road a man was curled in the shadow of a shuttered doorway. He was in a foetal position slumped against the door's hinges, back against the plastered wall, hands around his head, knees tight to his chest. He was shrinking. With every blow the man grew smaller, as if his diminishing size would make his attacker lose interest. But the soldier who was beating him did not stop. Oblivious to the suffocating heat, he continued to drive the butt of his rifle down, gun strap slapping with each savage stroke.

Lucas dropped out of sight and considered how he had got himself in to this position.

Before his arrival in Port au Prince, he had done his research, read widely, studied the maps. He knew this city was a spiralling web of narrow passageways, which twisted through the slums. He had already seen furtive figures emerge from these alleys, stumbling into the boiling glare of the street.

So, when he had reached the junction with the demonstrators and was suddenly confronted by soldiers with rifles raised, he knew what to do. If in trouble, you ducked out of sight. You fled like a thief, zigzagging your way through the back corridors of poverty, where outlaws recognised their own, and pursuers quickly became enmeshed in the threading pathways which narrowed and twisted and sucked hunters into dark corners until finally, they gave up the chase.

And yet today, there had been no opening, no alley, no beckoning shadow. The heat and the shuttered doors had stared back at him. So, Lucas had run. What else could he do? He ran straight up the centre of the street behind the fleeing protesters.

Suddenly, the air around him had erupted. The road spat stones. Bullets gouged brick like rain on water, and the impact was so close it had blown the air out of his lungs. For a moment, he thought one of the bullets had hit him. The imagined impact bent him double. It was only then, with his head down, he had seen the drain by the road. It was covered with concrete slabs to form a rudimentary pavement but two of the slabs had broken away, leaving a gap large enough to fall in to. Propelled by fear, he had jumped, landing in the filth at the bottom. He stayed low, his hand over his mouth against the sickening stench, willing the danger to pass.

So here he was. Listening to the silence.

Silence.

The beating had stopped. Perhaps the soldier had finally become bored.

Carefully, slowly, Lucas peered again over the edge of the trench. The soldier had gone. The man, having finally got his wish, had disappeared. The dusty road running up the hill to his right was empty.

Lucas clutched the bag that held his recorder. On it was the breathless commentary he had been making. In his flight, he had pushed the machine out of sight, fearing it would attract too much attention. Now, he determined to go and finish his report but as he put his hands flat on the ground to pull himself back up on the street, his eye caught movement to his left.

Walking towards him was another soldier: heavy boots, dark green uniform, rifle diagonally across his chest, finger flat across the metal band which cradled the trigger. His face was set hard, eyes looking directly in to his, coming straight at him.

There was no time to get out of the drain. The man was already too close. A desperate inner voice urged him on.

Talk to him. Show him you're not a threat; you're a man like him…

"Je suis journaliste!" His shouted words fell into the space between them. They sounded feeble but surely, he wouldn't shoot *un blanc*, an unarmed foreign journalist on the streets of his own capital. Think of the outrage – the revulsion in the international media.

Lucas held out his empty hands, but the soldier did not falter. He walked the last few steps to within five feet and stopped, still staring down at him. He raised his rifle and took aim at the centre of Lucas's chest.

The certainty of his imminent death brought a clarity that suppressed Lucas's rising panic. If he were to die in a drain in Haiti, thousands of miles from home, he wanted the bullet in his back not his chest. So, anyone who came to find him would know he had been murdered.

Instinctively he turned and, in the second it took the soldier to pull the trigger, Lucas's perception ruptured…

He detaches and, looking down, sees not himself but his sister Zoe on a high landing at the top of a staircase, brilliant light flooding from the tall window. She is turning to him slowly, defying time, her eyes on his. He's reaching for her, desperate to stop her cascading away, drawn by some hand he cannot see. Her fingers brush his, but still she falls, toppling backwards headfirst forever.

And then there was only blood: blood on the bricks in front of him, a searing pain in his head and a shattering explosion.

CHAPTER 2

"I'm so sorry. I'll bring you another glass. Let me clear this away."

The waiter stooped between them, busily gathering the white tablecloth into a shroud to contain the spreading red stain. Lucas sat stiffly in his seat, hands held high above the table as if the waiter had a gun.

The waiter quickly swept up the shattered contents of the cloth. Lucas looked across at Catherine and found her smiling at him, amused by his pose. He lowered his hands, pushing straggling locks back from his youthful face, as if that's what he had intended to do all along, then looked away. He hoped to deflect her gaze onto the empty restaurant. The large window to his right was brilliant in the spring sun. It was barely twelve o'clock. Silence hung from him, as oppressive as an unanswered question.

He glanced back and found her eyes still on him, searching. She was just as he remembered, animated even in repose, her fair hair drawn back over her shoulders, the light catching strands of gold which only the sun could reveal.

"It's good to see you," he mustered. "Has it really been three years?" He offered the question to fill the space between them and quell his anxiety, not sure he believed her when she had said they could still be friends. "Tell me what you're doing," he said. "I thought you were working at Campaign?"

"I am." Catherine looked pleased with herself. "This is my second year and I'm loving it. It's the creative sessions where we all get together to work on new ideas. I find them so addictive. The partners make us all speak. My boss Steve won't let me leave the room without offering ideas, and he dismisses nothing. He's so supportive. He says it's like building a wall. Every brick matters – even if it's flawed – and in the end you don't notice the mistakes or daft things people say because the wall looks so good." She waved a hand to prevent any intervention. "And they really do listen. It's like…sometimes I drop a suggestion in to the conversation and a few weeks later, there it is…on a billboard or on TV…or some part of it is." Catherine's shoulders had risen with her enthusiasm. "I had no idea I could do this. I never thought work could be so much fun."

Her enthusiasms still stoked a fire in him. Lucas had always thought her clever and eager, and looking at her now, with her wide eyes, and long hair held back from her face, he felt a familiar yearning. But he had no intention of letting this meeting rekindle old embers. He was pleased that she was so animated about work. Her words tumbled around him. He hid behind them, not wanting the conversation to become too intimate.

"You've done well," he said, keen to keep up the momentum. "Campaign must be the biggest advertising agency in the country. Funny how things turn out. I was sure you were going to do humanitarian work or apply to the UN or something."

"Oh, I got seduced by them at the careers fair. All these different companies came up to Leicester in my final term. I was heading for the charities' section when I passed Campaign on the way and got chatting. They gave me all this stuff about how they supported good causes. Next thing I know, I'm sitting in an interview thinking they're going to hate all my ideas and my criticisms of big business. But they hired me. They have me doing all the not-for-profit campaigns."

It all made sense, he thought – making a difference, getting bound up with other people, committing, doing good. She was better than him. Always had been. And she had this talent for knowing what she wanted.

He had known her from home, but they'd only started dating when they met on vacation. He had come down from Oxford and she was about to start her first year at Leicester. Catherine had asked him out, brooked no resistance, and after that first holiday she'd visited him regularly.

She was energetic, irresistible, seductive. She volunteered with charities working in the poorer parts of Leicester. Where he would have simply seen poverty, she saw potential and did something about it.

Sitting in the centrally heated comfort of his room above the cobbled, gated streets of his Oxford College, he had subsequently reflected on what she'd seen in him. Perhaps she thought she'd change him. Perhaps she thought the longer they remained together, the more they would grow together. But the more he had thought about a career in international journalism, the more impossible their relationship appeared. Lucas had a growing desire to work abroad and explore new worlds because it led away from his past and a life that had been defined by others on his behalf.

"But look at you," said Catherine, fleetingly touching his arm across the table, forcing him out of his thoughts. "You must be the only arts graduate in the country who didn't want to work for the BBC…"

"Well, I didn't tell them that!" Lucas cut in, laughing.

"And here you are at the World Service. It's not fair, I say."

"Okay, okay," said Lucas, raising a hand to stop her teasing him. "It's true I was a reluctant recruit…"

"Reluctant? As I recall, you were furious at being pushed into it." Catherine gave him a look that told him he couldn't hide from her, and he looked down, recalling what an angry young man he had been.

"I did try at the interview, you know," he said. "I mean, you're right, of course. I wanted to work in print, to become a real journalist and cover foreign news, not do the donkey work for someone's else's glory." Catherine nodded, urging him on.

"I was mad with my tutor for interfering. I'd wanted to make my own way, but all my applications were rejected, and I felt corralled in to applying for this trainee job. I mean I'm grateful now, but I didn't like her interfering, using her contacts. It felt like cheating." Lucas gave an exasperated shrug. "I know I was stupid. I shouldn't have got so worked up about it." Catherine gave him a victorious smile. And Lucas defended himself from his own admission. "I really did try at the interview. I got a real grilling."

"Ah yes – that's right," said Catherine, as if the final piece of the story was falling into place. "The man who interviewed you – the editor – he was a close friend of your tutor wasn't he?"

"Yes, he was. And I wasn't about to embarrass everyone by being honest. But you know something? It's proving to be better than I expected. I think I was just mad at the cronyism."

"Cronyism?"

"Oh, okay – too strong a word. I thought I had done enough to get a job without any help – you know, with the freelance work I'd already done, and my degree. I didn't need a leg up. But I know I'm lucky. I suppose I hadn't realised how hard it was to get into journalism."

So, tell me Lucas. What is it you actually do?" Catherine propped her chin on the back of her hand in an exaggerated pose of a star-struck teenager. "I mean apart from sitting there looking dashing with your brown eyes, that lovely auburn hair and your sexy smile…" She grinned, enjoying the effect she was having on him. "Are you meeting famous people? Are you travelling? Do you wine and dine young ladies every day?" She laughed, leaning forward, eye to eye, challenging him.

"Well, young lady – actually, no." Lucas couldn't keep the smile off his face. "It's been mostly training, or it was until a few months ago. I spent loads of time trailing people, hanging out in studios, learning how to use the equipment. Playtime really. And then I got picked up by this production department and the wonderful Carla who makes International Report."

"International Report," repeated Catherine. "Sounds rather dull."

"Far from it. She investigates people in power. She finds the stuff they try to hide. She makes headlines. Last week she had this interview with a Nigerian State governor who had no idea she knew where he was hiding his money."

"And you do the leg work?"

"Well, I dig out facts and background and do preliminary interviews to make sure we know what people are going to say before Carla sinks her teeth in to them…"

"Do you get a credit?" Lucas shook his head. "Surely you get a credit?" Catherine looked as if an injustice was being perpetrated.

"No." He laughed. "But it's great experience. And I can make my mistakes behind the scenes – which is cool. I kind of hide in Carla's shadow. I still want to go abroad and report. I have a proposal to travel, to research a documentary of my own…"

Lucas trailed off. Sunlight had flashed across the wall behind Catherine. It drew his eye away. The light slid along the wall, and he realised it was a reflection from the glass door which had opened. A short, thickset man entered with an immaculately dressed woman, considerably taller and infinitely better-looking than her companion. They were being shown to a table in the corner. The man looked over at Lucas and then said something to his guest and before walking towards them.

Lucas rose to meet him, but the man put a hand on his shoulder to keep him seated.

"Lucas, I've been thinking about your note. Come to the newsroom after lunch and let's talk about it. Between me and Flo, we might be able to work something out."

"That's great," said Lucas. "I'll come up as soon as we're finished." He was about to introduce Catherine but was cut off.

"No. You stay here and enjoy your lunch." He looked at Catherine with approval. "I'll be around till late. Just come and find me." And he quickly withdrew to where his companion was consulting a menu by the bright window.

"Who's that?" asked Catherine, following his retreat. "He looks a bit scary."

"John Carrick. He's head of News."

"Did he fight his way to the top?"

Lucas laughed. "He may have the look of a prize fighter but he's quite the intellectual. He was a foreign correspondent for years and if he's not God then certainly part of the Trinity."

"Well," said Catherine in a conspiratorial whisper. "He's not the Father – no beard – and certainly not the Son – too old. Maybe the Holy Ghost? What happened to him? He looks as though he's stepped out of purgatory."

"He's not that bad." Lucas chuckled. "Too many late nights, booze, and cigarettes. He was overseas for years. God knows what he got up to."

"Is he your boss?" asked Catherine, sitting back in her seat.

"No. Flo's my boss. She's the one who's encouraged me, especially with this reporting business but if it's going to happen, I need his support. Next to Flo, he's my greatest hope of getting out of the office and into the field,"

"Well, he looks like a hard man to please," observed Catherine.

"He's okay," said Lucas. "My future sort of depends on him. If he doesn't buy into this Haiti proposal I've been

18

working on, then I'm condemned to another year of stuffy offices…" Lucas looked at the table, contemplating this fate.

"Poor Lucas," said Catherine, "tied down in a boring old job at the BBC, which anyone else would kill for, and still not satisfied." Her gentle mockery rolled over him, and he was about to respond when she added, "But then you were always restless, always moving on…" She was no longer teasing. "Still seeing your sister?"

"Yes," Lucas responded quickly, without thinking.

Catherine stared intently, a note of bitterness in her voice. "I could never really compete with Zoe, could I?"

Lucas suppressed the urge to defend his sister. He stared back at her. He was not going to have this conversation again.

They had been destined to part, he thought. He always struggled to handle the conflicting emotions she generated, and his ambition had set him on a singular path that denied company.

The waiter reappeared and, as the Turkish meze was laid out before them, he decided that this lunch would go much better if he asserted control. So, he practised his interviewing skills.

Catherine told him how she'd moved to London and the flat she shared with friends, whom Lucas had never liked, and how she'd turned down other offers to join Campaign and how she was happy.

But the more talkative and animated she became, the more Lucas felt he was being lured back to a past he needed to escape. He wanted to be free from this. Free from others' expectations. Free from the sense of letting people down. Free from guilt about his sister. And that meant leaving.

19

CHAPTER 3

"You disappoint me, Lucas."

The words were preceded by a strong smell of cigarette smoke and a wrinkled hand which gripped Lucas's shoulder from behind. He was walking through the huge bronze doors which led to the central reception at Bush House, the iconic home of BBC World Service. He was keen to get to the newsroom not too far behind the editor, who had left the restaurant twenty minutes before.

"You spend your lunch wining and dining beautiful women. I can't have that. I need you focused on the job. You've got to chase that Freedom of Information request you sent to Armaments UK." Carla's voice was a growl from behind clenched lips that were hermetically attached to a cigarette, which she had pinched out at the door. "Dedication is what's needed, my boy." Carla unhooked her hand from his shoulder and fell into step alongside him as they walked past the commissionaires who greeted her with a salute. The cigarette drooped, as much a part of her face as her nose. "I'm depending on you Lucas. I have a small wager that you will make it into the field before the end of the month." Lucas glanced down at Carla, whose head only came up to his shoulder. "It's a long shot but the odds are irresistible, and I have a dozen takers already." Carla's breathing was short, and she walked with a slight limp which was eased by a pair of immaculate, white Nike sneakers. The shoes, together with today's smart three-piece suit and white lace top belied both her sex and age but the weathered face suggested she was well beyond a retirement that her superiors were afraid to mention.

"I'm touched by your faith, Carla. Really, I am," chuckled Lucas, "but I'm a little concerned that you're risking your money on my future."

"Don't worry on my account darling," she said. "It's just a little office sweepstake. I take ten per cent of the pot as the organiser and wager less myself. But that's our secret, isn't it?" She slipped another sly look at Lucas. "Just go and get that duty trip. The other punters seem to underestimate your chances, so there's some money to be made."

"Perhaps I should put a small bet on myself?" suggested Lucas.

"Oh no you don't," returned Carla. "That would be most unethical." And with that, she quick-stepped up the broad staircase to their right.

Lucas watched her ascent. She had shown him the ropes when he arrived in the department and chided him through a rapid learning process. She had done this while churning out a series of revelatory reports on the nefarious activities of politicians from New York to Kuala Lumpur, setting Lucas on a steep learning curve whose incline had at times unnerved him. Carla had her own weekly radio programme on BBC

21

World Service and a podcast which attracted a large UK audience. Quite how she'd secured her niche in the department, and where she fitted in to the BBC hierarchy, was a mystery. She appeared to have a status which defied all seniority.

Watching her go, Lucas felt curiously unsettled. Over the last year, he had spent more time with this woman than anyone else. Beneath her thick hide, he had discovered a warm, inquisitive mind that probed him at every turn. Their incessant talk of work only thinly disguised the more fundamental questions that kept recurring. What was real? What was illusory? And could you ever really tell the difference? He would catch himself searching her face. It was an endlessly fascinating engraving. Every line etched by some past experience or some lingering hope, still an unfolding story and one he knew he would never quite grasp. *Maybe it's regret,* he thought. *This feeling. Maybe my apprenticeship is about to end. Or maybe it's just time passing by.* He'd miss her. Miss her challenge, her intensity, all the things he didn't know about her. All the things he could still learn.

And he turned slowly to the lift that would carry him to the fourth floor and the newsroom.

"Delhi is on line 3 for bulletins," a woman's voice intoned as the door sucked shut behind him. Across the expanse of floor were rows of workstations around which journalists sat, some bent over their work, some leaning back, listening on headphones. Above their heads, long rows of digital clocks declared the times in all the major capitals of the world. Beneath the clocks on a long bar, an electronic news ticker displayed the latest headlines. Close to Lucas two technicians were staring at wave forms on monitors, as they checked the latest reports which had come in from reporters around the world.

"I have Brussels on line 6 to talk to Home News," came the woman's voice again, cutting through the background chat. On the far side of the room, Lucas could see the editor's glass booth.

John Carrick was on the phone. He waved Lucas in while talking at a volume which suggested the phone was not up to the job of conveying his message.

"Look, I know it's your patch, but I don't want you leaving Miami just now. We've got Congressional elections coming up and we'll need you on standby. I don't want you off base." Carrick looked up again and seemed irritated that Lucas was still standing. He waved him to a solitary chair in front of his desk.

Whoever was on the other end of the phone was speaking rapidly, and Carrick let the receiver drop from his ear for a moment. His free hand reached across the desk to grasp a large mug of tea which sat at the base camp of a mountain of paper. The mountain and a stack of filing trays occupied most of his desk. A split screen computer was relegated to one side, tolerated out of necessity. Carrick took a gulp of the tea.

"Look, Julian," he resumed, "I hear what you say, but this isn't a pissin' contest, nor am I running a democracy. You know how this works. You don't move without my say-so." More pidgin crackled from the other end of the line. "Nobody's saying Haiti's not your patch. You know you're my first choice, but it's quiet at the moment and we have bigger fish to fry in the States right now. So, stay put and wait on the call from Washington. Right?"

The response seemed to satisfy Carrick, and he hung up.

"Right," he said, still at full volume as he looked at Lucas with a critical eye. "Tell me, why so keen on Haiti? It's not exactly the epicentre of the world right now. And don't give me any crap about Haiti being a voodoo portal to a spiritual world or some such shit. I run a newsroom, not the Religious Affairs department."

For a moment, Lucas panicked. *Had Flo mentioned voodoo to Carrick? Of course not. He'd barely mentioned it to her. Don't be stupid.* He pushed the thought out of his mind and focused on what he had written in his proposal, which he hoped Carrick had read. But perhaps he hadn't.

"Well, it's a critical time," he offered, sitting up in his chair. "The Duvaliers' dictatorship ended long ago. The army keeps promising to stand down but – in spite of the promises – has failed to deliver. Every time they've tried to have elections, it's ended in failure. They flirt with democracy, but the army or people with guns always end up stepping in and taking back control. Haiti's one of the few places in the Caribbean that's not stable, and it's in danger of falling apart completely. America doesn't want chaos on its doorstep, with all the problems that could cause in the rest of the region. It's a story we should be paying more attention to…and there's no foreign correspondent based there."

Lucas paused, wondering if he had said enough.

"Yeah – alright," said Carrick, "but we covered the last attempt at elections." He rummaged around in the papers in front of him, not immediately finding what he was looking for.

"When was it…sometime last year… we reported on voters being hacked to death when the polling stations opened. We saw the whole process collapse. We got the story. We covered it already. Now they're back to military rule again. Business as usual."

"But if we fail to mention Haiti between disasters like that, it's the same story every time: a disaster. Our audience will never really understand what's happening if all we do is report the catastrophes. It becomes repetitive and boring…just another basket case."

Carrick cut him off, irritation never far from the surface. "Yeah okay. I buy it. Flo says you show promise and I owe her one, so we're going to share the costs of this one."

Lucas was taken aback. He had not expected Carrick to succumb this fast. He stumbled some thanks but was stopped.

"Let's get one thing straight, okay? This is a research trip. Things are quiet now. You can make the contacts you need and prepare this documentary for Flo – or whatever she wants – but while you're there you need to give me something, okay? I need a holding piece at least."

"A holding piece…" Lucas repeated, wondering whether he understood the phrase correctly.

"Yeah, give me a straight audio report on whether there's any sign of elections being reinstated. They said they would organise them again didn't they? But where's the evidence? Are they serious? You're going to see the Electoral Commission, right?"

"Yes," said Lucas, picking up the cue. "Flo and Carla have fixed me up with contacts. I want to do as much of the groundwork as possible, so we can make the programme quickly later in the year after a second trip. The Electoral Commission will be one of the main players... I can find out what they're planning now..." Lucas was exhilarated at Carrick's reaction. "Thank you," he said. "This is a really great opportunity..."

Carrick waved as if a spider was descending from the ceiling.

"Yeah, yeah. Just get me some facts, Lucas. Give me facts. I don't want promises or thanks or vague statements from the Commission." He jabbed his finger onto his desk. "Have they got ballot papers printed? Are they setting a date? How many candidates will there be? Have they banned opposition parties? Get me some facts we can stand by. And get your contacts. Prepare the ground. Then get the fuck out of there."

"Will do," said Lucas, adjusting to the pace being set. Carrick's tie had been neatly knotted in the restaurant. It now hung below an open collar. His sleeves were rolled up. He looked ready for a fight. Lucas offered more.

"There's a daily flight to Miami. I can go on from there..." He hesitated, aware of the phone call he had just witnessed. "I had been thinking of dropping in on Julian Headley. He knows the place better than anyone."

"Oh God. Don't do that," fired Carrick. "He's not in a good place right now."

Lucas tried to suppress his disappointment. He had been hoping for guidance before arriving. Julian Headley's work had originally sparked his ambition to become a reporter. His clipped factual style and the brusque, almost brutal language he used in his reports for TV and radio had fascinated Lucas. This was the life he had wanted: raw experience, unvarnished reality, a lone voice in a troubled world. He had been looking forward to meeting him, but that opportunity had just been blown out of the water.

"Okay, I'll steer clear, if you think it wise," he said. "I heard his reports during the election violence last year. He was good."

"Yeah. He's a great reporter alright, but he won't exactly welcome you with open arms right now," said Carrick. And he lowered his voice, sensing Lucas's disappointment. "Look, he's got some domestic problems. His wife's left him and took the kids. It's eating him up. And he's not going to like someone treading on his patch. Your turning up will be a red rag. He'll be alright but steer clear for the time being. I've told him I don't want him off base. He needs time to get his head together." He indicated the phone. "I've told him to help out with the Congressional elections." Carrick paused, checking his message had hit home.

Lucas nodded. Some of the gossip he had heard about Headley must have reached Carrick. For a second, he considered repeating some of it.

It was rumoured that Headley carried a handgun when on his tougher assignments, and Carla had repeatedly mentioned his capacity for bourbon. He was as legendary as Billy the Kid, known for his ability to turn up in the most dangerous of places and come out unscathed. He'd made his name in Guatemala's civil war and gone on to report on gangs and cartels across Central America. To Lucas, Headley's ability to remain cool and file graphic reports under the most intense pressure, was something to aspire to: something to give him purpose, counter uncertainty, something that might even keep ghosts at bay.

Lucas felt Carrick's eyes on him but stayed silent, keeping his thoughts to himself. If Carrick had reservations about Headley, it wasn't Lucas's job to dispel them, and he certainly wasn't going to argue about contacting him.

Carrick grunted and started again to rummage in the foothills of paper. He dug out a document which Lucas immediately recognised.

"Look," he said, "I liked your proposal. You've put a lot of thought into it. And I agree. We only ever cover Haiti when there's a coup or a hurricane. Every time disaster strikes, we act surprised. If you want to go and do something more considered, that's fine by me. Use this trip to dig into the guts of the place. I've said I'll share the cost. So that's sorted. Have you got a broadcast date?"

"Next January. It'll be two years since the last aborted elections. The idea is to revisit what happened, get into some of the historical background and take the temperature again nearer the time; assess if the army's promise of elections is any more than talk."

"Okay – sounds like a plan. Flo's a good editor. We're not all boring hacks. She's one of the good 'uns. She knows people make stories. Me, I just want the bones – she can add the flesh. That's why she gets her share of the documentaries on the network."

"I'm looking forward to it," said Lucas. "We just needed the funding confirmed. So, your support will make it all happen."

"Yeah – well don't thank me," said Carrick – back to full volume. "Thank Flo. She won me over." He stood up. He had somewhere else to be. "Give me something I can use while you're there." Carrick walked around the desk. "Steer clear of Headley. He's a good reporter. But good reporters are shits, and Julian's no exception." He took Lucas's hand and pulled him close. "And just remember. This is not all about you. It's about those poor benighted fuckers and whether they'll ever get their votes counted." Carrick's eyes bored into him. "And I don't want any social media crap in your reports. Stick to the facts. Keep your opinions to yourself, okay? If you start telling people what you think, you'll just be talking to yourself. If they believe you, then you're only reinforcing their existing prejudices. But if you tell them what you see and hear, what you're witnessing, there's a chance, just a chance, they may start to see the world as it is and not as they wish it to be."

Carrick released his hand and clapped Lucas on the back, propelling him, as if on casters, out of the door. "Right," he barked, simultaneously closing the conversation and demanding attention from the desks by the door. "Where are the headlines?"

A hand shot out from the nearest person, offering a piece of paper which Carrick snapped up, immediately absorbed in its contents.

CHAPTER 4

Lucas did not take the lift. Instead, he chose the broad marble staircase. Elation bore him down its shallow steps. Yesterday this had all been depressingly familiar, too much like the halls of his school and university. He had come to hate institutions with their stone stairwells, unadorned plaster, and imperious corridors. But today he was unbound.

Told you! Sunshine broke through a high window transforming the scene before him. *I told you it would all work out. But you never listen to me!* The laughing voice bubbled up in him.

"Push off sis," he muttered under his breath, imagining her reaction even when she was absent. But as he descended the stairs, the sunlight sparked the marble into a stream beneath his feet, glistening as he went, light bursting off the walls, warmth touching his shoulders. He was back at home, a child playing on the stairs, his sister dancing round him, their hands refracting the colours that streamed from the stained-glass window above. Happy. They were happy, lost in a world of light, fingers rattling the banister rails, laughing in the light…He loved her then and he loved her now. They were all each other needed, all they loved. Inseparable. A world unto themselves in a world that threatened to fall apart.

"She's waiting for you," said Carla as he walked back into the newly refurbished, open plan office that was home to a half a dozen programmes in the department.

Tables with workstations and phones were scattered across the space between the door and a giant window which overlooked the entrance to the building. Only a few staff were visible. Carla was at the desk nearest the door, the same unlit cigarette firmly clenched between her lips.

"She's in her office," she growled, flashing her thick-framed glasses at the smaller rooms to his left, immediately returning to her work.

He turned and put his head round the first door. Sheila, the trusted assistant, looked up.

"Ah Lucas. Flo was asking for you." And she waved him through an inner door which stood ajar.

Flo swivelled in her chair away from her desk as he entered.

"You've seen Carrick?" she said in a low voice that belied her thin frame. Lucas nodded. "Good, then you know you're off to Haiti. He's putting up the money, so I've got Sheila to fix the tickets for you. The flight leaves tomorrow. You can pick them up on the way out." Flo put out a hand to direct him to the little sofa that adjoined her desk.

She looked tall, even when seated. She sat straight with a dancer's poise, head up, looking down at the now seated Lucas. Her posture created an air of expectancy. One hand suspended, a tilt of the head to invite an answer, her torso ready to rise, she sat always in anticipation of what was to come, as if waiting on an invisible conductor.

"Carrick said he would like me to file a holding piece for him…something to show that News haven't forgotten the story. And perhaps I can do more when I return to do the final interviews later in the year." Flo's expression invited more. "I'm so grateful for your support, Flo, and for the time you've allowed me for all this research."

She smiled her approval. Sheila came in and handed Flo a large envelope, which she opened and laid out the contents on her desk.

Florence Burns was only ever known by her abbreviated first name. Everyone simply called her Flo. There was never any danger of her being confused with another, such was her presence. She wore flowing skirts and floral cheesecloth blouses, which in the 1960s would have been accompanied by long hair, but Flo's hair was always tied up in knots of great complexity, pierced with wooden shafts to keep them secure. She had an easy-going warmth, which did little to lessen an air of mystery. Her contacts spanned continents. There was no story or location that did not prompt some anecdote or observation, apparently acquired from first-hand experience over a long and undefined period.

Legend had it that her father had been an East European émigré, who had been an interrogator for British intelligence during World War II. He had raised his only daughter to converse in a range of languages, including Russian, French, German, and of course English.

There was speculation her family name had been shortened to conceal a Jewish heritage, which had caused her family much suffering. One thing was undisputed: she displayed a knowledge of world affairs so sweeping that her peers invariably acquiesced in debate.

"Now Lucas, you must make the most of this visit. You must take the time to get under the skin of the place. These first trips are so important. Yes, this is research for the documentary, but it's also time for you to see another world, learn to absorb what you don't know, experience a different take on things, open yourself to the unpredictable".

Flo's eyes were steadily fixed on Lucas – checking her words were registering.

"I plan to take full advantage," said Lucas. "I'll stick to research. I know the interviews can come later when I return." Lucas knew what was expected of him. He had worked up his proposal with some help from Carla and re-worked it extensively on Flo's advice. The story of the attempted election, the violence and the dictatorship which dogged the country, was meticulously planned. Flo had directed his reading from French historians to the great Trinidadian C. L. R. James and she'd insisted that, as far as she was concerned, this was a familiarisation trip and there would be time later to do all the interviews needed for the programme once they were nearer the transmission date. "I've been reading up on the culture as well as the politics and you're right, there's so much more to the country than the violence and poverty. The books on voodoo you lent me…I had no idea. My head was full of Hollywood nonsense about dolls and horror and evil hexes, but voodoo actually shares the concerns of all the other major religions like resurrection, eternal life, trying to make sense of the human condition. I thought in some ways it seemed more relevant. I mean, it feels more rooted, more connected – you know, part of everyday life not just for high days and holy days."

"Yes, it's fascinating," said Flo, reaching for a file she had on her desk. "And important. I find the spiritual aspects of Haitian religion quite challenging – helpful, even. Carla's very keen on it." Flo looked across at Lucas about to say something but thought better of it and returned to the file, which she had now opened. "It has elements that can be useful, especially for people who've suffered loss. I'd tell you more, but now isn't really the time."

Lucas was not sure whose loss she was referring to. Carla's? Perhaps. But he had long thought Flo's family history had a dark side. She never referred to it directly, and he had only gleaned snippets from hints that Carla had dropped in some of her more conspiratorial conversations. Both Flo and Carla, he decided, had pasts that only patience and time could reveal.

"I've had Human Resources badgering me," Flo continued. "They always do this when producers travel, and this is your first trip, so I suppose they're dotting the 'i's." She flipped through the pages in front of her. "They've pointed out that there's no next of kin on your file." Flo shifted in her chair, no longer comfortable. "Carla's been telling me you don't like talking about your family – so I'm sorry to bring this up, Lucas. Particularly sorry if they're no longer alive. Is that the case? I fear I had rather assumed that, but Carla – who I have to say fights your corner with an admirable tenacity – got quite cross with me the other day and said I should talk to you directly." Flo looked almost embarrassed. "So, I stand corrected. Perhaps you could enlighten me? So I can put HR's mind at rest?" Lucas had never seen Flo look awkward, and it made him feel bad that he had kept things from her.

"No, no," he said quickly. "They're still alive. They're in Port Moresby, but I haven't seen them for ages. We're not in touch."

"Really?" said Flo, one eyebrow raised. "Surely, they would want to know if something happened to you?" Lucas hesitated. He completely understood why Flo's family history was not a topic she felt happy to share and he felt the same way, but he had not intended his omission about his parents to cause her any problem.

"Well, it's difficult. My father was a member of the Bah'ai community…mother too. It's their whole life these days. We never saw eye to eye. They sent me and my sister away to boarding school and then they kind of moved on."

"Moved on?" Flo sounded puzzled.

Momentarily, Lucas wondered whether his parents were fleeing him or he them.

"They're essentially missionaries, and we…well we never really bought in to their beliefs. Once we were away from home, they put all their energy into work abroad. I haven't seen them for ages."

"I'm sorry to hear that Lucas," said Flo.

Lucas suppressed a rising anxiety. Having fallen out with his father he had gone and kept going, never stopping for long, keen to make his own way. Stasis made him uncomfortable. Momentum kept the past at bay.

"I'd rather their details weren't on my file. I think we're all better off as we are."

"Well, if that's how you feel, of course that's okay." With a sense of relief, Lucas watched as Flo crossed something off a list on the large notepad on her desk. "It's not a problem. It's an HR thing. We can live without it. No other close relatives alive?" Momentarily, Lucas thought of his sister.

"No, There's no one else."

"Understood," said Flo, moving on quickly, sounding a little relieved. "I had to ask. I'll put my name down as a reference. Computers hate blanks."

She closed the file and picked up the large envelope and put a sheet that contained his itinerary into it. "Now, I expect you to call me on arrival and to stay in touch each day." Airline tickets joined the contents of the envelope, which she folded over and presented to Lucas with an air of finality. "Go and get yourself an advance, pick up your equipment and then get off home for some rest before your flight."

Flo looked towards the door where Sheila was hovering.

"Your four o'clock is here," she said. And Flo gave Lucas a look that suggested she'd rather he stayed but stood, giving him a valedictory nod.

"I take it I can call in my winnings," growled Carla as he emerged, her unlit cigarette bobbing in time to her words.

"You can," said Lucas. "It seems your efforts with me have not been entirely wasted."

"Too right," she removed her glasses, the better to see him. "Star pupil. I'll be dining at Rules. So, you're on your way?"

Lucas nodded, unable to suppress a smile.

"Good. I shall call you Dick from now on."

"Dick?" Lucas said, nonplussed.

"Not that thing between your legs," scoffed Carla. "Whittington."

"Really?" said Lucas, unconvinced.

"Spitting image," Carla went on, "except for the cat of course…and the knapsack…and you're already in London." She feigned disappointment at the failing analogy. "But you do have it all before you darling." She reached for an antique lighter which sat upright on her desk and then adopted a pose that suggested the point of greatest interest was far beyond Lucas. "When you're young, time stretches out before you." She flicked the top of the lighter until it crackled to life. "At my age, it's mostly in the rear-view mirror." The flame hovered at the blackened end of the cigarette. "Go grab it all. Do all the things I wasn't allowed to do. Life's too short to regret missed opportunities." The cigarette spluttered into life, and she inhaled deeply.

"I'll do my best," said Lucas, sensing her regret was real. An industrial column of smoke clouded over Carla's head. A passing secretary, on her way to the stationary cupboard, scowled.

"For God's sake, Carla," shouted a male voice from one of the production desks behind her. "You can't light that thing up in here. You know the rules. It ain't legal."

Carla winked at Lucas. "Take care on your travels. Dictators don't like journalists." And she leant back and boomed, "It's the fascists you really have to look out for." Then to Lucas: "But seriously, don't go upsetting them. Use those charms which are so appreciated here." She indicated exactly where 'here' was by inclining her head in the direction of Flo's office. She closed her eyes, inhaling again through the cigarette. Then, with practised motion, she flicked it away so that it arced gracefully into a metal bin by the wall, hissing faintly as it hit the bottom. "In fact, nobody likes journalists these days – dustmen are more valued. So, take Flo's advice. Go and suck up the culture. Chasing down dictators can come later." The secretary passed again on her way back. She glanced at the bin and coughed pointedly as she retreated.

"Yeah, but if an opportunity arose…" Lucas said, only half teasing.

"Don't go there," said Carla sharply. "That's not the brief – right? You're not investigating the President. There's a lot of anger directed at him on social media, but he wasn't the one in charge when those people were killed at the polls. Your topic is the prospect for new elections, so don't get diverted down some rabbit hole. This isn't a diatribe against dictatorship. Get the facts, set up the key interviewees, get under the skin of the place and come home."

"Yes," said Lucas. "I understand. I'll do that but – just to be clear–– we're not impartial about dictatorship are we? I mean, dictators aren't exactly a good thing, are they?"

"Some things are worse than dictatorship. And does anybody want to know what you think, Lucas?" He already knew the answer to that question. "Oh – nearly forgot." Carla leant over and picked up a letter from the desk. "That Freedom of Information request came back. Guess what? Turns out that special advisor at Number 10 does have shares in Armaments UK…"

"…the company that just secured the arms deal with the Saudis," Lucas said, finishing her sentence.

"Indeed," said Carla. "I've got a contact on the Select Committee who's just dying to out our Mr Grant Keller and his dodgy connections." She pulled another cigarette from the pack by the lighter. It took its natural place unlit, muffling her words: "There's something rotten in the state of Downing Street."

She brought her foot up and pushed an office chair towards Lucas, which he caught before it could spin past him. "So, tell me, master Luke, have you been turned to the dark side? Is this now all about you and making a name for yourself?"

"No," said Lucas, sitting down. "It's still the proposal we worked on: find out whether elections are really possible and get the story before the next crisis hits. But who knows what I'll find? If something else comes up, I won't ignore it – if that's what you mean."

"Good." Carla flashed what would have been a smile had her lips not been otherwise occupied. "The best stories start with that," she said, pointing at Lucas's gut. "Don't listen to the accountants." Lucas took this as a dig at the BBC's new director who spoke mostly of planning and value for money. "Don't go with it all planned out. Look for the unexpected. Look for the things that don't fit. That'll tell you what's really going on."

"Don't worry, Carla," said Lucas, "I've had a good teacher. The best." He pressed his palms together as if in prayer. "I have learned well, master. Who, what, where, why, when and remain impartial," he intoned. "I've practised my devotions and had my opinions surgically removed."

Carla's eyes narrowed. "You can take the piss, but to break the rules you have to know them." She raised her hand. "And it's not easy." She took the cigarette from her lips and inspected it. "Since we're in the land of movies and fairy tales and you're my prince about to set sail…" Carla's eyes were swimming slightly from the smoke that still hung in the air. "You will recall that our great leader once said that it's our job to hold a mirror up to society." Carla looked at Lucas to check his attention was unwavering. "Well, sometimes we have to step through the looking glass to get to the story." Lucas sat up. The conclusions of conversations with Carla were always the best bits. "We've covered a lot of ground in a short space it time, Mr Lucas. You've got potential. In fact, I'd go so far as to say I see something of myself in you." Carla turned the unlit cigarette in her hand, eying it lasciviously. "Hard to believe, I know. Me being an old witch from Macbeth and everything." Some reflex made Carla take a drag at the unlit cigarette, which produced nothing but irritation. "Sod it!" she exploded and tossed it on the table. "Look! I know a thing or two about loss, which I'm not going to bore you with, but I figure you're alone in this world."

"But I told you -"

"Yeah, yeah," said Carla, cutting him off. "Your parents, I know they've gone off to La La land to convert the heathen, but – sister or no sister – I fear you are alone in this world Lucas. I sense it." Carla flashed Lucas one of her fiery looks. "You can't hide it from me. I've been there. And it's not good to be alone. Trust me, I know." Her piercing directness made Lucas want to confide more, but she held up her hand. "I don't want to know. I don't need to know. We all have our secrets and our demons. But it's no coincidence that your reading list included a book about Haitian culture and religion.

40

A subject that seems to have caught your imagination." Lucas was silent, and Carla gave him a slightly exasperated look. "In spite of all the venal stories of corruption and avarice we've worked on, some of our best conversations have been about what our senses tell us and what's really out there – that's the very stuff of voodoo, Lucas. So, her majesty – with a little encouragement from me – is sending you somewhere special. Take it all in, Lucas. Got me?"

Lucas was mute; unsure of what Carla knew or did not know; unsure if during their expansive conversations he had let too much slip about Zoe or said more than he intended about his growing interest in voodoo. But her intuition was unerring.

The more he had read about Haiti, the more he had been drawn to the place. Here was a world where voodoo seemed to permeate everything, where the dead and the living could walk side by side, where spirits and ghosts appeared commonplace. As fascinated as he was by Headley and his bloody minded, factual reporting, the thing that gnawed away at him was a feeling that he was missing something, looking in the wrong place. He invariably found his eye drawn not by what was in front of him, but by something off to the side. Drawn to the peripheral, he was becoming distrustful of his senses, anxious that what was just out of reach was more important than what was staring him in the face. And whenever his sister appeared out of nowhere, crowding into his imagination, it somehow felt more real than the solid world around him. Here in London her appearances were unnerving. Maybe in Haiti they might seem more natural. But such thoughts could not be shared. Carrick would never invest in a reporter who talked about spirits. Even broaching such a subject with Carla was too great a risk, although it was becoming clear to him that her intuition was as good as her interview technique. She'd never reveal what she actually knew, and experience suggested there was no point in trying to extract from her things she did not volunteer. So, he just nodded.

"Got it," he said.

"Good," replied Carla – a smile now visible thanks to the cigarette's absence. "Make the most of it. Immerse yourself. Seize the day but stay in control. Don't let your dick overrule your brain."

"Never," said Lucas with a grin. "It has a brain of its own."

Carla laughed and kicked him off the chair. "Go get the bastards," she said and went back to work.

CHAPTER 5

Lucas opened a beer when he got back to his flat, flopping on to the scrawny sofa allowing himself a moment. After the weeks of writing and refining, he felt pure relief. The vote of confidence from Carrick was a real boost. *No leg up. No favours,* he thought.

"So, it went well then, this proposal of yours?" Zoe slid down next to him on the sofa.

Her presence rarely surprised him. They had always been close, even after he'd been sent into exile by his father. She had followed him to boarding school two years later, just as he was moving on to university, and that was the point at which his parents finally decided to put missionary work before their own children.

One day, with no notice, they'd packed up the family home and left, leaving only a small and temporary stipend for the two of them. Thank God they'd gone, he thought. He hated them and their obsessions. Caring for others was one thing, but putting strangers before your own flesh and blood? That cut to the quick. Maybe he could have forgiven them if it had only been him, but Zoe as well…

She cuddled up to him. "By the way, talking to yourself is the first sign of madness."

"I'm not talking to myself; I'm talking to you." He smiled, feeling her presence, letting her fold in to him. Allowing himself this luxury.

"You talk to me all the time, even when I'm not here," said Zoe. "You're potty, but I love you."

A silence followed, as it so often did between them. Whether on the phone when she was away at boarding school or when she was with him, they always had long silences. Presence was enough.

Eventually, Lucas voiced his thoughts: "I hope I can make a success of this."

"Don't be daft. Of course, you can. You've wanted it for ages. You've worked hard and you deserve it." He let her answer sink in, gratefully believing it.

"Thanks," he said quietly. "Your faith is unjustified, but welcome…"

"What?" Zoe leant closer. "What is it?"

"I should have called you more when you were at school."

"You did call. Or I called you. We talked every week."

"Yeah, but somehow it wasn't enough. And it's my fault – you're being dumped there. If I hadn't caused so much trouble at home, I wouldn't have been sent away…and then you wouldn't have had to follow. Perhaps I should have just knuckled down and humoured Dad. At least we wouldn't have been separated."

"I don't think you had much choice, Lucas," came the reply. "It was stifling at home. It was the same for both of us.

But we didn't ask to be sent away. Dad forced that one on us. And I knew you and I wouldn't overlap at school."

In the silence that followed Lucas walked the panelled corridors again. He felt the chill draughts that chased away any warmth from the single hot water pipe that snaked through the common areas. He inhaled the smell of old polish and stale food. The inmates had called it The Rock. Lucas had loathed it and shuddered at the thought of Zoe being subjected to it.

"At least I'm going somewhere warm," he said.

"You're going to be hot, hot, hot!" laughed Zoe, and then, as she always did, she playfully pumped him for information, unpicking Lucas's brain. What was the story? Was this a fight for freedom against dictatorship – another example of a greater and continuing battle between the haves and the have nots? How would he get to the truth of what was really happening?

"Carrick says there's no such thing as truth," Lucas said out loud, bringing an end to the stream of questions. "He says it's just a platonic concept." He sensed Zoe listening intently, and he deliberately recalled the precise phrases Carrick had used. "Time changes truth," he repeated in a crude approximation of Carrick's gruff manner. "And time itself is a chimera. We measure it in hours and minutes as though we control it, but we don't." Zoe curled up beside him, considering this aphorism. "And he's right. What's true one year isn't the next. We call a man a terrorist one moment, the next he's a freedom fighter. We build statues to celebrate empire builders only to tear them down because they were slave traders. A woman murders her husband, but it's only in court you discover he beat her senseless…"

45

"The person you can't stand becomes your lover," added Zoe.

"Yes," said Lucas, wondering whether she had anyone in particular in mind. And then he remembered the lunch with Catherine. "I saw Catherine today. She said she could never compete with you."

"I thought you two were no longer an item."

"We're not."

"I rather liked her," said Zoe. "But I can't disagree. She can't compete with me."

Lucas laughed and went back to his theme.

"Carrick's quite the philosopher when he's not driving the news agenda."

"A news editor who doesn't believe in truth." Zoe considered the idea. "That *is* news. Sounds like a headline."

"He doesn't exactly shout about it. I think it came up in a Q&A over drinks at some training session." Lucas recalled the room full of eager young things, all excited having completed their first news programme – not for broadcast but for playback to the visiting Head of News. The drinks trolley which accompanied his entrance had loosened tongues. "It's not that he doesn't believe in it, he just said it's unattainable. He was pretty forceful on the subject." And Lucas resumed the manner so familiar to the staff outside Carrick's door. "Truth isn't a stone you can pick up. It's not a fucking fact. It's like water." Lucas leant forward absorbed in his recollection. "It runs through your fingers, stretches over time, changes its shape and meaning, confounding your convictions. Those who claim to know it are either liars or zealots."

Zoe's laugh echoed round the room. "Not a mantra to get journalists out of bed in the morning." Her presence spread a glow through Lucas that nobody else could generate.

"No." He grinned. "It's not the classic text for reporters."

Silence descended again like a blanket, wrapping them together until Zoe's young voice said softly:

"You should go to bed. You've an early start and a long flight."

Later, Lucas tried to summon sleep. He turned his head on the pillow to find a more comfortable spot, wondering whether his sister would always materialise when his thoughts turned to her. In the last few months, these visits had become more frequent and vivid, leaving him increasingly troubled. So, when he had found the book on voodoo in his stack of background reading, he had devoured it in one sitting – transported by what he read. The fact that an entire culture believed that they were all haunted by spirits somehow made his hallucinations less disturbing and further fuelled his determination to travel to Haiti. And now here he was only hours away from departure, a final night in his own bed, thoughts and voices clamouring in his head like a pack of hounds, keeping sleep at bay.

*Close your eyes. Get some rest…*He was not entirely sure whether it was his own voice or Zoe's exhorting him to sleep. *It'll be more than a day's travel and you'll not get any shuteye on the plane…*No. It wasn't Zoe. She was gone, leaving nothing but the sense of loss and guilt that always trailed in her wake…*You've got to get some sleep! If you get your head down now, you'll get four hours before you leave…*He turned over and pummelled the pillow, trying to block out unwanted thoughts…*Leaving…You're always leaving.* He knew that voice.

That's what Catherine had said in the restaurant. *Always leaving. Always moving on…*

He rolled on to his back. This was impossible. He gave up, eyes now wide open, unable to do anything other than watch as Sleep turned and ran, pursued by the baying hounds.

CHAPTER 6

Time flexes.

A few seconds can define a lifetime. Years pass, immediately forgotten.

Lucas stood at the top of the aircraft steps, all preoccupation dispelled by the vaporous heat that smothered him. He descended, eyes lidded against the sun, and paused at the bottom, allowing his lungs to adapt to this new medium.

Two spectral figures, heads bowed by the sun's rays, pointed the way. Across the tarmac, a low concrete building simmered. On one side, a ramp led to a battered door, which hung limply, exhausted by repeated use.

"Your business here?" asked the immigration officer. He sat at a simple desk, below a broken ceiling fan. He spoke with a French accent and was staring at the passport in his hands, turning the pages, looking for the visa which Sheila had secured from a non-descript building in London which acted as the Haitian Embassy.

"I'm visiting Radio Rèv."

"Journaliste?" The officer looked up. Lucas stared at his own reflection in the thick, dark glasses.

"Yes. I'm a journalist."

"You have a letter of invitation?"

Lucas handed it over and the officer's head went down again as he looked carefully at the headed notepaper with its signature and official-looking, round stamp.

Radio Rèv, Flo had told him, had done great work. It was one of the brave stations to cover in detail the fall of the dictator Baby Doc Duvalier many years before, when he had been forced into exile. She had got to know the station manager while on one of her many visits. For a brief period, the station had provided a platform for political debate. Politicians and some army officers had argued on air about what should happen next. In the event, the debate had been curtailed. The commander-in-chief announced 'with sorrow' that he had to intervene to 'protect the people' from squabbling politicians.

"This is your first visit to Haiti." It was a fact rather than a question. "Where are you staying Monsieur Gould?" Again, Lucas's reflection stared back at him.

"At the Hotel Etoile in Port au Prince."

"Then you will be a comfortable man…Mr Gould" the pronunciation of the English form of his title was slow and precise, the officer savouring the words. His hand moved to a stamp. He picked it up and punched it down on the open page of the passport, before gathering up the other papers, offering them back as a bundle.

"Enjoy your stay in my country."

With a flick of his wrist, he dismissed Lucas to the passage behind him. It led to the baggage hall where a handful of passengers were staring wearily at an empty and unmoving conveyor belt.

Paint peeled from plaster on the windowless walls. The smell of urine emanated from a door-less frame in one corner. A few airbricks failed to compensate for the absence of air-conditioning.

A noise approached. An old tractor with a broken exhaust, Lucas guessed. Black smoke wafted through the airbricks and then there was silence. The conveyor still did not move. With a bang, a door next to it swung open, and a man started to deposit bags on the concrete floor. Lucas's rucksack followed, and he was thankful that he had carried his recording equipment. He checked his mobile phone. No signal. No messages.

Outside, he found a crowd waiting at the edge of a large parking lot and in among them he saw a sign with his name on it.

"Jean Pierre?" A grin appeared on the man's face.

"Mais oui, vous êtes içi! Welcome. Let me take your bag." Lucas tried to hold on, but someone had relieved him of the weight. A porter, with ripped jacket and filthy cut-off leggings, had appeared behind them.

"It's good of you to meet me, Jean Pierre," said Lucas.

"JP please," his host responded. "Everyone calls me JP." He was tall and fit with cropped afro hair, and a fatigue jacket which was all pockets.

"You must be tired," JP pushed ahead through the crowd "I'll take you to your hotel but first I have a short stop to make, oui?" He talked over his shoulder as they moved. JP's

English was excellent. His complex accent and demeanour hinted at an African hinterland which went back centuries.

"Flo said you'd like to see the station and you can visit in the morning. But today you get some rest."

"Sounds good," said Lucas, longing for a cool shower.

They reached the car, and the porter lifted the heavy rucksack into the boot with no effort. JP offered some grimy bank notes. The ragged helper took them without comment and backed away.

The car was a big American four-wheel drive. Its engine roared quietly through a stainless-steel muffler, pointing at the sky. To Lucas's relief it had air-conditioning.

JP drove fast, weaving down the narrow track out of the airport. Soldiers were stopping incoming traffic and JP drove past the long queue to the perimeter fence where he turned right on to the main road. It proved to be little wider than the track they had left, although it was at least surfaced. JP kept the car firmly to the right as other vehicles swept past in the opposite direction.

There were many lorries, heavily loaded and covered with tarpaulins, flapping with the tortured motion of the frames beneath. They passed breathlessly close, but JP sped on, unfazed.

"This is where all the imports come into the country," he shouted above the noise. The scrub to their right fell away, revealing a vertical drop and a landscape of cranes and containers. "It's our only commercial port. Just about everything comes through here. It never stops."

The road twisted, and they skirted the base of a hill to their left. It was covered in the low, flimsy shelters of the slums, all at crazy angles to each other. Lucas had seen pictures of these shacks, which covered huge swathes of the city, encroaching on every piece of vacant land until, tortoise-like, they formed a thin, corrugated shell against the elements.

Intermittently, he spotted tall poles supporting cables that drooped like skipping ropes. From one of these poles, a bunch of thinner wires scrambled up the hillside into the slum. Some fearless person was tapping the power.

To the right, there was now level ground and fields covered with dense canes. Men with machetes slashed at their base, toppling them in rapid succession, tossing them aside as they moved forward.

JP saw him looking.

"Sugar," he said. "We still export it. The cane cutters come down from the slums." He gestured with his hand to the rear of the vehicle. "Then it's all taken to the refinery further back along the road. We still grow the stuff – even now. We lived off it three hundred years ago. But the world has moved on!"

And Lucas knew then what the strange smell was. It was here, and it was at the airport, and it had grown stronger as they drove. It was the sweet smell of sugar with a bitter edge of filth. The two smells mixed to a cloying cocktail of poverty and hardship. It sat in harsh contrast to what Lucas had read about Haiti's history.

This country had seen the first successful slave revolt in history. These were the people who had defeated one of Napoleon's greatest armies, sent to crush their revolt. This place had been the source of such riches that France prized above all its possessions – for a while, anyway.

Haiti must have seemed like paradise to the pale Europeans who had first set foot in the 15th century. And yet here it was, proudly independent, but desperately poor; crushed by dictatorship and corruption, deprived of its past glories, as if punished for its presumption of freedom.

"We still do everything by hand," shouted JP. "These guys break their backs to cut cane Europeans no longer need. Now they grow their own sugar beat in colder climates. They don't need our cane, and the price has fallen. What made us rich now breaks the hearts of our young men, who sweat and toil for next to nothing." JP pointed at the wooden shacks appearing by the road. "We're not far from the city," he said and slowed the car.

He pulled the car over, rolled his window down and called to a tattered boy who was loitering nearby. After a few words, the back door opened, and the boy slid on to the seat. JP drove back the way they'd come for a short while and then turned on to a deeply rutted track running in to one of the slum areas.

"I thought you should get a glimpse of Cité Soleil on your first day," he shouted over to Lucas. "Thousands of people live here. They come in from the countryside in search of work. Most are disappointed. There's no power, no running water, no drains. When the rains come, this place becomes a sewer. But still they cling on."

Lucas gripped the handrail above his door as the car plunged forward. And then JP pulled up and got out. He left the boy behind as a guard.

Lucas eased himself down and followed JP who had dived up a narrow alley.

"Watch your step," he called over his shoulder. "These potholes are deep. Take it easy."

As soon as Lucas entered the alley, the sun disappeared. In some places, the track was no wider than the width of his body. It twisted from left to right, snaking round the irregular dwellings made from a jumble of old branches and crates, capped with corrugated sheets.

Ahead was a junction where the path split. The remains of an old tree stump stubbornly sat on one side. JP bent to speak to an old woman who was squatting beside it. She was trying to coax a tiny flame from a pile of twigs.

Behind the woman, a dark door frame stood with its two vertical posts driven into the ground. It appeared unconnected to anything else since there was a distinct gap between it and some draped cloth on one side and a ramshackle wooden fence on the other. Within the frame, all was black, and Lucas peered at it as if it were a painting.

"C'est bon," JP said to Lucas. "She knows me. She won't mind if you look."

Lucas put his head through the doorway. There was nothing, just bare earth. The room was so small and dark that Lucas had not been able to see any walls from the outside but, with his head inside the frame he saw it was a narrow coffin-like structure made from earth bricks running straight back from the door frame. You could just about have lain down with your feet pointing towards the door. At the back there was a small mound of earth, maybe a pillow.

Lucas looked at JP.

"It's her house, said JP. She sleeps and eats here. It's one of the few places made of brick in the slums. At least when the rains come, she has somewhere to hide."

"How does she manage like this? asked Lucas.

"How do any of them survive in this place?" JP swung his arm at the hillside. "Her husband died last year, but he was a hard worker and built this. She has children and relatives who look out for her. The younger boys go off in search of work every day – mostly around the port. Whatever they scavenge or buy they share with her, but if they're unlucky, then everyone goes without."

Lucas stepped back, scanning the hillside. "There are so many."

"Mais oui, my friend. Nobody knows how many live here. Take a wrong turn and it could take you a month to get out."

JP bent and gave some notes to the lady who took his hand and put it to her forehead.

"How do you know her?" asked Lucas.

"She's related to one of the girls who helps at the radio station. One day she brought me here to show me where her money goes. We gave her a salary raise after that. What we pay isn't much but a little can mean a lot here."

JP put his hands together in a mark of respect for the old woman before he stepped back.

"Let's go. We mustn't stay too long. It will be dark soon and you're a little…too visible, my friend." JP laughed a low laugh and Lucas quickly followed his guide down the track to the car, where the boy was now sitting – a gargoyle on the bonnet, forward leaning over the radiator.

56

Again, some blackened notes and the boy slid off to the back of the car again. Once they were on the main road, Lucas heard the rear door open. Not waiting for JP to slow, the boy jumped, swinging the door closed behind him.

Lucas heard the snap of the central lock as the door shut.

Once in the outskirts of Port au Prince, the streets filled with people and the car wove its way through the crowds. Just when Lucas thought the way impassable, they rounded a corner into a wider avenue lined with stone houses. Some were single story with flat roofs, but most had balconies edged by iron railings with faded, swirling patterns that spoke of better times. The walls had a mustard hue. Everywhere, people sat on the curbs or walked along the cracked pavements beneath the balustrades. Children swarmed around a cart selling ice and sticky fruit syrups.

JP saw Lucas eyeing them. "I'd avoid the street food here if you want to keep your guts inside your body." He grinned. "The food at the hotel will be okay, but don't drink the water. I know where it comes from. Stick to bottles if you want to enjoy your stay my friend, and of course the rum should keep the devil at bay." JP laughed his deep laugh and Lucas was grateful to be by his side.

CHAPTER 7

The Hotel Etoile was an art deco creation, with an imposing entrance. A small, semi-circular driveway led to a neo-classical arch which sheltered guests from the sun. An enormous square stretched out before it which eventually formed the main approach to the Presidential Palace.

Lucas got out of the car and JP bounded round to lift the rucksack from the boot. A doorman took the bag.

"You should rest now," said JP, producing a small mobile phone from his inner pocket. He tried to share his contact details, but Lucas's international mobile still had no signal.

"Don't worry. I'll call you at the hotel in the morning and you can come to the radio station, oui? I'll have a local SIM card for you. Perhaps then your phone will work."

"That's great, JP. I look forward to it."

"This is my number. It rings at the station," JP produced a crushed business card. "They'll know where I am, if I'm not in the office…" He reconsidered. "Non, no worry. I'll come for you in the morning. I can't have you getting lost!" He returned to the car and Lucas went to reception.

There on the high, mahogany front desk to the left of the entrance, stood a huge cut-glass bowl, full of a cool, purple liquid and next to it a receptionist. Lucas was beckoned forward.

"Monsieur Lucas, we've been expecting you. Your room is ready but please – a glass of our rum punch of the house – our speciality. The bar's always open. Feel free to call for room service or come down to the restaurant as you wish."

The man picked up a large glass ladle and delivered a generous portion of the dark liquid, complete with some of the fruit floating in it. Lucas took a sip from the ice-frosted glass and was immediately seduced by its rich scent. He took a sip and its flavours flowed through him: burned chocolate, oak and a warmth that spread from his stomach straight to his head.

"You can sit and finish it," said the receptionist with a smile, pointing to the extensive lounge which ran away from the desk towards a sunroom, wafted by ceiling fans and bordered by french windows that looked on to a courtyard garden. Through the garden, Lucas glimpsed a swimming pool. "We'll take your bag to your room."

Lucas was tired. He would enjoy this delicious drink and then head up. He moved slowly through the lounge towards the garden and the windows that were closed against the heat. Soft armchairs and sofas, bracketed by low side-tables, beckoned him across rich rugs, and he chose a large leather chair, lined with little cushions.

As soon as he relaxed, unwanted thoughts crowded in.

Since leaving Flo's office, rest had eluded him. He had not slept on the long plane journey and his head ached. He missed his sister and seeing Catherine again in London had unnerved him a little. Breaking up with her had been hard. She had been more upset than he expected and, although she now seemed settled and confident, it had left him with a sense of guilt. It was a feeling he had expected to pass with time. But rather than fade, it had simply hidden away, to return unbidden.

He had a deep draught of his drink, the vapour blurring his senses and bringing a deceptive calm.

"It's made from 21-year-old rum – unique to this place." He looked to see who had spoken and there, his head framed by the high wicker armchair in which he sat, was a lean dark-skinned man in a cream suit, legs crossed, a thick cigar in two fingers of a hand that also held a glass identical to his own. He spoke slowly in accented English, considering each word carefully.

"To make this punch, it is essential to use only Haiti's best Guildive."

"Guildive?" Lucas queried.

"Ah – how would you say… *Kill the Devil*," said the man. "Our voodoo priests use it to keep spirits at bay." He raised his glass, inspecting its contents. "We have an excess of it since the tourists departed. Some connoisseurs say you should only drink fine rum on its own, but what do they know? They've never tasted this."

"It's excellent," confirmed Lucas, lifting his own glass, acknowledging his new companion.

"You've just arrived," the man observed.

"Yes," said Lucas. "It's my first visit and," he looked at his glass, "I'm feeling at home."

"You've made a good start," said the man with a faint smile. "It's important to understand the spiritual nature of this place." He took a sip of his rum to indicate the spirit he was referring to. "Haiti is not for the faint hearted. You must drink deeply if you want to know what happens here. You can't simply apply your white reason and think you understand." He paused, taking in Lucas. "This is a land of shadows, where souls cross from this world to the next. Some return. Some do not," he said with a chuckle. "Don't worry though, we have all the means to help you on your way…" And again, he lifted his glass, tilting it towards Lucas. He took a long, slow drink and returned it to the side table next to him. "So, you're a journalist," he said, as if Lucas had just offered this information.

"Is it that obvious?" Lucas responded in surprise.

"You must be," replied the man. "No other white man would bother to come. The tourists left after the killings last year. Our dear charity workers stay in their compounds and rarely come out. They are like exotic birds – only glimpsed when the moon is full." He glanced over to where the concierge was hauling Lucas's rucksack up the stairs: "And the labels on your bag show you came off the Miami flight. The question is: why are you here now?"

"Well," started Lucas: "I'm doing research ahead of next year's promised elections -"

"Perhaps you've already heard something? Perhaps your editor has told you what to write…" the man cut in, opening his arms wide to embrace the room.

"I'll write what I see, if I write anything," said Lucas, not liking the presumption.

"That's good," came the cool response. "But I wonder what will you write? What will your eyes see? Will you, as others before you, write about our famous poverty or about les Duvaliers and what terrible dictators they were?" He paused again, but Lucas could see there was no point in trying to explain himself further. "They come here and tell their readers how the blacks cannot run a country; how the blacks have enslaved themselves to autocracy. Is that what you'll write? Or will you speak of the true spirit of Haiti? A spirit greater than the Russians who burned Moscow in front of Napoleon; a spirit that burst the chains that bound them; a spirit that defeated slavery with no help from anyone; a spirit that defies all those who would have us back under the very same yoke from which we broke free?"

Lucas assessed the man, who sat so regally, cigar in his hand. Despite the passionate words, he appeared only mildly interested in what he said. He seemed distracted, not entirely present. And Lucas himself was feeling detached. The rum was doing its work accentuating his weariness, blurring the edges of his world. He decided he was not really up for this conversation. He swallowed the last of his drink. It was time to find his room. He stood, a little unsteady, to find his companion also rising.

"We shall meet again. I feel sure Monsieur Lucas," he said, cigar in hand gesturing farewell. "I wish you a good night."

Lucas retreated, not knowing how to respond. He couldn't recall having given his name or whether the man had introduced himself earlier. He nodded a goodbye and moved towards the stairs, realising halfway that he had no key. As he stopped, the receptionist who had taken his bag, reappeared, holding it out to him.

Muttering his thanks, Lucas started up, holding the handrail, the wood reassuring under his palm. He let it guide him to the landing above.

He stood briefly to get his bearings. To his left, a single windowless corridor led away towards the back of the hotel. It was brown, dark and straight. On either side was a series of large wooden doors, set back in their frames, like sentries in their boxes. Each door had an ascending number. His room was number 17. It was the last one, facing him at the end of the corridor.

His antique key slid easily in the lock, and he entered a substantial room, furnished with a double bed, bordered by two low cabinets. At the foot of the bed was another door, leading to an old but reasonably well-appointed bathroom. He checked the power sockets and found one by the bed. Another was connected to a standard lamp, which spilled a feeble light.

He placed his recorder and laptop on the bedside cabinet, next to a square white telephone of American origin. To these things, he added a leather pouch holding cables and connectors and his notebook, letting his shoulder bag from which they had all come fall to the floor.

He then swiftly undressed, hanging some clothes in the wardrobe and taking his sponge bag to the bathroom. He washed and lay down on the bed, more comfortable than he had expected.

His eyes were heavy, and through their veiled curtain he watched an old ceiling fan turn hypnotically until it carried him off to a fitful slumber where two figures he half recognised bade him a translucent farewell through a haze of heat.

CHAPTER 8

Lucas stared at a dark shape on the other side of the square. Its form swam in the air that shimmered above the cobbles. He shaded his eyes and slowly focused. It was a tank. Its sleek turret sat squarely on its tracked body. Its gun was pointing over Lucas's head towards the high hills that rose behind the hotel.

He had been woken early from a fitful sleep by the bedside phone. It was JP, telling him he wasn't coming to the hotel. Something had happened and he couldn't leave the station. But then the line had gone dead, and when Lucas dialled the number on JP's card, there was no response. So, he had decided to get a taxi and find the radio station for himself. The doorman understood Lucas's French and had gone seeking transport, leaving him to acclimatise to the heat and the light. He was still puzzled about the tank when a battered American car pulled up and the doorman, with some difficulty, pulled the rear door open. This evidently was his taxi. Lucas slid on to the battered rear seat.

Before he could say anything, the car took off at speed, shooting out of the hotel's shallow drive.

Lucas shouted the address, trying to assert control. He held out JP's business card and waved it next to the driver's right ear, which was as far as he could reach with the car in motion.

The driver let go of the rotary knob on the steering wheel, which allowed him to steer with one hand and took the card. With the wheel unattended, he looked at it. Immediately he spat a stream of invective in Creole, tossing the card on to the dashboard before grabbing the wheel again to stop the car careering off the road. He then swung the knob violently down towards the floor. Immediately, they veered left into a small side street and lurched to a stop.

Lucas was flung forward and back, and a young face twisted round, revealing that his driver was little more than a boy. He was dressed in a T-shirt and shorts, both well worn, and he was grinning at Lucas as if he was his long-lost friend.

"Me Henri!" he shouted, laughing through his broken English and he held out his left hand – the same one he used to grip the knob on the steering wheel. His other one was missing. Henri's right arm ended in a stump, which was currently propped on the front passenger seat to prevent its owner from toppling sideways.

Lucas gently took the offered hand and squeezed.

"Your driver...I'm your...Guide...you need guide in this city. I look after you!" exclaimed Henri, still grinning.

Lucas smiled back but felt hijacked. This was not what he wanted. He was not comfortable in the back of this ramshackle vehicle with a one handed, teenage driver.

"Look," he said. "I need a taxi, not a guide. I need to go to Radio Rèv," and then spelt it out "R-e-v" to try to get the boy to understand that he wanted to go from A to B and not on some unsolicited guided tour of Port au Prince.

Lucas pointed towards the dash and the card, which Henri retrieved. He stared at it uncomprehendingly. Lucas repeated the station name and the street address.

The boy's face dropped, then slowly brightened as he finally repeated the name of the radio station. Lucas pointed his finger and said, "Yes – now. Radio Rèv. Maintenant!" and Henri nodded vigorously, finally understanding his mission.

And they were off. Henri took another turn to the left, down a street of shuttered shops, set back under stone verandas. Then it was left again down a longer road. Lucas realised they'd gone almost full circle and were now on a route parallel to the great palace square.

The road was busy, and it slowed Henri's progress to a steadier pace. The houses on their left were substantial and detached. Through the gaps between them, Lucas caught glimpses of the great white palace.

It was enormous. It occupied one entire side of the square. A gleaming dome sat atop a huge central portico. Two long white pillared wings ran off on either side. The whole edifice had a classical grandeur which would not have looked out of place in Versailles.

Behind tall wrought-iron railings was an expansive lawn with small black cannons sitting like guard dogs. The central gates were closed and there, in front of them, sat the tank he had seen earlier. It was revving its engine. A plume of black smoke poured from its rear. Soldiers in crisp uniforms stood to attention near the gates.

The picture disappeared as Henri manoeuvred the old car through a busy market, loose cobbles rattling as they negotiated their way.

On a corner, Lucas saw another one of the little wooden carts selling iced drinks. The cart had wheels and two long handles sticking out to one side. It reminded Lucas of an old street barrow in London. Sitting on top was a huge block of ice, nearly covered by a filthy piece of damp hessian to stop it melting too fast in the heat. When a customer approached, the vendor took a plastic cup, added some syrup from one of the many coloured bottles sitting on a narrow shelf and, with a large machete, he expertly shaved slivers of ice from the block into the cup.

Another turn and the car slowed, stopping in front of a dilapidated hardware shop. It was part of another terrace of faded stone buildings, all with shop fronts set back from the street and shaded by a first-floor veranda. Yesterday everything he had seen had appeared alien, but the more he looked at these streets, the more Lucas caught glimpses of old London, Paris and New York all thrown together and blasted by the sun into a dishevelled tableau. What had seemed utterly alien held fragments of a world he half recognised.

Henri indicated their arrival and Lucas struggled out of the rear door on to the cracked pavement.

He had never seen so much rubbish and filth in a street. The drains were blocked with all kinds of detritus: plastic bags, bits of rag, sticks, shredded pieces of car tyre. Everything falling across the gutters, blocking the drains, which seeped a dark repulsive liquid.

Across the shattered pavement was a stone staircase. On the wall beside it was a faded metal sign with a picture of a rusty, red, rising sun in the top corner. Underneath were the words 'Radio Rèv'. The lettering might have once been green.

Lucas took the stairs to the first floor and a wooden door. He tried the handle. It didn't move. He knocked, then noticed a small brass doorbell to the left.

After some time, he heard footsteps. The door opened. There, easily filling the entire frame, was a huge man with ballooning afro hair above a full-face beard. Two sharp, brown eyes shone brightly at him from a face that seemed narrower than it should have been, accentuating his height.

"JP," said Lucas, wondering if his English was going to be understood: "JP invited me over to see the station…"

"Did he?" said the giant. "Then you'd better come in." An enormous hand reached out and pulled him through the door.

"JP's been on air for eight hours straight and I've come in with some breakfast." The man's voice had a deep rumble to it and Lucas, looking at him, decided he was not quite as intimidating as he had first thought. He introduced himself as Michel Jerome, the local reporter for Agence Presse Mondiale, and he spoke with an accent that was not local.

"You're American?" guessed Lucas.

"No, no, I'm Haitian. Born and bred in Port au Prince, but I went to university in Canada. It's where I learned my English and the accent's kinda stuck. But I live here – have done all my life and I sure aim to stay."

Lucas looked around. He was in a narrow hallway. Through a half-open door, he could see an old library with tapes and newspapers piled on a desk. Behind were some rusty metal shelves with thin, multicoloured boxes in rows. Amongst them, he recognised an early BBC logo.

There was loud music playing on the other side of a door at the end of the corridor.

"Sounds like JP's filling time. Let's go through, if he's expecting you," said Michel, leaning his shoulder against the padded door and easing it open. The music immediately grew louder, and Lucas followed his host into a small studio.

Lucas recognised little at first. He was used to professional studios with a window looking on to a cubicle, where studio managers mixed the sound. But this room had a simple wooden table supporting some domestic sound equipment and an old-fashioned cantilever table lamp. It should have had a bulb in it, but instead it held a microphone suspended on a large ball of elastic bands. The sound proofing on three of the walls was provided by dozens of little sponge pyramids, which collectively reminded Lucas of the inside of an egg box. The humidity was causing them to peel off in chunks. There was no window.

JP leapt up and shook Lucas's hand in welcome. He couldn't say anything because the music was so loud, and he subsided immediately to attend to a little sound mixer. Lucas stared at the wall behind JP's desk. Unlike the others, it had no sponge coating and the plaster looked like the surface of the moon, deep pock marks running in arched patterns across it.

JP followed Lucas's gaze and reduced the noise level.

"Eh voilà," he said. "We had a visit during the last elections. They shot the studio up pretty bad. We were off air for two days."

Lucas looked incredulously at JP. "Bullets?" He pointed at the wall.

"Oui. They came at night and broke in when nobody was here. We'd left music playing." JP nodded towards a large reel-to-reel tape recorder with a ten-inch tape which was rotating painfully slowly.

"I knew something was wrong when the music stopped. I was listening at home. When I got here, they'd machine-gunned the place. It looks bad. They mainly blasted the walls. We salvaged a lot of the equipment. But most of our staff left," he said, glancing over at Michel appreciatively.

Michel laughed. "Yeah – you'd have to be mad to work here."

"Do you know who did it?" asked Lucas.

"No. But it was probably the army – it usually is. They're the ones with the guns."

Lucas was quiet.

JP sprang up again from his chair, dropping headphones on to the wooden desk in front of him.

"Monsieur Lucas…I'm being rude. Soyez le bienvenu! Welcome! You managed to find us. I'm impressed. I'm so sorry I didn't get to the hotel this morning, but as you can see, I was on my own here until Michel arrived. Have you two been introduced? Michel is Haiti's most famous correspondent for Agence Presse Mondiale. He's a Haitian prince. He tells the world what's happening here, and he's my good friend."

Michel said he and Lucas had already made introductions at the door and the three of them sat down to talk – with JP producing two more wooden chairs from beneath a curtain in the corner and three small bottles of water from a battered cardboard box, one of which he offered to Lucas.

"I hope you had no trouble this morning," said JP. "The soldiers were on the streets last night. I've been trapped here."

He further reduced the sound levels to a murmur.

Michel picked up. "Yeah, they closed the airport at midnight. I don't know when you thought you were leaving, Lucas, but it won't be any time soon. They've imposed a curfew: midnight until 6.00 a.m."

"Ah yes – and you can have this," added JP, handing over a small card containing a local SIM. "But it isn't going to work. The whole mobile phone network went down in the night."

Lucas took the card and got his phone out of his shoulder bag. No signal. He inserted the new SIM and noted the number – still no signal. With a shrug, he returned it to his bag and tried to find out more from his two new friends.

Michel said the situation was hard to read. Since the last attempt at elections, which had ended so violently, the country had been under a new military government led by General Ignace Auguste. This much Lucas knew, but the fact that troops were on the move and the airport had closed was unexpected. He had thought General Auguste had taken over because civilian politicians couldn't agree on an orderly transfer of power. He had assumed the army was fully in control.

"Well, that's certainly what Auguste would have you believe," said Michel. "But there's tension. We think the Presidential Guard is loyal, but the Dessalines Battalion is led by officers who may have different ideas. Their commander is the general's number two, Major Chambert. He's publicly committed to Auguste, but who knows whether he can control his junior officers or other units in the army. What we do know is there's a lot of corruption. A lot of drugs come through Haiti and some elements in the army may profit from it."

JP interjected: "This place is difficult," he said. "Haiti's vulnerable. The planes come in late at night from the mainland and the drugs go to America. Security is weak. There's much money to be made if you know the right people. Some people favour chaos. It suits them. It makes it easier to do bad things."

"Has the President said anything today?" asked Lucas. JP handed him an official-looking statement marked with the presidential emblem. It was in French. Lucas started to work through it. Michel leant across to summarise: "The Presidential Guard had been deployed to protect public peace; a curfew from midnight until morning will be in place until further notice."

"Eh bien," said JP. "And now today the opposition say they'll have manifestations… demonstrations…"

Michel chipped in again: "Yeah, some of the politicians have been whipping up support. It looks like they've had some success. There's a growing frustration with the army – not that people love the politicians much either," he added. And then he looked at JP:

"Hey, who are you putting on air? Who have you called?"

And JP talked rapidly to Michel in Creole, explaining what he had in mind for the rest of the day's broadcast. After a long exchange, Michel turned to Lucas.

"JP has the key ones lined up. What are you going to do? Are you filing for the BBC? I'll be putting out a story on the wire this afternoon."

Lucas said he would contact London and fill them in, although he wasn't yet sure what they would want.

Michel offered some useful contacts, and Lucas greedily copied them into his notebook. If it was background Lucas wanted, Michel said he should go and see Leslie Laguerre, a veteran of the political scene who was now retired but still held an important role with the Electoral Commission. He had been a key opposition figure who had spoken out, first against Papa Doc, the first dictator, then his son, Baby Doc. It had done Laguerre little good. When Baby Doc had finally fled under pressure from the Americans, the divided opposition ignored him and squabbled among themselves. Unable to form a government, they gave the army the excuse to step in. Michel wrote Laguerre's address down.

"You must come and see me. I live in Petionville. It's a safe area and my daughter's home from university in the States. We dine alone tomorrow, and we'd be happy to see you." Lucas said he'd be there. But now he should check in with London.

The three parted and Michel accompanied Lucas out onto the street. He shook Lucas by the hand, glancing over at his battered taxi and driver.

"Give him my card and he should be able to find it. It has my address and landline on it. See you tomorrow evening – say seven o'clock."

Michel got into a gleaming Mercedes. Lucas watched him drive away.

Standing there in the hot sun, he had a powerful sense that he had lived this moment before, that he had some connection to this man. Maybe it was just a lack of a decent night's sleep or dehydration, or the familiar way Michel had said goodbye, but Lucas was certain that he was where he should be.

CHAPTER 9

Lucas arrived back in his room to find it newly cleaned and tidied. He sat down on the edge of the bed and wondered whether the hotel phone would handle an international call.

"Lucas, is that you?" Flo's voice was surprisingly clear. She sounded anxious.

"Yes, and I'm fine," he reassured her. "You've heard about the airport closing?"

"Yes," responded Flo. "I phoned the airline to make sure you'd landed safely, and they told me all flights had been suspended. I couldn't get through on your mobile. What's happening?"

Lucas explained about the curfew and the presidential statement.

"The mobile network's down but this landline works, and I've met the local APM correspondent, who says he's filing this afternoon. So, there'll be something on the wires later."

"Ah yes, Michel Jerome," said Flo, rarely caught off guard by a name. "His reports are worth reading. Too many of the others just spout the government view." Lucas said he was thinking of filing for News and there was a short pause at the end of the line: "Why not?" came the considered reply. "You're not going anywhere with the airport closed and you're the only person we've got. Why don't I put you through to the newsroom? I was at the morning meeting today. Haiti wasn't on the agenda, but Carrick was there. I'm sure he'll be interested. Hang on, I'll transfer you."

Lucas heard a crackle on the line, and then Flo was back. "And Lucas, take care. I want to hear from you every day, okay?" He managed a quick yes before he heard another voice.

"Who's this?" The tone was curt, typically Carrick. In the background, Lucas could hear the PA system sounding off about the Middle East.

Lucas explained what had happened as quickly as he could.

"Okay, Lucas," said the voice, a notch less brusque. "Sounds like things are kicking off. If I'd known this was going to happen, I'd have sent Headley. Looks like we've rather landed you in it."

Lucas said he was alright and could file.

"Well, since we've got you…give us a minute today about the curfew. I can't promise it'll run but, if the Middle East quietens down, we might use it later. Let me have it as soon as you can. If things develop, file again for the midnight bulletin." Lucas agreed. "And stay off social media. All the usual suspects will kick off about the evils of dictatorship. There'll be loads of inflammatory crap from expats and stooges. You're our man on the ground. Just give me the facts. Report what you see, okay?"

Carrick then rattled off deadlines for the various news programmes on the schedule before the line went muffled. Lucas could faintly hear some four-letter instructions being issued to someone who had dared to interrupt. Then Carrick was back asking if Lucas was still there.

"Good – thought I'd lost you. Give me your local numbers." Lucas gave the hotel and his local SIM, reminding Carrick the network was down. "That doesn't sound good," he said. "Look, don't go sticking your neck out. Tell me if it gets too sticky. You know how quickly things can blow up. Don't be the spark that sets it off. Got me?"

"Got you," said Lucas.

"Good lad – stay cool." And Carrick was gone.

Adrenaline lifted Lucas to his feet. It seemed his gamble of focussing on Haiti was paying off. This was the wave he had been waiting for, and he wanted to ride it as far as it would carry him.

He looked at his watch. It was already past midday. He had a copy of the President's statement and what JP had told him. It was enough to write a short report, but he might learn more by seeing Leslie Laguerre.

He went down to the reception again, intending to get a taxi. There, hovering by the front door was Henri, where he had left him.

"You go…?" Henri asked eagerly, walking up to him. And Lucas thought, 'why not?' He had exchanged his dollars for an exceptionally large quantity of local gourdes. The taxi was costing him a pittance. He followed Henri out into the sun, handing him the address on the way.

Leslie Laguerre's house was close by – Lucas could have walked, had he known. So, quietly congratulating himself on bolstering the local economy, he pushed through a large wrought-iron gate which led to the front garden of one of the stone houses on the far side of the square from the palace.

Between the dusty bushes by the front door, he was met by an elderly lady, whom he took to be the housekeeper. In his halting French, he explained who he was. The woman made him wait on the doorstep in the sun while she went back inside. Two minutes later she invited him in.

The hallway was dark and cool after the fierce midday heat. She led him towards the back of the house, where she stood aside to let him enter a large study. To the right of the door was a broad writing table, overshadowed by a bookcase crammed with old volumes. At the desk sat a thickset, grey-haired man in a dark suit. He was reading. His large shoulders were hunched, and a pair of wire-framed spectacles rested halfway down his broad nose. He looked up and immediately rose.

"You're from the BBC?" Leslie Laguerre's English was excellent. "Jean Pierre said you might come. You'll have something to drink?" He looked past Lucas at the woman who was still standing in the door. Lucas declined.

"I listen to BBC World Service," Laguerre said, offering his hand. "The Internet comes and goes, so I listen on shortwave. Your news is excellent, but you say very little about our poor country."

Lucas apologised, shaking the proffered hand, and said he wanted to try to put that right. Laguerre showed Lucas to one of the wide armchairs bordering the ornate fireplace, which was the focal point of the room.

As he moved, Lucas noticed that all the walls were lined with books. They overflowed and pooled on the floor. One lay open on the small table by the chair in which he now sat.

"You're a man of letters," he said.

"Mais oui, I studied in Paris for years. I have doctorates from la Sorbonne in politics and philosophy, but my most important work has been here." Laguerre took a deep breath and straightened his back in the chair. He slipped into French and then corrected himself:

"I have worked for the betterment of the Haitian people. Always they try to silence me, but I write and speak and walk with the poor." Laguerre's phrases seemed practised, as though repeated many times, and as Lucas listened, he pieced together something of the old man's past. It became clear that Leslie Laguerre had worked under Papa Doc Duvalier and had fallen out for reasons he did not explain. When his son Baby Doc took over, there was no rehabilitation. Laguerre had written tracts about the need to establish a democratic government and what the proper role of the army should be. Although some of these had to be published outside the country, they circulated locally, and they did not win him any favour with Baby Doc or the senior officers around him.

However, young people from the middle class found his ideas compelling. They chimed in with a growing desire for change, current among students at the university. They resonated with other movements in the Caribbean, where politicians whipped up passions and raised expectations that corruption could be stopped, and wealth better distributed.

"This country…" said Laguerre, expounding his thesis, "this country has the capacity to govern without intervention from the military. The army is corrupt. The generals steal our money. They work with the gangs and the drug lords on the mainland to enrich themselves." The words poured out of Laguerre and droplets of sweat gathered on his forehead. "It's time for Haitians to take control of their lives. This is a country that rose from slavery. Ordinary men and women fought off the French tyrants and the British and the slave owners. Why should we enslave ourselves again to men with guns? It's time to put our faith in our own civilian leaders once more…"

Lucas finally intervened. "But the President says he's against corruption. He says he won't tolerate drug runners. He says he wants democratic elections. Don't you believe him?"

"That's what he says." Laguerre shrugged. "But what's he doing? He promised us elections, but when? There's no date. And his predecessor killed voters at the polls. They shot them down like dogs in the street." Laguerre quickly drank from a glass tumbler by his chair. "Auguste is an army man. He has spent his whole life in uniform. He's grown up surrounded by corruption. How can he not be part of it? How can he know anything else? His words mean nothing without action."

"And what about the politicians?" Lucas asked. "Why have they failed to persuade the troops back into barracks?" Leslie Laguerre drew a deep breath and studied the fireplace.

"Monsieur Lucas, I can only tell you the opposition groups are very divided." He waved a hand at the window, as if they were all gathered outside. "There are many of them – led mostly by citizens who are educated and well known but they're only popular within their own faction. They are largely ideologues, égoïstes – not all but many of them – and I'm sorry to say that the corruption, practised by the dictatorship for many decades, has seeped into every corner of this country. It runs from top to bottom. The population is poor. The government's agents are everywhere. They pay money for information and what they cannot buy they beat out of people. If there's money to be had – by any means – you're regarded as stupid if you don't take it." Lucas must have looked sceptical because Laguerre quickly continued. "You surely don't doubt this? If our leaders are mired in corruption, what other example do people have?"

"But is there no chance of the opposition uniting?" asked Lucas.

"Yes, we try!" exclaimed Laguerre, raising both arms. For a moment, Lucas thought Laguerre was going to stand. "But there's so much to do and we have so few levers. Our press is weak, our parliament is undermined and our army…" Laguerre produced a handkerchief and wiped perspiration from his forehead. "…Well, it's an army. It's not trained to govern or empower civil society… That's not what armies do." The handkerchief was pushed back into a pocket. "But we try. Even the Church has tried. There's one opposition figure – a Catholic priest, who is himself poor. He's very popular. But the poverty…" Laguerre bent his head, rubbing his eyes to ease some sudden ache. "Of course, it's the poverty as well…so many have so little." He paused before looking up and when he did, his focus was not on Lucas. His eyes searched the bookshelves over Lucas's shoulder. "For many here, poverty strips everything away. The struggle to survive is the daily preoccupation." He was quieter now, no longer addressing an audience. For a while, Lucas watched him as he sat there wrestling with his thoughts and then slowly Laguerre continued, his voice little more than a whisper: "And then there is the fear. It trumps even the fight for life. When fear runs loose, all people can see is death. Death comes in the night." Laguerre's eyes narrowed. "Yes, he comes in broad daylight. He lives among us. He walks with us, sleeps with us, waits for us... He becomes...our familiar." For a moment, the breath seemed to leave him. "He even becomes a friend..." He stopped. A silence descended, as if Laguerre had followed his gaze and had gone.

Then gradually, the old man stirred again. "So," he said, pulling himself upright, "where do we begin when faced with all this? When death and corruption are everywhere?" And he was fully present once more, his voice regaining its forcefulness. "Well, I think we start by speaking out and condemning the leadership that has allowed it." He waved his hand as if turning a page. "But frankly, my friend, my time is running out. Many people want change, but they need new leaders, young leaders – brave ones who will stand up against the forces that rule us. It's good that you're here," he said, looking Lucas in the eye. "We need you. All we have here is a diet of rumour and fear. The truth is, we don't know about Auguste yet – he's only been president for a matter of months. He wasn't in power when the killings happened. There's no proof he was involved. But you can't trust anyone. You must be careful. Every person is an informant. Lies are everywhere. Our business leaders are only interested in money. And who suffers most? Always the poor."

Lucas was stirred by Laguerre's returning passion, but he was worrying about his report. Where was he going to find the facts that Carrick wanted? Then the old man came to his rescue.

"We will march tomorrow," he said. "We'll march all week. We have no power, but we can protest. We have no guns, but we have our voices. We can show them how many we are. We can show them we'll stand up against oppression."

Lucas was scribbling in his notepad.

"So, are there no preparations for fresh elections?" he asked. "Has the Electoral Commission started drawing up voter lists?"

Laguerre shook his head vigorously and reached for a large document, which he retrieved from under the open book on the table next to him.

"After the last attempt at elections, the Commission drafted this for the government. It lays out all the things that need to happen to secure fresh elections, all the improvements that need to be made. But the army ignores us." Laguerre handed the document to Lucas. "There's no approval for new elections. Just this paper."

"So, what will the demonstration achieve?"

"Maybe nothing." Laguerre shrugged. "But if we go on the streets, the Americans will see us. You're here. You can report what happens. You can tell the world we don't want to live like this, that we demand free elections."

Lucas took all this down, and Laguerre went on to explain where and when the march would begin. When he finished, he urged Lucas to be there.

Time was running out. If Lucas was to file for News he had to move. With London five hours ahead, he could wait no longer if he wanted his report to be used. He stood to go. They shook hands as Laguerre unsteadily raised himself from his chair, only to subside again as their hands parted. "À demain," he said as Lucas turned to the door, where the woman had reappeared. He glanced back at the old man, now slumped in his chair. Having spoken for so long he was spent, staring at the fireplace, his black suit crumpled in on his frame, visibly diminished. The woman touched his arm and led him out into the heat. In English she said: "He's tired but he was pleased to see you."

Now that Lucas could see her face properly, he realised she couldn't be the housekeeper. She was slightly stooped, and her dress was faded and there was a warm intelligence in her eyes. As they faced each other, she tucked a stray wisp of hair back into a hairclip, a gesture which Lucas took to be an echo from her youth.

Then he noticed Henri off to one side. He had brought the car to the gate and was waiting to take him away. He made his goodbye and started to go but as he did, he felt again her hand on his arm.

"Monsieur," she said, looking up at him through lids veiled against the sun: "My husband is a good man. He has done much for this country. We are living peacefully here. If you're going to report for the News, can you please not mention his name?"

Lucas considered her carefully and saw for the first time her fear. She must have been sixty years old and Leslie, he guessed, was older. Something stirred in him. He wasn't familiar with this world. He didn't know its rules. At home, it was different. At university everyone was free to question. At work, everything was discussed, agreed, and planned. Even on the streets of London, there were common codes of behaviour. Vehicles were licensed; they stopped at traffic lights; people gave way, acknowledging the rights of others. Here in Haiti, the individual was obscured by poverty. If rights existed, they were for the privileged and powerful. If you spoke out, men came in the night.

Looking at Madame Laguerre, Lucas wondered at the audacity of this old man in his faded house, so close to the palace, reading his books, connected to a world far away in Paris.

"I understand," he said. "I'll be careful." And he walked to the waiting car.

He started work on his despatch as Henri drove him back to the hotel. He finished it in his room and then laid out his equipment and committed it to his digital recorder. Behind the hotel phone, he found an ethernet port and attached a long cable from his accessory bag, which he had been given by the duty engineer before he left.

With great precision, Junior – as he was singularly known – had carefully selected a range of equipment to meet any eventuality and, in the process had left a strong impression on Lucas.

"You can use dis for connecting to your laptop – just like you do here." Junior spoke with a lilt that came from Jamaica via East London and was waving the long grey wire over his equipment of choice, which he had laid out in front of him on the bench. His face and a good part of his upper body were framed by his dreadlocks, which affirmed his connection to Ras Tafari. He was a broadcast engineer and there wasn't anything he didn't know about field work in far flung places.

The workshop in which he stood was his pride and joy. "You can record directly to your laptop or use dis digi-recorder," he said, putting one down on the desk. "Then you send your audio and video files to News Intake – no problem, man." Junior fed adapters and more leads into a string pull bag. "But specially where you're going," he continued, "de Internet can just disappear, yah know? You might have to read your reports down a telephone line." He lifted a small black box which had two crocodile clips dangling from short wires at one end. "So, here's my magic box." Junior produced a small, black, square object from a drawer on the counter. "I only have a couple. I made dis one myself, so you take care, yeah man?"

Lucas nodded and focused on the tutorial unfolding before him. The box was shiny black plastic with two short cables. A tiny red light lit up when Junior touched the crocodile clips and there was a small socket to connect a microphone. "Dis my man, will make any old copper cable sound like fibre." Junior held up the two crocodile clips. "You just unscrew de mouthpiece on the phone and attach them at the back ..." He picked up a dismembered handset he kept to one side and demonstrated where to place the clips. "Easy as that," he said, and grinned at Lucas. "You're my man!" and Junior's hand rose in a whipping action that loudly cracked his second and third fingers together to affirm his complete satisfaction. "Not everyone goes to de back of beyond, but you're going." The laugh that followed had drawn its twin from Lucas.

The computer hummed on Lucas's lap. The connection was made, and the file sent. There had been no need to delve further into the bag of tricks that Junior had given him. Back came the confirmation, 'file received'.

Lucas spent the rest of the time before the curfew reading Laguerre's document and tracking down maps of the city, on which he traced the likely route of tomorrow's march. Lack of sleep was catching up on him and he wished he had drunk the water offered at the radio station. He flipped the bedroom light off and flopped down on the bed, thinking he would rest before going down to the restaurant. Above him in the gloom, the ceiling seemed to be behaving erratically. Was it the ceiling moving or the fan? He closed his eyes to stop the spinning sensation and thought about the report he had sent.

He had written it quickly, and it seemed straightforward: the government announcement of the curfew, the lack of preparations for elections and the promise of demonstrations tomorrow.

"Facts," Carrick had said. Well, the curfew was a fact – he had the government statement. But for the rest he only had Laguerre's word and, conscious of what his wife had said, he had not mentioned him or the Electoral Commission in his report. What if the demonstration didn't happen? What if the demonstration was an old man's wishful thinking?

He wondered what a subeditor back in the newsroom would make of it when writing a story for the bulletin. News scripts always listed sources at the bottom. The government statement would be one source. The rest would be attributed to 'our correspondent' in Port au Prince. Laguerre had better be right. Lucas didn't want to be dragged into a world of speculation, where political theories were committed to paper only to be blown away. He wanted proof. He wanted to witness this promised demonstration – see things for himself. But for the time being, he was trapped by the curfew and four walls. He lay there increasingly feeling his confinement: he hated being stuck in one room, in the dark, no longer able to leave, wondering what tomorrow might hold. It felt like being back at school, lying in bed after lights out, yearning for escape.

Tap, tap, tap.

He thought at first it was someone clearing cutlery from an adjacent room, but there it was again: a rapid tapping noise and a thump. He rose from the bed and followed the sound which was coming from the bathroom. He opened the door.

The feeble overhead light was still on. Perhaps it was a rat scuttling across the floor. Thank God he still had his shoes on. But he could see nothing on the floor.

Tap, Tap, Tap.

Lucas looked up and there at the little window, high on the wall was a bird on the other side of the glass, head moving from side to side, looking askance into his prison. The little window was hinged at the bottom, sloping inwards, slightly open. Lucas, thinking the bird might squeeze through the gap, gently pushed it closed, careful not to cause injury. The bird, with its sleek dark body and white chest, gave him a long look. He put his hand against the glass and tapped, and the bird tapped back. He turned and pushed at the switch on the wall and the dim light went out. The bird stayed for a while, staring at the now dark glass and then slowly turned before flying off. Lucas knew where he'd rather be. Out there, under the cover of a warm night, soaring up on the rising air.

He returned to the bed. Too tired for the restaurant, he flopped onto the counterpane, drifting away, staring at the ceiling, thinking about the bird, flying free. And suddenly Zoe was there beside him, lying on the bed as silent as she had been during that last phone call to the school.

Silence was the very stuff of their calls, but this time it had gone on too long and eventually he had coaxed her to speak. When she did, it had only been to talk about the birds. She had been watching them from the window in her dormitory – her favourite retreat…

"Swifts, I think they are. They swirl round the roof." Her voice had been clear down the line. *"Sometimes they even come to the window. They're beautiful. I can watch them for hours. Flying into the long summer twilight playing hide and seek with the setting sun. So fast. So beautiful. They twist and turn. They swoop and soar, circling the chimney pots. The eye can't follow. They take my breath away…"* Then the silence hovered between them again, trembling on the line. *"You know they fall asleep in flight? It's true. Even as they fly, they sleep. Even as they fall…"*

He should have called her more. That's what he had thought at the end of the call. He should call her more…

CHAPTER 10

A rapid knocking dragged Lucas to his senses. There was a faint square of sunlight by his bed. The rays had escaped from the bathroom, where faded tiles had dulled their brilliance before projecting them through the half-open door to flop exhausted on the floor.

The knocking was repeated urgently.

Lucas hauled himself up to open the door, still in his clothes.

Henri was talking fast while holding out a small bottle of water. Lucas took it. His head was throbbing. Almost overcome by thirst, he gratefully drank and tried to listen. It took some time, but he eventually worked out that Henri was excited about the demonstration and was urging Lucas to go. He checked his watch. It was early. He was not sure how long he had slept but his mental fog suggested it was not enough. Lucas stared at Henri, puzzled by his insistence. Up to now he had showed no interest in anything other than his next fare and here he was urging him to see the 'manifestation'. Perhaps he had worked with a journalist before. He made a mental note to ask him, held up his hand to stifle the torrent of words and said he would be downstairs shortly.

Lucas grabbed another bottle of water from the bathroom and drank it with some paracetamol. He gathered everything he needed for the day and then thought 'coffee'. At the bottom of the staircase Henri was waiting, secure in his new role of personal assistant.

Although Lucas had no great liking for the boy, he had to admit he was useful. So, he invited Henri to join him in the restaurant where he sat and shared the coffee while Lucas ate the croissant from the basket between them.

It was impossible to have a proper conversation, but as far as Lucas could make out, Henri had not worked with a journalist before. He wondered about the boy before him. Perhaps he too had a mother and family in the slums and the money he earned found its way back to them. Lucas pointed at the stump where Henri's right hand had been and asked what had happened.

"Macoutes," came the key word in the reply. Henri made a chopping motion with his remaining hand, like a machete coming down.

What had provoked such violence from the secret police remained a mystery, the detail was beyond either of their linguistic skills. All Lucas could gather was that Henri had been pursued and caught. Whether the cruel amputation was punishment for something he had done Lucas couldn't tell and Henri did not encourage further enquiry.

The demonstration would start soon so Lucas went to the reception to check the directions. He explained that he wanted St Joseph's Church and showed them the map he had brought with him. They knew the place, and instructions were issued to Henri in Creole, who swiftly led the way from the lobby to the battered car which was perched at an angle on the kerb by the hotel entrance.

St Joseph was about half an hour's drive. To get there, Henri took the car through a succession of dirt tracks riddled with potholes. The ramshackle buildings along the route were all low, single storey affairs, marginally better than the meagre shelters Lucas had seen in the slums.

The closer they got to the church, the more crowded the streets became and when Lucas finally got out of the car, he had trouble making himself heard. He told Henri to go because he intended to follow the demonstrators and find his own way back to the hotel. Henri looked worried. Lucas thought he wanted money and so paid him from the wad of blackened gourdes he had purchased at the hotel, but still Henri lingered.

'What now?' thought Lucas. He needed to get on – he had no time to stand there with this raggedy boy in the heat and the dust. He briefly considered terminating their new-found relationship, but pragmatism got the better of him, after all what other option did he have? And perhaps it was just money. So Lucas offered a day rate to ensure Henri would always be available.

Henri looked happier. He tucked the gourdes in to his pants and launched the car back in the direction they'd come, weaving dangerously as he waved goodbye with his one good arm. With some relief Lucas turned his attention to the church.

He pushed his way through the crowd and reached the shade of the portico. Despite the hubbub around him, he could hear a raised voice echoing inside. Someone was making a speech and Lucas burrowed his way through the throng.

Inside, he passed under a broad balcony and emerged into the body of the church where he could see up into the impressive interior. Above him was a high-pitched roof, ornately decorated and supported by stone walls punctuated by a generous number of gold effigies. The scene was curiously at odds with the poverty outside and Lucas wondered where the money had come from. It was certainly not from the poor people crushed up against him. But they appeared oblivious to these riches. They were all focused on what was unfolding in front of them. He pushed further up the nave until he could see the altar and there, standing behind a broad wooden rail which separated the church's heart from the congregation, were four men facing the crowd.

One of them was a young priest, and he was holding everyone's attention. His head was bare. His long black vestments cascaded from his shoulders to the floor. A pair of gold-rimmed glasses flashed as his eyes searched the faces before him. His clerical collar shone white round his neck. He spoke rapidly in Creole, striding first one way, then the other, heads following his every movement. His arms swirled through the air, grappling with a demon that struggled to evade his clutches.

The crowd breathed in his words, mesmerised. They hummed and chorused the phrases he used. They called out to him, and he caught their cries, incorporating them into the rhythm of his speech. He conjured their responses, catching them as he darted from side to side, wrapping them up in the billowing folds of his vestments.

And then he stopped, his gown gradually subsiding and out tumbled the words he had caught – deftly revealed for all to see. He was a magician, as engrossed as anyone in the room, hypnotised by his own illusion.

Lucas looked around, wondering if anyone spoke English. His silent appeal was met with bewildered looks by those nearest him, but from close behind came a voice that said: "I speak English. I can help if you like…"

He turned and saw a striking, dark-haired young woman in her twenties. She wore a simple summer dress of a shade of blue that caught the colour of her eyes and there was a sheen to the long curls that cascaded to one side over her bare shoulder. She carried a small handbag on her arm. Her skin was the colour of café crème, her features finely drawn. She would have turned heads on Maddison Avenue and here in this church she had the same effect.

Young men in the crowd, who thought nothing of hanging off each other or holding the hands of their companions, somehow held a respectful distance. Lucas heard himself speak his half-framed thoughts.

"What are you doing here?"

She smiled brightly and laughed.

"It's okay," she said, moving closer to make herself heard. "It's not just the poor who want to see the back of this government, most of the middle classes who live up in Petionville are also fed up with dictatorship. My father, for one, would love to see change."

With a smile still on her lips, she looked at Lucas's recorder and microphone and said: "You're the journalist?"

Lucas nodded and asked her name.

"Marie," she said offering a gloved hand, holding his gaze. Then she leant in. "They're saying they're going to march to the palace, and this is the beginning of the end for the government. They want Auguste to go. They want the promised elections now."

Lucas could hear the priest still speaking behind him, but he couldn't take his eyes off Marie.

One phrase he didn't understand stuck in his mind: "La découpage… faire la découpage…" and as he gazed at her, he heard the phrase again.

"La découpage…what does it mean?"

"It means cutting down. It's Creole," she said. "It's what the farmers do to clear the fields for new crops. They pull everything up by the roots. He's telling everyone here to be a farmer and prepare Haiti for a new beginning…"

Lucas tore his eyes off her and looked back at the priest, who was calmer now, standing alongside the other three men. One of them was Leslie Laguerre, as transfixed as anyone in the room by the impact of the diminutive figure in front of him.

"His name's Père Baptiste," said Marie in his ear. "He may look small, but he's the one that puts fire in their belly."

As if in response to her words, the priest was on the move again. There was electricity in the air, and everyone was craning to see the man who was generating it. Heads were raised in expectation, awaiting a sign. Marie translated, her lips close to Lucas's ear.

"He's saying everyone must be orderly and not be violent. He wants a peaceful march …" Her translation lagged behind the priest's words because he was now punching the air with his right hand, repeating a phrase Lucas could understand: "To the palace, to the palace…"

The crowd turned and surged, pouring towards the door of the church, propelled by the priest's exhortations. Lucas too was borne up by the crush. He was squeezed off his feet and carried a few inches above the ground, no longer in control of his body. Panic flooded through him and involuntarily he grabbed Marie's hand, fearing either he or she would fall and be trampled.

Locked together, they were swept back through the church to the door until they burst out into the sickly-sweet air of the boiling street. The light sprayed his eyes, momentarily blinding him, but he felt the ground once more beneath his feet, as people scattered left and right out of the door, some falling to the side like flotsam.

Swiftly, the panic of the exit receded. Those ahead led the way up the road dragging a long line of jiving humanity behind them, heading towards the city centre moving as one, not fast but in a practised fashion, like warriors in some ancient ceremony, feet lifted high, swaying, pounding through the dust and collectively, steadily advancing on their objective.

Lucas pressed the red button on the side of his recorder and put the microphone to his lips. He started a commentary, trying to paint a picture, using the short sentences beloved by his instructors.

"*We're at the Church of St Joseph in Port au Prince. The demonstrators are marching to the Presidential Palace. They want an end to military government…*" he spoke above the noise, keeping the microphone close. "*Ahead of me in the street, I can see burning tyres which have been set alight by the crowd. Black smoke is pouring up into the sky. It's impossible for anyone in the capital not to know something is happening here.*"

He broke off, paused the recording, and walked on in silence with Marie for a while following the long meandering route of the protesters. From time to time, he drifted away from her to record more commentaries, but he was always drawn back.

He was puzzled by the unpredictable turns they took. Perhaps it was to keep an element of uncertainty, so the authorities couldn't be sure of their destination. But the energy and determination of those who walked in front did not ebb, despite the searing heat.

After a while, he became conscious of Marie looking at him. The sun was at its peak and the heat was intense. He could feel the sweat running off his forehead and down his cheeks.

"You should drink," she said. "You'll be no use if you pass out."

Lucas had brought nothing with him but a notepad and his equipment, which hung in the bag from his shoulder.

"You can get water here," Marie said, pointing to a wooden hut by the side of the road. A small door was open and inside in the black interior Lucas could just make out a table with a few meagre items on display. Some others from the crowd had also stepped inside. Lucas, easing himself into the confined space, saw some triangular plastic bags of water.

He pulled out some bank notes, but Marie laughed and pushed his hand down.

"You don't need those," she said. And quickly she produced two small coins from her purse. She handed them to the man behind the table and picked up one of the waters. She made a little tear in one corner.

"Here, drink like this." And she held up the bag, tilted her head back and squeezed. A steady stream of clear water curved down between her parted lips.

She handed it to Lucas, who had marvelled at the ease with which she drew liquid from the air. There was a grace about her. Her movements were effortless. Nothing about her struck Lucas as studied. Everything was as natural as her smile and the silk of her skin and her hair which caressed her neck, curling round it like a lover's hand.

Marie offered the bag so Lucas could follow her example. He tried, but the water spilled to one side, and he chased it with his mouth. It splashed on to his shirt. Laughing, Marie stepped forward and held his hands to steady the stream so that finally it eased his thirst.

"Thank you," he said. "I'll pay you back at the hotel." Marie swatted the idea away and ducked out into the heat again.

They walked on, following the growing crowd. Most were young men. A few were older in suits, some were students carrying books bundled together with string, but many looked like cane cutters, stripped bare to the waist. These bare-chested ones had large machetes hanging from their belts. Marie explained that a machete was essential equipment for any poor young man seeking work in the city. They were muscled and lean from physical labour, and they made a formidable escort. It was an eclectic mix of people fused together by an apparent passionate dislike of dictatorship.

"What do they think will happen?" he asked Marie by his side. "What do they expect? Do they really think the army will go back to barracks?"

"I'm not sure they have expectations," replied Marie. "They just want change. They have nothing. Things can't get any worse. If the army goes, then new possibilities arise."

She seemed coolly unaffected by the heat. Lucas continued:

"But if the army steps down, who will take their place?"

"Some politicians could do a better job, but they need the space. First, the army must give up power. There's talk of a general strike, so the whole city could come to a standstill. Perhaps things will really change this time."

Lucas looked up around. There was no questioning the size of the protest and he lifted his microphone again:

"There are hundreds of people on the street now. They are converging on the Presidential Palace, and they're unified in their demand for change. The demonstration is peaceful, and their message is clear: the military government should step down and make way for democratic elections."

They passed another row of burning tyres and Lucas stopped recording as the acrid fumes hit the back of his throat. He briefly came to a standstill. The smoke, the exertion of the long walk in the sun was taking its toll, and he was short of breath.

He looked down at his feet. His black leather shoes were covered in thick, brown dust.

Lucas wiped his face with a handkerchief he took from his pocket and then noticed one of the slit-alleys which ran off from the street.

"These paths into the slums are so narrow," he said, coughing at the smoke. "It's amazing anyone can get through them."

"They need every inch of space for their families," she said. "There's no room for anything else." They were pushed forward again by the crowd.

"How many live like this?"

"You can't count them. Every day, people come in from the countryside and disappear. Nobody knows how many."

Up ahead, Lucas could see the route was broadening out, and he realised they were close to the hotel. To his left must be the palace, but his view was obscured by a long, high, rendered wall, and just ahead were a pair of heavy metal gates. Set back was a watchtower, where two soldiers were surveying the crowd.

They continued up the road, and finally turned in to the square, taking a route diagonally away from the hotel with the demonstrators who were fanning out in front of the palace. People surged past him and, as he tightened his grip on his recorder and bag, the first shots rang out.

Suddenly, like a shoal of fish confronted by a predator, the crowd split apart, fleeing the gunfire. Lucas stood still, watching the scene until someone ran past him, striking his shoulder. The impact spun him around and he realised he was on his own. Marie must have been carried off by the tide of people.

He instinctively pressed the red button and spoke into the microphone.

"The protesters have now arrived in the main square, outside the Presidential Palace. And soldiers are firing to clear the crowd."

He looked round again. Sporadic shots echoed back from the large houses on the far side of the square and many protesters were crowded in front of them, seeking a way through the gaps that separated one property from another. These narrow paths acted as funnels, leaving the protesters exposed as they jostled to get away.

Towards the palace, Lucas could see that most of the soldiers were by the gates. They had their rifles raised in the air, firing at the sky. But a few had walked forwards, across the space left by the fleeing demonstrators. Lucas's recorder was warm in his hand.

"The demonstrators had intended to take their demands to the very gates of the Presidential Palace, but the army won't tolerate their presence. These civilians are unarmed. The demonstration has been peaceful. But they're being met with force. It's clear that this government won't tolerate peaceful protest."

He paused again, checking the scene before him, thinking his last words might make a good conclusion.

To one side he saw a low trough about four feet long and a couple of feet high. It might once have contained water for animals, but now was empty and he crouched behind it, still looking towards the palace from behind his shelter. Now he was lower, he felt safer. More shots. He couldn't tell where they were coming from. It could have been an echo or from some unknown source behind him. In the confusion, he didn't know whether to move or stay where he was.

He then noticed one of the soldiers from the palace advancing towards him. He was a hundred yards away and had his rifle pointing forwards at the ground as he walked. He must have seen him take cover. Lucas just watched. Time slowed. It felt like the still moment before a crash, when you know there is nothing to be done.

Lucas glanced sideways. He was completely alone. He looked back at the soldier still advancing and gripped his recorder.

"Shots are being fired but it's difficult to tell where they're coming from. It's all around. Protesters are fleeing the square and the march is effectively being broken up -"

There was a firm hand on his shoulder and a voice behind him said, "I think it's time to go…you should come inside now." Lucas looked up and saw the stranger he had met earlier in the hotel. He was standing behind him, still in the same cream coloured suit.

"Monsieur Lucas," he repeated with increased urgency, looking at the soldier, "I think you should come with me. You can't stay here…" Lucas stood and together they walked side by side, away from the trough and towards the hotel entrance.

By the time he got to the door, his pace had increased to something closer to a run. It was, he thought, like being released from a trance. A few seconds ago, he had been locked in the event, unable to break free. His presence had given it meaning. To turn away was to break-up the story, to disrupt fate and interfere with an inevitable force. He had felt curiously elated by being so involved in the moment. He knew it was beyond his control, but somehow to be part of it was to become one with it and it brought a kind of resolution for which he yearned.

"I wouldn't wish any harm to come to you," said his saviour, as if absolving him from some indiscretion.

"I should thank you." Lucas was still looking at the door that was now behind them. "But you see I'm here to report. If I don't see things, I can't do my job and what's happening…is out there."

"I agree my friend. I don't deny its importance, but I felt you looked a little…" and the man stretched out his hands, "… alone."

"Let me introduce myself. My name is Alfred Toussaint, but people just call me Toussaint. I own a small printing press near here, and this hotel is my second home."

Lucas introduced himself in return. He knew it was unnecessary because Toussaint already knew who he was, but it completed a circle of expectation. And as they went to find a seat, Lucas realised that his heart was pounding. He took several deep breaths, forcing himself to consider more carefully what had just happened. It was slowly dawning on him that he had lost all perspective out in the square.

He had become so fixated on his report that he had felt immune from any consequences. Why would anyone hurt him? He was not a demonstrator. He was not trying to bring the government down. He was simply an observer, and the important thing was to record what happened not take part in it. But now, sitting on this comfortable sofa, all his reasoning sounded increasingly naïve. Then he remembered. That cameraman. The one who had filmed his own death. Where was it? Beirut? Somewhere in the Middle East. He had carried on filming long after the shooting started. Somehow, he had become trapped in the lens, detached from reality. And there it had ended. A blank screen. The conclusion to his story.

Perhaps, he thought, there was no way of remaining truly objective or impartial. Simply by being there you became part of the story. Being present affects everything. People are like planets. They exert influence on each other even when they try not to.

Lucas wiped the sweat from his forehead and looked at his hand. It was trembling slightly, and he reproached himself.

You're going to get yourself killed. Headley wouldn't have got himself exposed like that. He'd have got the story and got out. He wouldn't have lingered, made a target of himself. He'd have moved faster. You've got to survive to report. You need to be like Headley. That's what you want – to be like Headley.

Toussaint was watching him from his chair. "You need something to drink, my friend." He signalled a passing waiter and quickly ordered. The waiter scuttled back with two glasses of the purple punch from the great glass bowl at the reception, clinking with ice, softened by fruit, chilled by tears falling from the tumblers' lips. Lucas drank gratefully and let the tension fall from his shoulders. It was only then that he focused properly on Toussaint who was sat, upright and unruffled in his white suit, cradling his own drink.

"What do you think will happen?" Lucas asked. "The protesters seem so determined."

"Ah, my friend, who knows?" he replied. "I've been here long enough to know nothing is certain and change is a yearning that's never satisfied."

"But how can a president rule a country where so many people reject him?" Lucas's question hovered in the air.

"Well, that's a question," said Toussaint, staring at his glass, still untouched. "The Hougans here have a saying—"

"The Hougans?" interjected Lucas.

"Hougans, my friend are the spiritual guides of the people. They're the priests of voodoo. They understand the mysteries of how to pass from this world to the next and return. They understand a man can be alive and dead at the same time, here in body, but spiritually absent."

"And the saying?" prompted Lucas.

"The saying goes: 'You can call a chicken a bird, but it still cannot fly'."

Lucas laughed aloud but Toussaint didn't look amused.

"Forgive me, but how does that help in this situation?" asked Lucas, kicking himself. He sat up in his chair, focused on the man before him. Toussaint leant forward. "General Auguste is President in name, but can he truly lead this country?"

"Well, that will be hard if he doesn't have the support of the people."

"You learn quickly, my friend. I heard your report on the BBC last night. You tell the world what's happening here. You do us a great service." Lucas let the compliment pass while registering that his report had been used.

"We're all prisoners in this country. You can't leave. I can't leave. We're all trapped by a man who promised us elections but doesn't deliver…"

Lucas looked at Toussaint, this strangely detached man, and decided he had underestimated whom he was dealing with. Toussaint's demeanour suggested he had inside knowledge. Perhaps he even knew some of the individuals.

"That's very interesting," he said, hoping to draw more from Toussaint. "I've been thinking of approaching the

President for an interview. He is after all the centre of this story."

"I think you're right, Monsieur Lucas. The President himself was on the radio today. He talked to the people directly, but he didn't answer questions." Toussaint sat back in his chair: "We hear what he thinks, but I'm not sure he hears what we think."

"But it's going to be difficult to reach him." Lucas wondered if Toussaint knew anyone in the President's office or in the military senior enough to help. "I can't just walk up to the gates and demand to see him. I'm a foreigner. I don't have the necessary contacts."

"My friend." Toussaint smiled at him, relaxing further back into his chair, "The President's in the phone book. You simply pick up the phone and call the palace. He has a press secretary, I believe."

Lucas remembered seeing a crumpled A4 phone book in the drawer of the bedside table in his room. It seemed to him incredible that calling the President could be so simple and wondered if Toussaint was teasing him.

He glanced at his watch, anxious about the time. It was still quite early in the afternoon, but if he was to get to Michel's house while there was still light, he needed to be on his way. He rose, thanking Toussaint for his help.

"Of course," came the reply and Toussaint took his hand and held it firmly for a moment. "You must take care, my friend. Not everyone will be pleased that you're here."

Lucas returned the firm handshake, but Toussaint was no longer looking at him. His eyes had fixed on something behind

Lucas, who did not turn or ask any more of his saviour. He went straight up the stairs to the shelter of his room.

CHAPTER 11

Lucas switched on Junior's shortwave radio by the bed. There was nothing about Haiti on the news. The BBC was leading on a big European story. If his report had been used, it had now been dropped.

He sat down and wrote a sixty-second despatch and then a longer piece, using extracts from the commentary he had recorded during the demonstration. He listened back to the final cut and was once again swept up by the crowd, their progress to the palace and the echoing gunfire in the square. He pressed 'send' and checked his emails. One had just arrived from Carrick, thanking him for his first piece and asking for more. And there was a second from the BBC's Caribbean Service with a number for him to call.

The man who answered was Courtney James, the head of service. "Hey Lucas, we heard your piece, but if you can give us more about what's actually happening on the streets, we'll run it at length." Lucas explained what he had just filed, and Courtney sounded pleased, his resonant voice rumbling down the line. "That's perfect, man. We've been phoning round and you're the only international reporter there. We can see some local stuff on the wires, but you're the only guy we've got on the ground, so we're depending on you."

Lucas had been so focused on winning support from the newsroom for his trip that he had forgotten about this specialist unit which broadcast in English to the Caribbean. It was run by another department at World Service, and he had overlooked it. But he happily confirmed he would do more detailed reports for them. Courtney gave him all the contact details and said they would be checking the system regularly for anything he provided. He was still talking when the line clicked dead, but Lucas was left in no doubt that Haiti was rising on the news agenda.

Down in the lobby, he found Henri lounging against one of its broad pillars.

"You see...shooting?" he asked, clearly relieved to see Lucas again.

Lucas assured him all was well and gave him Michel's address. Henri considered it for a moment and then pointed to a new watch he now sported on his wrist, indicating the need to set off immediately.

The way to Petionville lay up a steep hill which ran off the airport road.

As they ascended, Lucas saw the capital spread out below them. With each kilometre, he could see further across the city. At the centre was the white Presidential Palace bordered by its few streets of stone and brick houses. There were the barracks off to the right and the broad palace lawn and the square, but beyond this central grandeur lay mile after mile of low-rise dilapidation punctuated by the few recognisable roads.

Rising from the shambles of the city were thin strands of smoke from charcoal fires. Collectively, they spiralled up to form a brooding canopy.

Lucas realised this hill was one of a series that separated Port au Prince from the interior of the country. It was as if a giant lay buried on the outskirts of the city with only its great arms visible, spread wide as a barrier against whatever lay further inland. Lucas had read accounts of the fertile soil and lush vegetation that had typified this Pearl of the Caribbean, but now all he saw was wasteland. Where were the trees to make the charcoal that burned in the slums below? Where was the soil to grow the meagre amounts of food in the markets? It seemed everything that had made this country great had eroded into myth. He didn't know Haiti at all, he told himself. He was not sure he ever would.

The old car's engine, which had been straining under the effort of the long climb took on a lighter note. To his surprise, Lucas found the plateau at the top of the hill was green and lush. Set back from the road he glimpsed some substantial properties.

After a while, they entered a square and Henri swung the car down a small avenue running off one corner. He stopped after a hundred yards near a pair of black, newly painted gates supported by two stone columns and switched off the engine. The sun was low, its rays red across the car's bonnet.

Lucas got out and walked towards the gates. As he did so, half a dozen youths who had been lounging by the side of the road ran around laughing and shouting at the novelty of a white man's arrival.

Lucas waved at them and tightened his grip on his shoulder bag, which contained his recorder. He strode forward, trying to look as though he knew where he was going. The younger boys sported Paris Saint Germain football shirts. They gathered behind two older youths who were walking towards Lucas. They were bare-chested, tall, fit, strong. Lucas put his head down and continued towards the gates and the overgrown garden beyond them. He hoped this was indeed his destination. It was the closest building, and he needed a familiar face.

The two bigger youths were now in front of him, preening. They were standing in his way, but slowly retreating. Lucas tried to ignore them. He looked over at the football shirts and said: "Manchester United." This drew a big grin and a laugh of recognition from the younger ones, but their leaders now stopped in front of him. They weren't laughing.

What now? How was he going to get past? Then there was a hand on his bag. He turned to slap it away, and when he looked up again, they were on top of him, their faces in his. That's when Lucas saw the knife. The tallest youth held it flat across his lean stomach, angling the blade, showing Lucas who was boss, showing him what would happen if he resisted.

Suddenly, a terrible roar brought everyone up short. At first, Lucas thought the sound came from one of the boys. But then it burst on them again – louder and much closer. The leaders in front of him wheeled round to reveal a black swirling apparition from which a fearful cry once again erupted, scattering the boys in all directions. All Lucas could see in the fading light was a twisting pillar, turning like a tornado. And from its centre, he glimpsed suns and moons and stars, catching the rays of the setting sun as they spun. He squinted at this advancing galaxy and for a moment considered following the boys in flight. The whole, towering mass appeared to be suspended above the road, moving over a cloud of dust billowing from its base.

Then Lucas saw above the dark column, a thick mass of afro hair and where the column met the road, barely visible through the dust cloud, were two sandaled feet.

The vision now gave off a sound, so deep Lucas thought Henri must have started revving the car, but he suddenly recognised it as deep-throated laughter. It was Michel. And as he came to rest in front of him, Lucas realised he was dressed in a voluminous, black sorcerer's gown with long flowing sleeves, adorned with brilliant astrological symbols.

One enormous hand gripped his. The other encircled his shoulders. Lucas was swept up in a torrent of material as he was whisked through the open gate and into the crazy garden which lay beyond.

Michel guided Lucas along paths that segmented overgrown bushes on every side. "Sorry about the reception committee," he growled, his large hand still on Lucas's shoulder. "Kids don't have much to do round here." A bird – not unlike the one Lucas had seen at his bathroom window – sat on a bush in front of them, head cocked, waiting for them. And as they approached, it flew further along the path ahead. "I'm glad you made it. It's been a busy day what with the demonstrations." The path bent and twisted from left to right, as if the garden had been laid out as a curious maze. There were continuous intersections, often followed by squeezes through which they went single file, foliage closing in and then releasing them on to broader paths that allowed them to glimpse a seat or a fountain – but always briefly. Lucas had the feeling again that he had been here before. It all felt familiar somehow, although he had no idea where they were or where they were going. Then the house appeared in front of him, made of stone, surprisingly grand for a family home and there was the bird again waiting for them. It flew off as they walked up the four steps which led to open French doors.

They entered a long living room with plush sofas lining the walls and a broad, dark Persian carpet. At the far end there was an altar, framed by tall wooden poles which had been fashioned into serpents, their heads surveying the room. Between them, complex symbols had been chalked on to the wall with circles and arrows. Michel saw Lucas take it all in and then look again at his cloak.

"I like to play the Hougan." He smiled. "It keeps everyone round here on their toes. I put on the robes and people don't disturb the house or my work."

"It's very effective," chuckled Lucas as Michel rolled up the broad sleeves of his gown and swept the hair back from his eyes to reveal more of the man Lucas had met at the radio station the previous morning.

And then a more melodic voice chimed in behind them, brought in by the breeze which had set the trees murmuring in the garden.

"You're not dead then?"

Lucas turned to see a translucent figure by the door. The last rays of the sun framed this new vision against the garden beyond. She wore a light flowing dress, streaked blood-orange by the setting sun. As she walked into the room, the overhead

114

light dispelled the colour, revealing her in a simple white dress tied round the waist with a golden sash. Lucas, taken completely off guard, spoke without thinking.

"What are you doing here?" he asked.

"That's the second time you've said that today." Marie laughed and moved closer to offer her hand – this time ungloved. It slid coolly in to his.

"I'm sorry," he said. "It's the sunset; I was dazzled."

"I think I'm the one who should apologise," Marie said. "I told Papa I'd keep an eye on you." She looked at Michel, explaining herself. "It was all the confusion, everyone running in all directions. I lost him." She turned back to Lucas. "I'm sorry. I'm glad you're alright."

Then Michel intervened. "I did ask Marie to look out for you. She was determined to go on the demonstration – much against my advice." He frowned at his daughter. "But then I thought she might catch you at the hotel before you set off."

"We caught up at the church," said Marie.

"So, you've seen our mad priest?" Michel said, turning back to Lucas. "He's quite a force of nature."

"You mean Baptiste?" managed Lucas before Marie picked up again.

"Yes, he was there. Wasn't he marvellous?" She was suddenly animated. "He looks so fragile, so vulnerable in his simple black gown, but his presence magnetises a room. He outguns the army with his words. I've never seen a man who can command attention the way he does. The politicians argue and divide people, but he brings everyone together, gives them all purpose."

Michel cautiously agreed, putting his hand gently on Marie's shoulder as he spoke.

"I try not to get too close to the opposition, but it's hard not to be swept up by the emotion generated by Baptiste and his followers. He is extraordinary. Rome hates it, of course. The fact is, he's brought us liberation theology. He tells the poor they don't have to put up with oppression; that God doesn't intend them to accept their lot; that the poor will inherit the earth, not in the next life, but in this. Rome hates being dragged into politics and controversy."

"He's wonderful." Marie's eyes glistened. "We've seen nothing like it." Her head pitched up defiantly. "At last, there's someone who gives people a voice, who feels their pain, who stands up for justice against oppression. He speaks the truth. Haitians have heard too many lies and suffered too long. I'm no Catholic, but I can see why the poor think he's been sent by God."

Lucas stared. Her tanned skin was glowing. Her long dark hair embraced her shoulders. Her gestures, serene and controlled, only emphasised the passion in her words.

It must be wonderful, he thought, to be swept up in a cause, to have something to live and fight for, to believe you were so firmly on the side of right.

Michel ushered them through the long room to an alcove, where a silent Haitian maid had laid out drinks on a low table. Lucas sat and Michel excused himself, saying he had to finish his report for the Agency. Marie followed, saying she'd return in a minute. The maid poured a dark liquid in to a glass and offered it to Lucas, who drank the rum with an ease that worried him. He stared at the shadow beyond the door and thought of the priest and the power he had exercised over the crowd earlier in the day. It was more than a simple demonstration. It was more like a revolution, and Lucas was already thinking of how to chronicle it.

"You still with us?" Marie was by his side, her hand lightly touching his shoulder. "Michel's just coming. He's finishing his article. He's like a spider, sitting there contacting everyone. He gathers up all these threads and spins them out over the telex to APM and the world gets to hear about poor Haiti…" she hesitated. "…Well, only if the papers print it, of course. Living in the States, I'm amazed at how little gets into the newspapers. We're kind of in our own time zone here…The shooting starts, someone dies, everything speeds up, the world takes notice. Then the shooting stops, everything slows down, and we're forgotten again."

"Well, that's why I'm here," Lucas said. "If all we do is report when terrible things happen, then we never take a more considered look at what the causes are. I came here to make a documentary not report the news. I've kind of been overtaken by events, but I plan to do something more considered."

Marie sat down opposite him. "Take a longer view," she said approvingly. "That's good. Nothing's going to change unless we take a long view, work away at the issues – for years if necessary. That's why I admire my father. He's here all the time. He lives it. It's why I'll be coming back here next year after university."

Lucas felt they were falling into step, as they'd done earlier in the day.

"What university?" he asked.

117

"I'm at NYU, living the high life in Manhattan." She smiled brightly. "I'm studying anthropology and doing my doctorate on voodoo. I come back here of course. I come to see papa, but I spend time with the Hougans and try to get them to explain it all to me."

"And do they?" asked Lucas.

"Actually, yes. They're remarkably tolerant. I don't know why. Perhaps it's because they know my father, and he respects them. And of course, I was born here. I'm half Haitian. They include me in their rituals. I'm going to one tonight. You should come!"

Lucas laughed, surprised. "Really? That would be great. I've read a bit about it, but to actually experience it would be extraordinary."

"That's good," said Marie brightly. "And what have you learned so far?"

"Well, it's been difficult. Where I come from, people associate voodoo with horror movies, but from the little I've read it seems to have more in common with Catholicism than Hollywood. The idea that a spirit can live on, even after death and influence us – that's pretty familiar to Christians. Everything from the resurrection to the power of the Holy Spirit all seem to have a mirror in voodoo." He paused, not wanting Marie to take him for a committed Christian. "Don't get me wrong. I hate the institution of the church. My father was very caught up in it and it pulled our family apart. But something about the mystery of it rings true with me. That it's possible to feel someone's presence when they're not physically with you." He hesitated, wondering whether this was all getting a little too serious too fast, but Marie was sitting forward, clearly engaged.

She laughed. "Well, you've come to the right place. And yes, there are elements of the Catholic faith that have been taken up by voodoo. I think it's because the Europeans tried to convert their slaves who had their own beliefs rooted in their own experience. But there's a lot more to it. Voodoo is based on a spiritual view of the world that's rooted in Africa, and it's simply how the world is here. If you don't understand voodoo, you don't understand Haiti. It's how people... survive all this." She waved her hand towards the garden and what lay beyond. "It's how they communicate and understand the significance of the world around them. It's key to everything."

"Sounds fascinating," said Lucas, quietly thanking Carla for feeding him all that reading material. "It sounds really relevant. In London so many people seem to think of religion as something separate from everyday life or something for other people."

"Yes," said Marie. "I see it in New York all the time. People put their beliefs in a box. They keep them to themselves. They only roll them out on formal occasions – often funerals. And there's huge emphasise on the physical stuff – that seems to be all they focus on. You know, the body, the funeral, the grand memorial, but here life's more mystical and death isn't so final. The body may die, but of course that's not the entire person – not everything they were. And those elements that aren't physical can live on. It's not that strange an idea. Everyone has moments when they sense things they can't see or touch. Don't you sometimes feel a presence of some kind? Like someone's watching you?" And suddenly

Marie sat up straight, pointing at something next to Lucas. "What's that? Who's that next to you?" she asked, her eyes wide with surprise. Lucas quickly looked round and then, catching the amusement on Marie's face, realised the deception. She was smiling happily at having fooled him. "You know, it's Eliot in *The Wasteland*," she laughed. And Lucas half remembered what she was referring to. "He's walking along a road with a friend, and he sees a third person walking beside them, but when he counts there are only two: whatever it is that he sees, it's in his peripheral vision. When he looks ahead – up the road – he's aware of the third person with them, but when he looks directly, he's not there. I think it happens to all of us. And it can happen anywhere, anytime, when you're not expecting it. Suddenly, some presence overtakes you. It can be triggered by a memory or a story. Maybe a parent or a friend, someone who's died, but something lingers, and you feel its presence. That's the way it is here, but all the time. Spirits are always with you, always influencing you. And people embrace it: the dead are here to guide you, warn you, show you the way."

Lucas leant forward. He felt his heart quicken, not quite believing what he was hearing, eager to grasp her full meaning. "You mean it's like history's always with us, and only fools ignore it?"

"Yes – history. But this isn't just something to be studied." Marie put her hand to her breast. "It's something in here." And then she looked straight at Lucas. "I mean, who are you?"

The question took Lucas off guard, and he laughed again. "That's a tricky one. I'm not sure I've nailed that yet. I can't explain myself to other people; don't even understand why I do things sometimes or why things happen. I'm not sure I know myself."

"Well, there you are." Marie looked satisfied with his answer. "It's hard. It's hard to understand what life throws at us. We get confused, afraid, and we struggle to understand ourselves and how we feel. We need others to help us. Sometimes we only get to see ourselves clearly through the eyes of others. It's almost like we don't exist on our own and it's the attention, the perception of others that brings us to life."

Lucas gazed at her, struggling with her stream of thought. "And what's that got to do with voodoo?"

"Well, that's my field." Marie leant back, pulling her smooth legs in to her body and wrapping her bare arms around them. "People here understand that others help them make sense of the world. It's just the others aren't always alive. The fact that someone's dead doesn't diminish the influence they have on the living. They're still part of who we are." Marie chose her words carefully. "Their knowledge…their perception of us is key to who we are. People here understand this better than anyone. It's only through others that we come to know ourselves properly."

"And voodoo captures this?" Lucas drank it all in like a man emerging from a desert.

"It's an instinctive way of life for people here. To practise voodoo is to recognise all the forces that make you who you are." Marie shook her head. "It's weird studying it because it's not something learned. It's a belief system, not a rational thing. But it's real enough. All these spirits roam freely in this world. They can even possess you. And you don't have to search them out. They're here now…" She glanced back towards the garden… "in this room, but *you* won't see it. You come from Europe." She smiled. "Such things are forgotten there."

Looking at this beautiful young woman, so natural in this room with its pagan altar and Michel in his magical robes working silently next door, Lucas found himself seduced by the conversation. Everything that had seemed so strange and unsettling in London no longer felt out of place here.

"Perhaps that's why we're so fascinated by love," he ventured. "When you love someone, they almost become part of you. You lose yourself in them. It's a bit like letting a spirit take you over. It gives your life meaning. It's exhilarating. It makes you feel… more alive…"

Marie smiled at him. "Perhaps love is all you Europeans have left. Perhaps love is just a remnant, a fragment of an understanding people here still have. Here you can move in a world of spirits as easily as go to the marketplace for food. Both bring life. Both make you who you are. Without them, you won't exist."

For a moment, Lucas had a strong urge to tell Marie about Zoe and their strange connection, but it was too soon – too personal. Anyway, he wanted to know more about this person who had dazzled him with her entrance and now intrigued him with her talk of spirits.

"You said you were only half Haitian?"

"Actually, I'm more Haitian than anything else, having been brought up here. But my mother's French. She's a musician: Celestine? She's famous." Lucas apologised, not recognising the name. "Oh, if you were French, you would have heard of her," said Marie, "And she's popular here too. She plays Zook

122

and Funk and mashes up Creole influences with jazz and rock – it's world music. She tours all the time, and she met Michel when she came on a visit to Haiti years ago. They fell in love and Michel went off with her...he followed her on tour." Marie looked a bit distracted.

"And then?" prompted Lucas.

"Oh, well they got married," she said as if that was the end and Lucas waited until she was ready to go on. "Michel wanted to come back here and settle. This is his home. And Celestine came for a time, playing with local musicians and of course they had me." She shrugged, as much to say that she was not the point of this story. "But she became disillusioned. Not with Michel, but with all the oppression and the violence. Now she lives in Paris and only rarely comes back." Marie brightened. "But I see her in America. She still tours there with her band and when she does, she comes to New York. She's pretty cool... well, more than cool. She's brilliant. People love her music, but she can't bear to be here. She says the government has stripped Haiti of its dignity and will never really change."

Lucas wondered how Michel felt about this and at that moment he re-entered the room – appearing out of the shadows leading to his study.

He sat down next to Lucas and immediately started asking questions about the demonstration and what had happened. Lucas relayed the key events. He described how the priest had fired up the young men before they set off and explained the running commentary he had recorded.

"We should check to see if the BBC has your report," said Michel, springing out of his chair. He went across to a table that stood against the wall. On it was a huge shortwave radio with wires running from the back and up the wall to form a makeshift aerial. One thin strand ran the full length of the room and out of a small window.

Lucas glanced at his watch. If Michel was intending to listen to the news, it must be coming up to the hour. But his watch said quarter past.

"You've missed the news," Lucas said, as Michel flicked switches and twisted the chunky black dial in the middle of the instrument.

"I know," said Michel. "Your report won't be on World News until midnight GMT. For some reason the BBC saves News about this region for the late bulletins, but Caribbean Report will have it. That's what we listen to. They do the in-depth stuff and they've been featuring Haiti a lot recently."

Lucas recalled the rich Jamaican voice on the phone and realised that this regional programme, not made in the newsroom but by a handful of Caribbean reporters in another part of Bush House, might have the most impact here.

The radio crackled into life. It sounded like the sea crashing against some faraway shore, and then whistled like a bird before a signature tune of pounding drums took over. When it faded away, Courtney's voice was introducing the lead story. The clamour of the protesters came surging out of the receiver and then that deep voice again:

"Lucas Gould witnessed the demonstration today and sent us this report…"

They sat silently as the day's events resonated round the room. There was the priest exhorting the crowd, the burning tyres, the tumult as the procession approached the square, the shooting and finally a stranger's voice. "Perhaps it's time to take shelter…"

Gunfire echoed around them as Courtney concluded: "Our reporter taking cover in Port au Prince this afternoon."

Michel switched off the radio and Lucas turned to Marie, wondering what she'd made of it. She was still sitting with her arms around her knees, her eyes wide.

"We were there, Lucas. It was like being there again. I saw it all again."

"Thank you," Lucas said softly. "It was quite a day."

"This is good, Lucas," said Michel with a clap of his hands. I write my articles, but newspapers cut them down or spike them. But what goes out on the BBC hits home. The government will be listening. It matters. It can make a difference."

"I'm not sure about that," said Lucas. "I'm not here to campaign. I have to stick with the facts."

"Facts can be the most powerful thing," responded Michel.

"Well, yes – but I'm finding them hard to come by here."

"That's true. They can be elusive – especially with all that's going on at the moment. There's so much rumour and fear; figuring out what's true can be an impossible task. It's like trying to do a jigsaw puzzle when the pieces have been scattered or lost. You pick up bits of information but on their own they make little sense and getting them to fit together…well it can take years to get the true picture."

"But worth the effort," said Marie, proud of her father. "Worth the years of work and the risks. That's what journalists do, isn't it, Papa?"

"Yes, yes," said Michel, as if picking up previous conversations. "It's true. We live our lives in pieces. We pick them up and report as we go." He looked at Lucas. "You and I, we may work alone, but if there's value in what we do, in the end it becomes a collective effort. If enough of us dig deep enough for long enough, then one day someone may pull all the pieces together and make good use of it."

Marie was no longer looking at Michel but at something in the distance… "It's all about ideas," she said. "The power of ideas to change the world and create the future. It's there in voodoo. It's everywhere. In the end, ideas are the most powerful thing. Great ideas are irrepressible. They have a life of their own, unstoppable. They'll outlive us all. And you journalists," she said, looking at them both. "You spread ideas like viruses. That's why you frighten dictators. They know that ideas are the one thing they can't control."

"Well, you did good today," said Michel, turning to Lucas. We must work together, share material. Pool our resources. I'm told more protests are planned. We must be ready."

The silent maid reappeared, and Michel guided them through to a dining area where the table was laid with chicken and rice and a large bowl of fresh salad. They sat down to eat and, under Lucas's questioning Michel explained that he sent his stories to Caracas, where an Editor then sent the final version to Washington. If there was enough interest it was distributed all over the world. Michel seemed to like his editor, who visited once a year and generally kept an eye on his welfare. Lucas asked about Michel's wife and was touched by the way Michel spoke about her.

"Celestine's a great musician. I knew when I married her that Haiti couldn't contain her. It's only right for her to live in a great capital like Paris. It's the best outlet for her work. We see each other when we can but now Marie's grown and living in the States, I couldn't ask Celestine to stay here. I married her for love, and I can't confine her or stifle her."

"But *you're* still here," said Lucas, wondering how he couldn't be with the woman he loved.

"This is my life," said Michel. "I'll die here because I don't have a choice. I can't simply walk away. And I'm lucky. APM's one of the very few wire services that show any real interest in what's going on in Haiti and they're good to me. The American reporters fly in and out, but I must stay. I live this story. It's part of me. It's what I do."

Lucas felt a sudden urge to say he too might stay. Who else was going to pay attention to this country? Flung out into the sea, too far for America to care very much and too close to be totally ignored. But somehow this geographical position condemned the country to a form of stasis, which could only be changed if something dramatic happened to force its plight onto the world stage.

"You should be getting back to the hotel," said Michel, pushing his plate away. "You should leave well ahead of the midnight curfew. The Macoutes will be out, and they won't tolerate stragglers."

"I thought the Macoutes had been disbanded?" Lucas had read about these security police, set up by the dictator Papa Doc Duvalier to keep everyone subservient to his will. They had roamed the country, instilling fear into the population. Some of them were even Hougans and Duvalier had encouraged the connection to voodoo to fuel the fear they spread. They had no formal uniform but sometimes wore blue shirts, or red neckerchief and always dark glasses. Such shadowy figures had rapidly become infamous. If you crossed them, you were beaten. If you plotted revolt, they would come for you. They would rip out your tongue or rape you, so everyone saw the price of rebellion. Michel didn't answer the question, so Lucas continued: "I know Duvalier used them to kill political opponents. Didn't he have them in every village? But I read they were disarmed after he died."

"Well, you barely see the blue shirts anymore, that's true. And the army said they were disbanded but even if you wanted to, it's hard to get rid of a secret police force. Many of them are still loyal to their commanders and they in turn maintain close links to the army or they've hooked up with gangs. They're everywhere. I guess the money for them still flows somehow. After all, if you don't pay you lose control of them. If anything, the situation is worse than before because now they're harder to identify."

Michel took a drink and continued: "They don't call them Macoutes for nothing. They come at night like shadows." He was looking quizzically at Lucas. "You know how they got their name? They took Macoutes from the children's tales. Tonton Macoute was the uncle who came in the night to steal children away from their parents. They're the figures from our nightmares."

"Well, I certainly don't want to meet them on the road tonight," Lucas said with a laugh.

"Dead right," said Michel, glancing at his watch. "The curfew applies to the whole city, so you don't want to be heading down the hill too late. You'd better get going." Michel began to stand, and Lucas was pushing his chair back when Marie stopped them.

"He's not going back. He's coming with me," she said,

Michel looked down at her in surprise, still seated at her place at the table.

"I'm invited to the *hounfour* tonight. You know De Beauvoir invited me." Michel was about to protest, but Marie quickly continued. "Lucas wants to understand voodoo. He can't report Haiti and not understand voodoo culture. He can come with me. De Beauvoir won't mind. He says I'm always welcome." Lucas felt Michel's eyes on him, checking his reaction as Marie pressed home her argument. "It's a regular meeting and there are no initiates – if there were, then De Beauvoir wouldn't have asked me." Marie stood, with an air of finality and said, "Anyway, it's nearly dark, and it's risky for Lucas to go back to the city. Even now it'll be dangerous."

This last thought seemed to sway Michel, who gave in.

"Okay Lucas, it looks like you're staying the night. Your driver can take you back tomorrow."

"It sounds like the safest option," said Lucas, hoping Michel didn't think he had conspired in Marie's plan.

"Come," said Marie. She beckoned to Lucas as she moved to the door and the garden. "We can walk. De Beauvoir's visiting the temple below the village, and we can go down through the fields....Goodnight, Papa," she said, reaching up to give her father a swift kiss on the cheek. Then she turned and Lucas felt her hand slip into his as they crossed the threshold, on their way.

CHAPTER 12

They looked spectral in the fading light as they emerged into the garden. Lucas was sure they took a different path from the one when he arrived. He recognised nothing as they turned down an empty alley, past a concrete pool, empty of water and on, twisting and turning, covering a lot of ground to reach the gate, which Lucas thought must have been closer than their route suggested. When they finally emerged, he looked around to see if the youths were still there, but the shadows had chased them away. The rough road that led to the house was empty except for the car.

Henri was virtually invisible inside. The driver's seat was reclined so low only the outline of his face was faintly visible through the open window.

Marie put her hands on the door and leant in, speaking to him in Creole. Henri, startled out of his doze, stared at her in wonder – a study in concentration, listening to every word.

"We stay?" Henri said to Lucas who nodded approval. "Okay. I sleep here," he said, pulling his seat upright.

"I've told him we're going to the temple," Marie said. "He can drive down the road behind the house and park by the entrance. But we can walk." She pointed to a track that led past the house. "It's cooler now, and it's not that far."

Marie moved off, tugging at Lucas's sleeve to encourage him to follow. She set the pace, walking ahead of him down the ill-defined path through parched shrubs and thorn bushes. Their progress was accompanied by the constant chatter of cicadas, punctuated only by the bleating of a goat below. By the time they were halfway down the hill, it was completely dark. Lucas called to Marie to wait because he was losing sight of her white dress. She turned.

"Hang on Mr Lucas." She took his hand and slid it into the small of her back through the band of gold encircling her narrow waist. Lucas could feel the warmth of her body through the thin material and thrilled at the touch. She set off again slowly, and he fell into step behind, gingerly at first, careful not to trip her and end the contact. "Stay close," she said over her shoulder as they passed rocky outcrops and needle-sharp thorns. Lucas held tight to the band and carefully rested his other hand on Marie's hip, steadying himself, feeling her easy sway as she walked, savouring the descent. Her perfume wafted over him, teasing his senses until – all too soon – the ground levelled out, and they arrived in a clearing of flattened earth.

Marie released his hand to walk next to him, her long dress floating around her feet. Freed from her touch, Lucas noticed wavering lights ahead, faintly revealing a long-whitewashed wall which ran across the width of the clearing.

They approached the wall and Lucas saw candles recessed in the render. Two wooden doors stood open, and a woman came forward. Marie spoke to her, and Lucas heard the name

De Beauvoir again. She bowed and led them through the entrance into a courtyard, half covered by a roof of woven leaves propped up by wooden staves. Beyond the yard, there was a large circular building, with a conical roof made of wooden slats and banana leaves. Another whitewashed wall formed the circumference of the building. Light and the sound of voices spilled out from its narrow entrance.

"We must wait here," said Marie. "The ceremony usually starts at sunset and we're late. We must hope De Beauvoir can still see us."

Lucas looked at her. She was perfectly calm and cool despite the walk down the steep hill, comfortable in her own frame, in control. Certain in this uncertain world.

"Won't I look a bit out of place?" he whispered.

"No. I know this man. He wants foreigners to understand voodoo and take it seriously. He'll welcome you, I'm sure. De Beauvoir's like family. I can't remember a time when I didn't know him. My father and he go way back…"

"I'm not even sure what to call it," mused Lucas. "Is it a religion?"

"I suppose Christians might think of it as a religion, especially with its connections to Catholicism. But I don't think religion is the right word." Marie leant towards him, and he could see the smooth swelling of her breasts against the white cloth of her dress. He consciously kept his eyes on her face. "It's a philosophy, religion and culture all in one and it doesn't have the same boundaries that you have in your world. For the people here, spirits are as real as the ground you walk on."

"So real you could talk to them? See them?"

"Yes. See them, talk to them. It's not so strange." Marie laughed, trying to put into words what required no explanation in Haiti, but was so important to Lucas.

"Perhaps it's easier to think of it as philosophy. It's a different way of looking at the world. It redefines what's real. In London or New York, people think of themselves all the time. What's real to them is limited by their own preoccupations, their own thoughts. But here, what we see in others and what they see in us can be more important and more revealing."

"Well, it's true that where I come from people put themselves first," said Lucas. He thought of his break with his parents and Catherine and his own ambition. "We pursue the things we want for ourselves. I suppose it does look a bit like a cult of the individual."

"It's the same in America," said Marie. "But not here. Here, if you reduce everything to the individual nothing makes sense anymore. You could end up entirely alone. I mean, imagine you really *were* alone in the world. No one to criticise you, no one to praise you, no one to love you. Would you exist? How would you know you exist?"

"Well, I'd be me," said Lucas, smiling.

"Would you? Aren't we who we are because of others?" asked Marie. "You're born because someone gives birth to you; you're nurtured to become who you are; you're taught by someone else. What people think of you and how they respond to you help define you. If you were completely alone – all those things that make you who you are would disappear – would you even exist?"

"But I'm often alone," said Lucas. "I'm alone all the time when I'm not at work."

"Ah, but that's not the way this world is…you're never alone, because the spirits are always with you. They never leave you – the departed, kindred spirits – they're always there, influencing you." Marie stopped, searching for some analogy to make her meaning clearer. "It's like Descartes, or rather the opposite of Descartes," she corrected. "Not so much 'I think therefore I am.' It's more: '*You* think therefore I am!'"

"Very good." Lucas laughed. "Not *Cogito ergo sum* but *cogitant ergo sum*. So, without others an individual is just someone who thinks they exist – perhaps they don't."

"Well maybe not literally," Marie smiled happily at the thought, "but it's sort of true. What are we without the affirmation of others? It's hard enough to understand yourself and why you feel the way you do. Sometimes others' perceptions can confirm a more solid reality…"

"I hadn't thought of it quite like that," said Lucas. "We get so caught up in ourselves, we can miss what's really important."

"Here everything's connected," said Marie. "People see themselves bound up in a spiritual world, bound to family, friends, past and present, both the dead and the living."

As she stopped speaking, Lucas realised the cicadas had fallen silent. All that was left were the voices inside the building softly chanting, hushed in expectation.

"And these spirits," he asked. "Are they benign?" ·

"Not all. Some can be dangerous. Those who die violently or don't receive a proper burial. But most are kind. I hope you'll see tonight. If you're open to it, you'll see *lespri*, you'll feel them when they come."

Their conversation had drawn Lucas and Marie closer to each other and their voices had hushed to a whisper. The chanting from the building died away, and a stillness wrapped them round like a cloak. He could feel Marie almost touching him. Her presence filled his senses, and he suddenly caught himself wanting to slow time, to hang on to this moment with her. But he checked himself. *How foolish,* he thought. *You can't control time. You know that. It's unruly. You have to let it flow round you. Give yourself to it if you really want to live.* And he looked at Marie, open and ready for whatever lay beyond the walls in front of them, her passion for life tangible. Her energy evoked a liberation that was irresistible. It made him think that perhaps he had indeed been too wrapped up in himself. Maybe that was what Carla had sensed when she'd said he was alone. And it was true, wasn't it? For months now, his life had been like a prison. The very presence he longed for had confined him.

The truth was that his sister's visitations had left him feeling isolated. Her presence, unexpected and inexplicable as it was, was a secret he had felt unable to share. How could he possibly explain it to anyone? What was he supposed to do? Turn round and casually say: *Oh, by the way, my dead sister drops in and talks to me occasionally.* It was just too weird. How could you possibly say that to anyone? And not being able to speak of it had brought a terrible loneliness.

So, maybe that's what he was seeking, he thought. Tonight, standing next to Marie outside this *hounfour*, he hoped for release. Not release from his sister's visitations – he loved her. He relished her presence. But release from the guilt that followed in her wake, that left him wretched and isolated, obsessing about what he could have done differently. If he could only see this world that Marie described...a world beyond normal perceptions. Somewhere beyond the objective world of facts which bound him round and made anything else so hard to talk about. Somewhere more fundamental. Somewhere closer to a truth he sought; a truth which beckons but never waits...

A woman approached. Like Marie, she was dressed in white, but with a red neckerchief wrapped tightly round her hair. She offered two small wooden cups and invited them to drink. Lucas looked at Marie who took hers and drank in one swift movement and he followed her example, keen not to offend. With the cups returned, the woman stooped before them and with a long twig she drew in the dust at their feet. The twig circled several times, creating symbols which looped and trailed off in the direction of the door. Lucas thought he saw a goat's horns, but before he could untangle the pattern, Marie's hand was at his back pushing him forward and they followed their guide under the arch into the large rotunda, ringed by a mud wall. An unbroken circle of about fifty villagers were facing inwards.

A man stepped forward and greeted Marie with outstretched arms, and she made the introductions. "De Beauvoir, this is Lucas. He's a journalist. I hope you don't mind, but he's staying with us, and I've brought him to you because he's telling the world about our country. He wants to understand."

De Beauvoir took Lucas's hand, immediately dispelling any sense of intrusion. "I'm glad you've come."

"I'm honoured to be here, Monsieur De Beauvoir," Lucas said. "I'm here to learn."

"And if you have an open heart, you shall," said De Beauvoir, squeezing the hand which he still held. And then he looked at the assembled villagers. "Forgive me, it's time we started. You must stay. You're most welcome." And he walked away towards the middle of the room.

All eyes were on him and as he walked he started to chant, drawing imitative responses from the onlookers. De Beauvoir raised his hands, inviting more interventions. His words became rapid, and his voice rose. The crowd mirrored his movements, vibrant in rhythm, responding in unison whenever he paused for their contributions.

He circled a large wooden table adorned with fruits and other foods. Smoke rose from two saucer-shaped stones at each end and a woman stepped out from the crowd carrying a baby in her arms. She offered it to De Beauvoir who carefully cradled it and walked around the table wafting the fumes over the child as he passed. The baby was then returned to its mother and from somewhere off to the side drums started a rhythmical pattern, at first simple and subdued but gradually growing in volume and complexity.

De Beauvoir followed the curve of the outer wall of the chamber, calling out as he went. Marie stayed close to Lucas and whispered in his ear. "He's calling *lespri*. He's asking us all to help him invite them in."

The villagers gradually fell into step behind him. They followed closely as he led the way, his body propelled by the rhythm of the drums. As the pulse accelerated the procession broke and each person became more absorbed in their own

137

dance. Some raised their hands to the ceiling, others held their heads, some spun on their heels and toes as the whole body of people continued to circulate, each driven by their own interpretation of the pounding rhythm.

Lucas could feel the vibrations through the soles of his feet. His senses sharpened; his skin tingled. Everything around him appeared more vivid. The percussive pulse travelled up through his legs to his stomach. He felt the pressure in his chest and head as though some great object was speeding by, forcing a passage through the air. If he had not known better, he would have thought the musicians were pounding out their beat directly on the walls and floor around him.

Marie danced next to him, having given up trying to speak against the noise. Lucas too was moving to the drumbeat, unable to remain still in a place where everything was in motion. The music generated its own gravity. It pulled people towards it and dragged them out of shape.

Marie drifted away, following three young girls who circled past her, moving off on a trajectory not of her making. Lucas gradually gave way to the forces at play and followed in the same direction, slowly rotating, losing any sense of where he was or how much time was passing. It became an endless dance, a circle of rhythm, a commotion which spun everyone away from themselves. They were no longer constrained by the walls around them or the ground beneath their feet. There was only this moment and the motion. Here was space without limits, energy unbound, a place for the spirit, not the flesh.

Then a woman close to him fell. Something about the way she lost her balance and toppled backwards – her loose dress cascading from her, arms flailing – made Lucas stand and stare. The fulsome dress billowed up, inflated by her fall, as though it no longer contained a body. It was just a pile of clothes, dropped where they lay, disembodied, discarded. A man came forward. His horn-rimmed spectacles caught the candlelight. He knelt to help, but Lucas was focused only on the crumpled dress. The man looked up at him, returning his stare, questioning his presence.

***

"Why are you here?" He was standing in the headmaster's study at his old school, staring at the pile of clothing which lay on the broad desk in front of him. The clothes were twisted in a heap carelessly thrown down. "You should have given us more time." The headmaster was glaring at him through a thick pair of glasses, his eyes oddly magnified by the lenses. Stale air hung in the room like a shroud.

Lucas had insisted on coming at short notice to pick up his sister's possessions, meagre as they proved to be. The Matron had brusquely dropped them on to the desk in a crumpled sheet too big for the task. Lucas eyed the contents: pieces of discarded uniform, a toothbrush, two pairs of shoes, games kit still muddy from some recent fixture…

The headmaster's gaze was still on him. There had been no greeting at the door. No handshake. Just this glassy stare and suspicion oozing from every pore.

"You do know it was suicide?" He was blunt and defensive. "The handrail's too high on the top landing for someone to simply fall from such a height."

Lucas found he was unable to speak, his blood raging through him. Some fuse in his brain had caused his fists to clench. His body taught. He wanted to throttle this man, but his limbs wouldn't obey.

"We had an independent expert review the case. He checked everything. The findings were unambiguous. Nothing like this has ever happened before. There's nothing to be done."

Lucas, in disbelief at the man's cruelty, had finally turned away, fearful of what he might do, shattered by his loss, overwhelmed by guilt that he had been the cause of his sister's banishment to such a hateful place. He fled the room haunted, unable to accept she was no longer there talking to him, teasing him, answering his questions.

***

Lucas felt a hand brush his face. The sound of the pounding drums rushed in once more, and he turned to look. A girl was spinning away, smiling back at him, pulled by the pulsing rhythm and Lucas was once again caught up in the wild dance that bound him round on every side. Nobody could remain still for long in this place, so he wove and twisted his way back through the throng, until he stood dazed and breathless with his back against the encircling wall, facing in on the scene before him.

He searched urgently for Marie and glimpsed her on the far side of the room. He stood watching, determined to retain some semblance of self-control while everyone around him appeared to be abandoning theirs.

Marie disappeared, swallowed up in the crowd and then reappeared as if nothing could contain her. She made him giddy, her long white dress flying up from her feet blurring across the ground, floating free as if one leap would be sufficient to carry her forever.

He tried hard to focus only on her, unconsciously holding his breath, letting her presence dispel all thoughts of his sister,

140

the wall a reassuring presence at his back. As long as he concentrated on Marie, he could remain detached – a lone observer. But he knew it couldn't last. He couldn't stay like this forever. Not if he wanted to fully grasp what was happening.

Have an open heart. Wasn't that what De Beauvoir had said?

He had to let go, give himself up to the energy in the room. He'd hate himself if he didn't.

Just take that step. Get past this frozen moment. Acknowledge the fear. Face it. Because once you take that step there's no going back. Close your eyes…step through…let the adrenalin take you…surrender.

In a moment, everything changed, no longer solid, all opaque. Forms swirled round him, stretching out before him. *So many! How could there be so many?* And that sound … like the rustling of a million leaves, every soul in the world whispering, all different but all together. And one form reaching out, a familiar laughing, bidding him welcome, pulling him forward. And it was like falling, except there was no rush of air. No constraints. Only release, until the noise stopped, and all was still – profoundly silent: no weight, no tether, no compass, only this irresistible force stretching out forever from the beginning of time to its end. All past present. All future here. All accessible. All eternity held in this still moment, dazzling, breathless, unbearable…terrible.

It was the impact that brought Lucas back, wild-eyed, frightened, staring at the man in front of him who had pinned him against the wall. "You were falling," the man said. Lucas was transfixed, still not comprehending why he was immobile, somehow suspended above the floor. "It's okay. You're safe now. I've got you." The man eased the pressure to allow Lucas to take his own weight. And as his feet touched the floor time restarted. He felt once more gravity beneath his feet. In a gasp, his breath returned, and he managed to focus. It was then he saw, over the man's shoulder. He saw Marie. She was toppling backwards, arms outstretched before her, way beyond his reach. His whole being snapped to attention and all his thoughts locked firmly into the present.

He was on the move before he knew it, rushing to her. But another man who had been watching had also seen her and by the time Lucas was with her she was held in two strong arms cradled like a child being carried to bed. The man seemed to recognise Lucas. Perhaps he had seen them enter together. He gently put Marie's feet to the ground, holding her slight frame with his other arm so that Lucas could move behind her and take his place. As the man withdrew to continue his watchful patrol, Lucas wrapped his arms around Marie and gently dropped to his knees, letting her cascade against him as he eased himself down to the floor, where they lay locked together; she with her head against his chest, perfectly still, life suspended. He held her tight, as if without his presence she might spin away down through the earth and on into darkness.

Now he had her in his arms, shock curled round him like a wave. For a moment, it overwhelmed him. His chest heaved, and he buried his face in Marie's hair, trying to anchor himself in the present. Even though he could feel the earth under him, he had the notion that the ground might suddenly give way. It was only brief, but in that moment, it was not Marie in his arms but his sister Zoe. These arms should have held her; these hands should have saved her. On this hard floor she lay before him. Lucas held on tight, pressing his cheek against hers, her hair tumbling across his face. Drums drowning out the sound of his grief. Eventually, he came up for air – his vertigo slowly abating.

He loosened his grip to raise one hand to wipe his eyes, and then he looked at the girl before him. She was so still that a fear gripped in him. He touched her neck, brushed her hair away from her face and put his hand close, searching for life. All other thoughts dispelled. The wavering light from a hundred lanterns shimmered around her. And then relief flooded through him because he saw Marie's lips part. She stirred. Slowly, she opened her eyes, finding her focus, reluctantly returning.

"Are you alright?" he mouthed at her. She nodded and closed her eyes again to hold some memory close.

Lucas did not know how long they were there on the floor. The room moved, but they remained together at the fulcrum of the rhythm. Around them, time and space stretched and diverged endlessly, only to be reunited when the drumming finally faded as dawn chased it away.

Slowly, people dispersed, drifting away on a trance of exhaustion.

Lucas and Marie eased themselves to their feet and went out into the sharp air. They stood together, Lucas with his arm around Marie's waist, bathed in the milky light that heralds the sun's arrival.

They made their way in silence across the compound towards the hill back to Michel's house. Out of the corner of his eye, Lucas caught sight of Henri, who had parked the car up against a tree and was sitting next to it. He scampered to his feet, but seeing them so close together, held back. He got into the car and Lucas heard the engine start.

CHAPTER 13

Marie was lying full length on the couch in Michel's living room, hair falling across the cushion beneath her head, breathing gently, eyes closed. Lucas sat opposite her his head filled with the night's events.

"Are you alright?" asked Marie dreamily without opening her eyes.

"Are *you*?" replied Lucas. "You're the one who fell." Looking at Marie's slim form laid out before him, he knew she was even now lingering with the spirits. She could be Ophelia, drifting between worlds, letting the currents take her. "I thought I'd lost you ... when you were unconscious on the floor. I couldn't tell if you were still breathing."

"I'm fine," she whispered, her words barely audible. "I've been there before. And when it happens, Ezili protects me."

"Ezili?" asked Lucas, mystified.

"She's a spirit – a *loa* – that always seems to come." She paused, hovering somewhere between sleep and waking. "But there were spirits everywhere last night. I didn't want to come back." She stretched, long and slow. "I could feel you though, feel your arms around me."

Marie slowly rolled on to her side towards Lucas, trying to pull herself out of her reverie, eyes still barely open. "And you. What happened to you?"

Marie's drowsiness only made her more beautiful to Lucas. Watching her gradually wake up from this dreamlike state felt so intimate. It was as if they'd slept together, not just spent the night in each other's company. But how could he answer her question? He couldn't tell her that when he'd held her in his arms, he had seen Zoe, that momentarily she'd become Zoe. *Jesus! What kind of freak are you? You can't tell her you were thinking of someone else when you held her.* He shivered. *Who wants to be compared to a sister? Go there and it will end in disaster.*

"Well, I saw them too," he replied, picking up what Marie had said. "All the spirits. So many and they were so real. It was like they knew me. They took me. I saw…I don't know how to describe it. The place where everything comes together. Their world? Where is it? Out there – beyond our eyeline…" Lucas ran out of words, careful not to say too much.

"Ah good," said Marie yawning. "I'm glad something happened. It's always so hard to describe. You have to experience it…the void, no constraints, letting the spirits buoy you up, letting them take you away…carry you off."

"It sounds almost like death. I suppose that's what it felt like. It was as if my soul left my body and I with it."

Marie lay there a while still apparently toying with consciousness, before appraising his thought.

"But death has many forms, don't you think? We love people. We lose people. We leave our childhood behind. We

145

grow out of our skins and become new people. We forget who we were and who we're supposed to be." And there she was, eyes open, looking directly at him. "All these things are forms of death, but we're still alive, aren't we?"

"But death takes us in the end, doesn't it?" countered Lucas.

"Well, yes," said Marie with a smile. "That's not in dispute. But is death the end of everything?"

"Ah – that's been disputed for centuries, and the conclusion seems to have eluded just about everyone. Even those who thought they'd found the answer struggled to assert it with any real certainty. Even Christ had his moment of doubt on the cross." He thought of Carrick. "It appears that truth and certainty make awkward bedfellows."

Marie lifted her head, her eyes still on his.

"Yes, but this place has its own answer to that question. And nobody here needs to assert it. They live it. They accept it as a fact and then everything else seems to follow.

"Here, people think they're more than the lives they lead. They're the impact they have on others. They're expressions of the influence others have on them. They are not simply or solely themselves. Their self – if such a thing exists independently – is a kind of prism where all these connections coalesce and become something distinct and recognisable. But the self never stops changing. For better or worse it's always in motion. You and I may think we come to an end with death, but for people here the self is inseparable from others. So, your self connects with all that's been and all that will be. As long as there is life, there it is. Still observably You, reverberating …"

146

All Lucas could do was look at her, and she held his gaze. Gone was the mystery of the night, only this girl before him. And as he stared, he felt his breath leave his body. A wave of exhaustion broke over him and he let his head fall into his hands, bleary with the lack of sleep. He had to fight it off. He pushed the palms of his hands into his eyelids, feeling the blood pulse, seeing stars burst. And when Lucas looked up again, he felt a fierce longing. He had a sudden desire to hold her as he had done on the floor of the hut. But he knew he couldn't touch her now. Here in this more solid world, in Michel's house in Petionville, different rules applied, and Lucas was once again bound by the norms of a place where time is measured in seconds, space in metres and where a body confines a spirit which would otherwise float free.

There was a stirring from the direction of the study, and footsteps heralded Michel's arrival.

"So, you're back." Michel wore loose cheesecloth leggings belted with a simple white cord and a Che Guevara T-shirt. His hair was wild. He might have been emerging from a storm.

"Have you heard?" said Michel to Lucas. "The army's on the streets. It's a good job you didn't go back last night. There was shooting at the barracks near the palace. Army units have been taking positions around the capital, although it seems to have calmed down a bit. I've been taking calls half the night. It seems some army units exchanged fire with the Presidential Guard."

"What's happening?" Lucas pulled himself upright, responding to Michel's energy. "Is it a...coup?"

"Not sure," said Michel. "But we've known for a long time that there's unrest in the army. They may have control of the country, but they're far from unified themselves. Perhaps Auguste is consolidating his position – or perhaps he's losing control…hard to judge at this stage."

Lucas found all this unsettling. Just when he was getting an insight in to this world a new development obscured his view. In some ways, it was all so simple, and simplicity was so seductive. There were two clear sides: the people living in poverty with no weapons other than their voices, opposed by an overbearing army ready to use violence to retain power. But now it seemed the army was not united. Neither were politicians. And the general population was infiltrated by spies and informants who might be connected to the army or might be in the pay of those who simply wanted chaos. There was division on all sides.

He looked to Michel, who had lived here most of his life, had roots in this place, and sought some clarity.

"This is more than a fight within the army, isn't it?" he said. "There's something more important happening. The demonstrators are so committed. The people on the streets yesterday had a determination that cuts through petty, political squabbling. I mean there were so many of them…It's their concerns the army has to address." Getting no immediate response, Lucas continued. "And in the end, a regime can't fight everyone – even if those who protest are unarmed." Michel was still silent. "Anyway, the soldiers here must know these people, don't they? This isn't a big place. Surely a soldier won't fire on his own kind? How can the generals keep control if they've no public support? Are they going to kill everyone?"

"They don't have to kill everyone," said Michel. "Just a few."

"But how can a young soldier shoot the very people they're supposed to protect? For all they know, if they fire into a crowd, they could be killing a member of their own family."

Marie sat up and shook her head. "It's true this is a small place, but the army plays by its own rules. They've always thought of themselves as the defenders of the nation. This isn't like England. The army doesn't defend us from foreign invasion – although it has had to in the past. The army thinks it *is* the nation. This country was won by force of arms against the slavers. We only exist because they fought for our freedom. So, the army feels it has to defend the country from all its enemies – at least that's their mentality."

"But they prevent civilian politicians from doing their job!" said Lucas, exasperation cutting through his weariness.

"No, they think they stop corrupt politicians from pursuing their own selfish interests. They defend the country from those who'd do it harm. That's the way they think. And the soldiers you see, they all come from the rural areas." Marie sighed wearily. "They hate the city people. They think the rich of Port au Prince just want to exploit them and keep all the money. They think they're the true Haitians and we city people are looters and thieves."

"So, the army has set half the population against the other, and they use Macoutes to spy on everyone?" Lucas looked from Marie to Michel, seeking affirmation.

Michel too was looking tired. "Well, there's some truth in that," he said.

Lucas checked his watch. It was still early.

"So, what's happening today?" he asked Michel.

"Well, the demonstrations aren't going to stop. An opposition politician phoned me an hour ago and said they aim to march again today. He's calling for a general strike. They're asking everyone to stand and be silent or go to church to pray at midday."

"Then I'd better get back and see what's going on."

He stood and held out his hand, which Michel immediately gripped. They said a quick goodbye, agreeing they would call each other later. Marie walked him to the door.

"Thank you for a fascinating evening," he said. She moved closer, close enough to kiss but he wasn't sure where to begin. But then she took his right hand in hers and, leaning across their joined arms, she gently placed a kiss first on Lucas's left cheek and then the other.

Lucas did not let her hand go. He raised it slowly, brushing it with his lips before releasing it, conscious of Michel looking on.

"I hope I'll see you later," he said quietly, not wanting to leave but letting his feet carry him out to the garden, now clearly visible in the morning light.

As he walked, his stomach tightened and a familiar feeling ran through him. It was as though his whole life had been one long departure. Leaving his home, his sister, Catherine, moving from place to place. He felt he'd always been away – somewhere else. He couldn't remember the last time he had seen his parents. He had thought time would inure him to these absences, but here he was again with a nagging sense of separation.

Standing at the gate and looking across the dusty road, Lucas could see the car parked where it had been yesterday.

Henri had driven up the hill and gone back to sleep. The car looked empty, but as Lucas approached, he could see Henri flat out on the reclined driver's seat. Stuffing seeped from the upholstery, curling round his form.

Henri awoke as Lucas rapped on the driver's window. He struggled upright.

"À l'hotel?" he asked, shaking the sleep away.

Lucas nodded and walked round the car to the passenger's seat. Henri drove carefully back the way they had come the previous day. He took elaborate care, keeping to a speed that wouldn't attract attention, checking every corner for soldiers.

CHAPTER 14

The road hugged the hillside. As they descended Lucas looked out across the capital, which was crouched beneath a charcoal sky. On the horizon was a streak of white light where the sun had risen, only to disappear into the dark clouds that reached across the sea to brood over the city. The touch of Marie's cheek lingered, and he leant his face to the breeze, letting the car's motion clear his head.

'Facts,' Carrick said. 'Give me facts ...' Lucas rallied what he knew. He was trapped and going nowhere. People wanted an end to military rule and without elections they were out on the streets, causing chaos to make their point. The army stood for order, but without popular support their response was risking a terrible escalation. It seemed to Lucas that this paucity of facts dissolved far too rapidly into speculation. What was he to do?

What was it Carla had said? Sometimes you have to step through the looking glass...Perhaps the only way to find out more is to dive deeper. Take the plunge. You can only remain an observer for so long. You have to commit to really understand what's happening. Maybe Carla was right. She usually was.

***

Lucas was back on the pavement outside the entrance to Bush House, staring up at two stone statues which stood above the massive portico when Carla had appeared out of nowhere, as she often did in moments of reflection when you weren't expecting her.

"What do you make of that?" she enquired, always probing.

"A symbol of undying Anglo-American friendship?" he ventured. He knew the architect had been an American. "Isn't that an eternal flame they're holding between them?"

"Yeah – that was the intention." Carla removed her cigarette from her lips as if it had developed a sudden sour taste and exhaled. "But the BBC's got other ideas." Lucas, head still raised, was reading the chiselled inscription at the statues' feet. He could feel Carla next to him, persistent, always challenging. If she'd been a dog, she'd have been a Staffordshire bull terrier: compact, fearless and only audible when moving on concrete. "Don't believe all that stuff about friendship between English-speaking people," she spat. "We don't believe any of that crap." Lucas looked from the inscription to Carla. What was she up to now? "Stuff friendship. It's truth, Lucas. That's what we're about."

Carla and Lucas had walked back from interviewing the Nigerian State Governor at his five-star hotel. Lucas had operated the equipment and Carla had asked a series of increasingly hostile questions, which had culminated in her accusing the governor of moving large amounts of cash from Nigeria to a British bank, which she named. Taken off guard, there had been no denial or protestation of innocence, only a spluttered: "Who told you that?"

"I thought the BBC motto was 'Nation shall speak peace unto nation'," said Lucas, wondering why those were not the words on the inscription.

"We wouldn't get very far with that would we?" Carla blew the idea away on a stream of smoke. "Imagine. If we put peace first. We'd never ask any awkward questions or offend anyone." She looked up at the statues high above their heads. "Peace is for the birds. It's truth we're after."

"Hang on a minute." Lucas laughed, knowing every dialogue with Carla was a lesson. "I've read the BBC's editorial guidelines. I don't recall a section on Truth. It's all about accuracy, balance and fairness and stuff."

"Yeah – clever, isn't it? The one thing we're actually about and the buggers barely mention it."

"Well then, it can't be our purpose, can it? Anyway – how do you define truth? What's true today isn't true tomorrow. The world's not square. It turns out the earth isn't the centre of the universe. And how many people today believe the British Empire brought enlightenment to the colonies? One man's truth is another man's delusion. It's not truth we're after. It's facts – ask Carrick."

"Facts are okay, but they only get you so far." Carla waved her cigarette skywards before re-inserting it. "Sometimes they don't get you anywhere. Take our state governor – it's a confession we need or a conviction in a court. Facts are always deniable and these days there are plenty of people who are in denial."

"True enough," Lucas conceded. "Even if you accept the facts, you can string them together to make different truths. Take Dresden. The RAF bombed it to hell in '45 and killed tens of thousands of civilians. Some say it was justifiable after the blitz; some say it shortened the war; some say it was plain murder. You can take your pick of the truth."

154

"But that's the point." Carla looked triumphant, as she usually did at the end of their exchanges. "Time stretches truth on the rack. It changes its meaning; confounds our convictions. That's because truth is not a fact. It's not a conclusion. It's something you strive for because you want to be better than you are. You debate it. You have a dialogue about it because you know it's so hard to pin down. So yeah. It's truth we're after, but it remains irritatingly out of reach. Those who want to write it down or turn it in to a slogan, they're the ones who kill it. They turn truth into a lie and stop the dialogue. It's why we make endless bloody programmes; why we come back to events again and again, it's another point of view, another step towards understanding what the truth is." She was already walking towards the door. "You just have to keep going. Don't ever stop…"

Her last words were delivered as a Parthian shot as she stalked into the building, leaving Lucas still staring up at the portico far above his head, and its crazy mix of Celtic, Roman and Americana. Beautiful though, he thought.

***

The car came to a sudden halt. They had crept round the last corner at the foot of the hill to find an armoured personnel carrier parked square across the centre of the road. There were soldiers on either side to stop them passing. Henri had his one good hand on the steering wheel and was holding up his stump, muttering furiously under his breath.

One of the soldiers walked up to Henri's window. "Papiers!" he demanded.

They were at a junction. A smaller road ran off to their right. A sign pointed to a village. Set back from the junction was a school: a small, simple structure made of wood with a veranda that ran along the whole frontage. There were books

155

and papers scattered across the ground and Lucas could see that the building was splintered by gunfire.

The soldier reached in through Henri's window and turned off the ignition. Henri was scrabbling to extract papers from behind the scruffy sun visor above his head. Another soldier appeared next to Lucas, demanding ID. Lucas pulled his passport from his bag and explained who he was, but the door jerked open.

"Venez! Venez!" He was pulled from the car and pushed towards the armoured vehicle. The soldier spoke in a mix of Creole and French: why was he here; what was he doing? Lucas protested, repeating that he was a journalist, but the man seemed indifferent, all the time pushing him firmly forward. When Lucas turned to check on Henri, who was still in the car, he felt the sharp jab of a rifle in his back, making him stumble into the side of the carrier. He moved along it, putting his hand out to steady himself against the huge rear tyre.

A few more steps and he received a final shove which propelled him round the corner towards another soldier who was definitely not Haitian. He was dressed in fatigues, a black flack-jacket wrapped tight round his torso and he was alert, on top of the situation.

"He wants to know who you are and what the fuck you're doing in his country." The American's right hand rested on a snub-nosed, semi-automatic strapped round his chest. A handgun was holstered on his thigh. A peaked cap tilted down over sunglasses obscured his face. The cap bore the faintest imprint of some letters which had been removed: DEA.

"And you are?" Lucas had not meant the question to sound as cheeky as it did, but he wasn't sure whether he felt relief or alarmed.

"I'm asking the questions, buddy," came the reply. "Don't get cute. These guys want to know what you and your friend are doing coming down their hill. The curfew's barely ended."

"I'm a journalist. With the BBC. Henri's my driver. I'm researching a documentary about prospects for an election."

"BBC?" The American sounded surprised. "What the fuck are you doing coming down from Pétionville at this hour?"

"I stayed over because of the curfew. I'm heading back to my hotel. Are you really drug enforcement? Are you supporting the army here?"

The American was now square in front of Lucas, leaning forward, inspecting him. He was thickset, heavily tanned, and he was reading Lucas: the bag, the loose shirt, slacks, accent. He spoke rapidly in Creole to the soldier who had taken Lucas from the car. The soldier nodded and moved away.

"They take orders from you?" Lucas's question drew a sigh from the American, who put his face next to Lucas's ear and whispered.

"Look buddy. Stop asking questions. Don't mess with these guys. Just get in your car, go to your hotel, and stay there. There are geeks out on the road you don't want to meet. And you've not seen me. Got it?"

Lucas hesitated. If the DEA was here, then perhaps someone in the army was really trying to suppress drug running. *And why the roadblock? And the school? What had happened?* The questions kept coming. He searched for an insignia on the fatigues, but there was nothing apart from an empty strip of Velcro.

"What's happened at the school here? I saw the damage on the veranda…who did the shooting?"

The American looked closely at Lucas and seemed to have second thoughts. Lucas held his tongue. Hoping his silence would invite more.

"You really BBC? You got ID?" came the reply after some thought.

Lucas produced his BBC pass. "Yes BBC. I'm reporting on the demonstrations."

"Well, if I tell you what happened here you move on, right? You go and you don't come back, and you don't say anything about me or these guys or the roadblock or nothin'"

"Sure," said Lucas, seeing that he had little choice.

"Off the record, yeah?"

"Yes."

The American drew a deep breath. "Well, there's been stuff kickin' off all night. You heard the shooting. The curfew was supposed to be lifted at first light, but not every goon with a gun got the message. Kids here they walk everywhere. They set off early for school. And some turn up really early to be sure they don't get locked out. And today there was this kid…this girl." The American turned his head and spat on to the road. "She was sitting on the veranda over there early this morning. She must have been doin' her homework or something when two factions let loose at each other down the road. There was all sorts of shit flying around and the school got hit… And some stray bullet took her out."

"She's dead?" asked Lucas.

The American nodded.

"You know who did it?"

"Hell no. Could have been anyone. They were all out last night."

"You mopping up then?" asked Lucas.

The American took another deep breath. "No, I'm not mopping up. We're here on other business and your business ain't here now. So, get goin'."

Lucas started to move but thought better of it. "So, why are you telling me this?"

The American was pushing Lucas in the direction of the car, but the question made him pause.

"Look, I joined up to shoot bad guys. I get pissed when it gets indiscriminate. She was just a kid. Never hurt anyone and we had to pick up what was left of her." The American's index finger slid onto the trigger of his semi-automatic. "If I knew who did it, I wouldn't be here talking to you."

Lucas thought he might be on a roll and started asking more questions but got only a shake of the head, a gloved hand on the side of his neck, and a firm squeeze which made him aware of his carotid artery.

"You wanna get out of here?" Lucas nodded.

"Then get in the car and don't look back. I don't wanna dead journalist on the road, but some people round here may have a different idea. So, fuck off and remember – I don't exist."

Lucas turned and made it to the car just as Henri brought the engine back to life. They drove in silence and did not look back.

CHAPTER 15

"Lucas, darling." There was relief in Flo's voice. "I was sure you were alright, but I was beginning to wonder." The phone had been ringing when Lucas got back to his room. He sat down on the bed, wiped the sweat from his forehead and assured Flo all was well. She was evidently following events closely.

"One of the wires has just put out a story about a schoolgirl who's been shot. Killed on her way to school. Can you confirm? Have you heard about this? I'm not sure where they're getting their information from."

Lucas relayed what he had just seen and explained that demonstrations were already under way in the main square. "Newsroom want a piece from you," said Flo. "This girl's just the sort of thing that will capture imaginations, but newsroom only have the one source and they won't run with it unless you can stand it up. Can you file for morning and evening bulletins?" Lucas said he would start as soon as they were off the call. "Darling, you were the main topic of discussion at this morning's news meeting, and I was able to say you work for me. You're at the heart of things. You're the only foreign reporter on the ground, so everyone's feeding off your material. Newsroom is very sceptical about all the other sources."

Lucas confirmed he was working with Michel. "That's great," Flo enthused down the phone. "But you must promise to take care. No silly dramatics. We don't want you getting shot, do we?"

Lucas laughed, flattered by the affection with which the message was delivered.

When the call ended, he immediately wrote the despatch about the girl and fresh demonstrations, recorded it and transferred the file to his laptop and sent it off.

He then lay down on the bed for ten minutes, closed his eyes and briefly let the tiredness roll over him as he assessed his situation. A crisis loomed. The troop movements, the determination of the demonstrators, the sense of anticipation he got from Marie and Michel. There was a momentum to it.

Just how far was the government prepared to go to restore order to the streets? There was only one person who could answer that question.

He went to the phone book, turning the pages. There was nothing listed under the presidency, so he tried government of Haiti and there was Le bureau du President. He picked up the telephone and dialled the number directly. It rang, and a man answered. In French, Lucas explained who he was and what he wanted.

"Un moment," came the reply, and there was a long silence while the line remained open. After several minutes, another voice came on, this time speaking English with an American accent.

"You're the BBC reporter?" asked the voice. Lucas gave his name and repeated his request.

"Mr Lucas, we've been listening to your reports with interest. I'll be happy to put your request through to the President. Where can I get you?" Lucas gave his details at the hotel and asked who he was talking to.

"Colonel Jean Claude Chambert," came the reply. "I work with General Auguste and will talk to him this afternoon. I should be able to come back to you today with an answer." Lucas wondered whether the President's English was as good as the Colonel's and asked what language the President would use in an interview. "General Auguste speaks only French and Creole, Mr Lucas. Any interview would have to be in those languages. But you speak French…"

Lucas wondered whether he would fully understand the President's answers. So, he said he would need an interpreter and asked if he could bring a French-speaking journalist to act as translator. The Colonel said he would relay the request, and the call ended.

Lucas then called Michel to update him and asked if he would act as a translator.

"Of course, happy to, Lucas. If we get this interview, we'll be the first journalists he's spoken to since the demonstrations began. It's your interview, but I'll happily share it."

"Well, he has to say yes first," said Lucas, and then mentioned Colonel Chambert by name.

"He's no ordinary Colonel," said Michel. "Chambert's in charge of the Dessalines Battalion. They were one of the units on the streets last night. After the Presidential Guard, they're the most influential corps in the army. If anyone can get you the interview, he can." Lucas's hopes rose. "Lucas," said Michel quickly moving on. "Marie left for the city soon after you this morning. She says she wants to go to today's protests. She might drop by the hotel on her way. Can you look out for her? She knows Port au Prince so well, but I still worry about her. She's headstrong."

Lucas said he would, and the call ended. He wanted to get out and see what was happening himself. He picked up his equipment from the bed and went on to the landing.

The sunlight bounced up the staircase at the end of the corridor. Its brilliance made him realise just how dark his room was. It was like a cell, just four walls and a door leading off to the bathroom, whose solitary window was too narrow and too far up to shed much light.

He started down the stairs to the bustle of reception and the large glass windows through which the sunlight blazed. This day was going to be as hot and oppressive as the last. Lucas found himself longing for something green, for rain, for even the chill of an English winter.

He reached the bottom of the stairs. He knew Henri would be lurking somewhere between the pillars, jealous of his prize client making and sure no thief stole his possession. But when Lucas looked up, it was Marie he saw. She moved from the french doors overlooking the pool and came towards him with both hands outstretched.

"You mustn't miss the demonstration," she said. "And everyone's talking about this schoolgirl who's been shot. I don't know if it's true, but it's galvanised everyone and they're out there now in the square. Come and see…"

"Oh, it's true," said Lucas and he told Marie about his encounter on the road.

Marie's eyes filled with tears as she listened. "The poor girl,' she said. "It's always the innocent who suffer. This has to stop."

And she took Lucas by the hand and led him to the doorway where he finally caught sight of Henri staring at them. Before he could acknowledge him, Marie had him through the revolving door and out into the square.

She walked close by his side, loose-limbed, a gentle sway to her hips, her hair shining, flowing back from her face as she moved. She was extraordinary. Her skin was as smooth as gold leaf. Her lips were full, her eyes were wide over high cheekbones. Every feature was unique, the whole composition compelling.

Unconsciously Lucas slowed in the heat as she moved ahead of him, watching her part the crowd. He drifted. To his left, the brilliant white of the palace rose towards the sky and the sun burned down. He narrowed his eyes, barely able to take in his surroundings. It was like looking through a gauze. Images distorted in the heat bouncing off the cobbles. The light teased him, reflecting something more solid beyond his reach. And for a moment he stood there consumed by the haze and the heat until there she was again.

"Lucas, you disappeared," she said. "What happened?"

"Marie," he heard himself say. "Sorry – I lost you."

Passers-by in the crowd jostled them and they moved closer to stay together. Marie produced a small bottle of water from her bag and offered it. He drank gratefully.

"What's wrong? Do you feel faint?"

"No, no… It's all this… I mean," and he paused trying to articulate his feelings but afraid it would sound wrong or dispel the exhilaration he felt. "It's you… I'm glad I'm here… with you…"

She looked at him, holding his hand, and there was something in her eyes that drew him in. The kiss was soft, the touch exquisite. He did not breathe in case the moment was lost and afterwards he remembered no sound.

It was then Lucas knew he had made the right decision in coming to Haiti, despite the chaos. He finally had a sense of real purpose. Marie held out so much promise. She had all the passion and conviction of a liberator, and she filled him with hope.

"We should see what's happening," she said, smiling up at him. "See what I see every day. I want to show you. Together. This is what's important now."

He put his arm round her shoulder to turn her back in to the crowd and towards the centre of the square. They walked together for a while and then Lucas reluctantly shook his recorder from his bag and started to record the sounds of the demonstrators around him, Marie staying close.

After a few minutes, Lucas started asking questions of people as they passed by, and Marie quickly took on the role of interpreter. She spoke in Creole and repeated the same question: 'Why are you here?' And as each one answered she translated, so Lucas could capture their responses.

"We are sick of brutality… we want democracy… we want control over our lives… I don't want to be afraid of the night and the Macoutes… they beat us and suck us dry…"

The replies came quickly, fading away as people passed, like travellers on their way to some destination that would tolerate no loitering.

Everyone responded to Marie, and Lucas knew these recordings were the best he had made. He could hear the desire in people's voices, the conviction that what they were doing might at last make a difference.

"This is good!" he shouted to Marie, having captured more than enough for his report.

Marie put her lips close to his ear. "One of them told me they were going to the Church of St Mark. It's one of Père Baptiste's churches. Maybe he'll speak. Shall we go and see?"

Lucas nodded. They pushed their way through the crowd towards the houses on the far side of the square. As they got nearer, Lucas recognised where he was and pointed out Leslie Laguerre's house. Marie said she knew it well. Laguerre was a friend of her father and she'd visited several times.

He told her about his meeting with the old man, and he wondered whether he might now do an interview. It would be good to have him on the record, explaining what was happening. Together, they went through the gate and up to the front door. When they reached it, Lucas could see it was ajar. He knocked, and it swung back on its hinges. There was no reply.

"That's odd," said Lucas.

"Perhaps he's gone to see the demonstration," Marie replied. But looking at the open door, he suspected that even Marie did not believe what she said. He called out and still getting no response started forward.

Marie gently pulled Lucas back and went in front of him. She walked down the corridor to the study where Lucas had sat with the old man when they first met. He held back and called again, looking up the stairs in front of him.

The house was completely silent. He could no longer hear Marie, so he quickly went down the corridor and into the study where he found her stock-still and staring at the wall over the fireplace. At first, he couldn't see what she was staring at and moved to get a better look. The piles of books that had been stacked against the walls were strewn across the floor. And over the fireplace ran an arc of holes that Lucas recognised from the radio station. There was no sign of the old man or his wife.

Lucas went to the desk and looked down at the papers. They lay where the professor had left them. Across a couple of sheets was a scattering of little dark droplets. Ink? He looked more closely and saw it was not ink but dried blood.

"They must have come for him after the first demonstration," said Lucas, looking up at Marie and pointing to the stains on the desk. She came over to see for herself.

"It wouldn't be the first time," she said. "Laguerre was in prison for years before he fled to the States. He came back after Duvalier fell. I think he had reassurances from the government, but now..." she trailed off. "Michel will be worried. They're good friends."

Lucas suggested calling Michel to let him know, and he reached for the telephone on the table, but Marie stopped him.

"No. Don't call from here. Don't touch anything. They listen and they'll know we've been here."

They looked at each other. And Lucas felt a pang of anxiety, thinking of Laguerre's wife in the garden.

"His wife stopped me as I was leaving," he said as the image of the woman came back to him. "She told me not to give him away."

"You haven't, Lucas." Marie was shaking her head. "Your reporting makes us safer. The world needs to know what's happening. In the end, we can't fight this on our own. I'm sure she doesn't think you betrayed him. She knew the risks Leslie ran." And then, after the shortest of pauses to let her words sink in, she said, "We must go. We can't be found here."

And the two of them walked quickly back outside into the crowded square.

CHAPTER 16

Marie led the way to the Church of St Mark, taking Lucas through the decaying colonial colonnades close to Radio Rèv, only to quickly turn off through a series of alleys which wound their way between the closely packed shacks of the slums. They walked single file. Occasionally, inquisitive faces peered out at them. They probably assumed Marie was lost. Lucas, on the other hand was clearly from another planet. They rounded a corner on to a small clearing where a shoal of tiny children was running and playing. One shouted, "Heh blanc!" and the others gazed up at this strange new creature. All joined in the chorus of "blanc-blanc-blanc" and ran along behind them, amazed at their discovery.

Then suddenly they were out on to a market street, bustling with carts and the occasional car. Lucas stopped as a heavy wagon piled high with bricks tied down by ropes passed in front of him. It was pulled by a single man stripped to his waist straining between the shafts, bearing the entire load on his own, muscles defined sharply across his arms and torso.

"PB says they're treated like donkeys," said Marie, looking on, "while our leaders watch from horseback."

"PB?" asked Lucas.

"Petit Bondyu. It's what they call Père Baptiste. It means little God."

She pointed towards the end of the long road, and Lucas could see a large church in the distance. "That's St Mark's. I think we may have missed them. But let's go and see…"

They set off down the street, navigating their way through the traffic, dodging people carrying crates and jars on their heads, until they finally stood before the great west door of another neo-classical monolith, open to the public but with no sign of protesters.

They went up the broad steps into the shade. Marie looked cautiously through the door and then disappeared. Lucas followed. An enormous heavy curtain hung inside, which they pushed through.

All was quiet except for a huddle of men talking at the far end before the altar, all wearing the long black robes of the Catholic church, their heads bowed. They were circled around something Lucas couldn't see.

They walked up the nave at a respectful pace and stopped well short of the group. Lucas looked up at the tall pillars that supported the gorgeous, vaulted roof. In the half-light, he could make out decorated scenes from the bible in gold and blue and green. There was a huge painted figure scattering seed.

Marie whispered, "Wait here. Let me find out what's going on," and Lucas watched as she returned to the door. She had seen a man who was not a priest standing in the shadows and after a short exchange she quickly returned. There was urgency in her voice.

"He says Baptiste spoke out against the army and then sent everyone away, so we've missed the protest. He says the police are coming. We should leave…"

Before she could finish, there was a crashing sound at the back of the church. The man in the shadows stood aside as a large group of men burst in through the great door, pushing the heavy curtain aside with thrashing arms. Pausing only briefly to adjust to the meagre light, they started down the nave.

The leading men carried cudgels and at least one had a machete in his hand. Some of them wore the red band of the Macoutes, and behind them were half a dozen policemen in uniform. They moved quickly, shouting as they came.

Marie and Lucas were standing at the end of a pew two-thirds of the way towards the altar and the group swept past them with barely a glance, heading straight for the clergy.

The priests parted, and Lucas saw what had been holding their attention. There in the middle was a thin, diminutive figure. A black cassock fell straight from his neck to his feet, and he wore the same sharp gold spectacles Lucas had seen the day before.

Père Baptiste stood calmly, looking straight at the approaching thugs. His fellow priests fanned out on either side, standing their ground.

"You should go… go…" a voice urged at their side. It was the man whom Marie had spoken to. So as not to argue and attract attention, the two of them moved back down the nave towards the great door and the shadow of the curtain. The man carried on towards the altar and joined the back of the group confronting Baptiste.

Lucas and Marie watched. They could only catch the odd phrase in the commotion that followed. Two or three Macoutes were shouting, and their abuse echoed up to the rafters and down to the floor again. It was all a mixture of Creole and French, and Lucas could only make out the odd phrase.

"You don't speak now, do you?" shouted one. He raised a large cudgel high above his head as if to strike Baptiste, but it did not fall. It hovered and gradually came down to his side while others took up the cause, bellowing their threats.

One young man was more animated than the others. He was waving his arms and working himself in to a frenzy. He wore the red that marked him out as someone to fear. Suddenly, those closest to him recoiled, and a space opened, enabling Lucas and Marie to see both the boy and Baptiste as they stood face to face.

The priests all froze at the sight of the weapon, which had suddenly appeared in the boy's right hand. It was a pistol, and he was waving it wildly in Baptiste's face.

Baptiste himself was stock-still, his hands clasped before him as if in prayer. His eyes were wide, looking directly at the boy.

"Non, non, non…" shouted one of the priests, who still couldn't move but was clearly terrified by what the boy was about to do.

Lucas felt Marie stiffen beside him and start forward. Instinctively, he grabbed her and pulled her back. She seemed to think better of it and slipped her arm through his, gripping him tightly.

The boy was still shouting and waving the gun. It flopped crazily in his hand, like a snake ready to strike. Lucas could see the finger on the trigger, a fulcrum around which the weight of the gun rocked. Whether intentional or not, the outcome seemed inevitable.

Then one of the policemen – a large man – pushed forward with a speed that belied his age and size. He stepped right up to Baptiste, whose diminutive frame was briefly obscured. He turned to face the boy, who was still cursing, the gun careering in front of him.

"You can't do this!" Lucas heard the words cascade down from the great roof above his head.

The policeman was holding out his hand for the gun.

The boy's other hand rose to steady his weapon, but now his whole body was shaking. He had not expected one of his own to get in the way – a priest possibly – but not this man.

The boy screamed at the policeman and Lucas could feel Marie taut at his side, still gripping his arm, urgently whispering: "He's threatening to shoot if he doesn't get out of the way…"

But the policeman remained where he was. He said something low but clear which travelled around the church. The painted figures on the walls seemed to be listening to his words, and Marie quietly repeated them:

"You can't kill this man. We may disagree with him. You may hate him. But I can't let you kill him. Not here. It's not right."

An awful wail went up from the boy. It was as though he had been waiting all his life for this moment only to be thwarted by one of his own, one of the people who had encouraged him, who had fed his hate, who had brought him here. He couldn't believe what was happening, and although the words he heard from the huge figure opposing him were rational and calm, they seemed to feed his anger. The gun settled more steadily on the policeman he had to kill to reach Baptiste. His hands tightened on the butt of the pistol. Lucas felt Marie's intake of breath and his own heart faltered because he knew what was coming.

A tremendous explosion blasted up into the cavernous roof.

Marie and Lucas clung to each other. The sucking, echoing eruption burst on them from every corner of the vaulted chamber. It poured down from the ceiling, ricocheting off the walls, breaking from one side to the other. It was a furious, blind outpouring of hate and bile, a tormented demon searching for an exit, unable to find release.

Lucas looked towards the altar, expecting to see bodies slumped on the floor. Instead, he saw the figures still where they were. Slowly, the huge man moved. The boy's arm was held straight up, pointing at the rafters. One of the other men had it in a firm grip, keeping it vertical, away from the two figures in front of him. Then the big man's hands reached up and enveloped the pistol. Carefully, he bent the gun out of the boy's grip and slipped it into a cavernous pocket in his jacket.

As he moved to do this, he revealed Baptiste, who was still standing behind him, looking straight ahead, hands gripped as before. He was trembling so badly that Lucas thought he was on the verge of a seizure. Then, once again, the priests closed in.

There was no shouting now, only a dreadful silence. The clergy moved as one, with Baptiste at their centre, and disappeared into a vestry.

The thugs, together with the boy, turned back towards the door, where Marie and Lucas were standing. "Let's go," Lucas whispered and quickly, like fugitives, they felt their way along the heavy curtain until they found a gap through which they melted.

The great door was still open, and they went out on to the portico, down the steps into the sunlight, immediately turning right so they would be out of the eyeline of anyone exiting the church after them.

CHAPTER 17

The sun was sinking. Higglers and stall holders were packing up their meagre offerings. Carts were heading home. Animals scavenged for food in the rubbish which lay in the gutters and piled up on the corners.

Lucas had his arm round Marie. Outwardly, it was a gesture of protection. But it was partly to quell a fear in him, not her. He feared the hate they had just witnessed. He feared the unknown. He feared the feelings this woman was unleashing in him.

They walked through the late afternoon light, back towards the hotel, cooled by a rare breeze coming off the sea. His hand on her shoulder – hers was wrapped round his waist.

"Why do you do this?" she asked quietly.

"Do what?"

"Reporting." Her hand tightened. "You don't have to be here. You must have a good life back in London." She looked at the detritus piled up on either side. "You don't need to get caught up in all this. I come back because of my family. It's my home, but you have a life of your own in a place where everything works, and corruption doesn't steal the food off your plate…"

Lucas felt a pang of guilt. The closer he got to Marie and the more he saw of her determination the less deserving of her affection he felt. They walked in silence for a while, Lucas wrestling with his thoughts, wanting to be honest, but fearing the consequences. So, he changed the subject.

"Can I ask you a question first?"

Marie tickled his side, making him laugh and squirm.

"Well, you can," she said. "But don't think for a moment I'll forget the question you're avoiding."

"Okay," said Lucas, struggling to regain control. "But me first. Why here?" Marie looked puzzled. "What is it about this place that makes people see spirits? It doesn't happen elsewhere, but here it seems commonplace. Even you, who live half your life in the States, get carried off in front of me. And I…well I end up in some kind of parallel universe that I can't explain…"

Marie thought for a moment.

"Perhaps it's the poverty," she offered. "Perhaps it's fear. These things strip everything away. They pare life to the bone, and it feels as though death is everywhere. People live with it all the time. So much so that death no longer seems the worst thing, or the end, or some kind of defeat. I suppose its presence opens their eyes…" She stared straight ahead, a study of concentration. Then she turned to him again. "But it can happen anywhere Lucas, not just here – and for any reason. Sometimes missing someone, longing for them is enough and then you see them…it can be enough. You can be apart from someone but still feel their presence, still hear their voice, see their gestures, talk to them…"

"Yes," said Lucas, thinking of Zoe. "I know what you mean. I've talked to people I miss. It's like you're so used to them being there that they simply appear where you expect them to be…"

"And not just the living," said Marie. "The dead too. People you know who couldn't possibly be there, but they are. Like at the ceremony. The spirits there were real. They weren't the product of our collective imagination. They really exist." Lucas felt Marie's hand give him a squeeze, willing him to understand. "I mean, we know this from science, don't we? Scientists tell us we live in a world where nothing ever really dies. They call it half-life. I hate the term because it implies that anything not fully present or conscious is inferior when we know that our most creative and authentic ideas come from the subconscious. But you know what they mean. Things never disappear. Atoms fade away but they don't die. Sounds don't stop. Their echo goes on forever. Light doesn't go out. It travels so far that you can see things millions of years old. Things that may not even be there anymore. And it's the same with us. We're a bit like stars. We're observed, and that observation gives us meaning and relevance and who knows? As long as the light lasts so will human memories and desires. Everything you strive for has meaning because it resonates." Lucas felt her eyes on him. "And that's why you're here Lucas. Observers matter. They really matter. They bring things to life for those who never knew, who never understood, who weren't there, who thought they were alone, but they weren't

…they were always part of something much bigger. Something glorious."

Lucas was stunned. What he'd meant to be a diversion had led straight back to the question he had wanted to avoid.

"So, Mr Lucas. That's *my* answer to my question. But what's *your* answer?"

Lucas was back where he had started. This brilliant young woman had pinned him like a butterfly. He desperately wanted to be the person she described – this great observer. But the truth was not as noble, and he was afraid the truth would make her think less of him.

"I love your answer, Marie. It's admirable and principled, and I'd be proud to be that person. But I fear I'm not. I'm more selfish than that… and I lack your conviction…" There, he had started and immediately he felt control sliding away from him. He was setting himself on a path that could only lead away from her. But surely he owed her the truth? He owed her that, at least for opening the door on his confinement, for sharing her knowledge, for showing him her world.

"The truth is, I'm not like you. I can't commit the way you do. You live this place, breathe it, love it." Their walk slowed. "I feel a bit like an imposter." He kept his arm firmly round her shoulder, trying to keep her close. "I'm just a journalist, an outsider, who'll report and move on." He felt her tense, but he felt compelled to be honest. "This is what I want to do, and I'm ambitious. The truth is, I came here because Haiti's under reported, so I stand a chance of gaining the kind of experience to help me move on and become a correspondent." They came to a stop. "I think that's the truth," he added, knowing it

179

wasn't the whole truth, but it was bad enough and the rest was too painful. "I mean, yes, of course I think the violence is awful, that people here deserve better, that you shouldn't be ruled by the gun, but I'm supposed to be impartial, remain objective…not take sides nor get emotionally involved." He almost spat these last words out, so conscious was he of Marie's presence, of her body touching his, of the reaction his words might provoke.

Then, just as he feared, she broke away. When she moved, he felt a sudden emptiness, as if beached by a retreating tide. Lucas stood there, stranded, floundering in his own veracity, inexplicably wanting to say more, wanting to move. Stillness would suffocate him. If this was her reaction now, what would she do if he told her the whole truth? He looked down the empty road, which stretched out bleakly before him.

So, this was how it was to be: always alone, always the outsider, always apart. An observer of other people, always the reporter, never the story.

Marie studied him, stony faced.

"I don't believe you." Her words were like a slap. "There's nothing wrong with ambition, Lucas. I'm sure you'll go on to be a great correspondent. I can see that in you. But you don't come to a place like this simply to impress your boss. You don't come just to make a name for yourself. At least *you* don't. You don't take these risks unless you care, unless something else is driving you." Lucas was silent. Not wanting to stop her, but still fearful of saying more. "You're not alone. I've been watching you. You went to the ceremony. You didn't just watch. You gave yourself up to it. Let the spirits take you. You let them in." Still, Lucas was silent. "I think something else brought you here, some spirit led you, something you're looking for."

Lucas felt the panic rising in him. Only this morning he had kissed her. Last night he thought he'd lost her. If he told her the whole truth, she could only think less of him. He started to turn away, but as he did, Marie put her hand on his arm.

"It's alright." He saw concern in her eyes. She pulled Lucas round, forcing him to look at her. "Really, it's okay. We need you. I need you. We need your independence. Everyone out on the street is taking a terrible risk. People have died here simply trying to vote. We need people like you to bear witness, tell the world – without that such sacrifices become meaningless." And Lucas recognised the same look he had seen in Laguerre's wife. She was afraid. Afraid that all this might be for nothing. That people might die, and it would make no difference, that mothers might lose their sons, that brothers and sisters would be separated forever, and for what?

Moved by her honesty, he took her hand in his. It felt so soft and warm. He turned it over and ran his fingers across her palm. Beautiful. She was so beautiful. He ached in her presence. If anything happened to her, Lucas would never forgive himself. He couldn't just stand back and watch while she was involved. Why should she take all the risk on her own? This must be how it was for Michel. This must be how he felt every time she left the house. Wanting to keep her safe but knowing she was a free spirit, ungovernable.

"I'm sorry," he said.

"Sorry? What for?" Marie gave a little laugh. "You've got nothing to be sorry for."

"But I have. I'm sorry. Because…you're right. There is something more. I haven't told you. I haven't told anyone."

And he stopped, holding back, just like at the ceremony, standing on the edge, afraid to let go, scared of what might follow…but still hoping…He felt Marie close her fingers round his, tight. And before he could say more, she was speaking.

"I'm sorry too." Lucas looked at her not understanding. "I didn't tell you. I don't know why. But something happened at the ceremony, and I didn't tell you. I didn't really know what it was. I didn't understand and I couldn't explain it at the time. But now I see…maybe it's why you're here…" Lucas stared at her, his hand still firmly enclosed in hers. Could it be that she'd seen the same thing? Felt the same? But she couldn't possibly know. He'd said nothing. Nobody knew. But here she was telling him.

"It was all so confusing at the ceremony, with the drums and the rhythm and music and the movement, but there was someone there. When I was taken. Someone came…" Lucas could see that she was back in the hut, recalling everything that had happened. She leant against him, steadying herself, her hand on his chest. "When I fell, she was there, but it was you she was looking for." Marie was speaking into his body, distracted, trying to recapture what she'd seen when she'd slipped from the known into the shadows. "It was a girl, a young woman. She reached out when I was taken. She was there." Lucas felt his heart pounding. It was so strong he must have been able to hear it. "It was as though my life was slipping away and she stopped it, gave it back to me, and when she did, I was sure she knew you. She was there for you, and she was so close I touched her…It was so powerful, and then you were holding me. I could feel your sadness."

Lucas knew then who it was. Who else could it have been? And he knew he had to tell Marie everything, but each word was a weight, to be hauled out of him by his need for her to understand.

"Yes, yes. I felt it too. When you fell… when I held you in my arms, I could see her." Marie looked up at him, urging him on, demanding to know. "It was Zoe…she's my sister." He moaned with the effort of pulling the words up. "She haunts me. I see her all the time… but she's not alive. We talk. We talk endlessly. But it's only with me. Nobody else sees her…You see, she died…" He stopped. He had to breathe. Lucas consciously sucked air into his lungs, horribly aware that every word he uttered couldn't be taken back. "But it's worse than that. I don't just see her. I'm there. I'm there when she falls. It's a memory…No, not a memory. It's what happened, but I wasn't there. Somehow, I can see it. I see it again and again. And I can't bear it. I feel responsible. It's my fault. I should have seen it coming and done something. I mean we talked so often…" Lucas buried his head in his hands, fearful that his words would conjure the very sight he dreaded.

***

And Lucas is there once more, staring at Zoe at the top of the stair high on the fourth-floor landing. She is looking only at him, smiling, not paying attention to her surroundings. The smell of polished wood and stale food conjure cold corridors and isolation. Lucas sees her clearly, her back to the banister on the landing, at the end of the corridor that leads to the

183

dormitories where Lucas is standing. Curlew and Kite, Swallow and Swift, the name-tagged oak rooms where generations of children have slept, are seared into his mind's eye together with Zoe staring straight at him. Behind her, the huge skylight attracts a flock of birds and a curious one pecks at the glass, eyeing the interior, stabbing at the translucent barrier that separates it from what lies within. Zoe looks up, craning to see the source of the scratching noise, to see what's at the edge of her vision. She takes a step back and stumbles. The handrail, too low, only acts as a fulcrum for her slender frame and she swings back and over. As she falls, her arm reaches up, and she cascades into the stairwell, leaving Lucas transfixed, nailed to a cross of his own making: twin planks of the unsaid and the undone. He screams but his cry falls from him, void of sound, void of release, void of anything that might bring relief. Its silence hangs like a veil between him and a world which is now beyond his comprehension.

***

"So she was there at the ceremony," Marie said softly. "She was with us. I saw her. You saw her. This is what happens when they come. They cut through everything. Spirits connect you to what's real…" But Lucas could barely hear her. Marie was a blur to him, an apparition calling to him. He was wrestling with the demon in his head. "Lucas, you understand? It's alright. People think spirits are from some kind of dream world. But it's the other way round. They show us the things that really matter. It's everyday life that feels unreal, as though we're detached from it, like it's all happening to someone else."

Lucas still clutched his head, unable to speak, trying to hold back tears as she continued.

"I think it's our senses. You know, everything we experience comes through our senses – touch, smell, sight. It can make us feel cut off from the world. It's as though our senses get in the way, and you end up feeling separated from everything around you. But when a spirit comes, it shatters all that – you're no longer bound by your senses. It can be terrifying."

Marie's hands were on his, pulling them away from his face. They felt wet. His face was wet. And her touch stripped away the last of his resistance. He was a child once more. His mother holding him, forcing him to focus, making him look forward, pulling him out of some dreadful nightmare. "Listen to me Lucas. When a spirit comes, you have to embrace it. Nothing else matters. Give yourself to it. It will show you the way. You must hang on to it. I mean, you knew she was there, didn't you?" She was shaking him, staring up at him.

"Yes, yes!" The words exploded out of him. He knew this was Marie in front of him, trying to help, but he was overwhelmed by the dam bursting inside of him. "I know she was there. She's more real than she was when she was alive. But I can't bear it…Sometimes it's Okay. Sometimes we just talk. Sometimes it's just as we were, but then…" And he sobbed, sickened by the thoughts he had tried so hard to suppress. "I hate her. Oh God! I can't help it – I feel so angry." And Lucas pushed Marie away, trying to fend off the emotion but floundering hopelessly, hating himself. "I can't help it. She makes me angry. Angry that she died. Angry that she took her own life. Angry she'd do this to me. Take herself away like that. I should have done more. Called more. Gone to the school. Taken her out. *Done* something. If only I'd known she was so desperate. It's no excuse not to have known. How could I not have known? I loved her! I'm inhuman – I disgust myself. First, I fail her and then I'm angry and somehow, I know it's not her fault but—"

"Lucas, Lucas, it's not her fault, and it's not *your* fault." Marie's hands were on him again. She was smoothing his hair back on his head, forcing him to look at her, forcing him to listen. "It's not your fault." Her eyes burned into him. "I was there. I saw her. She came to me. But she was there for you. She wanted you to understand and she couldn't reach you. So, she showed *me…*" and he could see it in her eyes. He saw how sure she was, how utterly convinced of what she was saying.

He grasped her hands and held them, like a drowning man held by the strength of another, lifted. And then there was just Marie: no street, no cobbles under their feet, just the two of them and all he could hear was what she was saying. "She didn't fall out of despair. It wasn't suicide, not a deliberate ending of her life. It was an accident. She simply lost her balance. Yes, she'd seen spirits, recognised them. She'd heard them calling her. She knew there was a place where we all connect, where we all coalesce. She's there now, but she didn't kill herself and she loved you. She loves you. It was Love that came to me on the floor. I felt it. I know it. And you have nothing to feel guilty about. I think that's why she came. Out of love – hoping you would recognise the truth and that there's nothing to forgive."

And there on the street, Lucas felt Marie's arms wrap round him. It was like a blessing. She held him close as the tide of his emotion slowly drained away, leaving only her presence and her breath upon him, like a gift: a gift that was his to keep no matter what the future held.

CHAPTER 18

In this place, evenings have no length. Days are relentless and unforgiving. Nights arrive swiftly, chasing the light away, leaving a darkness so complete that souls pass unnoticed.

Only the dim glow of a solitary lamp guided Lucas and Marie over the cobbles and the last few yards to the hotel entrance.

Once inside, a new reality awaited them, and Lucas reluctantly remembered how much work he had to do. Sensing the change in him, Marie took a step back. "I know," she said. "You must get on. I'll leave you to it."

Henri was loitering, looking worried. He rushed up to them and said in his broken English, "You go... I don't know where..."

"It's okay Henri. I'm back now." And then he realised that Henri thought he might have deserted him without paying: "It's okay. I'll change some money. Tell me how much gas you've bought..." As Henri rummaged around in his pockets for the scraps of paper on which he recorded his purchases, Lucas turned to Marie.

"Let Henri take you back. Better someone we know than a taxi." Marie spoke quickly in Creole to Henri, who nodded and immediately headed for the hotel entrance and his car, which they had seen parked at a crazy angle on the kerb outside. Marie gave Lucas a kiss on the cheek.

"À bientôt," she whispered and was gone.

Lucas walked briskly to the reception. He took a couple of $100 bills from his wallet to change into gourdes so he could pay Henri when he came back.

As the cashier calculated the day's exchange rate, another receptionist came over with a message which had been sitting upright in one of the little wooden boxes that lined the rear reception wall.

Lucas flipped the paper open and saw a telephone number with a short message saying the caller would phone again first thing in the morning and he should remain in the hotel until then. The number was the same one he had dialled for the Presidential Palace.

The cashier produced a large bundle of gourdes wrapped in a receipt and Lucas gathered them together. Upstairs, he went down the long corridor, past the doors standing to attention on either side, and slotted his key into the lock. He turned it and pushed.

His room had been cleaned. It smelt of disinfectant and the bed was neatly made, everything in its place. He moved round to the bedside table and put down his equipment. Opening his notepad, he wrote a quick introduction.

He picked up his recorder and fast-played the last recording. Chipmunk voices squealed out at him, wailing gibberish until Lucas flipped the speed back to normal.

Marie's voice filled the room, asking a question of a passer-by in the square. He listened to the answer in Creole and then Marie's translation. He found a good sequence and marked the beginning and end.

He wrote two paragraphs: the first outlining the scene in the square and the reported death of the girl who had prompted the protest. The second he would use after the demonstrators to underline their determination to continue their protest. He edited the piece together and sent the file to the BBC server. Checking his emails, he found a message to call the Caribbean Service:

"Hey Lucas – this story's buzzin' and you're on all the outlets. Newsroom's flagging your reports for domestic as well as world bulletins. We're really grateful that you're filing for us as well." Courtney's warm voice was a comfort. "You know, I heard you on Radio 4 this morning. Haiti displacing a British story – something of a first!" Courtney chuckled before returning to the job in hand. "Hang on. I'll transfer you to the studio." And after a short pause he returned, sounding thoroughly professional, and the interview began. "Which elements in the army were on the move? Where was Père Baptiste? What can we expect tomorrow?" The questions tumbled down the phone line, and Lucas took the opportunity to describe the scene at the church and the threat to Père Baptiste. Courtney came back after the interview, sounding pleased. "You must be tired, man. Why don't you let me write up the attack in the church as a news story? I'll use your quotes. Give you some time to get a bit of rest…"

Lucas accepted the offer gratefully, and Courtney said he would get right on it. "Take care, man," he said. "I'll listen out for you tomorrow." And with that he was gone, leaving Lucas to look at the second message in his inbox which was from newsroom.

"Lucas, this is the desk. We're having trouble with the numbers here. We've got reports of deaths during the demonstrations, but the figures vary. Can you confirm numbers for us?"

Lucas said he didn't have any firm figures and asked where the information was coming from and how many were being reported.

"The Times has a figure of three dead over the last two days, but it's not quoting a source. The story's by-lined Miami, so they may have been calling the hospitals from there but it's not clear. Can you check the hospital for us?"

Frustration welled up in Lucas. He was tired. He wanted to say no, he wouldn't go back out in the dark so close to curfew. But then he thought of Headley. What would he do?

Reluctantly, Lucas had to admit that Headley would go. He'd go after the facts, the details. He'd want to see the bodies. He wouldn't be afraid of the dark. *If you want to be a correspondent, then you have to go where the story leads.* That's what Julian Headley would say. He could hear his voice as clear as if he was sitting next to him. He'd never met the man, but Lucas had listened to his idiosyncratic reports so often that his delivery still resonated. Once he had heard him talk on the radio about his work as a foreign correspondent. The interviewer had asked how he'd got his biggest scoops. The laconic tone of his reply had stuck with Lucas: *You go the extra mile, track down that reluctant source, do the extra interview…and if the phone rings you always answer it. You never stop. Doing this job isn't work, it's a way of life.*

191

That drive, Headley's total absorption in his role, the places he'd been, the history he'd witnessed had all fed Lucas's ambition.

"Are you still there?"

"Oh yeah, sorry," said Lucas down the line. "Yes, I'll go and see what I can find out. It's getting late here, so I don't have much time, but I'll see what I can do." He hung up and grabbed his bag.

Lucas paused at the revolving door to check with the concierge where the nearest hospital was. He knew one was near the palace. The concierge said that if he followed the road off to the left, he would see it directly behind the palace walls. So, he pushed through the door. Within a few short paces, the darkness was complete. He stopped. The curfew was still an hour away, but the streets were already empty. He swore to himself but pushed on because the doorman had said it wasn't far and he had made the commitment to the newsroom. He put his head down and walked swiftly. He crossed over the cobbled road to the high wall by the Presidential Palace and followed it, getting some comfort from its shelter.

After two hundred yards, it veered off at a right angle behind the palace. A low fence continued to an open gate which gave on to a driveway. It bisected two stone buildings set back from the road. At the end, he could make out large rubber doors – the kind you see in warehouses. To one side there was an old wheelchair. He walked towards it.

Cut in to one door was a plastic window. Lucas could make out a man in a white coat moving across the room in front of him. He pushed and was immediately in a dimly lit corridor, calling after the retreating figure.

When the man looked back, Lucas could see that his eyes were ringed with fatigue. He was standing by two trolleys with rusty metal bars. Taut leather sheets were strung between them to make rudimentary stretchers. The walls on either side were chipped and dull with dirt.

Lucas approached and tried his French. The man confirmed he was indeed a doctor, so Lucas asked if he had admitted any people from the demonstrations and got an immediate response in a heavy accent.

"I speak English…"

Lucas thanked him. "Have you had any wounded people in today?"

"Oui, we have had five or six wounded."

"Gun shots?"

"No – not gunshots…no bullets… people fell…arms, legs broken." The doctor made a chopping motion with his arm. "Perhaps beaten… but no guns…"

"Any dead bodies?"

"No – nobody dead and no gunshots…" The doctor paused. "But if someone was shot by the soldiers, they wouldn't be here. There's an army hospital on the other side of the palace."

"There was a girl. I was told she was shot at the school…" Lucas flicked through his notebook for the name of the village he'd seen on the road sign when he'd been stopped at the roadblock. He showed it to the doctor. "She was shot here at this school. It's on the road that leads up to Pétionville." The doctor nodded in recognition. "Was she brought here? Do you know what happened to her?"

193

"Normally, any injured child would come here, but everyone says she was shot by the army."

"So, you know about her?"

"Mais oui. Everyone has heard about her. But they say she was shot by a soldier. They wouldn't bring her here in that case. They would take her to the army hospital."

Lucas thanked him and asked for his name.

"No name," came the reply with a faint smile. And he retreated from further questioning, quickly walking down the corridor out of sight. Lucas made his way back into the night.

The darkness seemed even more oppressive after the lights of the hospital. He went down the drive and turned back towards the hotel. The only way he was going to get facts about casualties was to go to the military hospital, but it was too late. The curfew would start any time now.

Up from the hills in front of him came a thump. At first, he thought someone had dropped a huge object. It was followed by the crackle of fireworks – except there were no lights in the sky, no stars falling.

He listened again, and two more thumps echoed down from the hills and across the city. It sounded like artillery, or a tank firing, and he realised the crackle he was hearing was automatic gunfire. The detonations were some distance away, but the rapid fire was much nearer.

This is crazy, he thought. *I'm not going to try to count bodies because some sub in London asks me to confirm numbers that I never gave him in the first place. It's my life. This is my story. I make my own decisions.*

He picked up his pace and followed the wall back along the side of the palace until he was in front of the hotel again with its revolving glass door and dim lights. He entered and breathed in the warm, rum-flavoured air. Across the broad lounge in the far corner was the familiar face of Toussaint, securely framed by one of the high-winged armchairs, cigar in hand, looking at Lucas as though he had been expecting him. Lucas raised his hand in acknowledgement and received the faintest of nods in reply.

He did not want conversation tonight, he thought, overcome once again by a strong desire to sleep. He went to the stairs. Lucas had his foot on the bottom step when a hand touched his shoulder.

"Monsieur Lucas," said Toussaint, still sporting his cigar. "Have you heard about the journalist?"

"What journalist?"

"A journalist was killed today. I'm sorry but I must tell you. He died in the square. He was shot by the soldiers."

"Lucas examined Toussaint, who was standing side on, staring obliquely back at the foyer, keeping a watchful eye out. Lucas assumed Toussaint did not want to be overheard, but he could detect no anxiety. He appeared as confident as ever, as if what he was telling Lucas somehow gave him authority.

"Are you sure?" asked Lucas.

"Yes. I'm sure. I didn't see it myself, but I am told one of the soldiers fired a shot and the journalist was killed."

"A local man or was he a foreigner?" asked Lucas.

"I don't know sir, but everyone is saying it's dangerous for journalists now. You must be careful."

Toussaint offered nothing more and retreated across the room to where his glass of rum awaited him.

Lucas continued up the stairs. He went to his room, closing the door behind him. He turned the key and looked at his private space, grateful for the lack of windows. On one of the bedside tables, the hotel had placed a bottle of aged Barbancourt, courtesy of the manager. Lucas pulled the cork and poured himself a generous helping. He savoured the rich, oak-flavour and relished the effect of the liquid as it slid past his heart and lungs and warmed his stomach. He poured another glass, took a large gulp and lay down on the bed.

The heat and the strain of all the things he did not know were taking their toll. He was not sure what to make of this new piece of information nor of Toussaint's demeanour. He did not know if the numbers the newsroom had given him were accurate. But he knew the soldiers had guns and used live rounds. He had seen the fate which had so nearly befallen Baptiste in the church and he believed the American soldier's account of the schoolgirl.

He finished his drink, letting it fog his senses. He flipped on the small shortwave radio beside the bed. Haiti was top of the news bulletin and his report led the despatches that followed. He heard the voices of the demonstrators saying they wouldn't give up until the President left office and there was no hope for Haiti without democracy...

He lay still, the sound of the radio filling his head, adrenalin slowly giving ground to the rum and a fitful sleep.

CHAPTER 19

They came for him as soon as he lost consciousness. Carefully, quietly down the long corridor, wary of the sentries who slumbered invisibly in each shadowy doorway, they gathered at Lucas's door.

His room, so secure a few minutes ago, was now a trap. Its position at the dead end of the building with its solid walls and solitary window, gave no other egress. He listened intently: a floorboard groaned, a key turned slowly, slowly and then there was silence, a silence so long that he turned his head to look. Only then, as he moved, did the door fly open.

A terrifying roar enveloped the room. Contorted forms flew at him on the bed, flaring into his mouth and nostrils, sucking the breath from his lungs, claiming his body. He writhed as he struggled for air, shackled by these forces and a rhythmical pounding which grew louder and louder until all was lost.

When he came to, he was bolt upright in the bed, fighting for breath. It took him a moment to understand where he was so he could chase the demons away. He looked at the door. It was firmly shut. The radio was blasting out some brazen military march, and he put his hands to his face to wipe the sweat from his forehead; the touch confirming some kind of reality.

Barely an hour had passed, but all the spirits that haunted this country had roared round his room to torment him. The blaring military music had come to an end to be replaced by a persistent ringing. A calm male voice spoke to him from the radio, and only then did Lucas realise that the ringing came from the phone on the bedside table. He swung his feet round to touch the floor. His head thumped, and he turned the radio off. The telephone persisted, and he picked up the receiver. He raised the handset to his ear. Finally, the room was quiet, and the hotel telephonist was telling him she had a call for him. It was Michel.

"Lucas, I thought you must be there. Only a madman would be out of the hotel now. I hope I haven't woken you." Lucas stuttered a reassurance. "I was just phoning to say thank you for lending your driver to Marie. She's back safely and Henri is sleeping in his car. He said he would be in the lobby first thing in the morning."

Lucas was reassured by the sound of his voice, and then remembered the message.

"Michel, the palace is going to call in the morning. Maybe we've got the interview with the President."

"Great," said Michel. "Just let me know when you hear. I'll go with you. And Lucas… It's great working with you. It's good to have you here. And Marie seems very fond of you too."

Lucas was grateful for Michel's acceptance. "At least if I get this interview, I can pay you back for your help. I'll call you in the morning when I know what's happening."

A voice in the background said, "Give him my love and tell him to get a good night's sleep."

"You heard that?" asked Michel down the line. "She seems happy, which is good. Normally, she's berating me for not preparing the world for the coming revolution. It's good to see her a bit more relaxed."

"You must miss her when she's in New York," said Lucas, extending the conversation to bring back a sense of normality.

"Yeah – but this is no place for her really. She should make a life in the States where she can be anything she wants to be. As much as I'd like things to improve here, there's not much cause for hope. She should be somewhere safe, where she can grow. I guess I'm tied to this wheel now, but she shouldn't feel obliged to come back all the time."

Lucas said he didn't think that Marie was acting out of a sense of obligation. "It's her passion which brings her back," he said. "You must be very proud of her. She comes because she cares."

"Yeah, she's the real deal alright," said Michel. "Beautiful, intelligent, driven. This place can't contain her… I think she'll fly off at some point and quite right too."

Lucas had no response to this.

"You know about the students tomorrow, Lucas?" Michel's voice broke in on his thoughts.

"No. What are they planning?"

"There's a meeting at the university at ten o'clock and then they'll march on the palace. It'll be the usual thing of speeches beforehand. They probably won't set off for an hour or so but there'll be more trouble, that's for sure. I had a call from someone at the Student Union tonight. We can go together if you like. Although I'll need to be back to file early afternoon."

They agreed that working together would be best, and the call ended with the promise to meet in the morning.

Lucas showered and fell into bed, longing for a sleep. His first thoughts were of Zoe and everything that Marie had said and the comfort it had brought him. For once, sleep was not driven away by a sense of guilt or shame. Then thoughts of what the morning might bring came tumbling in. Would the President do an interview? And if not, what then? What would Flo or Carla do? They'd ask the tough questions. The two of them differed in so many ways, but they invariably took the same approach to a story. Endlessly inquisitive. Always asking the central question. Their relationship intrigued Lucas. Carla the challenging, testy one and Flo the conciliator and counsellor – the one who subtly exercised control.

Lucas lay there his arms around his head, seeking oblivion, memories turning in to the stuff of dreams.

From the first day he had met Flo, she'd surprised him and chased away any reservations he had about the work. The training he received on joining the BBC had emphasised detachment, impartiality, accuracy in reporting, and then instilled studio discipline. It was all so rational and dispassionate that when he had finally met Flo he had been taken aback by her humanity and her intuitive insights into the lives of those around her.

So, when one morning Carla had burst into the office and disrupted the planning meeting, swearing and cursing, billowing smoke like a locomotive, it was Flo who quietly calmed the storm which threatened to overwhelm the room.

Nobody knew much about Carla, but she had a complexion cured in the desert sun during numerous visits to the Middle East and a tongue that could lacerate.

"She works to get away from home," Flo had said later to Lucas, seeing him watching Carla, who was berating one of the producers for yet again prioritising a UK story over an international cataclysm.

"She smokes cigarettes here, but never touches them outside the office. Her husband can't stand it…" Flo corrected herself. *"Couldn't* stand it…He was killed on assignment in Somalia several years ago, but she still respects his wishes." Lucas was shocked. Carla was such an indefatigable presence; he had never thought of her anywhere other than in the office. Flo, on the other hand, had clearly been to her home. Flo had placed a hand on his shoulder and manoeuvred him down the corridor so as not to be overheard. Lying on his bed, he recalled the conversation that followed:

"Not for general consumption this…" Her words came with a look that demanded discretion. "Carla still lays a place for him at the table. I don't think she's ever really come to terms with his absence, never really accepted he's no longer there." She sighed. "I see she's rather taken to you Lucas, which is good. You can learn a lot from her. But I fear you're the exception, so tread softly. More often than not, she fills the void with strangers." Flo was still guiding him down the corridor of discretion.

"You know why I come in so early in the morning?"

Lucas shook his head, wondering what possible connection there could be between Flo's timekeeping and Carla's erasable behaviour.

"In the winter, when Carla leaves the office late, she goes and collects the homeless from Charing Cross and lets them sleep on the floor. She can't abide the fact that people sleep rough on cold streets when there's a warm building just up the road. She's an amazon and a radical, but she has a heart of gold…" she paused: "…and she's a great producer. I just need to clear up after her occasionally."

With a knowing look, Flo had sailed off to her next meeting, always calm, always one step ahead of those around her and Carla became Lucas's mentor, testing him, always challenging his assumptions, sending him off to truffle for facts, probing him about what was true and what was not.

But, where am I going to find the truth in Haiti? The question hung hazily in Lucas's head, whispering like a spirit, keeping him on the edge of consciousness, hovering for an answer, inviting in other spirits. *On the streets? In the hospital? At the palace?*

'*At the palace. Too bloody right. That's where the answers are.*' The voice in his head was no longer his, and he could see himself approaching the palace gates. There was a man with him. He should have been Michel, ready for the interview but, he had somehow mutated into Headley. '*If you want answers, go to the top.*' He seemed pleased, no longer the hard man of his reputation, nor the bastard whom Carrick had described. Lucas tried to look at the face again. Was this really Headley? The face was too indistinct to be sure, and Lucas sensed that the good humour was evaporating, replaced by frustration. '*Is someone going to answer that phone?*' They were walking past a guard room where a soldier sat, ignoring the persistent ringing of a telephone next to him. 'For God's sake, *answer the bloody phone!'*

And Lucas, in response to Headley's urgent command, found himself with the receiver in his hand, upright on the bed.

"Good morning, Monsieur Lucas. This is Colonel Jean Claude Chambert from the palace."

CHAPTER 20

The clipped tone on the line snapped Lucas to attention.

"Colonel," Lucas struggled to get the words out and dispel the notion that he was still asleep. "I'm sorry I didn't return your call yesterday…I got back to the hotel late."

"I understand Monsieur Lucas. We live in unsettled times. I'm sorry to wake you so early but I wanted to tell you that yesterday I put your request to the President. He agreed to see you this morning at nine."

Lucas's watch on the bedside table read 7.30 a.m. He rubbed his eyes with his free hand, still trying to focus. Chambert repeated himself: "The President says he'll talk to you at the palace today. Can you be here at nine?" There was impatience in his voice.

Lucas immediately accepted. "I'd like to bring a journalist with me, who speaks French and Creole. He can do the translation, so there'll be two of us…"

"Who do you want to bring?"

"Michel Jerome. He's Haitian and works for Agence Presse Mondiale. You know him?"

There was a pause and then the Colonel came back. "But you will do the interview yourself? Monsieur Jerome is only here for translation? Yes? And you will broadcast the interview on the BBC?"

Lucas confirmed.

"Then Monsieur Lucas, we shall see you both at the gates to the palace at nine. Just give your name to the sentry. He'll be expecting you." The phone clicked off.

Lucas had no sooner put the receiver down when it rang again. It was Michel, sounding anxious. Lucas wanted to tell him about the phone call, but Michel did not let him get his first word out, so keen was he to talk about Marie. He had called to impress on Lucas that she should not go on the student march.

"She's insisting on coming, and I don't like the way the army is reacting to these demonstrations. I've told her I want her with me. We'll meet you at the hotel and show you where the students are gathering, but then I need to go to the Church of St. Mark and Marie will come with me. Baptiste will be preaching. I want to hear what he says. I just wanted to agree this with you before we arrive…"

Lucas was relieved by Michel's insistent tone. He did not want to be in another dangerous situation with Marie alongside him. When they had first met, and the crowd had swept him off his feet, he had momentarily forgotten all about her in his bid to stay upright. Now he was afraid that if events took a turn for the worse his instinct for self-preservation would obliterate his desire to make sure she was safe. So, he agreed and then broached the subject of the President.

"Michel, I had a call from Colonel Chambert just now. They want us there at nine this morning. The President has agreed to the interview."

"Great Lucas. Congratulations! I told you Chambert's a man who can make things happen." Lucas could sense Michel checking the time. "We're on our way. See you in the lobby." Lucas busied himself with his equipment, refreshing the batteries in his recorder, transferring files to his laptop, clearing the hard drive. He sat and worked out questions. He tried to imagine what Auguste might be thinking. What sort of man becomes a military dictator anyway? thought Lucas. Soft, warm, pliable, concerned for the poor? He steeled himself for a tough exchange. In battle, generals expected casualties and this general no doubt thought using soldiers to control unarmed demonstrators was a perfectly reasonable thing to do, as long as it kept him and his cronies in power.

Having completed his preparations, Lucas put everything he needed in his shoulder bag, cast a final eye around the room and went downstairs, past the guarding doors, which had proved so ineffective the night before.

Michel arrived shortly afterwards. He was wearing an old sleeveless jacket with limitless pockets, every bit the seasoned reporter. Marie was by his side.

"We should get going," said Michel immediately. "It's nearly time."

Michel's sense of urgency was cut short by Marie, who stepped forward to greet Lucas. She offered her cheek, and Lucas kissed first one and then the other.

"Ah non…three kisses are the custom here for good friends," she said and presented herself again for the third kiss. Lucas glanced at Michel but saw no note of disapproval.

"As you can see, Lucas. I couldn't keep Marie away. But she's here on condition that she comes with me."

Lucas nodded, and Marie looked resigned. Appearing satisfied, Michel put his massive arms round them both and ushered them to the door.

"Now let's go and see the President," he said.

Marie accompanied them across the square to the palace gates. She made her goodbyes in front of the sentry and returned to the hotel to wait.

Having ascertained who Michel and Lucas were, the sentry picked up a phone in the guard room, spoke briefly, and then waved them through. Other soldiers lounged on benches behind the guard house and one of them rose to take them through one of the great doors which stood either side of the palace's central façade.

The building shone. It radiated glory, as if the Sun God himself had placed it there to protect its inhabitants from the stench and grime of the city beyond. They were led up the steps through the entrance to a large assembly room where they were told to wait.

Lucas couldn't believe he was still in Port au Prince. Massive maroon marble columns rose from the oak floors to touch the ornate ceiling, which was covered with a beautiful stucco painting. A blue sky shone down through cascading clouds. Emerging from the cumuli were Romance figures. Warriors with golden tridents bestrode chariots that raced above their heads. Looking on from each corner were scantily robed, cream-skinned beauties, watching the action. With blue eyes fixed on the striving men, they reached out with bare arms, their loose robes falling away to reveal generous bosoms. An enormous crystal chandelier, suspended from the high ceiling, scattered a galaxy of lights.

The inner door clicked open and a house servant in a gilded uniform appeared and stood to attention. Through the door marched a tall Haitian officer, the braid across his epaulettes reflected gold on his skin and half a dozen medals glinted on his chest. He clicked his heels.

"Gentlemen, you're welcome. I am Colonel Jean Claude Chambert. Monsieur Gould?" He offered his hand to Lucas. Lucas took it and introduced Michel.

"Colonel, how long will we have with the President?" Lucas asked.

"You'll appreciate he's very busy. You're scheduled to have fifteen minutes. Please don't hesitate to ask anything you want. You've seen what we face here. The President wants only what is best for Haiti."

The Colonel walked stiffly back through the door, signalling them to follow. Down a corridor, they passed through a gigantic gallery. It ran across the width of the palace. High arched windows overlooked great lawns at the back. They followed the marching Colonel and saw that opposite the windows, a series of doors led to rooms at the front of the palace. The walls either side were covered with oil paintings of Haitian heroes.

The Colonel eventually stopped at a tall door at the far end. He knocked and entered. There was a brief exchange with the person inside and then he showed them in.

General Ignatius Auguste was standing in a small circle of chairs on the far side of the room. He was solidly built with a broad nose and high forehead and was wearing a tight, light grey uniform. Blue and red braid looped round his left shoulder and his stars of rank shone, newly polished. On his lapel, a rectangular black badge, like one worn at international conferences, simply said 'Auguste'.

Chambert led them over and the President greeted them while Chambert retreated to a chair against the wall. Lucas explained briefly how he would do the interview, with Michel providing translation. Auguste nodded and sat straight-backed, legs apart, with the two journalists either side. Lucas pressed the red button on his recorder, raised the microphone and asked what the President thought of the demonstrations.

The General spoke in Creole, and after each phrase he paused to allow Michel to translate. Lucas quickly realised that this process of translation would condense even the short time they had.

"You must understand," the General said. "Many of these demonstrators are misguided. They are whipped into a frenzy by politicians who can't agree among themselves what they want for this country. Demonstrations will achieve nothing. What this country needs is clear leadership and an end to corruption—"

"But Mr President," Lucas cut in. "You yourself have promised a move to democracy. When is that going to happen? You haven't set a new date for new elections."

"I will. I have promised a transition will take place. But first I must get agreement from the civilian politicians. They must promise to take part and urge their supporters to act constructively so this transition can take place."

Lucas thought the renewed promise of a return to democracy might be the news line he was seeking.

"So, Mr President, you're still promising a return to democracy. But are you making it a condition that these demonstrations must stop?"

"Of course; how can we hold elections when there are people on the streets and the city's not secure? This country needs peace and security."

Auguste had paused again for Michel to translate, and Lucas was about to ask another question when Auguste leaned forward, suddenly less formal, apparently confiding in Lucas.

"I didn't seek this job. It was my duty when my fellow officers came to ask me to take over from my predecessor." He shrugged and opened his hands. "What choice did I have? Watch this country descend into chaos? I love my country. I have an obligation to do my duty if I'm asked." He stiffened, his back once again straight in the chair. "I want to make it clear: I want peace and I want a democratic transition."

Lucas was surprised by the President's candour. He seemed to speak from the heart. But was he to be believed? Here he was in a palace fit for the wealthiest of royalty, presiding over a country with a level of poverty that beggared belief, leading a military government which was apparently set on suppressing an unarmed population. It forced a tougher question:

"You say you want to lead a transition in Haiti, but these demonstrations show no sign of ending. What will you do to stay in power? Are you prepared to kill?"

There was a sharp intake of breath and for a moment Lucas thought the interview was over. Instead, Auguste spoke in French, as if to make himself better understood.

"Oh non, non, non, je suis Chrétien…" And Michel picked up the translation. "I'm a Christian. I would never shoot unarmed civilians. I wouldn't harm anyone, but we need some stability to do what must be done."

Michel finished and looked at Lucas, his expression suggesting they had what they needed, and Lucas stood, clicking his machine off.

The President did not linger. There was no handshake. He walked straight to the door which Chambert quickly opened for him and then returned to escort them out. "I think you have what you need." His tone was cool and clipped, and he turned and walked ahead of them down the long gallery.

Michel asked what the Colonel thought would happen next.

"Ah, who knows? Our President is an honourable man. I don't know. He has the answer, but does he have the means to deliver it?"

The Colonel handed them over to the doorman, who in turn showed them out into the palace courtyard and the heat.

"That was an odd way to put it…" Michel said to Lucas as they walked. "Not exactly fulsome support for his president."

"Not exactly," agreed Lucas. "And what are we supposed to make of Auguste? Is this the tyrant everyone wants to get rid of?"

"Whatever he is," said Michel, "We have him on record. We should hold him to his word."

CHAPTER 21

Marie was waiting for them at the hotel, impatient to set off for the university.

The sun was high, pouring its heat over them as they walked. Michel, a well-known figure, attracted glances and nods from passers-by – his huge frame unmistakable. Lucas could see he was in his element on the streets, looking around, always attentive. Nobody questioned his presence. Marie, as independent as she was, held his hand as she must have done as a child and stayed close, trust and love tangible.

They reached the university. Access to its compound was through a narrow door, blocked by the crowd around it. A speech was being relayed through a pair of rusty loudspeakers on the ground by the door. From the sound of it, the gathering was reaching a climax, chants from students beyond the door already obscuring what was being said.

"Viva Haiti!" "Democracy." "Tous pour la découpage!"

Within a couple of minutes, young people poured onto the street, clustering together, preparing to march up the hill and away. Everyone seemed to know where they were going and the three followed on, keeping pace as the procession gathered momentum.

They stayed together until the march was well under way and the street was one long mass of humanity. Michel and Marie then said farewell, and they all agreed to meet back at the hotel in the afternoon. Lucas watched them go, catching one brilliant smile from Marie before she focused on weaving her way through the milling crowd.

Lucas was the only person standing still, and he could hold his ground no longer. He let himself be carried along by the students. Together they flowed up the road as it climbed the hill, their direction of travel away from the Presidential Palace. It was at least a mile behind them. But at the top, they took a sharp right turn, which led down again towards a distant main road. Lucas could see vehicles criss-crossing in both directions. The demonstrators moved en masse towards the junction. He asked those closest to him the name of the road they were approaching. 'La Rue Jean Jacques Dessalines,' came the reply from someone behind him and the crowd surged down, students moving together four and five abreast, some linking arms, all chanting.

At the high part of their descent, Lucas had a view across the city towards the sea. Plumes of thick black smoke were spiralling up towards the blue sky from burning tyres elsewhere in the city. Now, as the road levelled out, he could see that some marchers ahead of him had already reached the junction and were rounding the corner on to the main street. If everyone followed this route, it would take them back towards the palace. The climax would once again be before the President himself.

Lucas was ten yards from the corner when he saw the army truck cross from left to right. It was full of soldiers, crouching in the back, ready to jump.

Those in front of him saw the truck as well, and immediately turned and ran past him back up the road away from the threat. Instinctively, Lucas followed them. He ran some ten yards before looking over his shoulder, back at what was now an empty street.

He slowed. There were no soldiers. No demonstrators at the junction, just a few stragglers. There was no sound of shooting. Why was he running? He was there to report. The further he ran, the further he was from the story.

He had to go back.

He switched on his recorder and, bringing the microphone to his lips, started a quick commentary as he turned.

"This is Lucas Gould in Port au Prince. Today, the students are marching from the university in opposition to the military government. Once again, they're calling for the resignation of General Auguste, Haiti's military leader. The demonstration has been peaceful..."

He was nearly at the junction. Now he was talking, he wished he had brought some water. Despite the lesson Marie had taught him, he still carried none with him. But his commentary would be short. When he got to the corner, there would be the truck, empty of its occupants. Further away would be a crowd of protesters running away, soldiers at their heels.

But this expectation was shattered by the two soldiers who suddenly appeared in front of him, rifles raised, intent on firing at the retreating demonstrators.

His stomach heaved as he recoiled. He turned and again he was running, microphone still at his lips.

"I'm at the Rue Jean Jacques Dessalines and the troops have just turned up…"

He went as fast as he could, words spilling into his recorder fearful that time was running out. He managed one more sentence and then the rest was blown away by the shock wave that erupted round him.

The bullet passed so close to him he felt its passage. His recorder captured the sound of his breath exploding from his body, as if someone had actually struck him, but he was still on his feet focused on survival.

It was then he saw the broken drain, a deep trench dug by the road, covered with concrete slabs. But here the slabs had broken away, leaving the drain exposed and Lucas, desperate for cover, jumped. He hit the bottom hard, surprised to find he was still intact. He kept his head down and waited, stuffing the recorder and microphone into his bag to keep them out of sight. With his bag secure, he looked up to see the man in a doorway being beaten with the rifle butt. Lucas immediately ducked down again and listened intently.

After a while, the beating stopped and there was only the distant sound of voices further up the hill – all receding. This was his moment to move. He looked again, putting his head to street level, checking all was clear. The man in the doorway had gone, but then he sensed the soldier moving to his left, looking directly at him.

Momentarily, he thought of flight again, but he had no options. The soldier was going to reach him before he had time to get out of the drain.

A still, reasoned voice in his head told him. *He won't kill you. You're a foreigner and soldiers don't kill foreigners on demonstrations – not in cold blood.*

So, he stood up and shouted 'je suis journalist' and immediately questioned his wisdom. They may not kill foreigners, but had he not been told a journalist had died the day before?

He looked at the face beneath the metal helmet and saw no hesitation as he came to a stop a few feet away. Lucas raised his arms and then all his reasoning was swept aside as the soldier pointed his rifle directly at Lucas's chest. There was to be only one outcome.

A spasm ran through him, bringing a cascade of half-framed thoughts. He thought desperately of a sign he could leave for anyone who might come looking. His recorder was switched off in his bag. Saying anything was useless. So, he instinctively turned round. If he was going to be shot, he would rather take the bullet in his back, unarmed in this hot, stinking place, like an animal. Not a threat, but a victim.

Before him was a low wall of bricks at the bottom of the drain. He thought of Marie and felt something which might have been regret, but the thought was obliterated by a thunderous blast which ripped away all thoughts, breath, feeling, as he toppled forward.

CHAPTER 22

Lucas was on his knees in the drain. Slumped down, his body compressed. There was no pain, no sound. The heat, the dust and the smell had all evaporated. He was staring at the low wall in front of him and the blood spattered across it.

He didn't move. He waited, searching for some sensation other than sight. Only gradually did he become aware of the throbbing heat on his back and the sharp pain in his head. Even then, he stayed on his knees, trying to comprehend what had happened.

For a while, all he saw was the wall. Why would you block a drain with bricks? He gave this question his full attention, seeking something reassuringly mundane. He noticed a pipe poking through by his feet, allowing effluent uninterrupted passage. So, he reasoned, the wall had been built as reinforcement not as a dam. This understanding brought a little comfort, and his focus widened.

Carefully, fearing that movement might provoke more violence, he looked more closely at what was in front of him and saw a fist sized crater in one of the bricks. At its centre was a perfectly round bullet hole. The soldier couldn't have missed from so close a range. He must have had second thoughts before he fired, thought Lucas. But what about the blood? Was it his? He moved his arms and felt his chest. No evidence of any bullet wound there. He looked at his hands, caked with mud, but otherwise okay. Then a drop of red liquid dripped. He touched the side of his head and felt the sticky oozing. His fingers cautiously traced the matted trail that ran above his ear to his forehead. His scalp burned and his head throbbed, but his skull was intact. Perhaps the bullet had grazed his head and hit the wall, felling him, producing enough blood to stain his shirt and spray the wall but otherwise not doing serious damage. This conclusion brought further reassurance, and his confidence rose.

He stood up stiffly and peered out at the street. It was deserted — no sign of life in either direction. He gathered up his bag and clambered out of the drain. Shakily at first and then faster, he walked up the hill. When he reached the top, a car passed and then stopped. Two Haitians looked back at him. The car reversed, and the passenger leant out and said: "You need help?"

They were two local journalists from Radio Soleil, the Catholic Radio station. They said they'd heard shooting and had come to investigate. One of them got out and produced a first aid kit. He wiped Lucas's head with lint bandages and antiseptic. When he had finished, he showed the stained dressings to Lucas as he stuffed them into a plastic bag. Then he gave Lucas the thumbs up and illustrated the trajectory of the bullet by grazing the side of his head with his finger and then pointing off into the distance. Some pain killers were produced, and Lucas wolfed them down with a bottle of water from the car.

They drove off, with the two local journalists firing questions. When they finally worked out what exactly had happened on la Rue Jean Jacques Dessalines that day, they gave each other a long look that did not go unnoticed in the back seat: it was a look, thought Lucas, of disbelief that he was alive.

In a quarter of an hour, they pulled up outside his hotel and Lucas went directly to the bar, where he ordered a ladle of the rum. He then went to his room and changed his shirt, inspecting his head in the bathroom mirror and marvelling at what a good job his new friends had done in cleaning him up. He then took more pain killers from his bag and returned to the bar where he ordered another glass of rum and carried it in an ice filled, rattling glass, to one of the deep armchairs near the doors leading to the pool. When he had finished it, he ordered another one.

It was there that Michel and Marie found him sometime later.

"My God!" said Marie who immediately sat down next to him on finding him ashen faced, bent forward on the sofa. She went to touch his head, but he caught her hand and held it. "It's okay. Just a little tender."

"You should see a doctor," said Michel.

"No, not necessary," said Lucas quickly. He had already thought the situation through. He knew this was his opportunity to make his mark and transition into reporting. He wasn't going to do anything that might jeopardise his ability to carry on working. "I'm fine. I've already been patched up. It's been cleaned and I'm fine. A couple of days of painkillers and

I'll be right as rain." He said this with such conviction that Michel seemed reassured. Marie appeared less convinced. She bombarded Lucas with questions about what had happened.

Suspecting that she feared concussion and that her questions were a test of his memory, he gave a more detailed account than he would otherwise have thought necessary. As he talked, Michel prowled the carpet in front of them, listening intently.

When he had finished, Marie was the one who broke the ensuing silence. "We should have stayed with him." She was looking up at Michel reproachfully. "The streets are too dangerous now."

"I'm not sure it would have made much difference, but it's dangerous alright. You can't use live rounds against unarmed civilians," Michel went on, muttering his contempt at the President's claim to abhor violence.

Lucas was not sure he wanted to be the focus of their attention much longer. Too much concern, and he might fall apart entirely. So, he diverted the conversation elsewhere:

"Come on," he said. "Fill me in. What happened at the church with Baptiste?"

Marie understood what he needed and quickly recounted what they'd seen, keeping close to Lucas.

"Well, Baptiste was there," she said. "He was in full flight when we arrived, preaching to a packed church, in his element. He was quoting the psalms saying right would prevail against wrong and those who've been wronged would receive justice, but really what he was doing was calling for a general strike."

"And people lapped it up," said Michel, who stopped pacing to focus on the two young people in front of him.

"Everyone was really fired up by the end of it. It was all Baptiste could do to stop them marching on the palace there and then. But the plan is to strike tomorrow. I talked to some of the politicians who were there, and they said they're determined to bring the city to a complete halt, close everything down and get everyone out on the streets again in the morning."

One of the waiters came over to offer drinks. Michel ordered more rum for them and as the man turned to leave, he said something into Michel's ear. As he retreated, Michel repeated what he'd heard.

"The internet's down," he said. "Apparently, there are radio announcements saying the curfew's being extended. It'll start at dusk instead of midnight and end at six in the morning. This is getting worse."

"How am I going to file my reports?" asked Lucas, not expecting a reply. Michel stood, motioning to Lucas to stay where he was.

"I'll go and check what's happening at reception. They'll know more about what's going on. But either way, Marie and I had better stay here. There'll be troops out preparing for the curfew already, and we may not be able to get back to the city in the morning. I'll go and get a room." He walked off towards reception.

Marie put her hand on Lucas's arm.

"Are you alright?"

"Yes, I'm fine. Lucky, I guess." He took in the comfortable lounge with its soft chairs and carpets. Marie looked doubtful, and he smiled at her. "Really, I'm okay. Although I'm not sure I'll be leaving here entirely intact."

"I'm not sure you were entirely intact when you arrived, Lucas," said Marie, and their laughter released some of the tension.

"Michel told me about your interview with the President. Did he really say he was a man of peace?"

"Yes," responded Lucas. "That was pretty much it. He sounded quite offended by the suggestion that he might have to kill people. I need to file the interview...but with the internet down..." He trailed off, thinking about options, but Marie continued.

"Well, the President has set a standard and we must hold him to it." She lowered her voice to a whisper. "It seems to me you're no longer an observer, Lucas. Today you became part of the story."

"I'm not sure about that," replied Lucas, but he knew she was right. He understood what his job was, what he had to do, but now he wanted more. "I know I told you I was here to report and move on, to make a mark and prove I can be a reporter. But part of me now feels I shouldn't leave. Everyone here has such purpose. Takes such risks. They struggle so hard for a better life. And the outside world barely knows about it. Most people have never even heard of this place still less care... There's so much more to do. I mean, look at Michel. Haiti needs more like him. He lives it. He's not going anywhere, and this story needs to be lived to be understood. I think reporters who stay in a country and live it every day are so much better than people who fly in and fly out and move on all the time, always looking for the next story..."

"Then stay," said Marie calmly. "Why don't you stay? Michel's the only local journalist whose stories get reported internationally. None of the news organisations care enough to base foreign correspondents in Port au Prince. You could commit to it and make a difference…if it's what you really want to do."

Lucas stared at her, wondering whether she meant to stay with her or stay on the story.

"But you live in New York now," he said.

"I go to university in New York. I live here. I'm Haitian. I'm part of all of this." She lifted her head, looking around the room.

"And beautiful," added Lucas, staring at her. Marie threw her head back, suddenly irritated.

"Don't tell me I'm beautiful. I'm just me. I am what I am. I don't want to be admired and I'm not what's important here."

Lucas smarted at the retort, kicking himself for misjudging her mood. She had a towering independence that only made him want her more. He wanted to hold her, possess her but he knew no person could possess another. It was foolish, like chasing a shadow.

Michel returned, looking concerned.

"It's not just the internet. They're saying the international exchange is down as well. So, no more phone calls to London…" Lucas dragged his attention away from Marie, not wanting Michel to think anything was wrong. "So, the President grants me an interview and then stops me from filing?" He watched Michel, who had started prowling again. "It doesn't make sense…"

"Unless," said Michel, "he didn't think the interview went well. Or perhaps he's not making the decisions. Perhaps someone doesn't want Auguste on the BBC. Who knows?"

Michel paused to meet Lucas's gaze, searching for answers. "At least I have a telex machine in my office. I should be able to file using that and if all else fails Lucas, you can use it to send written reports back to London."

"Doesn't sound like great radio," Lucas quipped. "But thanks for the offer. It may be my only option."

Michel said he had got a room and said they should eat. Lucas, still feeling the sting of Marie's rebuke, declined and said he should work. He picked up a sandwich from a tray on the bar and went upstairs.

He spent the next hour going through his notes, burying himself in his work. He listened back to the interview, wrote an introduction, trimmed the audio for an illustrated despatch and then wrote a straight voice report for news bulletins. But how was he going to get anything back to London? A written report could go by telex, but he had to try to find a way to get audio back. He tried the phone. There was a dial tone. He tried the international number for newsroom. An automated message in French came up saying no service was available. He tried the internet connection. It was dead.

Frustrated, he packed up his equipment and went downstairs to reception and asked for the manager.

"Monsieur, I'm so sorry. I can do nothing. The government has blocked the internet. I believe it's the same all over the city."

"And the phone lines?" asked Lucas. "I can't call anyone?"

"You can make a local call. I think that's still working. But I believe the international exchange is closed. It was announced on the radio this evening and I don't know how long this will last. I'm sorry sir…"

"Is there a problem?" The question floated over Lucas's shoulder, and he turned to see Toussaint looking at the manager who appeared taken aback by the intervention.

"Ah Monsieur Toussaint. How very good to see you. I was just explaining to this gentleman that the international phone lines are down, and the internet is unavailable." Toussaint took a step closer.

"Are you alright?" he said looking more closely at Lucas. "What's wrong with you head?"

"I'm fine," said Lucas quickly, not wanting to explain everything again. "I banged it earlier. It will be better tomorrow." Toussaint appeared satisfied and turned his attention back to the manager, who was shifting his feet nervously.

"So, Pierre, my friend. You say our friend cannot make an international call? Surely there's something you can do? Monsieur Gould here is an important man. He's been to see the President. We must do what we can to make sure he gets what he needs."

The manager looked astonished.

"Yes, but I don't control these things. You know this. It's not my decision..." He had his arms wide, expressing the size of the problem, looking quizzically at Toussaint.

"What about the DEL line?" asked Toussaint, as if this was the most natural question in the world.

"The DEL?" The manager's expression was blank.

"Before you put this fancy telephone system in your lovely hotel, how did you make phone calls?"

A realisation dawned. "Ah – you mean the old manual exchange? It's still there, but it's not connected," said the manager.

"I think you'll find," said Toussaint, "that in the same room you have an old phone with a direct international line. It was a back-up for when there was a fault at the exchange. I used to use it myself. Take a look." Toussaint withdrew, having placed a hand on Lucas's shoulder as if bestowing an honour that would ensure respect from everyone.

The manager, fumbling a set of keys, took Lucas to a little room to one side of reception and unlocked the door. There, was an old manual switchboard with rows of sockets and elasticated jacks which were sitting upright on parade awaiting their orders. Everything was covered in dust, including the frosted window which provided a meagre light. To the side of the switchboard Lucas could see an old-fashioned bakelite phone. He picked it up and put it to his ear, blowing a cobweb from the mouthpiece. There was a steady tone. He dialled the international code and then his home number. It rang, and he quickly hung up.

"I can use this. Can you let me have the key? I could make calls and log them. You can charge them to my room."

"I had no idea this was still here. But yes, sir, you can use it. I'll leave the key behind reception. Just ask for the operator's key." The manager turned, looking relieved that a resolution had been found and then paused. "Would you mind not mentioning this to anyone?" he asked. "I have great...regard for Monsieur Toussaint... Not everyone is as..." he searched for the right word... "*helpful* as he. You understand?"

"Of course," replied Lucas, keen to get on. "I won't tell anyone else." He plonked his bag on the desk to indicate he had urgent work to do. "If you don't mind, I'll use it now." The manager handed him the key, and Lucas took it. Immediately, he turned his back and rummaged through the pouch with all the cables, searching for Junior's black box. With relief, he heard the manager close the door behind him. He unscrewed the mouthpiece to reveal a metal disc. Junior had supplied a brief typewritten set of instructions on how to connect to 'traffic' and Lucas dialled the number.

"Control Room." The woman's voice was curt, expecting something urgent. Lucas explained his situation.

"Oh dear," came the reply. "Sounds like you're calling from history. We used to have traffic, to take telephone despatches, but we haven't done that for years… but hang on." There was talking in the background and some laughter. "Hang on," came the voice again. "We're just getting you hooked up." Lucas could hear someone flipping switches and then typing furiously on a keyboard. "Right Lucas. We're ready for you. Leave ten second pauses between takes. Say when you've finished, but stay on the line, please."

Lucas played the interview with the President. He counted to ten and then read his straight piece.

"Got that," came the voice down the line. "I'll flag it up for all outlets. It'll be in the system in about fifteen minutes. Are you going to do this again?" Lucas explained he had no alternative.

"Don't worry, dear," came the reply. "I'll leave a note for the next shift. By the way, I can see the Caribbean Service has put a note in the system to say they want to do an interview with you. I can put you through if you hang on."

Courtney was not there, but a producer introduced herself as Colette and expressed surprise that Lucas was calling via the control room. Lucas missed Courtney's warm Jamaican accent, but he recounted his experience at the hands of the soldier. After Colette had finished with her questions, she asked if Lucas had kept his recorder running when the soldier shot at him. She seemed disappointed he had switched it off. Then Lucas remembered he had some commentary from the street and played it down the line. This seemed to satisfy her, and the call ended.

By the time he finished, it was late. He packed his things and went back up to his room, leaving the key at reception. His head still throbbed, so he swallowed more painkillers and dropped down on to his bed in his clothes to wait for the headache to subside.

Outside his door, the sentries along the corridor rallied to keep the spirits at bay. Nobody came for him in the night. And eventually he slept an uninterrupted sleep.

CHAPTER 23

Michel met Lucas on the stairs as he headed down to the lobby, having woken only minutes before.

"I was just coming to wake you," Michel said. "I left it as long as I could." He wrapped a large hand around Lucas's shoulder and gave him a broad smile. "I thought you might need the rest after yesterday."

"That's good of you," said Lucas. "I was afraid I might have missed you."

Michel laughed. "No chance! We're not going anywhere without you."

"Good to know," said Lucas, hitching his bag back on to his shoulder. He felt distinctly bleary, unsure whether it was caused by too much sleep or too much rum or the graze to his head. Marie, on the other hand, looked cool and fresh as she rose from one of the big chairs, any tension from the previous day forgotten. When he got to the bottom step she was there to greet him, eager to check that he really was feeling better for his night's rest. Together, the three of them walked to the entrance and out into the boiling square. It was filling up fast with streams of people converging from all directions. Michel, wearing the same battered reporter's waistcoat as yesterday, notepad in his hand, spearheaded a path through the throng with Marie and Lucas trailing in his wake.

Michel greeted those he knew by name, nodding in turn to the many other people who recognised him. After a while, he paused to talk to a diminutive, bearded man whom he clearly knew well. He was firing questions in Creole as Marie and Lucas came alongside him. Michel explained that Monsieur Paul was a union leader and when Lucas pulled out his recorder, Michel started translating for his benefit. Paul said there had been a widespread response to the call for a general strike. The markets in the centre of town had not opened that morning and all the little buses which ferried people around were offering free rides to the demonstration.

"The whole city's on the move," Paul said. "The poor and disenfranchised of City Soleil are walking on the palace. They want Auguste to go. It's a great day for Haiti."

Lucas flipped his machine off and watched him disappear into the crowd.

The square was now a heaving mass of bodies, shoulder to shoulder, straining to see what might be happening in front of the palace. Chants echoed from one side to the other. In among them were the words with which Lucas had become familiar

"Découpage…"

"Liberté!"

Earlier, Lucas had glimpsed a squad of soldiers lined up behind the palace railings, but his view was now obscured by people pushing in from every side. It seemed the whole of Port au Prince was here, from the well-dressed middle classes to the poorest labourers all compressed together in the sweating heat, before the great white symbol of wealth, power and privilege.

Michel, who had his notebook raised above the crush, shouted, "Numbers?" at Lucas. They looked quizzically at each other with no way of coming up with a clear answer.

"Thousands!" shouted Lucas. "Definitely the biggest yet." Michel nodded before giving up on his notetaking. The weight of the crowd came in waves, rolling them from side to side. Chant after chant welled up to a crescendo to be hurled across their heads at the palace only to echo back unanswered.

With no hope of getting a good view of what was happening, Lucas cast around for a better vantage point. Looking back at the hotel, he saw there was a balcony high on the first floor above the hotel's entrance. He would be able to see everything from there and record a commentary above the noise of the crowd. Trying to make himself heard in his current position was nigh impossible. He shouted at Michel and signalled where he wanted to go. Michel gave him a thumbs up and turned to Marie to try to get her to go with him. But Marie immediately protested, shaking her head and gripping Michel's arm, determined to stay put. Michel gave Lucas a now-familiar look of resignation and waved him off. As he turned away, Lucas saw Marie's eyes glistening with excitement. Her head was high, relishing the defiance of the crowd around her. She was in her element. All the way back to the hotel and long after, it was that look on her face that was to remain with him.

Lucas intended to go straight to the balcony, but when he got to reception, he reconsidered. He ought to file immediately. With the protests escalating like this, newsroom might want coverage throughout the day. It would depend on what was happening elsewhere in the world, but he did not want to miss the opportunity.

He diverted to the operator's room, picking up the key from the front desk. He sat and wrote a summary and recorded it.

"The capital is today at a standstill. The call for a general strike has generated a huge response with shops and markets closing and public transport ferrying demonstrators without charge. Thousands of Haitians have gathered in the square facing the Presidential Palace. They continue to call for President Ignatius Auguste to step down. The people before the palace are unarmed and they're turning this demonstration into a battle of wills between them and the President. Yesterday the President said he wouldn't kill civilians in order to stay in power. Today the demonstrators are testing that pledge and sending a clear message. They want a return to civilian government."

Lucas called the control room and played the recording using Junior's black box. When it had finished, a voice came back on the line and said that News wanted to talk to him:

"Hey Lucas. I heard your report coming in. Thanks for that." It was Carrick. They talked briefly, with Carrick ordering more later in the day. "We'll use what you've just filed and expect you up again tonight. And good work finding a way round the lock-down." He sounded genuinely pleased. "Your interview with the President ran across all outlets yesterday, so Haiti's now our lead."

Lucas confirmed he would file again once the demonstration was over. And then there was a rare hesitation at the other end of the line:

"Look Lucas, I've been talking to Julian Headley, and I have him on standby to relieve you when there's an opportunity. He's been chomping at the bit since the demonstrations kicked off, and it's his patch. It's just that with the airport closed, there's been no way for him to get there to help you out. So, I just wanted to alert you to the fact that I've agreed he can take over from you when the airport re-opens."

"I'm fine," said Lucas quickly, his heart sinking. "I can carry on. I want to stay. I'd really like to see this through." But he knew the decision had already been taken.

"Look, you've done a great job Lucas," said Carrick, impatience never far from the surface. "You've gone above and beyond. But Headley's been covering Haiti for years. I can't deny him the story if there's a chance of getting him in. But keep going until you hear from him. You're still our man until the airport opens." He clearly wouldn't brook more discussion and moved on. "Did you know you were all over the wires yesterday? APM ran a piece saying you got cornered by the army and Reuters picked it up. Make the most of it while you can and take care."

And he was gone. Lucas put the handset down and swore quietly. So, his story was being taken away. Headley must have really piled on the pressure. But Carrick's last words lingered, and they brought him to his feet: *So, what's really changed? The airport is still closed. Headley can't fly in. I can't fly out. It's still my story.*

A new sense of urgency ran through him. He had to concentrate. It was all happening outside. He needed to get back. He gathered his equipment together and went upstairs, turning right at the top towards the front of the hotel. He followed the passage until he judged he was above the entrance and found a door that opened on to a high-ceilinged room with gold lacquered chairs up against the walls.

Opposite the door, tall sash windows ran from floor to ceiling. There, through the glass, Lucas could see the crowd and the balcony. He bent down and pulled hard on two brass handles and the window rose. The roar of the crowd flooded in, along with the baking heat and the sound of a car revving below.

Holding his equipment close, he ducked through the window and stepped carefully on to the tiled surface. It was the perfect spot. He had an imperial view across the square. The heaving mass of people below stretched from the hotel to the barracks on the far side with the palace off to his left framed by its huge gravel courtyard and lawn.

The soldiers were still lined up, some officers shouting at people at the front of the crowd through the heavy black railings. Lucas sat to one side on the low wall that formed the balcony's perimeter and lifted his microphone. He quickly described the scene, thinking his words could introduce the comments from Monsieur Paul.

When he finished, he noticed that the soldiers in front of the palace had come to attention. An officer wearing gold epaulettes of seniority was barking orders and in response they executed a crisp quarter turn and started marking time.

Guards at the gates were trying to clear a way, driving protesters back. The squad of soldiers marched forwards and as they reached the open gates, they broke step and fanned out. They held their rifles in both hands across their chests, ramming them into protesters who failed to retreat fast enough until they cleared sufficient space for themselves. Those at the front of the crowd were now pinned back, straining to stay on their feet.

The officer in charge had a megaphone and was hurling instructions, but the protesters could only retreat so far before the weight of people behind them made it impossible to move any further. It was only a short while before some started to fall.

The megaphone must have waved in Lucas's direction, because a clean, clipped command floated up to the balcony. Lucas watched as the soldiers suddenly raised their rifles. Then, in response to a second brief command, they fired a crisp volley over the heads of the crowd.

Immediately, there was total panic. Those not already on the ground ducked low. Some tried to run but many of them fell. At the sound of gunfire, those further back in the square recoiled and tried to flee. Another volley followed. On the far side of the square, Lucas could see the side streets filling up with people trying to get away. Lucas had caught the second volley on his recorder and was shouting a commentary over the crescendo of noise boiling over the balcony.

There were screams as people exhorted each other to get away. There was the sound of a thousand feet on cobbles. Cries of help echoed out from those who fell. As one went down so did another, sucking more and more into a deadly crush.

Individual soldiers fired at will. Commands meant nothing now. What had been an orderly line of troops become a ragged collection of uniformed men spreading out to clear spaces that closed behind them as people fought to get away in all directions.

On the far side of the square, two trucks had appeared at the gates of the barracks and men in darker uniforms were climbing down with their rifles. A bullet slapped into the wall behind Lucas, and he dropped low behind the stone balustrade.

He heard a warning whine from his recorder as it switched itself off. He packed it in to his bag. He had seen enough.

Lucas waited, heart pounding, crouched low to avoid any more stray bullets. After what seemed an age, the shooting reduced and finally petered out. He looked up. Most of the crowd had dispersed and some of the soldiers were forming up in the centre of the square. He went back through the window and down to the lobby.

Henri rushed up to him, shaking him by the hand. "You okay Mr Lucas…you okay?" Lucas told him to stay put. He checked the lobby to see if Marie and Michel had made it to the hotel, but they were nowhere to be seen.

He went to the hotel door to be revolved once more into the blazing heat. Some soldiers were being marched back towards the palace; some officers lingered reviewing their handiwork; two men who looked like doctors were moving from one huddle to another. There were dozens of people lying on the cobbles.

Lucas tried to reassure himself. He'd seen soldiers shooting into the air. *Michel and Marie were well back from the palace. Surely, they must be safe.* He walked forward, looking at anyone who was sitting or lying on the ground. An elderly woman raised a hand to him, and he took it. She spoke in Creole. He couldn't make out what she said, but she had no visible injury. After a minute, a medic appeared and took her hand from his and knelt to help. Lucas hurried on to where he thought he had left Michel and Marie.

At first, he did not recognise them because he couldn't see Michel. But there was Marie. She was on her knees, looking down at a crumpled heap in front of her. Lucas rushed over, calling her name. When he was within a few feet, she looked up. Tears were streaming down her face. She was cradling Michel's head in her lap, stroking his thick black hair, crushing it in her hands, rocking back and forwards.

Michel was on his back, legs at an awkward angle. His eyes were closed and there was blood on the cobbles next to him.

Lucas sank down next to Marie and put his hand on Michel's neck, feeling for some sign of life. Marie shook her head and sobbed in great heaving gasps, drowning. Lucas tried to calm her. He briefly put his hands on her shoulders, but she remained head down and rigid, consumed by what was lying before her.

Lucas felt utterly useless and somehow responsible for what was in front of him. Why had he gone to the balcony? Why had he left them there? It should be him in the dust, his body spread out on the ground with a bullet in him. It should be him, not Michel.

He looked up desperately seeking help. A few yards away was a medic in a white coat. Lucas shouted at him, but his back was turned. He was focused on someone else who had fallen.

Lucas stumbled towards him. He grabbed the man's shoulder and, as he turned, there was a moment of recognition. It was the doctor from the hospital. Lucas dragged him towards Michel with a combination of pleading and force.

The doctor bent and felt for a pulse. He frowned and moved his hands down Michel's body, feeling for injuries, finding none at first. He then slid his hands under Michel's back. As he did, more blood pooled in the cracks between the stones. The doctor withdrew his hands, wiping them on his coat and checked again for life. He was motionless for a while, and then looked at Lucas and shook his head. Marie let out a low moan, one hand mopping Michel's brow, the other stroking his cheek as if the contact would somehow bring him back.

The doctor moved away to help others, and Lucas remembered what had been said when they first met. He ran after him and pleaded with him to take Michel to the hospital. He did not want the troops coming to take him away. The man understood and within a few minutes, two attendants came. They gently prised Marie from Michel and transferred him on to a canvas stretcher and carried him to a vehicle at the side of the square.

With Michel no longer there, Marie grew quieter. She stood staring at the ground, blood on her clothes. Together, they walked slowly towards the hospital. There was nothing said. Lucas had no words and Marie was buried in shock, seemingly unaware of what she was doing or who she was with.

By the time they arrived, Michel was laid out on an iron bedstead in a small room by the entrance. Lucas was asking the doctor what they should do when Marie spoke. She had somehow collected herself and she told the doctor she'd make funeral arrangements and return for Michel as soon as she could. There was sympathy and then forms to fill in with names and addresses. All this Marie did, the activity pushing the pain away, providing a wall between the past and a future she couldn't bear to contemplate.

"I'll speak to Michel's friends. I'm sure they'll help," she said absently when they left the hospital. As the words left her, she started to shake. She took a huge gulp of air, as if all her grief had been suffocating her. She reached for Lucas to steady herself and stood there, struggling to stay upright. Painfully, deliberately, she regained control, and she walked, her hand still on Lucas's arm.

He was numb; helpless in the face of Marie's grief. He did not know what to do next. He had no words. Everything Lucas thought of saying sounded cold or inadequate. All he could do was walk, feeling the weight of her hand on his arm, struggling to understand his own reactions. Without Michel, everything was different, suddenly empty. Nothing was worth this loss. Nothing was worth seeing Marie so distraught. And then, as Lucas pushed through the door into the cool air of the hotel reception, something made him think of that moment when Michel had driven away from the radio station and he had thought he already knew this man, that he was renewing a connection that already existed. And as he looked back at Marie who was following him in through the hotel entrance, it was as though Michel put his great hand on his shoulder. He must focus on her. He must make sure she was alright.

Lucas stood before her and gently asked what she wanted to do, where she wanted to go. He would stay with her, do anything. She replied quietly that she wanted to go home. And Lucas could only do as she wished.

He looked around. There was Henri again, hovering by the reception desk, visibly afraid to approach. Lucas waved him over and told him to bring the car round and together they drove Marie back to Petionville and Michel's house where Marie made phone calls and talked and cried until eventually an exhausted sadness descended on her.

She did not want Lucas to stay. He tried to insist, but she firmly said no. She wanted to be alone. They would talk tomorrow, but she must be on her own tonight.

He reluctantly got in the car and Henri, driving slowly, took him back to the hotel where he went straight to his room and buried himself in work.

Lucas tried not to let his feelings infect his writing. He did not rant against the inhumanity of shooting unarmed civilians in the street. He did not say Michel was his friend. He did not mention his beautiful, brave daughter.

He wrote what he had seen: accurately, rationally, using a rapier that Carla had taught him to wield, with a precision that cuts before the victim feels the blade.

He filed the sounds of the demonstration. He filed the story. He did interviews for News and for the Caribbean Service. He told the world what the President had said: he wouldn't kill to stay in power. But today a journalist died on the street of Port au Prince, at the hands of an army, whose commander-in-chief was the President himself.

CHAPTER 24

Lucas had been awake for hours. He took the call on the second ring and immediately recognised Colonel Chambert's clipped voice.

"I hope I haven't woken you Mr Gould, but I thought you would want to know, President Ignatius Auguste left the country at four a.m. this morning."

Lucas was on his feet, his head throbbing.

"He's left the country. How?"

"The Americans flew him out. I believe in one of their aircraft but please – and I must insist on this point – don't quote me. If you want confirmation, call the US Embassy."

Lucas was sure it was the Colonel's voice, but he realised as soon as he put the phone down that he had not given his name. He looked at his watch. It was not yet eight o'clock. Still early, but he had to make the call. Lucas picked up the crumbling phone book in the drawer of the table by the bed and looked up the United States Embassy. Five consecutive numbers were listed for different departments. One was for the Ambassador's office and thinking he should go straight to the top, Lucas dialled.

It was answered immediately, and he explained who he was.

"I'm not sure whether the Ambassador's available, but I'll see if I can find her. Please stay on the line."

After a few minutes a new voice came back at him.

"Mr Gould?"

"Yes. Who's this?" asked Lucas.

"This is the Ambassador. How can I help you?"

"Ambassador, I've been told by a source at the Presidential Palace that General Auguste was flown out of Haiti this morning at four a.m. Is that correct?"

"That's right, Mr Gould."

"Can you give me a bit more detail? Like why and how?"

"Well, Mr Gould it's quite straight forward. A US military transport plane, I believe it was a C130, landed at the airport this morning and we advised the President it might be best for him to be on it, given the situation on the streets and the unfortunate events of yesterday."

"The airport's open again?"

"I'm told flights will resume later today, since this situation appears to be resolved. Now Mr Gould I'm busy, so unless you have any other questions…"

Lucas put the phone down.

It was the end.

He sat and wrote the story.

"After days of protests and public demonstrations the Haitian President General Ignatius Auguste went in to exile this morning at 0400 hours local time. He was flown out of Port au Prince airport in a military transport provided by the American government. His situation became untenable when, having promised not to use deadly force against protesters, troops fired on unarmed protesters outside the Presidential Palace…"

Lucas finished the report and recorded it to make sure it was word perfect and without emotion. He was transferring the file to his laptop when his mobile phone suddenly sprang to life.

"Lucas," said a man's voice. "Hello mate. It's Julian Headley. I'm at the airport in Port au Prince. Newsroom gave me your number and said you would know I was coming. I managed to hitch a ride on the first flight out of Miami. I gather you're expecting me."

Lucas, taken aback at the speed of Headley's arrival, told him where he was, and Headley said he'd be there as soon as he could find transport to the city.

Lucas knew he had little time but if he was quick, he could bring this story to its conclusion. The ethernet was live again in his room and he connected his laptop and quickly filed his report. Moments after he had finished his phone rang again. It was Flo.

"It works. Finally!" Her relief evident. "Look Lucas, I haven't got long but I wanted to say well done and we're looking forward to having you back. I'm so pleased you're coming home." Lucas was flattered she'd bothered to call so quickly and said he had just wrapped up the story. "Lucas, we've booked you on a flight out of Port au Prince tonight. It's been hell getting you a ticket. There are so many people trying to leave the country. We had to pull a few strings, but you should find the ticket waiting for you at the airport."

So fast. It was all happening so fast. A deadline had been set and he must go. Trying to delay his return would upset everyone who had helped him get to Haiti in the first place, but the thought of leaving Marie left him utterly dejected.

243

He started getting his things together. He was nearly packed when there was a knock at his door. Irritated, thinking it was Henri, Lucas opened it to find – not Henri – but a tall blond man in his fifties. He had a holdall and equipment bag and a big grin on his face. Out came the hand.

"Julian Headley. I see you've been busy, mate!" Before Lucas could say anything, he was swept aside. Headley immediately sat down on the edge of the bed and started to talk as though this was his room and Lucas the visitor. "You heard about the President flying out this morning?" Lucas said he had just filed that piece of news. "Well, you'd better get going then. You've a long flight ahead of you. I'll pick things up from here. I've not heard you doing any interviews with the politicians, other than the President, of course. I'll crack on and do the aftermath…"

Headley stopped and seemed to see Lucas properly for the first time. "You look knackered mate." It was a flicker of concern that passed as quickly as it came. "I called one of my contacts at the embassy this morning. The US Embassy. You know the kind, a man who has his finger on the pulse. One in every capital. I have to tell you buddy, the Americans aren't happy." Lucas sat down on a chair against the wall, trying not to let his immediate dislike of this man show. "Seems like Auguste was their guy. They loved the little shit. Thought the sun shone out of his arse… you see they have a big anti-drugs campaign, and all sorts of crap have been coming in through Haiti. Auguste was their answer to all that. He'd agreed to crack down on corruption, close the little airstrips, stop the army creaming off the top. You and your reports have wrecked their tidy plans. What's more they kinda thought he was going to hand over to a civilian government."

"But that's exactly what he wasn't doing," protested Lucas. "He had his chance and didn't do it."

"Yeah. Well, they reckoned he would've. And what's more his successor's known to be a real bastard, who won't think twice about shooting civilians in the street. I wouldn't be surprised if he wasn't in charge of yesterday's little fiasco."

"Successor?" Lucas asked, dreading the answer.

"Colonel jumped-up Jean Claude fucking Chambert – that's who," said Headley. He's a prick – always has been. And got himself rich, no doubt on the drugs coming through. Anyway…" Lucas thought the look on Headley's face was something approaching triumph. "You'd better be getting off. I mustn't hold you up. Mind if I take over this room? No need to pay. I'll charge the lot off to the Beeb." And he stood and held out his hand. "Good to meet you, Lucas. God knows it was unexpected, but you soldiered through, didn't you? Story of a lifetime. You won't find airports closing behind you very often." And that was it. Headley turned his back, as though he had flicked Lucas off like a switch.

Lucas hastily gathered the rest of his belongings, packed up his kit. As he turned to move to the door, he looked back at the man sitting on his bed. Headley was preoccupied, unpacking his equipment, laying it out on the counterpane.

Lucas had long anticipated this meeting. He'd even thought of what he might say to Julian Headley when they finally met. How he'd listened to his reports, admired him from afar, been inspired by him even, but looking at the self-absorbed bully words failed him. *Shit wasn't a bad word*, he thought. Carrick had been right.

Who wants to be Headley? Be better than him. Be a human being who doesn't see everything as a story to be reported. This is no way of life. If you become this self-absorbed, you miss what's really important; how everything fits together; how people matter more than a scoop or a headline; how those moments when two people connect can change the world.

Lucas left the room without saying anything. And as he went downstairs to the lobby, he surprised himself. He thought he would be angry at being dismissed like that. But he didn't.

He felt sorry for the man he'd left behind. Alone in that room.

He paused at the reception desk, rucksack in his hand, frozen in a moment of realisation. *You're not alone. You met Marie. And Zoe's no longer a ghost that haunts but a memory to be cherished.* And it was only then that it fully hit him. All this he owed to Marie but now he must leave her.

"Are you checking out Mr Lucas?"

The receptionist was looking at Lucas, trying to get his attention.

"No, no," stumbled Lucas, "Headley, Mr Julian Headley is taking the room over and he'll settle the bill."

"Ah, Mr Headley," said the receptionist, knowingly. "But we hope to see you again Mr Lucas. I hope you have a good journey home."

Lucas turned from the counter, disorientated, knowing he had to move but was reluctant to face the immediate future.

Flo had told him his flight was leaving at 3 p.m. for Miami with a connecting flight on to Heathrow three hours later. He looked around for Henri, who was loitering as usual, this time on a stool near one of the doors leading out to the pool.

As soon as he saw Lucas, he was by his side, taking in his instructions to go first to Petionville and then on to the airport. Together they drove up the hill, through the parched landscape and the treeless hills, Lucas letting the blasted terrain infect his mood.

Henri parked as before outside Michel's house. And Lucas trod carefully along one of the twisting paths almost obscured by the writhing stems and thorns of the unkempt garden until he reached the door. It was open, and he tapped on the glass.

The maid was at the back of the room and when she turned and saw Lucas, she quickly beckoned him in. She ushered him to one of armchairs and immediately disappeared into the interior of the house.

Lucas felt wretched. The last thing he wanted to do was leave. He wanted to be with Marie, but had to go home. He sat, trying to think of what to say. And then she was there, standing in the doorway that led off to the bedrooms and Michel's study.

She looked as though she'd not slept. Her hair fell about her face – a ghostly beauty.

He rose to greet her, and she offered her cheek gently nodding from side to side three times in the mirrored movement she'd taught him. Lucas let his lips touch her skin, feeling her warmth. She took him to the sofa.

"Thank you for coming," she said softly. And after a pause, the words Lucas had been struggling to find rushed out. He spoke as if a soldier was at his back, and he only had a minute to pass his message on, blurting out that he had to leave;

someone had come to replace him; he'd been sent a plane ticket to return to London. And then he paused, regretting he had put it all so bluntly, wanting to say more.

"Marie. I'm so sorry about Michel. I'll stay if you ask me to. I can't leave you like this. I can't simply get on a plane after everything that's happened…"

She sat straight and still and close, searching his face. Her blue eyes wide, taking in what he said. He gazed back at her, awed by her composure.

The maid brought two glasses and a large jug of sorrel.

Marie picked up the jug and served, pouring the ruby liquid in to the two glasses, her movements as deliberate and practised as a sacrament. And when she spoke, it was in the measured tones of a blessing.

"You mustn't feel you have to stay. Michel has many friends here who'll help me. It's the custom for friends and neighbours to take the weight at times like this. I shan't be alone, and you have your work."

Her calmness only accentuated Lucas's turmoil.

"Don't you want me to stay?" he asked, immediately regretting his clumsiness.

"Of course, you know I do." She leant forwards. Her hand touched his. "You have such a heart, and I know you care. I see it in everything you've done. But I can't ask you to stay."

At a loss and needing the time, Lucas reached for the glass on the table and drank some of the cool sweet liquid. The taste of flowers and wood and sun and sea flooded through him. Marie watched, perfectly upright, her hands back on her lap, her hair tumbling round her face, caressing her shoulders, lightly touching her bare arms.

"I feel," said Lucas, trying to find a rational path through his emotions, "as though I have a choice. I don't have to leave. I could stay and work here. I could cover this story as Michel did, try to make the world take more notice. I could make this my life and my work and not go back to covering stories other people choose for me. Perhaps here I could make a difference, do something good, do something better…"

"If that's how you feel, Lucas," Marie replied, "then you must do what your heart tells you. But I can't make the decision for you. I must stay with Michel and be with my mother, who'll come and…then I'll finish my studies…" It was a first glimpse of a life after Michel and Lucas could see her eyes brimming as she struggled to keep control. "But I shall return," she said, and Lucas again saw the proud, determined young woman at Michel's side in the square. "I shall always come back because this is my home. I feel complete when I'm here. You, Lucas, must go where your spirit takes you too. If it's here, then you'll know it in time. But right now, you must get on that plane."

And here he was again. This was the point at which he stood up and left. His instinct always led him away, and Marie was giving him permission to go. This is what he wanted wasn't it? This was his chosen profession: move on, get the story and go. This is what he had worked for. This is what he did. This is what defined him: restless, haunted, not wanting to be tied down… but this no longer felt right. Not here. Not now. Leaving was the last thing he wanted. Lucas needed to hold her, take her pain away, kiss her, bury himself in her, protect her, never let her go. But then he looked again at her face and saw her sorrow, her vulnerability, her determination to see this through, and he realised how selfish he was being. He shouldn't push himself on her. She needed time to bury her father and wade through the grief. She was asking him to go, but he could return. This was not final. Leaving need not be the end. If she'd taught him anything, it was that space and time were not sufficient to keep people apart who wanted to be together.

A car horn honked outside, and the maid disappeared to see what the commotion was. Marie stood up and putting her hand lightly to Lucas's shoulder to keep him seated. She moved over to a cabinet in the corner of the room and returned with something in her hand.

"My mother gave me this."

She held a silver pendant in front of Lucas and let it fall into his palm. Lucas studied it. It was a small filigree square of silver, with a rectangular cross at its centre, surrounded by spirals of fine silver work. They twisted and laced around the central cross, making it impossible to follow any one single strand to its conclusion.

"It's beautiful," said Lucas.

"My mother said a Hougan had it made for me. It represents *ti bon ange,* the spirit."

"I can't take this," said Lucas. "It's too valuable and too much part of you."

"Lucas, I give it freely. Whatever happens I want you to have it…"

Before Lucas could reply, they were interrupted by the maid, who returned and whispered to Marie.

"She says your driver's getting impatient. If you don't go now, you'll miss your flight. You must leave."

Marie raised Lucas up, holding his hand and pulling gently. They stood before each other, and this time when Lucas leant to kiss her cheek, Marie stepped in and took Lucas in her arms and held him. They folded into each other like the twists of silver in Lucas's hand until a sob welled up in Marie and she broke away.

"You must go Lucas. You must catch your plane. Think of us here. Think of Haiti. Think of all the people here who yearn for a better future and think of me when you can."

Tears burned his eyes and Lucas turned barely knowing where he was going. He struggled towards the garden, afraid to look back. Once past the glass door, he lost his way, stumbling through wild foliage, where tendrils clung to him, before thrusting him back on to an unfamiliar path, which led eventually to the gate and the waiting car.

Even with its windows wide open, the car was an oven. Henri was holding open the rear passenger door for Lucas. He had covered his hand with a cloth to protect it from the red-hot handle. Lucas slid past him and on to the seat, whose leather burned through his clothes.

Henri moved a blanket from the driver's seat and started the engine. Keeping his hand off the hot steering wheel as much as possible, he navigated back on to the main road which led down the hill to the city. With windows down, the heat gradually became bearable.

"This is goodbye?" asked Henri, glancing at Lucas through the mirror.

Lucas was staring out of the window at the sprawling slums of the city below.

"Yes. This is goodbye, Henri," said Lucas.

251

"You come back?"

"I don't know," said Lucas. "I don't know Henri…maybe. Maybe soon."

They drove on in silence, Henri pushing the car to its limits.

When they reached the airport, Lucas picked up his shoulder bag and rucksack, said a swift goodbye, and gave Henri his remaining gourdes. Henri smiled broadly, stood to attention and saluted as Lucas set off for the departure gate.

He reached check in just before it closed, watched his bag disappear and walked through to passport control. He stood before the uniformed officer, who went through his papers and found the stamp which marked his entry. Lucas looked around as the formalities unwound. Beyond the officer's desk and to one side was a room with a large glass window where security officials could observe passing passengers.

A group of uniformed men were standing behind it, talking. Amongst them was a civilian who seemed to be the focus of their attention. Lucas thought he recognised the figure.

The sound of his passport being stamped brought his attention back to the official in front of him who was handing over his papers and waving him through. Lucas walked beyond the desk. He passed close to the window, and he looked again at the men in the room. As he did so, he met the eyes of the civilian. For a moment, they stood in mutual recognition and then Toussaint gently raised his hand in a gesture of farewell and resumed his conversation.

CHAPTER 25

When Lucas arrived at the office in Bush House, applause broke out among the producers working at their desks.

"Well, the conquering hero returns," shot Carla out of the corner of her mouth.

"He appears to have swept all before him…" Flo said in an imitation of Carla's scolding. She had come up behind Lucas and he turned to see his boss.

She leant forward and offered a cheek for him to kiss, which he did only to find she repeated the process for a second and third time as if to let him know she knew where he had been and what the custom was.

"Have you had that head seen to?" she asked, inspecting the light dressing that was mostly covered by Lucas's abundant hair.

"Yes, I've just had it checked out. No infection. The nurse says it was cleaned really well, but she's put me on antibiotics just in case."

"I'm glad to hear it," said Flo, smiling. "Come into my office."

Lucas waved to his colleagues who were calling out welcomes and followed Flo back to her room. She sat him down next to her on the little sofa reserved for conversations of a personal nature.

"Lucas, I have to say, you've done a first-class job. So dramatic. Everyone says how well you did in Haiti. Even the director was praising your work at the morning meeting."

Lucas was still taking in the welcome he had received. He was only now realising how many people had heard his reports.

"Your credit is high." Flo tapped her desk with her pen. "I don't mean to rush you, but there's a senior reporter post which has come up in the News department. I think you should apply." She was looking serious. "I'll be sorry to lose you, of course, but I'm proud of the people who've passed through this department. I think it's an opportunity. You should seize it."

Lucas did not respond immediately, and Flo stared at him pointedly. He had managed to get a little sleep on the flight back, but his thoughts were still all of Haiti and Marie, and he was surprised to find things moving quite so fast.

"This senior reporter job is where many of our correspondents started out. If you do this well, you could have an overseas posting. You could build on what you've done and travel the world, follow the stories wherever they take you. You have it in you to be a good correspondent, Lucas. You've shown everyone you have that potential. You should consider this carefully."

Lucas had to say something, and finally he managed. "I'm glad my reports went down well." Lucas was wilting under Flo's gaze. He could see this was not the reaction she'd expected. He had to be more forthcoming. "Flo, this isn't easy, but I was thinking I should stay in Haiti. It's such an important and neglected story. The BBC will never place a full-time correspondent there, but I could resign and go freelance and work for different news outlets. Auguste may have gone but there's still so much injustice, so much poverty, the protests are bound to flare up again..." he trailed off, wondering whether he was expressing an obligation or a desire. He looked at Flo and the muscle that twitched in her cheek made him realise he had never seen her angry. Her hard-set jaw suggested that might be about to change. But what followed belied the expression on her face.

"I can completely understand why you might feel that way." She was speaking unusually slowly. "Powerful stories are like drugs or love; they suck you in. They're an addiction." She exhaled as if some safety valve had been released. "You've been through a lot. There's nothing like being on the spot, leading the news, standing at the focal point when the world is watching. But you know, Lucas, the truth is: the world moves on and Haiti won't be headline news next week and you surely don't want to spend the rest of your life in a backwater, when you could be at the centre of things."

"No," replied Lucas cautiously. He rubbed his eyelids with his hands, pushing the tiredness away, trying to explain. "I can see that. It's just I thought I was getting to the heart of the story... making a difference...changing things... and I'm not sure I've done anything of the kind..."

"Well, it's not your job to change things, Lucas."

"I know, I know," he responded quickly. "It's just something Julian Headley said...when he took over. He told me the Americans thought Auguste had been Haiti's best hope and now he's gone things will only get worse. His successor's supposed to be heavily involved in the drugs trade."

Flo scoffed. "You mustn't take any notice of Julian. He's jealous. I had him on the phone just the other day complaining you were covering his story. He sees Haiti as his patch and you're an interloper. He's hardly going to show up and greet you like an old friend. You're the competition, Lucas."

"Really?" said Lucas, wondering how many people Headley had lobbied.

"Look, Auguste was a dictator. There's no such thing as a good dictator. The army should stay out of politics. Nobody wants to be ruled by men with guns." Flo sounded brusque and matter-of-fact. "Any improvements in the world over the last fifty years have been the product of peace. You don't make the world a better place by oppressing and killing people. Progress is the result of education, growing prosperity, empowerment, giving people information to make informed choices...that's the business you're in Lucas. You're out there giving people what they need to make-up their own minds. If your reporting has fuelled people's desire to see the end of a military government, that's their decision, not yours. And if the army's still in charge, it's not your fault. If change is going to come, it's down to people to make it happen – not you. We're not gods, remember?"

Lucas was silent. He thought of Marie. He thought of her strength of purpose and her love for her country and the struggle she was caught up in. He missed her more than he could say.

"Lucas." Flo interrupted his thoughts. "Lucas, you must make a decision about this reporter role, because the closing date for applications was yesterday and I've asked them to hold it open to allow you to submit your CV."

"That's really good of you," said Lucas. "I'll think about it quickly. I'll decide today, I promise. Just give me a few hours and I'll leave my decision on your desk tonight."

Lucas stood. Flo, understanding his need for space, let him go. As he left the room, she said quite simply:

"Make the decision today. And Lucas…don't doubt for a moment whether you can do this. I have every confidence in you. Then take a few days off. Recharge your batteries."

He left the office to return his equipment. As he passed Carla's desk, she slipped him a sly look. "Top of the class," she said with a wink.

Lucas went straight out down the corridor to the lifts, thoughts of Marie running through his head. He was fooling himself to think he could be with her. He would never feel as she did about Haiti. All her energy and love of life was rooted in a sense of place. He'd never fully understand the spirits that stalked her world. Love, he thought, was no respecter of place, or time, or culture and all these things would come between them. And he thought of Michel's wife, whom he had never met, and who had loved a man who was rooted in a country not her own.

Junior was standing in the doorway of the equipment store when Lucas rounded the corner. "Hey man!" he shouted. "I heard you on de radio. Your voice was blasting out of my speakers every day. You sure put my kit to the test out there…"

"It did the job alright," replied Lucas, holding out his recorder, battered but still working well enough. He dug into his shoulder bag for the squawk box and Lucas offered it up along with the leads and adapters: "Your little black box was brilliant – it made an ancient line sound good and clear."

"My man!" laughed Junior, dragging Lucas into his room, taking the kit and laying it all out carefully on his wooden counter. "I was seriously impressed, man. You got decent quality recordings and everything…it sounded cool…Glad you made it back!"

Lucas scanned the well-ordered racks behind the counter, seeing the care Junior took over the equipment as he transferred it to the shelves.

"I heard you got you cornered. Dey goin' to kill you or what?"

"Yes. I had a little run in with the army," said Lucas, thinking he sounded hopelessly uptight in contrast to Junior's affable banter.

"Jesus, man! You're a lucky boy!" cried Junior, laughing in disbelief, staring hard at Lucas as if he might be a ghost. Junior put out his hand and felt Lucas's arm and poked him in the chest. "Damn you, man, you're alive!" and Junior lifted a loose index finger and cracked it loudly against its neighbour. "Hey! You're Lazarus man, dat's you. You're my man back from de dead!" Junior's laughter rolled round the little cubby hole as he moved behind the counter carrying the last item to its allocated slot.

"Well, it's good to see you, Junior. The kit was brilliant. I owe you. I'll be back for more as soon as I get a chance."

Lucas bumped the fist that was offered and went back down the corridor. Before he got to the heavy doors leading to the landing, Junior called after him, his voice echoing off the hard surfaces.

"Hey Lucas. You planning to go back to Haiti?"

Lucas hesitated and then shouted back, "No, Junior. I don't think so. I shan't be going back."

He was unaware of having made the decision until he said it. Immediately a wave of regret washed through him, but the chance of taking another step towards being a correspondent had been constantly in the back of his mind. He put two hands on the double doors and pushed his way through, feeling them sweep back into silent equilibrium behind him, leaving no hint of his passage.

He did not wait for a lift. He did not want to be in a box but on the broad stairs. The rouge of a setting sun poured down from the great window as he descended, spangling the old marble staircase under his feet. On the final few steps, he felt the urge to turn and look back. He paused and glanced behind him, half expecting to see someone, but he was alone.

CHAPTER 26

"Hello stranger."

Catherine was standing at the door of his flat in the morning sunshine, looking up at him. "And how's the famous radio reporter?"

Lucas laughed, surprised to see her.

"Not too famous to talk to you." he countered and invited her in, up the stairs to the small living area where she watched him make coffee in the micro kitchen.

"I heard your reports. They were all over the news – so exciting! The one when that soldier shot at you was really amazing."

"Oh?" said Lucas, taken aback. "Was it?" It had not occurred to him that the encounter might have sounded like a scene from a movie.

Catherine, seeing Lucas's reaction, quickly corrected herself, apologetic. "I mean, it sounded like you really had been shot."

Lucas laughed it off. "Yes, I thought so too. However, he missed – as you can see."

"Well, I'm glad you're still in one piece."

She sat at one end of the sofa, which was the only comfortable spot and looked around at the bare walls – evidence that Lucas spent virtually no time there. She placed her carefully folded coat over the arm of the chair as Lucas brought the coffee over.

"It's good to see you," she said, taking the offered cup.

"It's good to see you too," he said cautiously, recalling their last meeting in the restaurant and the feelings she'd provoked. It was always the same when they met. Memories crowded around them like unwanted guests at a party. He sat down at the other end of the sofa.

"Tell me, Lucas – what was it like? You seem to have brought down a government."

She wanted him to talk, but he was not sure where to begin. Last night, everything had seemed clear. He had gone to bed having decided to remain in London, but on waking he found himself beset by doubts and thoughts of Marie and then the doorbell had rung. This coffee was breakfast.

"It's difficult. It all happened so fast," he said, stalling. "I feel like I'm waking from a dream. You know – trying to sort out what's real and what isn't." He could feel the weight of Marie's necklace under his shirt. "One minute it was just a research trip and the next all hell broke loose. It was such a whirlwind, and I'm still trying to figure it out." Catherine sat forward, urging him on. "I did my best – you know, reported what I saw, tried to get both sides of the story, get to the truth but now I'm back I feel a bit of a failure. I think I got too involved, too close, too caught up in the drama of the demonstrations. Somehow, I became the story, and it wasn't about me…"

"But you're bound to get involved, aren't you?" said Catherine. "How can you go to a place and report and not get involved? Especially when they start shooting at you. Seems to me you didn't have much choice."

"Well, I was kind of thrown into it, and maybe I got swept away. Whereas I should've stepped back and seen the bigger picture – tried to work out what was really going on."

"Well, it all sounded pretty straight forward to me," said Catherine, sounding surprised at Lucas's confessional tone. "Your reports were all so clear. I mean it was a revolution. You know, a dictator toppled in a popular uprising? A bit of a classic, if you ask me. Why all the angst?"

"Well, that's it," said Lucas. "What you just said. The story sounds so simple the way you describe it – the way *I* described it. It seemed so straight forward, but now I'm not so sure. It was all incredibly intense, and the people around me were so impressive and passionate…I just don't know. And now there's this reporter job."

"What reporter job – where?"

"Well, it's based here," said Lucas.

"But that's great Lucas," said Catherine quickly, "and you've applied?"

"Yes – I put in my application last night."

"That's so good Lucas. That means you won't be abroad all the time?" She looked so pleased it brought Lucas up short.

"Not for now," he replied. "I mean, you know I've always wanted to work abroad. Nothing's changed. This would be a steppingstone, not a final destination." Catherine looked down at her hands. "Flo, my boss, thinks I should get it. She's really keen that I apply, but I still can't help thinking I should go back: I mean go and base myself in Haiti so the story would get more consistent coverage and maybe that could make a difference."

"But why Lucas? Surely, you've done enough?" Catherine rose and moved to the window.

"It just feels unfinished," said Lucas, "and you should have seen the protests. These people are risking their lives, desperate for change, and the world ignores them half the time. I know it sounds a bit arrogant but perhaps I could help… just a little."

Catherine's attention was firmly fixed on something outside.

"Well, I thought you wanted to report international affairs, rove the world. It seems a little rash to devote yourself full-time to the first story that comes your way. And anyway – wouldn't it be a good idea to get a bit more experience first? You know, perhaps start with this job in London?"

"Yes – well, that's what Flo thinks, and she's probably right, of course. She usually is," said Lucas. "But it's really hard. I still feel so involved. If you knew the people I met, you'd understand. They sacrificed so much. A friend died next to me. His daughter's burying him. And I'm here. You should have seen the risks they took, and now…well, I feel like some kind of deserter." Catherine was still transfixed by whatever lay beyond the glass. "You know what they did when I walked back into the office in London?" His question finally made her look at him. "They applauded me. But what have I done? You say I've toppled a dictator, but another one's taken his place. Nothing's changed and all those people who risked their lives are still there – burying their dead."

Unconsciously, Lucas's hand strayed towards the pendant beneath his shirt. Catherine saw the thin chain around his neck and her eyes narrowed.

"So, what really happened, Lucas?" The directness of the question hit home. It demanded a reply, but the reply was all about Marie. "Who was this friend? And who's this daughter that you left behind?"

Lucas hesitated. He had spent much of the last forty-eight hours trying to focus on the job and what Flo had said to him, trying not to let his emotions take over, trying not to think about Marie, trying to face reality in London, away from a world of spirits and shadows.

"Come on, Lucas. What aren't you telling me?" Catherine turned back to the window. "This isn't just about the story, is it? You've met someone out there who's pulling you back." Catherine's voice had risen, and she stopped herself before going on. "Sorry. I don't mean to harangue you." She looked across at Lucas and smiled weakly. "You see, we still care for each other, don't we? I know you care for me. I knew it in the restaurant when we had lunch. But you see, I have this life." She hunched her shoulders, her tension visible. "I have this life in London, these friends, this job, and I like it. I need to live it. And I can't if you and I are…" She faltered, staring back at him. "So, if there's someone else, I need to know." Lucas felt suddenly wretched.

"Yes – I'm sorry. I can see that. I don't mean to mislead you. I've never done that… I suppose I have met someone." Catherine was silent, but Lucas could see her eyes filling with emotion. "It sounds ridiculous," he said, hating the inadequacy of words. "Her name's Marie. I barely know her. She was one

264

of the protesters. And I've tried to stop thinking about her. She was with me on the demonstrations and was there when the shooting started. She saw her father killed in front of her, but still she goes on." For a moment he was back in the square, blood on the stones.

"But you can't fall for someone out of pity," said Catherine. "Someone that you have nothing in common with, who lives thousands of miles away, who you won't even see again…"

"It's not pity," said Lucas, suddenly defensive. "She wouldn't tolerate pity. She's the strongest person I've ever met."

"So strong you'd give everything up for her?"

"No, no. It's not like that. If I went back, it wouldn't be for her. It's more than that. I'd be trying to get to the truth, to understand it all better."

"To get to know *her* better?" Catherine countered bitterly. "So, what's to know? What's so special about her?" Lucas was silent, thinking a reply was not really expected, but Catherine persisted. "Come on, I want to know."

"I couldn't have done my job without her," he replied, irritated by her intrusion. "She's Haitian. She knew what was happening and where."

"Go on," said Catherine, stony faced.

"Well, she's studying in New York, anthropology I think, and doing a master's about local religion – voodoo. But she's not just studying it. She lives it. She's part of it." Lucas shrugged, frustrated at trying to explain to an unsympathetic audience. "It's as though she occupies this space between two worlds. Not just the new world and the old but…well this world and the next: it's like she can see the dead; see them, talk to them; like it's the most natural thing in the world…"

"Ah, the dead." Catherine took a pace towards Lucas, her face set hard. "You'd be an expert on that, of course." Lucas looked up at her, alarmed at the aggression in her voice. "I suppose your sister made an appearance as well?"

He stood up. "Look, Catherine, I don't want this argument again. Let's not do this, please. But the answer to your question is yes – there's someone else. I'm sorry – truly I am, but I can't help how I feel. And I know it's impossible. She's on the other side of the world and I'm here and ultimately, I can't be tied down to one place. We discussed this, you and I. We agreed we could never work if we weren't together."

"Well, go back to Haiti. Behave like a fool," Catherine said, all patience gone. She picked up her coat and started for the door.

"Look, I'm not going back," said Lucas. "I made up my mind last night. I'm in for this job in London and I'm not a fool. Marie's a free spirit and would no more give up her life for me than I would for her. It's not like that."

Catherine was back in front of him. "Interesting though, isn't it? That you would think of travelling halfway round the world for some girl, when you wouldn't contemplate staying with me once you set your sights on being a correspondent."

"I just don't see how it would work, in either case," said Lucas. "And you haven't been listening. It's the story. I was thinking of going back because I missed the real story – not for Marie."

Catherine raised her hand and swung it wide and hard at Lucas's face. He saw it coming but didn't flinch. He took the slap full on and, before Catherine turned and swept out of the room, he thought he saw a flicker of satisfaction cross her face. He listened to her footsteps clattering down the stairs to the front door. He heard the front door slam. Then there were brisk footsteps on the pavement rapidly fading away.

CHAPTER 27

Flo was in her office with John Carrick sitting on the same sofa that Lucas had occupied just two days earlier. Carla had witnessed their arrival, and she caught Lucas as soon as he walked into the office.

"They're in there, talking about you," she said, indicating Flo's office with the stub of a dead-headed cigarette before flicking it away theatrically. It arced towards the bin in the corner. "Don't be shy – go and find out what's up," she said, and then she was head down again over her computer.

Lucas went straight in, getting a nod of approval from Sheila on the way, and found them deep in conversation, two half-drunk cups of tea on the edge of Flo's table.

"Ah Lucas – just the man. Come in." She beckoned to him. "Something's come up and John's been asking whether I could release you to go back to Port au Prince."

Lucas closed the door behind him. "Really? I thought Headley had it all in hand."

"That's just it," said Carrick. "He's not filed. We haven't been able to raise him. I've called everywhere, a couple of his contacts, the US Embassy, the hotel and it seems he's disappeared. Did he say anything to you before you left?"

"We didn't talk much. He was chomping at the bit. He said he was going to talk to some politicians, report on the succession. He certainly didn't want me around."

Carrick frowned. "I shouldn't have let him leave Miami." He turned to Flo, who was all attention. "He's had all these problems at home. I knew he was stressed, but he sounded so keen to get back to Haiti, I thought it would be the best thing for him." Carrick came back to Lucas. "Look Lucas, you did a great job, and I had no reason to pull you out, other than this obligation we have to Headley. Besides, I thought you could use the rest, what with all the violence...But I'm worried. Something's happened. Headley's a pro. He doesn't go AWOL like this. He knows he should be filing. I need someone on the ground, and you know the situation."

Both Flo and Carrick looked to him for his answer, and a voice inside Lucas's head was screaming 'yes' but he suppressed it and looked at Flo.

"But we talked about me going back to Haiti and you said I should focus on the London reporter role."

"I did," said Flo, "but that was before Headley went missing."

Carrick chimed in quickly: "Look, Lucas. Going back to Haiti won't affect your application for the reporter's job, if that's what you're thinking. We can consider you in absentia. The interviews are tomorrow by which time you'll already be on your way. But we have your application, and we'll consider it after we've seen the other candidates. I promise you, the decision you take now won't put you at a disadvantage. If we have any outstanding questions at the end of the process, we'll see you when you get back before we make a final decision."

"And I can file reports while I'm there?" asked Lucas.

"Sure. It looks like this Chambert's now in charge of the army, but we've had no confirmation that he's taking over the presidency. Presumably that will come in the next few days. You could check things out and file if Headley doesn't show up."

Lucas looked from Carrick to Flo, who was nodding imperceptibly at him.

"Of course, I'll go," said Lucas, trying not to look too pleased.

"Good," said Carrick. "Grab a chair and let's go through what we know."

"Okay," said Lucas. "What's the hotel got to say?" Carrick shook his head.

"They haven't seen him."

"That's odd," said Lucas. "Headley told me he was going to pay the bill and would take over the room I'd been using."

"Well, he's not paid, and the desk says his key's been in reception for three days untouched." Carrick's eyes flitted to the door to check it was closed. "Look, there's something else you should know. Headley's been chasing down some story about the army. He's been working on it for ages. It's a lead he got from his work in Central America. You know his patch includes Colombia?" Lucas nodded. "Well, he's been using his contacts there to try to dig out some concrete evidence of the army's involvement in cocaine trafficking. We all know the army's involved. There's no way so much coke could be passing through Haiti without their consent. But proving they profit from it is something else." Carrick put his hand to his forehead and rubbed vigorously. "I've been thinking about why Headley was so keen to get back to Haiti." The hand came down, and Carrick's tired eyes fixed on Lucas. "Maybe he wasn't just being territorial or just trying to distract himself from problems at home. Maybe he had something he wanted to follow up locally. He was so insistent on getting back on that first flight." Carrick hesitated and then went on. "There are a couple of guys at the US Embassy. Headley always checked in with them, so I called one of them to check whether he'd seen him."

Carrick took a gulp of his tea while Flo and Lucas waited expectantly.

"And he said?" prompted Lucas.

"Well, he said he hadn't seen Headley, but I'm not so sure. He may just have been cautious on the phone. You know, calls are often monitored – the Americans are particularly paranoid about it."

"So, you want me to go and see him?"

"Yes. I think you should make him your first port of call. He's the first secretary – his name's Martinez. He's got the political portfolio."

Lucas wrote the name down in his notebook.

"I've already called JP," said Flo. "He's willing to meet you at the airport again. Just give him a call to let him know which plane you'll be on. We'll get going and book your tickets now. Can you go tonight?"

"Sure," said Lucas. "I just need to pick up some kit and pack a bag."

"Good." Flo looked pleased. "JP said they had the funeral for Michel Jerome yesterday. Apparently, there was a good turnout. People even flew in from Jamaica and Miami. APM sent someone, and his wife was there. It sounds like everyone's rallied round."

Lucas stood. "I suppose I'd better get going." Carrick and Flo followed his lead, and Carrick shook Lucas's hand.

"Thanks for doing this, Lucas. Take care." Lucas nodded. "Give us a couple of updates on what's happening and as soon as you get a whisper about Headley, let me know. I'll cover off his family in the States and I'll talk to the editor of the Miami Herald. This drugs angle he's been working on was for them as well as us."

Lucas left, ducking out of sight of Carla who was deep in some argument with a producer.

When he got to the engineers' office, he found Junior slouched over the counter talking to a tall, athletic looking man, whose voice Lucas recognised immediately.

"Courtney?"

The man looked puzzled until Junior straightened up and said, "Hey Lucas!" His fingers flicked so hard together they would have swatted a passing fly. "Yeah Courtney, he's de Haiti man."

Courtney immediately stretched out a hand.

"Lucas Gould! Good to meet you man. We used all your stuff. You going back?"

"Yes. I'm here to pick up some kit. I'm going back tonight."

Junior laughed. "I thought you was finished with dat, man. You want to get your head blown off?"

272

"Sucker for punishment I guess." Lucas couldn't help smiling as he looked at Junior, who was grinning broadly. Junior's eyes were red, and his face had a sheen that suggested he had been drinking more than tea.

"You okay Junior?" Lucas asked.

"Notin' time won't heal," commented Junior, giving Courtney a glance as he said it. "We maybe had one too many Appleton's, but I'm back in de land of de living now." His chuckle filled the narrow space. "And what's de idea with you? You going back to stir up more trouble or what?"

Before Lucas could reply, Courtney stepped in.

"Be good to have you there, man. I hear Headley took over from you, but he never gives us anything. He's only interested in filing for News."

"Well, I'll certainly do pay-offs for you and interviews and stuff. It was good talking to you on the line. I wasn't hearing the broadcasts much, so getting your feedback was really helpful."

Lucas looked at Courtney with his big frame and trimmed beard. "You're Jamaican, right?" he asked.

"Yeah man. Born in Jamaica but live here now. Got a family and I'm wondering what happened to your schools now I've got two kids. My school back home gave me all I needed. Hell, I speak better English than half the people who work here but finding a decent school in the East End is hard work. Sometimes I even think about going back. When you gave us our freedom in '62, we had the sense not to throw out the baby with the bathwater."

"Independence man," chipped in Junior, who did not seem fully present. "Dey gave us independence, not freedom. *I 'n I* always free." He tapped his temple with his index finger. "Freedom isn't something given. You have to take it. Haitians know," he said looking at Lucas, "Dey shook off de shackles demselves."

Courtney looked impressed.

"I stand corrected," he said and offered his flat hand for a high five, which was given a firm thwack by Junior. He winked at Lucas. "I always come here for a bit of philosophy."

"Yeah, and looking for a bit a relaxation," chuckled Junior.

"Junior, you're wicked man. You'd cause trouble in paradise."

And Junior laughed loud and long before directing his attention to Lucas.

"So, what do you need, man?"

Lucas was not entirely sure what Junior meant but focused on the task at hand. "I'd like one of your squawk boxes again and a recorder, mic – your usual Rolls Royce service…"

"Coming up…" Junior was off round the corner, still talking, gathering the equipment together. "You need one a those jackets de bullets bounce off…" he said in a raised voice as he moved around, returning with the various pieces of equipment as he found them "…but we don't have any! We just have these miracle boxes and wires… and bags… and microphones…" Junior placed the latest portable recorder on the counter. "Truth box, is what I call dis one…" he said, tapping the machine with his finger. "What comes out of dis is exactly what went in. Dey can't deny what dis baby picks up. She says it exactly de way it is."

"You always tell the truth, Junior?" asked Courtney.

"Na – not now, man. I told my wife de truth and she upped and went to her sister for a month. Man, I missed her. So, I don't mess with de truth. I leave it to you guys and de spirits."

"Spirits?" asked Lucas, wondering how much Jamaica had in common with Haiti. "I kind of got a crash course on spirits in Haiti."

"Yeah man. De spirits are all around. Always. Everything that ever was is stalking us wherever we go." Junior put out a hand in Lucas's direction as if trying to touch him. "It like di past is trying to catch-up with you all de time. You got to keep going my friend, or it'll overtake you and den…" His voice drowned in the thought.

Courtney leant up against the wall, listening. "You see what I mean? The man's a philosopher. He's got it all wrapped up. Me, I just focus on what's in front of me. It's easier to concentrate on facts and leave history and philosophy to others."

Lucas picked up the equipment and put it in the bags Junior had provided.

"Well, I mean to put this kit to good work," said Lucas. "And I'll see if can rustle up a few more facts this time round." He smiled broadly at the two men.

Courtney gave him a high five. Junior bumped his fist and Lucas was on his way.

CHAPTER 28

It was dark and a throng of people packed the area outside Arrivals in Port au Prince. Lucas searched the faces in front of him, but JP was nowhere to be seen. So, he started to retrace his steps towards the arrival's hall. He'd call him. And then suddenly, as he turned there was Marie – in his arms.

"So, you came back…I knew you would." Lucas could feel the curve of her body through the light fabric dress until she took a step back, smiling brightly, lighting up the dark.

"It's so good to see you." Lucas said, reeling at her touch. "I was expecting JP."

"He told me you were coming. So, I said I'd meet you…Pleased?" she said her face wide and searching.

"Surprised," said Lucas, laughing, "And yes…pleased. Very."

"I have the car," said Marie. "Come on."

Lucas slung his bag over his shoulder. Marie took his free hand, and they walked together across the ranks of parked vehicles to Michel's Mercedes. In the car, Marie handed him a SIM card. "JP told me to give you this. He said to make sure you use it." Lucas thanked her and inserted the new SIM in his phone and up came a local network. Messages immediately started to arrive, including JP and Marie's mobile numbers.

Marie was driving with care along the dark road towards Port au Prince, past the port with its containers and on to the fields of cane, listening to the purr of the engine and the crackle of cicadas audible through the car's windows.

"How are you?" he ventured. "I was told that the funeral's already happened."

"Yes. We buried Michel at the weekend," said Marie, her gaze fixed on the road. Both hands were firmly on the wheel. "Everyone has been so good. His friends, JP, everyone from the station – even staff from other radio stations – everyone came. And they said such wonderful things about him: about his bravery and his kindness and the hope he represented. So many people loved him. I hadn't quite realised. There must have been a hundred people there…" Marie trailed off. "And my mother flew in…And then flew out again. She's on tour in the States and took time out to come back."

"She didn't stay?"

Marie glanced over at Lucas, briefly taking her eyes off the road.

"I don't blame her. This isn't her home. I'll see her in New York. My last semester starts in a few weeks, and she's got gigs up there soon after." They carried on in silence, Lucas wondering how a mother could bear to be apart from her own daughter at such a time. "Please don't judge her," said Marie, reading his thoughts. "She's angry, and she hates this place. She always said it would never change and she couldn't do what she wanted here." The car drifted slightly, emotion rising in her voice. "Michel understood her. She was an artist and had to go wherever that took her. He loved her for it. It's just who she is." Marie's knuckles were white on the wheel. "And she knew Michel had to stay, that being here, doing his job was who he was." The car was slowing, and Lucas saw that Marie's arm was trembling. "She loved him. And she's so furious they killed him." Marie suddenly let out a little cry and immediately put a hand up to her mouth to stifle it. "She hates this place. I knew she couldn't stand it here…and now…" A lorry behind them blasted its horn, looming threateningly close in the dark.

Lucas reached over and carefully put a hand on Marie's. He let it rest there, making sure the car stayed on the road as they crawled along. She shuddered.

"She'll never come back. Never. She'll never forgive them. All she wanted to do was get out. And she wanted me to go with her but …"

The lorry sounded its horn again – long and hard – and Lucas swore under his breath as he looked back at the filthy headlamps: two threatening eyes staring in through the rear window.

As gently as he could, he said, "Pull over and let me drive." And his words seemed to revive her. She looked in the mirror and Lucas saw a tear on her cheek.

"No. It's alright. I'll be alright," she said and sat up. She wiped the tear away and accelerated into the dark, putting distance between her and the monster behind. They drove on in silence until they reached the city and before long, they were pulling up outside the hotel, where they sat for a moment.

"Marie, they've sent me back because the man who replaced me has gone missing. Remember when I told you about Headley. Have you seen him at all?"

Marie was looking at the entrance where a little queue of people was waiting for the revolving door to spin guests out on to the pavement.

"No, I've not seen him, but JP might have done. He's waiting for you inside." She climbed out of the car and one of the doormen took her keys and got in to park it. "I said I'd bring you here so the two of you can talk. Oh, and prepare yourself. This place is full of journalists now. Loads have flown in from the States."

They walked through the doors into reception, and Lucas saw that the hotel was no longer the quiet retreat he had grown accustomed to. Every comfortable sofa was occupied, and the room buzzed with conversation. As he walked up to the desk, someone shouted behind him.

"Lucas!" And there was JP, hand outstretched. He took Lucas's hand and in one fluid motion turned a handshake in to a fist – fingers locked together.

"I must teach you all our cool greetings, man," said JP with a chuckle. "Good to have you back." JP looked at Marie. "It's been a tough week."

"Easier because you've been around," she replied.

"Well, we all loved Michel," said JP and grinned at Marie. "And we especially love you."

Marie shoved him gently, then gripped his arm with both hands.

JP turned to the receptionist. "Look, you have a room for this man. He's Lucas Gould from the BBC." The receptionist had a key ready but held it back momentarily, asking if Lucas really wanted a second room because number 17 was already in his name. Lucas explained that he would be paying for both, and he saw that the key being offered was for number 15. The two would be next to each other.

"Do you have the key to my other room?" asked Lucas. The receptionist produced it from the hooks behind the desk. "Have you seen Mr Headley, the man who's been staying in it?" The receptionist thought for a moment and said he had seen him once, but the key had always been on the hook whenever he had been on duty. Lucas took both of them and the receptionist reminded him that there was the matter of an outstanding bill. Lucas put a dozen one hundred-dollar bills on the counter and was told that it would be added to his account. Then he was led away from the desk by JP, all of them accepting the inevitable glass of rum as they went.

JP took them through the lounge and out to the pool in the dark, where he had reserved a table by the deep end. They sat with their drinks and Marie listened quietly to JP's account of the funeral and the reaction it had generated. The station had been inundated with messages from the public in support of Michel and the work he had done at Radio Rèv.

"And now we have all the world's press here," he said. "General Auguste's departure has put Haiti back in the headlines and everyone wants to know what's going to happen next. Colonel Chambert is doing a good impersonation of a man who's going to be president. He's demanding airtime on all the news outlets, putting out statements extending the curfew and talking about enemies of the people. We all assume he's referring to the demonstrators. It seems that our own citizens are our enemies now."

"So why isn't he president? Why's he hesitating?" asked Lucas.

JP shrugged. "Search me. We've been debating that on air with some of the political leaders. They're all talking about forming coalitions ahead of elections. But nobody's actually doing anything. We can't even get the Electoral Commission to come on air. Leslie Laguerre's disappeared. Nobody knows where he is."

"When Michel and I saw Chambert after the interview with Auguste, he didn't exactly sound supportive. But if he wanted Auguste to go why not make his move? Surely, he could take the presidency if he wanted?"

"Well yes," replied JP, "he's definitely got the backing of a key part of the army. Perhaps he's waiting to be dragged to the altar. Perhaps he doesn't want to appear too greedy?"

"Maybe," said Lucas and he looked over at Marie, who, up to this point had listened in silence.

"Well, if you ask me, the army will only accept one of its own," she said. "But that person has to be credible or acceptable if not to the people, then to the US at least. Auguste had that. He was publicly against the drug traffickers and the Americans felt they could work with him. But he wasn't a democrat. He didn't trust the people – that's why we hated him. With Chambert, we simply don't know him. We don't know what he wants. Not yet anyway."

"We've asked him to come on the radio, of course," said JP. "We want an interview not another statement. But we've had no response." He looked exasperated. "But the way things work around here he'll talk to the foreign media before he talks to us. They're more interested in what America thinks than we Haitians."

"That's true," said Marie. "The one thing the army fears more than anything is the US. They'll push the boundaries all the time, but not to where they'll risk the Americans stepping in." She paused, looking at Lucas. "Lucas, you should ask JP about your friend…"

Lucas had been taking a drink of his rum. He put it down.

"JP, did you meet Julian Headley? The man who took over from me?"

JP shook his head. "No. I've not seen him recently. I've heard of him of course. He's been here before. We've used some of his reports on air. But I didn't know he's here now."

"Well, he is. That's why I've come back, really. I'm supposed to find out where he's gone. He's not filed since I left, which is really odd. Last time I spoke to him he said he was going to interview some of the politicians."

"So, aren't you here to report?" asked JP.

"Oh yes. I will, but London wants to know why Headley's gone quiet. So, I need to track him down too. But in the meantime, what's the army saying?"

JP produced the latest press releases and there was one from Chambert's office, outlining the new curfew arrangements, prohibiting all demonstrations, and offering some reassurance that a transitional government would be announced shortly. JP looked at his watch.

"The new curfew will be starting soon. I'd better get going and Marie, you should be heading home as well."

"He's right," said Marie. "I must go back." And they all made their way to reception where Lucas picked up his receipt for the money he had left and told Marie he would call her in the morning. JP impressed on Lucas that he was welcome at the radio station any time. They parted, and Marie offering her cheek three times, leaving him with a lingering sense of her presence.

Lucas went upstairs and took the corridor to his new room. Everything appeared the same. The same dark shadows, with the watching doors lining the way. He turned the key in the lock of Room 15, dropped his bag on the bed next to the towels and a dressing gown which had been laid out for him. Across the room was a tall window. He walked over to it. There was no balcony, just a long drop to the street below. Lucas picked up the phone by the bed and checked the ringtone. He replaced it and looked at the other key in his hand.

He went back to the corridor and knocked on number 17. All was silent. He knocked again and then rattled the key as he put it into the lock. It turned easily. The door opened on to complete darkness and he fumbled for the light switch.

As the bulb came to life, Lucas took a step back. This was not the room he had left. Nothing was the same. It looked as though a hurricane had swept through.

Someone had stripped the bed clothes down to the mattress. The mattress itself was askew on the bed frame. He couldn't see the bedside phone nor the little cabinet it sat on. Someone had thrown papers and equipment across the floor and the doors of the wardrobe hung open. There was a bag on the floor, gaping wide with its zips open. He gingerly walked in and eased open the bathroom door to find everything flung to the floor in there as well. Crumpled towels lay in the bath and a sponge bag's contents had been emptied into it. A tube of toothpaste had been squeezed out.

Back in the bedroom, Lucas found a notepad on the floor. It had half a dozen pages of notes, but most of the pages were blank. He went through what there was for any clue as to Headley's whereabouts, but there was nothing that stood out and nothing that suggested that any of the notes had been made in the last few days. There was no hint about where Headley had gone.

Dropping the notepad on the floor and turning his back on the mess, he returned to his own room, where everything was just as he had left it except for one thing. On the floor inside the door was a folded piece of paper with his name on it. He picked it up and saw it was on US Embassy notepaper. The scrawled message simply said: *Call me* with an extension number and it was signed: *Martinez*.

Chapter 29

Early next morning, having filed his first report, Lucas put in the call to the Embassy and was told Martinez would be in his office in half an hour. Lucas was expected. Would he mind coming to the Embassy in person? He wasted no time and went down to the foyer.

"Monsieur Lucas! I didn't know…you are here!"

Henri rushed over, waving his stump with a broad smile on his face, greeting his long-lost brother. "You need taxi?"

Why not, Lucas thought. "Hi Henri. You have your car outside?"

"Mais oui!" said Henri. "I take you anywhere. Where you go?"

Henri was wearing a fresh shirt and brand-new jeans, and Lucas wondered if he had been overly generous during his first visit, but he could hardly pay less this time. Resigned, he followed Henri outside, having handed over a thick wad of gourdes.

There on the pavement was Henri's car, no longer a battered antique but a Ford Sedan. Not new, but the colour was identifiably blue, and Henri had been polishing it. The rear door, which Henri opened, no longer required a herculean tug and the leather upholstery was smooth and shiny, devoid of volcanic stuffing.

"Nice car," observed Lucas as Henri drove off, spinning the steering wheel with the same round knob, which had survived the transition.

"You help me!" shouted Henri. "I work, I save, I buy new car, I get more work. All good. And now you back again!"

I sure am, thought Lucas, but said nothing as he watched the familiar street scenes pass by on the way to the embassy.

When they got there, a marine prevented them from stopping outside. He shooed them off to a car park fifty yards away, on the other side of open ground. The embassy itself was a modern, concrete building half a mile off the main route to the airport. It was surrounded by a high white concrete wall. Behind it stood a four story, flat roofed fortress. All the ground for about a hundred yards around it had been cleared. Tall metal posts supported flood lights covering the entire area.

Lucas walked back towards a concrete and glass guard house where a security man asked him his business while another made a call to check he was expected. He was frisked, relieved of his equipment bag, before a uniformed woman guided him across the compound to the main building.

Several anonymous corridors and a lift later, Lucas was in a large windowless conference room, which reminded him of a studio. The acoustic was dead. All the surfaces were coated with thick absorbent material, but there were no microphones or furniture, only a few hard-backed chairs scattered randomly.

When Martinez arrived, he proved to be a stocky man with greased, greying-black hair and a moustache which drooped around his mouth, giving him an expression bordering on sorrow.

"Señor Lucas, I'm glad you came. There are some things I'm afraid I can't say on the phone." Martinez spoke with a strong accent, but his English was good. He was holding a large file. "Please have a seat," he said, moving two chairs to face each other in the centre of the room. "I'm sorry, but this is the only place in the embassy where I can be sure we won't be overheard. And you must promise to keep what passes between us confidential unless I explicitly agree otherwise." Lucas nodded. "First, I have some bad news for you." Martinez sat upright, his back stiff. The file lay across his knees, with his hands folded on top. "You're looking for your friend Señor Headley?" Lucas nodded. "We also have been looking. I had an arrangement to see him when he arrived, but he didn't show. I've just learned that he's in hospital, close to your hotel. In a minute perhaps, we can go together to see him."

"My God," said Lucas, "what's happened?"

"I don't know. But perhaps if we see him for ourselves, we may find out."

"Well, at least we know where he is. How long has he been there?"

"I'm told he was admitted late last night, but he's been missing for three days. Or at least, he missed our meeting three days ago and hasn't been to the hotel since." Martinez shifted in his chair. "You should know that I and Señor Headley have known each other for many years. I have great respect for him. I used to be based in Bogota. He was investigating drug running from Colombia to the United States and that's something of special interest to me. When I moved to the Embassy here, we stayed in touch."

Martinez leant forward. "This is entirely off the record – yes?" Lucas assured him it was. "Good. The reason I'm telling you this is because the hospital says that Signor Headley's condition is serious." Martinez rubbed his forehead. "Very serious. We have alerted the editor of the Miami Herald – a newspaper I believe Headley works for – and we are helping them arrange a medical evacuation but the doctor I spoke to is not hopeful that he'll pull through."

"It's that bad?" asked Lucas, finding it hard to believe Headley could have become so ill so quickly. Martinez said nothing but simply nodded. "I see," said Lucas, "Well, thanks for fixing the evacuation. It certainly sounds as though he needs it. Did the doctor say what's wrong with him?" Martinez sighed and held a hand up:

"Well, he's Haitian…they don't use the same terminology we do… he said someone had stolen his soul," and seeing the look on Lucas's face quickly added, "he was speaking Creole. Even some of the educated people here believe in voodoo and they've their own ways of expressing themselves. You and I might say he's in a coma."

Lucas was discovering a sense of sympathy for Headley he had not thought possible. "I'll have to call London…and what about his family back in Miami?"

"Of course," said Martinez. "You must tell his boss in London, and I think the Herald are going to deal with his wife." Lucas was going over everything Martinez had said.

"But what do I need to keep confidential? What's happened to Headley is going to become public very quickly. We can't keep something like this quiet."

"Yes, I understand that," said Martinez shortly. "There's more. And I'm hoping you and I will come to an understanding when I've explained."

"Maybe," said Lucas not committing either way. "What else is there?"

"You see, Headley was working on a story. An important story." He chose his words carefully. "We have had a ...co-operation. I've been feeding him pieces of information and he's been working with his sources in Miami." Martinez took his hands off the file and became more animated. "You will understand Señor Lucas, that many drugs come through Haiti on their way to Florida. The cartels run their planes low over the sea. They land here to refuel, and then go on to the States. It's such a long coastline, it's very hard to police effectively. And people here help them of course – and take their cut." Lucas nodded, eager for more. "Part of my work in Bogota and here has been to try to track the ways the cartels move their money. As you can imagine, it's not easy. We've got a network of people globally all working on it and sharing information. But even with all our resources it's slow, grinding work. Finding witnesses who are prepared to talk is the toughest thing and even when they want to talk, they're scared; they're scared of the drug lords, of us, of the Feds. When you get tied into an investigation like this it either turns your life upside down forever, or you end up dead. Sometimes both. It's not an attractive proposition."

"So how do you get people to cooperate?" asked Lucas.

"Well, you know the score. We bargain. We offer witness protection, give them new identities, even get them set up in a new country. But it's still a big risk. There's always the chance the cartels will catch-up with you." Martinez stood up, "Forgive me. Sometimes I think better when I move…" He placed the file on the chair and paced around the room, with Lucas watching him. "… The thing is that in the last few years we've been having some success – particularly in the Far East. The cartels have been moving money out of Central America, through places like Guangzhou and Hong Kong. It gets laundered through different accounts and different companies, but we've managed to trace some of it. We know there must be a connection back here, probably through Miami because of all the activity we see. I gave some information to Headley, so he could ask the right questions of his contacts. He's built up a close relationship with some key people in the banking sector. And now he may have got a result."

"He told you that?" asked Lucas.

"Well, not in so many words. We've been doing this for a long time. We have our own way of communicating. But yeah. Before Headley arrived, he called me from the States. From what he said, I figured he had evidence of transfers from one of our cartel accounts to a beneficiary here."

"Why do you need Headley? Why aren't you approaching the banks directly about all this?"

"We are. But any bank that's moving this kind of money in these quantities is hardly likely to volunteer the information. It looks like Headley's got a mole who'll pass info, on condition of anonymity. It's some guy who won't stand up in court, but that's okay. All we need is the evidence and then we can go after the bank."

"And you think this is the reason Headley's in hospital?"

"Well, I wouldn't have dragged you in to this little hidey-hole unless I thought so. I suppose there's a remote chance he took too much zouk juice in some brothel, but he was living for this moment. We both were. We've talked about it many times. If the bad guys figured he had some real evidence, his life wouldn't be worth a dime round here."

"You know who's receiving this money?"

"Well, it's going to be someone in the army because you can't run an operation like this in Haiti without their involvement." Martinez put his hands out, palms uppermost. "You can see why this is kinda delicate. If Headley's in hospital because of this, then someone's on to us." Lucas looked around the room, which was already making him feel claustrophobic with its low ceiling, raised floor and blank walls. Martinez waved his hands at the space: "This is a kinda Faraday's cage, entirely secure…a spook-free zone, you might say…" and then with a chuckle, "present company excepted of course." Martinez gave Lucas a smile of sympathy.

"So, you want whatever it is Headley's got…" said Lucas, and suddenly the state of Headley's room came back to him, and he swore gently under this breath: "Look, I saw his room when I arrived. Someone's ransacked the place. His stuff's everywhere. It's a real mess."

"When was this?"

"Last night."

"Well, if he left anything in his room, they'll have it…" Martinez ran his fingers round the collar of his open-necked shirt and frowned, "…or they might not. Perhaps they picked him up, and he didn't tell them what they wanted to know… and then they go looking…" Martinez was talking to himself, working through the possibilities, "…but you can go looking and not find what you need…we've all been there."

He picked up his chair and returned it to the wall in one swift movement. "It's time you and I got down to the hospital. I'll give you a ride."

"I've got a driver outside," said Lucas.

"Ditch him," replied Martinez sharply. "Stick with me."

CHAPTER 30

The doctor who met them at the entrance spoke Creole and Martinez fluently asked where Headley was. They were led down a passage scarred by the motion of numerous trolleys. What little paint remained was peeling badly. At the end was a double door, which the doctor pushed through. Lucas and Martinez followed and found themselves in a ward with ten iron bedsteads on either side – all rusting and all occupied. A strong smell of urine permeated the place.

Headley was in the last bed on the left. He was lying face up, staring at the ceiling, barely breathing. The doctor started to speak but a scream from one of the beds distracted him. A man on the other side of the ward was thrashing his arms, and the doctor went over to restrain him. Martinez bent over Headley.

"Julian, Julian, how are you? Can you hear me?" Martinez was directly in Headley's eyeline, but there was no flicker of recognition. Lucas touched the arm that lay straight above the thin sheet. Again, there was no response. Martinez snapped his fingers in front of Headley's eyes. He put his hands on his shoulders and shook him. Headley's head lolled from side to side and for a few seconds his eyes closed, but once the shaking stopped, they opened again, staring straight up at the same point on the ceiling, as if his life depended on it.

"I've read about trances like this," said Martinez. "There was this guy in a village north of here. A group of researchers from the States came over to study him. I helped them with their visas. They wrote a report about it. The villagers said a Hougan had stolen his soul. Bit like this except he'd only respond to one person – some old woman he'd wronged. The team from the States had this theory that he'd been given some potion made from indigenous plants and animals."

The doctor returned, and they had a further exchange in Creole, with Martinez listening intently to the replies. "Yeah. He reckons someone's put some kinda hex on him. They've been trying to feed him, but with little success. He says his only hope is the medivac. Apparently, he was dumped outside the hospital last night. Nobody saw who left him." Martinez asked more questions, and the doctor pointed back at the doors and set off towards them. They followed. "I asked if Headley had anything with him like a case or a bag – but the doc says he just had the clothes he was wearing." Across the corridor was a storage room where the doctor rummaged through shelves stacked high with boxes and bedding. Eventually, he emerged with a bundle of clothes tied up with string. "This is what Headley was wearing," said Martinez, taking the package. He asked another question, and the doctor shrugged and walked back to the ward.

Martinez tossed the package on the floor and squatted next to it. He untied the string and systematically started going through the clothing: shoes, socks, underwear, shirt. He checked each item. The trousers got special attention. They were a pair of military style slacks made of light cotton with lots of pockets and a belt.

Lucas watched as Martinez worked.

"So, you've known Headley a long time," he said, wondering how close they'd become. "Yeah, many years, on and off."

"You knew him well?" asked Lucas.

"Professionally," came the reply. Martinez glanced up from working his way through all the pockets. "I don't think he's the kind of man you get so close to. He was very focused. Obsessive even. I guess the job can make you like that. But the one thing I'm sure of is that if he had some information for me, he would be sure to leave some sign, some clue. He would never want to lose a story or a lead. It meant everything to him." Martinez switched his attention from pockets to the belt, which was held in place by long squares of material, leaving very little of it visible. At first glance, it looked as though it was an integral part of the trousers. He ran his fingers round it several times, not feeling anything unusual. And then he snapped open a popper on the belt and the buckle came away in his hand. "I met his wife once," Martinez continued, thinking aloud as he worked. "She seemed sad. I think she hardly saw him. He travelled so much." He pulled the belt through the loops until it snaked out on the floor. He flipped it, inspecting one side and then the other. "And I think *he* was sad too. Never knew why… I hear he lost her."

Listening to Martinez, Lucas wondered if he too was destined to end up like Headley. He felt he'd already left so much behind: family; school; friends from university. If he moved abroad, the few that remained would fall away. And what of Marie? No matter how much he wanted her, his desire was tempered by what he knew of her parents' struggle to remain together. Maybe separation was an inevitable consequence of the life he sought.

Martinez was holding the belt up to examine it more closely.

"Perhaps Headley saw it coming," he muttered, looking at the two types of leather that made up the belt, one brown pigskin, the other black hide and polished. "Perhaps he knew his marriage wouldn't work out." He produced a small penknife. "I don't know. He never discussed it with me. But it seemed to me to have a kinda inevitability about it." He opened the blade and ran it carefully along the seam, which held the two sides together. The knife ran smoothly and then snagged. "It's tough," he said, scraping out slivers of glue as he worked the blade. "It takes so much time and effort to get it all together and then in a moment… it falls apart." With a grunt, he flipped out a small flat object which dropped on to the floor.

"One key," said Lucas, picking up the exhibit. "Number 31." He held it by its stem, so the number was clearly visible on the small, flattened grip.

"Yeah. It's too small for a room key," said Martinez. "Got to be something else. Looks decent quality. Maybe a case? Was there one in Headley's room?"

"Yes," said Lucas. "There was a holdall on the floor which might have had a lock or a padlock. I can go back and check."

Martinez was bundling up all the clothes again. He carefully threaded the belt back in to place and clipped on the buckle.

By the time he had finished, the bundle looked as though it had not been touched. He put it back on the shelf where the doctor had found it.

"Let's get out of here," he said, and they went quickly down the corridor. Outside, the Embassy car was waiting and with the two of them on-board, it moved off. Martinez turned to Lucas.

"I can drop you at your hotel. Check out the key and see if you can find out what it fits. Maybe Headley hid something and the goons who did this to him didn't find it. I've got to get back and finalise the arrangements for his evacuation. Call me, will you? But if you find anything don't tell me on the phone. Just say you want to meet, okay?" Lucas agreed, and Martinez looked distractedly through the smoked glass window as the car continued on its way. "It's funny," he said. "It doesn't feel right with his room being searched so late."

"What do you mean?" asked Lucas.

"You said his room was a mess when you were there yesterday evening. Well, hotel rooms are cleaned and tidied every day, so they only searched it yesterday. Headley's been missing for three days, which means he was probably picked up soon after he arrived. How come they're only searching his room now? If he'd given them what they were looking for, they wouldn't have had to turn his room upside down, would they? Maybe they don't have it yet."

"What am I looking for?" asked Lucas.

"Well, if he's got records of transfers then it would be lists of numbers or print offs. Headley knew what accounts we were suspicious of, so if he has any paperwork like that, I want to see it."

The car stopped outside the hotel. "I'll catch up with you later, Lucas. And take care, if you're going to file about Headley don't mention me or what we've discussed? I want all the pieces of this puzzle in place before anything goes public, okay?"

Lucas stepped out of the car. The heat pressed down on him, and he dived through the hotel door in to the cool of the lobby and went straight up the stairs.

Someone had cleaned Headley's room. The bed was made, and the clothes had been folded and put at the bottom of the bed. The holdall, which had been open on the floor, was now zipped shut and overlapped a chair by the bathroom door. Lucas went over and checked it. The main zipper had a travel lock, and he tried Headley's key. It didn't fit. Lucas moved round the room and looked to see where something might have been hidden. He checked the top of the wardrobe. He ran his hands underneath the table. He went to the bathroom and looked around the cistern, trying to recall every hiding place he had seen in spy movies. He even listened for creaking floorboards. He went to the bedside cabinet and flicked through the flimsy phone book which still lay inside. Nothing. In the wardrobe, he found a safe. The door was open, and it was operated by a panel of buttons on the front. No key was necessary.

He closed Headley's door behind him and returned to his room.

Sitting on the bed, he talked himself through the things he now needed to do. He wanted to see Marie, but he had to tell Carrick about Headley. That was the first thing. And he needed to file a despatch.

He looked at his watch. It was just past 1pm. He picked up the phone and called JP, who said nothing had changed since they'd last talked. There was music in the background and Lucas realised he was on air, so did not linger. He then called Carrick's office. It was answered immediately and gruffly.

Carrick's tone changed on hearing Lucas's voice. "Lucas! How are you? Any news on Headley?"

"Yes – I've found him, but it's not good. The doctor isn't sure he's going to make it." And Lucas explained Headley's condition and that the US Embassy was arranging his evacuation.

"Damn," muttered Carrick down the line. "He was good, but he always took too many risks. This is a nightmare. I'll have to talk to his wife…" Lucas told Carrick that the Embassy was in touch with the editor of the Miami Herald. "Good," said Carrick. "At least we'll have some support from them… Look, well done, Lucas. Sorry it's not better news, but stay on and keep filing. Hopefully there'll be some announcement about the new President and then we can bring you back… Oh – and congratulations."

"Congratulations?" asked Lucas, wondering what could possibly be worthy of congratulations in all of this.

"You got the reporter's job. We had the interviews today, and you were our first choice. Strong field, mind. But it's yours. There'll be a letter confirming it on your return."

Lucas felt a rush of pleasure. With everything that had happened, he had forgotten about the reporter job. But now he knew it was his. He felt his future clear. He wanted to tell someone. And immediately he felt his chest contract. What would he say to Marie? How long would he be here now? He'd have to go back. His elation evaporated.

"No need to thank me," barked Carrick down the line. Lucas hastily apologised and said how pleased he was and of course would accept. "Are you going to file again today?"

Lucas said he would once he had an update.

"Good. That's good. Hey and Lucas, don't go and do anything stupid. Losing one man's bad, losing two would be a bloody disaster. So, watch it, will you?"

The line clicked off. Lucas sent a text to Marie. He couldn't put this off. He had to see her. Somehow, he had to tell her.

"Monsieur Lucas. You left me!" Henri looked hurt. "I saw you go. I worried. So, I come back here. Wait for you. Why you go?" Henri seemed genuinely distressed.

"It's okay Henri. I'm sorry I left. We were in a hurry, and I didn't think. But I'm fine. We're here now. Can you take me to Petionville again? I just need to do something at reception and then we go. Yes?"

Henri nodded vigorously. Glad to be back in harness. Lucas went to reception and asked if they had any deposit boxes for the use of guests. The receptionist directed Lucas to the cashier at the far end of the desk.

"Mais oui, monsieur. What number? And you will need the key also."

Lucas gave the number as 31 and was ushered behind the counter, through a large wooden door and into a small room lined with metal boxes. "If you have your key, monsieur."

The cashier moved to number 31, which had two locks. He inserted his own key and then stood back for Lucas to use his. The lock was double sided, and the key slid in easily enough, but it didn't turn. The cashier stepped forward to see what the problem was.

"Ah monsieur. This is not right. Our keys look like this." And he retracted his own for Lucas to see. They were similar but the stub which displayed the box number was of a different design.

"I'm sorry," said Lucas, "My mistake. I must have picked up the wrong one. I'll come back later."

He was close, he thought. The keys had looked so similar. It might fit a safe-deposit box but if not at this hotel, where?

CHAPTER 31

Lucas could see Marie. She was standing deep in conversation with a serious young man at the far end of the living room. He was tall, with round rimmed spectacles, hands crossed in front of him, head bowed, listening carefully to what she was saying. When Lucas tapped lightly on the french windows, they both looked up, startled.

Marie smiled when she saw him. She waved and moved towards the doors as Lucas pushed them open.

"Lucas, I'm so glad to see you. This is Pierre Hérard. He's a good friend and lives nearby. He was such a help at Michel's funeral." She put a hand on Pierre's arm, encouraging him to say something.

"It's good to meet you, Lucas. I've heard your reports on the radio and we're grateful for all you're doing."

He was tall and slim, clean shaven and wore a simple black suit. He looked like a priest but wore no collar. Lucas shook his hand and wondered what they had been talking about so intently.

"Pierre works with Baptiste," said Marie. "He's one of a small group who support his work in the slums. He's an organiser." Marie did not go into detail, but having seen Baptiste for himself, Lucas could imagine him surrounded by people ready to do his bidding. She gestured for them to sit and continued: "Pierre was just telling me they're planning a day of action for tomorrow…"

"Yes," said Pierre: "We don't know why Chambert's hesitating. Everyone thinks he's in charge now that Auguste has fled. But there's still no announcement of a new President and still a curfew. His vague promise of elections is no better than we've heard many times before – there's no date, no call for parties or candidates to register."

"And Leslie Laguerre's still missing," added Marie, "and his wife too. How can anything resembling elections take place without a functioning Electoral Commission?"

"So, we're organising a day of protest," said Pierre, more animated. "The father says we should make our voices heard and show that the people want elections, that they're not happy with endless dictatorship. The army seems to think it can ride rough-shod over everyone all the time. But we shall show that it can't." Pierre had the same faraway look in his eye that Lucas had first seen in Marie. "Tomorrow, PB's calling everyone to the Church of St Mark early in the morning and from there we will march."

"Has Père Baptiste ever thought of standing in elections?" asked Lucas. "He seems to be one of the few people who has the trust of the people. And with the army saying they're only filling a vacuum left by the politicians – perhaps it's time he put himself forward as a candidate?"

Pierre gave a laugh of approval. "You should meet him! Ask him yourself." he said. "We've been trying to persuade

303

him to stand, but the church says he should keep out of politics. It's bad enough him speaking out in public the way he does. The Vatican's already warned him that he strays too far beyond his calling. But if you ask me – he should stand, and the people would follow him."

"Well perhaps a first step on the road would be an interview? Could you ask him for me?"

"I shall," said Pierre, standing to go. "I'll tell him today, and I hope you'll be with us tomorrow. It will be a big protest to match the ones that put an end to Auguste."

Marie showed Pierre to the door and as he quickly disappeared into the garden beyond, she said: "I'll have the money for you tomorrow."

"Money?" Lucas looked quizzically at Marie, as she walked back towards him.

"It's Michel's," said Marie, "He makes…he made donations to Baptiste's church. He didn't tell me, but it turns out he gave regular donations, and he left a significant sum in his will."

Marie sat down next to Lucas and placed her hand on his. "I'm so glad you came back, Lucas. I'm sorry I was upset in the car. I think the formality of the funeral kept my emotions at bay and seeing you sort of took me unawares and…well, you're here, and that's good." She looked at her hand, which had now slipped in to his. "I felt sure that you would return…"

Lucas felt suddenly sick. How could he not stay here? How could he even think of going back to London? But he had just accepted a job there – a job that promised everything he had wanted. The impossibility of his situation stared back at him, demanding a decision. He was not sure he could wrench himself away from Marie again. Whatever decision he made; it required too great a sacrifice. His innards cramped up as if some serpent was uncurling inside him reaching up to wrap itself around his throat.

"To be honest," he said, wrestling with the creature inside him. "I didn't know whether I was coming back or not…I was in such a state when I left…"

Marie sighed. "That's what this place does," she said. "It pulls everything apart, tears up the things you love…Just when you think there's some hope, it smashes it in front of you, drags you down…" She was holding back tears – all the pain of her loss weighing down on her – and then just as quickly she straightened up to face him. "But we must hang on to the good things. You're here now. I've wanted this so much. Today. This moment. Even if it's just a moment. These are the things that matter."

"Yes, yes. Every second matters," Lucas said, gripping her hand, desperate not to add to her grief, longing to pull her to him. "I'm so glad to be here too." He had tried so hard to stay rational while in London, to make the right decisions about his work, but now that he was in Marie's presence again, she was his sole focus. "I'm so glad to see you…just to be able to touch you," he managed before his voice gave out. His throat knotted. His face burned. He felt Marie's hand on his cheek, cool against his skin.

"It's okay Lucas." She was leaning into him, her eyes brimming. "Sometimes, all we can do is live moment by moment. Take it all one step at a time. That's what I've been doing. It's the only way. And it can be enough." She took a deep breath: "A moment, a lifetime, a month, a year.

305

Significance isn't measured in time. It's borne by some other dimension. Moments can last longer than anything."

Lucas searched Marie's blue eyes, wishing he could lose himself in them. Wishing everything else would just go away. She always seemed to be giving him permission, releasing him of some burden, allowing him to be himself – even when he struggled to understand his own feelings.

For a while, they just sat there, letting the silence speak until Lucas regained his voice. "I owe you so much," he said softly. "I owe you more than I can say." He reached into his pocket. "You've been so brave. You've lost so much, and I wasn't here to help. But I'm here now. Back with you. And you should have this. It really belongs with you." And he held up the chain, so it hung between them, its intricate silver work catching the light which span into the room from the garden. "I think you should have this back to keep you safe."

"I gave it to you to keep, Lucas. You don't have to give it back," said Marie.

"I know. But I don't need it to remember you. And I think it should be here, with you, where it belongs." Lucas searched for the right words. "You've already given me something just as precious." Marie opened the palm of her hand to catch the descending chain.

"I hope you mean Zoe," said Marie, closing her fingers around the pendant. "You do, don't you?" Lucas nodded. "Good. She wanted so much for you to understand. To stop you blaming yourself. Have you seen her again?"

"I haven't seen her since I left, but I still think of her all the time. And when I do, I feel…well it's different now." He thought for a moment. And it was true. It was different.

"Somehow, I feel liberated. You made me look at it all so differently. And I'm so grateful. But I think she'll always be with me and always a positive presence…"

"I'm sure of it," said Marie. "I too will never forget her…"

Lucas leant forward and kissed Marie's hand that held the pendant.

"You deserve the best, Lucas," Marie said, laying her hand on his head, easing her fingers through his hair as he bent before her. "We were together at the worst of times, and we trusted each other. Michel trusted you. He welcomed you here…You'll aways be welcome." She looked down at him and another sigh escaped her. "Tell me, what about your colleague? Is there any news of him?"

"There is," said Lucas, straightening up: "and it's all bad I'm afraid." He told Marie what had happened to Headley and how the embassy was helping with the evacuation. Marie looked shocked and shook her head when Lucas described Headley's condition as a coma.

"No, no. I've seen this before. De Beauvoir has let me attend some of the sessions where he's helped the sick. There's a malady here where the mind destroys the body. The few who know how to induce this condition have enormous power. But it only works with people who are vulnerable or isolated in some way. It's hard to describe, but Hougans say your spirit can escape your body. They say this sickness comes if someone captures *ti bon ange* so that it can't return. However you describe it, it's very real. A person can appear to be alive, but for all intents and purposes they're already dead. If Headley's been targeted like this, then it's very serious. He must have done something bad or provoked some dangerous people."

Lucas didn't doubt what Marie said, and he knew that if anyone could help him it was her.

"Marie, there's something I must tell you. But it must be our secret. We mustn't talk about this to anyone. Headley was investigating drug running. It looks as though he might have come across some evidence that links the Colombian cartels to someone here. The Embassy thinks he might have brought something incriminating with him. Maybe that's why he's in hospital now. So, it's really important that nobody knows I have this." Lucas reached into his pocket and produced the key he found on Headley. Marie took the key and had a close look. "I've tried it in the hotel's safety deposit, but it doesn't fit…"

"No, it wouldn't," said Marie, returning the key to Lucas. "It's not a safe-deposit box, it's a post office box."

"How do you know that?" asked Lucas, taken aback.

"Michel had one. They don't deliver letters to homes here. You have to go to the post office to pick up any mail you're expecting, and you can hire a box to store your post. But you could use the box for anything – like valuables you don't want to keep at home."

"The post office?"

"Yes. It's on Rue Nicholas. Les casiers postaux work on twin keys. There's one they hold and one you keep. This is one of them."

Lucas beamed. "You're brilliant Marie. What would I do without you?"

"Well, I won't argue with that," said Marie, smiling brightly. So, what are you going to do?"

"I'm going to pay the post office a visit," said Lucas, and then corrected himself. "But first I'm going back to the hotel to file about the protests tomorrow and the fact that Laguerre's still missing. I owe him that at least."

"Good," said Marie. "They might be holding him somewhere. It wouldn't be his first spell in prison, but the more people who know about it the better."

She walked with him across the room to the door and when they got there, she didn't offer a kiss. Instead, she put her arms around him and held him.

"I'll see you tomorrow at the demonstration," Marie said quietly.

"I'd have thought you'd never want to go to another one – ever," Lucas whispered back.

"I must," she said still holding him and speaking into his arm which cradled her to him. "I have to go and if I don't go tomorrow, I'm afraid I'll never go again. And I must. I can't let them beat me. I have to go on. Otherwise, what did my father's life mean?" She pulled back to look at him. "When my mother left, she pleaded with me to go with her. She cursed the people who killed Michel. I've never seen her so angry, and I loved her for it. But I couldn't leave with her. I mean...I'll finish my studies, but I have to come back again. Marie's hand moved to the necklace, which she now wore round her neck. "This is where I belong, and Haiti deserves better than this."

Lucas kissed her gently on the forehead.

"I'll see you tomorrow," he said.

Henri was parked in his usual spot. Lucas half expected him to be reclined and fast asleep but today he was sat over the front wheel, alert and keen to go. Lucas got in the back and Henri sped off down the hill to rejoin the main road back to the city.

They were on the outskirts of Port au Prince when Henri slowed the car and suddenly veered on to a side road which zigzagged up a hill. At first Lucas thought Henri was just taking a detour, but the direction felt wrong and after a short while the road turned in to a potholed track. The car started to roll violently from side to side over the unmade surface.

"What are you doing?" shouted Lucas at Henri, who showed no sign of slowing down. "Where are we going?"

"It's okay," shouted Henri from the front. "Some people, they want to meet you. You famous reporter. Not take long. Fast meeting. They just want to talk…"

They were now alongside a high wall at the end of which a pair of large iron doors stood open, giving on to a compound. Henri swerved through the gates and on to a large, paved area bordered by a newly planted flower bed. He slid the car alongside two others neatly parked to one side.

"Where the hell are we?" Lucas demanded angrily from the back of the car, but the boy was already out of the car and heading towards the gates which were closing behind them. There was a bulky man in fatigues at Lucas's door, pulling it open and telling him to get out.

"Who are you?" asked Lucas, trying not to let his alarm show.

"I'm a friend, Monsieur Lucas. There are some guests here who want to meet you. They'd like a few minutes, so they can talk to you. Everything's fine. There's no danger. Please come with me." The man moved off, leading the way into the large house. Lucas hesitated and looked around. The wall which ran around the entire compound was high enough to make flight impossible. He had little alternative but to follow.

The building itself looked unfinished and had three stories. To Lucas's left, and covering one side of it, was a lattice of wooden poles, providing scaffolding for builders who were rendering the walls. But there was no sign of any workmen. Spades, buckets and bags of cement lay around, left wherever they'd fallen.

He went up the few steps to the open front door. A cool marble floor stretched away in front of him. There was a small empty reception desk to one side, where his guide was standing waiting. A broad staircase led up to the upper floors. Wires hung from the centre of the ceiling and from holes in the plaster on the walls, awaiting light fittings.

"Your bag please," said his guide.

"I'd rather hang on to this," Lucas said swinging the bag in front of him across his chest, the strap firmly round his shoulder.

"I'll take it," said a voice in his ear. Another minder, wearing the same fatigues, stood behind him. He must have followed them in.

"Really, I'm okay," said Lucas still holding on tight. The man placed his hand on the strap and when Lucas did not let go wrapped his other hand round Lucas's upper arm and squeezed until pain shot up into his neck.

"Let go," said his guide. "You can have it back when you leave." Lucas let the bag slip away.

"Be careful with it, will you?" he said. "It's delicate."

"Don't worry," came the reply. "I've got it."

"Please – follow me." His guide moved to the stairs and Lucas trailed behind him up two flights to a large room at the front of the house. It was empty except for a long narrow table and a few chairs. Behind the table a pair of bifold doors had been pushed back to reveal a broad balcony. Lucas stepped on to it and looked down at the car and Henri, who was in conversation with a man in army uniform.

He turned to confront his guide, but there was no one there.

CHAPTER 32

Lucas stood on the veranda, his face to the setting sun. The crimson disc was sliding into the sea which was clearly visible over distant rooftops. Its progress made the horizon boil, and he watched the night hurry towards him. Below, an engine spluttered to life and Lucas saw Henri reverse the car and then swing it out of the compound through the iron gates which clanked shut behind him. Lucas swore under his breath. He had been a fool to trust the boy.

With the day now gone, the only light was a faint glow from a solitary, distant streetlamp. Why hadn't he stayed with Marie? He wished with all his heart he was with her and not here staring at the dark. But there was nothing to be done.

He turned and went back into the room and sat down at the long table. He ran his hands across its surface, feeling the grain beneath his palms and listened. He knew there were people in the house, but he could hear nothing. Strange, he thought, even the cicadas had stopped their incessant call. There was no wind, no movement, no traffic noise.

The silence grew more ominous with each passing minute. It held some threat for which Lucas felt ill prepared. The more he listened the more oppressive the silence became. He felt its pressure in his ears, the pulse in his body. The very absence of sound became an entity in itself – as alive and absorbing as if some tacit orchestra was playing. Its silent performance filled the room. Its intensity grew, every phrase and cadence building to a dumb crescendo. It was a climax that Lucas immediately recognised when it finally arrived – that penultimate moment when everything stops in anticipation of the final chord. And in this tense caesura, Lucas felt a familiar presence.

"You should tell her."

"Tell her what?" Lucas looked round to see where the voice came from.

"That you love her…." Zoe slid into the chair next to him as real as she'd been in his London flat. And with her presence, his apprehension at what the silence might hold fell away. "When you love someone, you should tell them. Don't wait. No time like the present. You never know what might happen. You may never get the chance again."

"Full of advice, as ever." He smiled, relieved to see her after what felt like an age. "Where have you been? I've missed you."

"Around, you know. And it's not been that long, silly. You knew I was there at the ceremony…"

"Oh yes. I remember alright," said Lucas, suddenly irritated. "Why didn't you speak to me? Why talk to Marie? Why did you go to her and not me?"

"You wouldn't have listened." Zoe leant forward, sliding her hand across the table next to his. "You were so bound up in that guilt of yours, blaming yourself for my death, tormenting yourself. You wouldn't have believed that what I was telling you was true."

314

"Really?" asked Lucas trying to recall exactly what he had felt on the floor when he was holding Marie.

"But you believed *her*, didn't you? I thought you would. Because she's real and present and you trust her."

Lucas thought a while.

"But I trust you. I always have. I love you."

"Yes. I know," Zoe said quietly. "I know you love me, loved me. Of course, I know. And I love you. But you're falling for Marie. It's obvious, and I can't keep turning up like Banquo's ghost at the table. How romantic would that be?" And she laughed the laugh that Lucas knew too well. "Tell her how you feel, Lucas. Be as true to her as you were with me. You can trust her. I did, and it worked out well, didn't it? She told you the truth. You believed her. And so you should. Don't let her slip away. You need a real friend and I think she's the one. You just have to ask."

Lucas stared at Zoe, loving her, wanting her to stay, wanting to prolong this moment, wishing again that time would stop.

"But I don't want to lose you," he said, fearing that this might be the last time that she came to him this way.

"You won't lose me," she replied. "You were there. You saw it at the ceremony. All past is here and all future present. These moments never end." Her voice was fading. "I want what's best for you, as you did for me, Lucas. Always..." and Lucas saw her hand grip his on the table, but even as he felt its touch, she was slipping away. "I'll always be here..." she said, but he could barely hear her.

And it was then that the invisible orchestra sprang back to life and the final chord crashed around him. The door flew

315

open, smashing the silence and in a rush all Lucas's anxiety about his predicament returned.

A single light bulb flashed on above his head. He squinted in its glare at the three men who walked in.

The first figure was unmistakable. It was Toussaint from the hotel. Still dressed in his immaculate white suit, he walked towards Lucas and offered his hand across the table.

"Monsieur Lucas. My sincere apologies for meeting like this but we live in dangerous times and my colleagues were keen to meet you. May I introduce Major Augustin? Head of Military Intelligence."

The major, who was in full uniform, said nothing and walked to the head of the table, some feet away.

"And this is Fritz Lazarre from the National Intelligence Service."

Lazarre too said nothing as he took a seat at the other end of the table. Toussaint remained directly in front of Lucas. With all of them seated, Lucas could only clearly see two at a time because of the length of the table. He looked from one to the other conscious of the strange tableau they must make.

Before anything else was said, the door re-opened and an old man entered with a tray, which he set down at the far end of the table in front of Lazarre. Lucas quickly checked the contents. There were three bottles of coke and a thermos of hot water, tea bags, instant coffee, and powdered milk.

Refreshments seem a little unnecessary if my time is up, he thought. *If this is an interrogation, violence doesn't seem to be on the agenda. You don't offer someone tea, and then kill them.*

Lucas then looked up at Lazarre's face and thought again. Fritz Lazarre had adopted the cinematic pose of a gunslinger who expected another gunman to walk through the door at any moment, right hand beneath the table, left hand above it, ready to steady himself if he had to rise quickly. At first, Lucas thought he was grinning, but then he saw the long scar which ran from the edge of Lazarre's mouth to his left eye. The pinched skin pulled at his top lip, making some of his teeth permanently visible. It gave him a locked expression of sneering amusement.

"You're probably wondering what I'm doing here?" Lucas's attention snapped back to Toussaint. "I'm afraid I wasn't completely open with you when we first met. I do own a printing press, but I'm also an advisor in the President's office. So, the three of us here work together in the interests of our country and we want to have a discussion with you– an exchange of ideas, you might say." Toussaint was sitting with his legs crossed, as urbane and relaxed as he had been in his high wicker chair in the hotel lounge. "I'm afraid we have few comforts here, but I can offer you tea or a cold drink?" Lucas accepted a tea and Toussaint busied himself pouring refreshments for everyone, while continuing to talk. "Lucas…you don't mind if I call you by your first name?" Lucas did not reply. "I'm here as your friend. I am – how would you say? – the facilitator of this meeting. My colleagues have a few questions. But please, you must ask us anything you want and of course you're free to leave. But I must make one thing clear. You must not report any of this. Yes? This is a confidential meeting. 'Off the record,' I believe you call it. We need – we *all* need – to be able to speak frankly."

Lucas felt some of the tension drain from him. While the invitation to leave was evidently not sincere, a conversation could do no harm.

"Why don't I start?" Lazarre turned square on to Lucas, pushing the tray away from him just as Toussaint finished pouring tea for himself. "You must understand Mr Lucas, I'm not like my colleagues here. I have little time for talk, I don't spend hours in debate when the facts are clear. I'm a man of action. I'm the man who gets things done when the talking's over. And I must say – I don't like your reports… I don't see why you mix with subversives – people who want to destroy the peace and order we have here. You talk as if the people who perpetrate violence on our streets have the same standing as the leaders of this country. But that's not right. We're the proper authority here. We're the people. You can't give time to hooligans who would overthrow a recognised government." He talked rapidly, impatient, not expecting a response. "You, Mr Lucas, are meeting with the perverts who won't stop their protests. You're talking to people who work for foreign powers. You're aligning yourself with enemies of Haiti – we see where you go and who you talk to. We don't allow our own journalists to behave like this. Why should we tolerate such behaviour from the likes of you?"

"Thank you Zar," said Toussaint, stepping in to quell the increasingly threatening tone. "I think what Monsieur Lazarre is saying…is that your initial reports about the demonstrations against President Auguste were completely understandable. It was most unfortunate that some protesters died, and we of course understand the President's decision to step down. But everyone thought the protests would come to an end when he left. Now it seems that they're continuing. And as you know, law and order are the prerequisite for any kind of democratic change or progress in Haiti."

Lucas glanced at the major at the other end of the table, who was listening intently but not offering anything.

"Well gentlemen," said Lucas, "I'm not here to take sides. I'm not here to foment disorder, nor am I here to simply repeat what the government says. I'm here to report what happens. I'm expected to report all sides of this story. I interviewed President Auguste because I wanted our listeners to know what the government was thinking, but I also had to cover the demonstrations."

Lazarre bridled. "Ah yes – you claim to be impartial. You stand above us all: always objective, like a God who miraculously remains aloof from the world where the rest of us have to live." He looked as though he might spit on the floor. "There's no such thing as your famous impartiality. How can you possibly remain unbiased when you come here with your own preconceived prejudices? You claim to be objective, but it's a lie. Impartiality is dead – if it ever existed."

"I'm no God," said Lucas. "I don't sit in judgement. I deal in facts and while I'm sure I've got my own prejudices and certainly my own opinions, I'm not stupid and neither are my colleagues. It's perfectly possible to set aside your own opinions and report what happens without overlaying your own feelings on what you say."

"But you know nothing of this place," Lazarre sneered. "We're not some playground where you can test your theories about balance and objectivity."

"You have people dead on your streets…" cut in Lucas. "Unarmed protesters gunned down by your army. This is no playground, Monsieur Lazarre." A fire had risen in Lucas, and he was up for a full-on argument, but he didn't continue because Lazarre looked as though he was about to throw himself across the table and attack him.

"Listen, you pup. Don't try to lecture me about what's happening here. You know nothing of Haiti. This is the real world where everyone has an agenda. This is not a place for journalists. It's a place for patriots. People who have a sense of destiny. We don't want collaborators or spies, or traitors on our streets wherever they come from and whoever they claim to represent."

The major tapped the table in front of him, making everyone look at him, taking the momentum away from Lazarre, whose snarling face loomed large at Lucas.

"Let me add something to clarify what Monsieur Lazarre is saying. Monsieur Lucas, you may think you're simply reporting facts, but you place too much emphasis on certain details. Like your colleague in hospital. It's most unfortunate that he's been taken ill, but why is your organisation reporting this in the news today?" Lucas had not heard anything broadcast about Headley. Perhaps Carrick had added something after their conversation on the phone. "Is it news that a BBC reporter falls ill? Or a local reporter is killed? People fall ill all the time. You know that. Journalists are not so special."

Lucas bristled. He didn't like being told what was and was not news and he was still smarting at Lazarre's patronising tone.

"I haven't heard the latest bulletin," he said, still wondering what exactly had been broadcast, "but if something happens to a journalist while covering a story, it's going to get reported. Michel Jerome was killed reporting the demonstrations. My colleague lies dangerously ill in hospital. He came to cover the aftermath of President Auguste's departure. What is it you don't want these men to report?"

Lucas immediately regretted his question. His irritation had got the better of him. He had no evidence that Michel had been deliberately targeted and what he knew about Headley, he couldn't repeat to these men.

Lazarre leant on his left hand, as if about to stand. "I hope you're not implying that we had anything to do with these incidents?"

"I'm not implying anything," said Lucas. He glanced at Toussaint, who still looked relaxed. So, he thought he'd take the risk of pushing Lazarre a little further. "Headley has reported from many dangerous places in Central America and nothing like this has ever happened to him. He's reported on the drug cartels in Colombia, for instance. As you can imagine, there are many people outside this country who might want him silenced or even dead. But to be clear – you're saying that the military here definitely had nothing to do with his current condition?"

Lazarre laughed aloud, his top lip pulling up further to reveal the rest of his teeth. "If we had done it, he wouldn't be lying in a hospital. He'd be dead. We aren't amateurs."

And that's when the light went out. The room was suddenly in total darkness. Lucas felt as though a blanket had been thrown over his head and he immediately thought of Laguerre.

So, this is how it happens. They come for you in the night or pick you off the street and nobody ever sees you again. Maybe you're found, maybe not. Maybe your body turns up in a ditch. Maybe in hospital. Maybe you simply disappear forever. But this is how it ends.

Lazarre shot out of his chair across the room. He headed for Lucas, who braced himself for the impact. But it never came because Lazarre ran straight past him onto the balcony, swearing violently in Creole – words that brought everyone to their feet.

"It's okay. Don't be alarmed," Toussaint said quietly across the table. "It's a blackout. The whole area's in darkness." And he shouted instructions that brought the old man back with candles which were placed at the centre of the table and lit.

The room was filled with a wavering light and Lazarre returned from the balcony, along with a faint breeze that wafted the flames. Everyone resumed their places.

"We have these interruptions I'm afraid," said Toussaint. "You won't notice the blackouts in your hotel. They have generators, but out here they're unfortunately only too common." He was trying to reassure Lucas, but even he looked a little unsettled and the atmosphere had changed. The flickering candles cast long shadows across walls. They became a ghostly group, multiplied by the uncertain light.

Lazarre was running a finger up and down the scar on his face, his body moving back and forward as though resenting its confinement in the chair. What little self-control he possessed was dissipating.

"I think what Monsieur Lazarre would like from you Mr Lucas," picked up the major, "is some assurance that you won't talk to certain people. There are troublemakers around this priest, Père Baptiste, and some politicians who are in league with foreign powers. We know who these people are. We know they're spies. They're not the kind of people who should be given airtime. They're criminals."

"I have a list of their names," Lazarre interjected. "I can give it to you, so you can avoid them. It's a simple thing to do. Simple for those who love Haiti."

Lucas bridled again. "I'm afraid that's not how we work," he said. "We don't have blacklists of people we don't talk to."

"Why not?" Zar asked, his eyes wide in apparent disbelief.

"I think the idea is," said Lucas, his seething irritation bordering on condescension, "we allow everyone to talk so a proper debate can take place and people can find common ground and resolve differences..." Lucas could see the look of incredulity on Lazarre's face. "Look, I understand that there are difficult issues here, but the way forward is to get them in to the open, so they can be examined properly... I think it's called democracy?"

"Don't preach to me about democracy!" Lazarre shouted as he rocked forward to bring his fist crashing down on the table. "We fought for our freedom! We didn't have a little shit like you to tell us what is right and wrong. We're not your colony. You can't come here and make out you know better than us. We're not your rich, privileged politicians in Britain. We want to build our country and take it forward and we're not going to have criminals or jumped-up journalists, put all that at risk."

Lucas tried to think of something to calm Lazarre down.

"But if these people are criminals, you should take them to court and convict them. I wouldn't interview convicted criminals about a political matter. It's for you to take the appropriate legal action and then of course I'd follow the law…"

Lazarre looked across at Toussaint with the air of a man who was not going to tolerate much more of this sparring and Toussaint cut in.

"Well Monsieur Lucas, I'm sure you're not going to be here much longer. We were grateful for the way you reported all sides when President Auguste was here. Soon there'll be a new President and stability will return and so your presence will no longer be required, isn't that so?"

Lucas wondered exactly what Toussaint's role was in the President's office, since Lazarre and the major both appeared to acquiesce to his authority. But rather than provoke further hostility, he took up Toussaint's invitation to ask questions himself.

"Perhaps you can tell me when a new president will be appointed? And will Colonel Chambert be the obvious choice? How will that choice be made? Are you planning elections?"

"Ah, these are political matters." Toussaint smiled broadly and spread his arms as if this was an area where he exercised no influence. "These are questions for politicians to decide. I'm sure there'll be consultations as there always are at times like this and if the politicians can't make up their minds, then the army has the duty to ensure order and provide stability. We're fortunate to have a man like Colonel Chambert, who won't allow chaos to fill a vacuum."

Lucas could see Lazarre nodding his agreement. He looked round at the major but was too late to see any further agreement from that quarter.

"But before we bring this meeting to a close, there's one thing you mentioned, Mr Lucas," said Toussaint. "You talked about these Colombians and the cartels your man Headley has been investigating. These are things we know little of in Haiti. We wonder why he's sent here to report about our country. I'd have thought his expertise would have been better deployed elsewhere. Drugs aren't a big issue here. And these demonstrators haven't been in front of the palace gates because they're worried about such things." Toussaint was looking pointedly at Lucas. "You don't intend to make this an issue, do you?"

Toussaint was clearly expecting an answer.

"Well, I can't tell you what I will or won't report. All I can say is that I'll be as honest as I can and report what I see as objectively as I can."

Toussaint shook his head, as though Lucas was not getting the message. "Of course, we wouldn't want you to lie, Monsieur Lucas. You must do your job. We simply don't want you to repeat misinformation or be misled by people who aren't acting in the best interests of Haiti. This is for your own safety – you understand?" Toussaint's expression was hardening, no longer the cool, detached figure at the hotel. "These drug lords, you must understand…we are a small country… we cannot control these people. These are dangerous men. When the authorities or the press go after them, they become violent. They do bad things. We wouldn't want to see you putting yourself in unnecessary danger here. Our country's reputation is at stake… you do understand what I'm saying?"

"I think so," said Lucas, returning the ambiguity. His heart quickened. "I appreciate your concern for my safety." He looked around the table. "I feel reassured that the army and the intelligence services here have my welfare at heart."

"We do Lucas. Believe me, we do. And I want you to fully appreciate that."

"It's our experience," snarled Lazarre, through his exposed teeth, "that these people are real bastards. When they get crossed, they do terrible things...Yes?" He was again rocking in his chair. "Terrible things... things we should not speak of...No. They don't just kill people, do they? They make you suffer. Yes." An eerie duet was unfolding between Lazarre and his shadow, which was nodding agreement on the wall behind him, a participant in the conversation. "They threaten family and friends. They go after your children. Yes..." His shadow affirmed the threat. "They find the ones you love. They do..." For a moment, Zar's eyes glazed as if he could see what he was describing. "They torture and kill the people closest to you...Yes." He paused, then his gaze refocused firmly on Lucas. "They keep you alive to watch the suffering...Yes. They make sure you know the cause of the terror they unleash." He rocked forward leering, the spectre behind him looming larger: "You must understand that the last thing anyone here would want is for something like that to happen to you... Yes?"

A drop of sweat ran down Lucas's back. A rare breath of air wafted in from the balcony and touched his cheek. He looked at the shadows on the wall, which now outnumbered the people at the table, and he felt the room closing in and his options disappearing.

"Thank you Lazarre," said Toussaint. "You understand, Lucas, that we're here to help you – to protect you." And Toussaint slid a business card across the table. "If you ever need me, you only have to ring this number. They always know where I am. I'll only be too pleased to help."

"I appreciate that," said Lucas, taking the card, willing all this to end. "I ought to be getting back to my hotel. I'm expected to file a report tonight, and they'll be worried if I'm late."

"Of course," said Toussaint as he stood. There was a scraping of chairs from both ends of the table and the three men moved towards the door. Major Augustin offered his hand and as Lucas took it, he said, "This has been a good meeting, Mr Lucas. Most informative. I'm glad you listened so carefully to what we had to say."

Lazarre did not offer his hand. He stood back with his leering face, staring at Lucas. Toussaint spoke for him.

"It's a pity you've been seeing some undesirable people, but we of course respect the job you do. On these broader issues, irrelevant to our country's political future, I feel sure you have taken on-board our concerns."

"Yes," said Lazarre. "Your safety is what matters. That should be your main concern."

Lucas nodded and followed Toussaint out of the door and down the stairs. The two men in fatigues were waiting, and Lucas retrieved his bag. Outside, the compound was deserted except for a Land Cruiser opposite the gate with its engine running. He had not heard it arrive. Toussaint put a hand on his arm and steered him towards it.

"You shouldn't be wandering around Port au Prince in the night. The curfew will be starting. Let me give you a lift back to your hotel. It's not far, but in the dark bad things can happen."

They got into the rear seats. The driver revved the engine and eased the car through the open gate.

"What have you done with Henri?" asked Lucas, still finding it hard to believe that the boy had betrayed him.

Toussaint studied Lucas in the dim light of the car. "You needn't concern yourself about him. He's been well rewarded." A faint smile crossed his lips. "Did you think you chose your driver? You underestimate your importance Mr Lucas. We couldn't allow you to be driven around by just anyone, could we? Henri's proved himself loyal enough. So really – you have no need to worry about him."

Lucas quietly berated himself. How had he not suspected him? Henri's incessant presence, the new car, the new clothes. He hadn't been paying that generously. And what choice would Henri have had? Everyone knew disobedience came at a price – Henri's missing hand was a testament to that.

In half an hour, they were outside the hotel and Toussaint turned to Lucas.

"You must understand," he said in a low voice that suggested he didn't want the driver to hear. "We can't control everything that happens here. You've seen the protests. You've seen how unstable things can become. Chaos attracts all kinds of bad elements. Violent men can do the most dreadful things to people who cross them. The important thing is that you and Marie stay safe." Not waiting for a response, he put his hand across Lucas to push open the door. "Call me if you need me."

Lucas slipped out. He walked into the bright foyer. Any doubt about the nature of the threat dispelled by the mention of Marie's name. How could they so blatantly threaten her? He looked at the bowl of punch on the reception counter and was tempted to take a large glass to his room but, ignoring the impulse, he went straight upstairs. He thought of calling Marie, but it was not a conversation for the phone. Instead, he filed a short despatch about the planned demonstration tomorrow and mentioned nothing about Headley.

CHAPTER 33

Lucas made the call the next morning. "It's me," he said, and the response was immediate.

"I'll pick you up. I'm on my way."

He replaced the receiver and went down to the lobby. He'd spent a sleepless night going over his encounter with Toussaint and his shadows. He had rehearsed the scene time and again, recalling every detail. It was no nightmare. It was all too real.

There was no sign of Henri in reception, which was just as well. Lucas was not sure what he would have done had he seen him again. He sat and watched the entrance.

A little later, through the revolving glass door, he saw an enormous black Chevrolet SUV draw up, and the blackened window in the back opened just enough for Lucas to see Martinez. Seconds later, he was in the car with the news that the key was for a post office box. He recounted the events of the previous night, but before Lucas could say who had been there, Martinez was issuing instructions to the driver.

"Hey, we've no time to lose. Let's go there now. The post office is only open a few hours a day, and we'll miss it unless we move. We'll drop you off and we'll stay close and take you back to the Embassy once you've established whether the key fits one of their boxes. But look – there's something you need to know now. I have some bad news."

Lucas immediately thought of Marie and blurted out her name, but Martinez cut across him.

"No. No. It's Headley. He died last night. The doctor said they did their best, but his heart gave out, and they couldn't revive him. The evacuation flight came in early this morning. I'll be seeing the body off. The guys from the Herald are going to meet it in Miami. They say they'll liaise with London and, of course his family."

Lucas was stunned. He had thought at least they were going to get Headley out alive.

"I'm sorry," Lucas said quietly.

"Yeah," came the response, and Martinez's head went down. "We worked well together. He was a brave reporter – particularly in Colombia. You should have seen him when he was on a story. He was relentless, fearless…" Martinez stared straight ahead. "Things got pretty hairy in Bogota, and he didn't back off, but I had not expected this here, not in Port au Prince. Usually these thugs kill each other, not foreigners."

"Well, perhaps he's still with us," said Lucas, holding out the key. "Perhaps he can help us find out who killed him."

Martinez punched Lucas's knee. "Let's do this." They were already pulling up outside the post office and Martinez was issuing instructions again. "Hey, look we'll park in front of the main entrance and handle any arguments about obstruction. You go and try that key. We'll be here when you're done."

Lucas jumped out of the car, having given up trying to tell Martinez any more about his encounter with Toussaint and his interrogators. It would have to wait. He dropped on to the street in the blazing sun and dived for the main entrance of the post office. He pushed his way in. Immediately, he was at the back of a clamouring crowd. A sea of people was pressing forward towards the counters, with parcels and bags tied round with string and tape. Some were waving pieces of paper or bank notes, trying to attract the attention of staff, who were pummelled by the demands being shouted at them. After staring at this tide of humanity for a minute, wondering how he would ever make it to the front, Lucas noticed a small door to the side. Above it was a wooden sign: 'Boîtes Postales'. He forced his way over to it and knocked hard. There was too much noise to hear a response, so he leant against the door, and it opened on to a narrow room with two long lines of metal boxes against each wall. They ran from floor to ceiling.

He closed the door on the chaos behind him and took a step forward. An ample woman appeared at the far end of the room. She shouted something indignant in Creole and came towards him, waving him back. She walked with the gait of a sumo wrestler. Her girth filled the corridor between the deposit boxes, and Lucas tried to check her advance by holding up the key in front of him. Her eyes widened, and she reached out for the key, muttering in recognition as it came into her grasp. She pulled at a long chain around her neck, which ran down her chest to disappear into a deep pouch in the front of her apron. At the end of the chain was an enormous loop of keys. She inspected the one Lucas was holding, nodded, and rummaged round until she found its match. Then she turned laboriously and rolled down the row, with Lucas following close behind.

Number 31 was waist height on the right, at the far end. The box had a narrow slot for letters and papers and beneath it were two round, brass locks. The woman put her key in and still attached to it, looked away. Lucas slid his key in to the second lock and turned. There was a click before the door sprang open an inch. The woman withdrew her key and moved off.

Lucas pulled it wide and looked inside. It was empty.

His heart sank.

If Headley had intended to use the box, he had run out of time. Or someone else had already got here. There would be no evidence to take back to Martinez.

To be sure, Lucas slid his hand in and felt along the sides and floor of the box. Something ruffed up under his hand. A thin piece of felt covered the floor of the cabinet. He patted it and felt something hard and flat underneath. Lifting the felt away, he saw a square piece of plastic lying at the bottom. Lucas prized it off. It was a blue floppy disc. At one end, it had a silver piece of metal which slid to one side when he pressed it and sprang back sharply as soon as he let go. He put it straight in his pocket, closed the door and locked it.

The woman was watching from a distance, not close enough to see what Lucas had taken. He moved towards her, and she led the way back to the door, where there was enough room for him to pass. Thanking her, he squeezed past and thrust a few notes into her hand. He plunged back through the crowd to the street. The car was waiting with Martinez leaning across the back seat, pushing the door open.

They sped back to the Embassy with Martinez cradling the disc in his hands. Within minutes of their arrival, he had Lucas standing in a basement computer room. The whole of one wall was stacked with servers, alive with flashing lights. Desks were laid out in the centre of the room with monitors on each one and a technician took the disc and inserted it into an oblong drive. "Jeez," he said. "Haven't seen one of these for a coupla decades. Just as well we never throw anything out round here." The screen flashed, and the man rattled off a series of keystrokes until a root map appeared on the monitor.

Martinez stood with his hand on the man's shoulder, giving a light pat every time he gave instructions as words tumbled across the screen. Page after page of figures appeared.

He turned to Lucas and told him to go with the driver to find some coffee. This was going to take some time. Martinez said the disc seemed to contain account numbers and transactions, but he would have to work through it all and see if he could match it all with other data he had on file.

Lucas left and was offered sandwiches in a ground floor canteen. He ate hungrily, having missed breakfast in his haste to get out of the hotel. His guide then took him back to the secure room where he had first met Martinez. Another two hours passed before Martinez joined him.

"Got it!" he said, bursting in. "This is what we've been looking for." And he dropped to his knees in the middle of the room and spread a dozen sheets of closely printed paper on the floor. Lucas knelt beside him and saw that there were figures circled and lines leading from one transaction to another across several different sheets. "This is what Headley found," said Martinez waving at a set of white computer sheets to his left, "and this is what we already knew." He pointed at the rest of the print outs on the floor, which were on pink paper. "We know this is a cartel account," he said, tapping one of the pink sheets. "And here we have sums of money moving every month…" his finger traced its way across the floor. "It goes from this account in the Far East, through several others …" The finger passed from white sheets to the pink ones and back again… "to this Miami account and on to this one in Port au Prince. There are regular monthly payments – well over a million dollars in one year."

"And this account in Port au Prince? Do you know who owns this one?" asked Lucas, pointing at the destination.

"Yeah – we know. This is an army account. It's not in their name of course. It's a local company, but we've double checked and the main beneficiary is Colonel Chambert. Looks like our man of the moment is on the take."

"What company?"

"Toussaint Printing – it has a printing press alright. We've checked it out. But it hasn't produced anything for years."

"Alfred Toussaint?" asked Lucas.

"Yeah, that's him. You know him?"

"He was there last night. He was one of the goons who picked me up for questioning."

"You serious?" Martinez looked puzzled.

"Yes. He and a Major from the military and some thug called Lazarre."

"Jeez, you need to steer clear of Lazarre." Martinez briefly looked up from all the papers on the floor. "Why didn't you say he was there?"

Lucas shrugged. "I tried, but – well you had the bad news about Headley – and we've been kind of busy." Martinez's head went down again.

"Sorry bud. I should listen more."

"It's okay," said Lucas. "But look, Toussaint's been tracking me since the first day I arrived. Every time something happened – there he was. He even got me out of trouble during that first demonstration, but everything's changed. I reckon that as long as I was reporting on the opposition to Auguste, he was cool, but now this whole drug angle has come up he's hauling me off to meetings with people who want to shut me up."

"Well, it certainly sounds like he's been protecting his investment," commented Martinez. "But look," he was bundling up all the papers, still preoccupied with the evidence in front of him, only half listening. "You've got this story now. This you can report. You can take these copies. I need this to go public. Now, before Chambert gets the presidency. But keep us out of it, okay? It's your story…"

"You don't want to be part of this? Why so coy?" asked Lucas, "And surely, you've got enough to bring a prosecution – at least in the States?"

"Sure, we can go after the banks, but right now it's better for us if you get the ball rolling. Nobody trusts us here. We've got a bit of a reputational issue. We're always cast as the bad guy: we flew Auguste out, we're accused of interfering all the time, of being heavy-handed and domineering. We've always got some selfish motive, never act in the interests of the people – you know the thing. We get so much flack it obscures the truth sometimes. This one's better coming from you."

Martinez put a hand on Lucas's arm and there was emotion in his voice: "Besides – Headley dug this one out and he deserves the credit. It's kinda… the least we can do under the circumstances."

"Well, that feels right," agreed Lucas. But then the impossibility of his situation struck home.

"No wait," he said. "I can't. If I start reporting on drug trafficking in Haiti, it's not me they'll go after. It's Marie."

"Marie?" Martinez looked mystified. "I thought they interrogated you and threatened you. Who's this Marie?" Lucas quickly explained how Marie had been his guide; how she'd helped him identify the key; how he wasn't going anywhere without her.

"It was what Toussaint said when he left me at the hotel. All Lazarre's threats of what they do to people who cross them – he was saying they'll go after Marie to get at me. I can't break this story knowing what they'll do to her."

They both fell silent, sitting on the floor, staring bleakly at the consequences of any action. Lucas was recalling how often Toussaint had appeared at the hotel, as if stalking him – always with something to say; some nudge to push him in the direction he wanted Lucas to go.

And then the shadows of the previous evening whispered in his ear; the ghostly spectre behind Lazarre on the wall nodding approval at the sadistic punishments meted out to those who betrayed the cartels. If it was just me, he was threatening, thought Lucas. I would write the report and damn the consequences. I'd get it all out in the open and take the risk. But Marie? He shook his head. He couldn't do that to her. He'd never forgive himself. Not after everything she'd done for him.

"Unless…" said Lucas under this breath.

"Unless?"

"Unless…they can't find Marie when the story goes to air. If she's somewhere safe, like here in the Embassy. They couldn't touch her."

"Nice idea," said Martinez, "but she's a foreign national – not American. I can't start turning the Embassy in to a hostel for Haitians."

"If not here, then out of the country – at least for a while," said Lucas.

"That's more like it. If you can persuade her. And I *could* help with that. But we'll have to move fast. We don't know how much these goons know about what Headley was up to. And look. It's not just Marie you should worry about. You can't be around either when this one breaks. It's time for you to go – and soon."

Lucas stood up next to him and picked up the papers, folding them in to a thick square.

"Can I take these?"

"Sure. Take them and go write your story but tell them not to run it until you're out of the country. There's a flight today at ten to five. It's the last one for two days. So, you've got under four hours before it takes off. I can get you two tickets – for you and Marie." Martinez rubbed his forehead. "No, wait a minute. I'll make two reservations for Embassy staff. If anyone's looking for you, they won't see your names on the manifest." Martinez was speaking slowly, working it out as he went along: "We can use the diplomatic channel in the VIP area, and I can get the tickets re-issued in your names at the last minute. I know the ground staff. I'll check you through to Miami and then you can travel on from there. It's an American

Airlines flight tonight – so they'll be okay. But you must only bring carry-on luggage. It'll all be last minute, no time for anything else."

Lucas had all the papers neatly folded up and in his bag.

"Okay," he said, looking at his watch. It was nearly 2 p.m. "If your driver can drop me at the hotel, I'll file and then go get Marie."

"Sounds like a plan. I'll see you at the airport at half past four, but not a minute later. Don't be late and don't go to departures. The VIP entrance is about twenty yards to the right. I'll be there waiting there. And make sure Marie brings her passport."

CHAPTER 34

The black SUV was in the courtyard when Lucas emerged from the Embassy building. The driver was the same, but there was another man in the front passenger seat who got out as Lucas approached and opened the rear door for him. He had a smart, loose fitting black suit, dark glasses, open-necked, white shirt and an earpiece. He might as well have had 'secret service' tattooed on his forehead.

Relieved that Martinez was looking out for him, Lucas sped back to the hotel, working out what he was going to write. He would use Headley's mysterious death as the introduction. He could then devote the body of the report to the documents and the links between Toussaint Printing and drug money.

The Embassy car dropped him at the hotel and Lucas went straight to his room to record his report – word perfect. At the top, he read out a warning, emphasising that it was not to be broadcast until midnight, by which time he and Marie should be safely on their way to Miami. His final line put an end to any thought of either Marie or him remaining in Haiti.

"The evidence which Julian Headley compiled from banking sources, shows Colonel Chambert to be one of the beneficiaries of money from cartel accounts known to the US authorities."

As soon as he finished, he saved a copy of the file and encrypted it before sending it off. He put in a call to Carrick. He wasn't there, but the duty editor came on the line and Lucas emphasised that his piece was to be embargoed. The password was his staff number and he'd have to get HR to look it up. The editor had lots of questions, and Lucas had to explain that he couldn't talk on an open line, but if he listened to the piece and talked to Carrick, they would understand. The delay, though, was critical. He said nothing of his departure and nothing about Marie.

He looked at his case and remembered the instruction from Martinez only to bring hand luggage. The bag was too big. He would have to go with only his equipment bag. And he must pay the bill. He went to the door and walked down the corridor to the staircase. As he reached the landing, he looked down at reception and there was the unmistakable figure of Lazarre. He was leaning across the counter, pointing at the room keys hanging from the hooks and shouting at a receptionist near the cashier's desk. With him were two other men carrying long batons.

Lucas stepped back against the wall. Surely, they didn't know about the report? They must have decided that leaving him free was too big a risk. He turned and ran back to his room. He locked the door. He left the key in, to make it harder for anyone to insert another key from the outside. He had to get out. He crossed the room to the window and opened the two glass frames outwards until they were flush against the building. Below was the side street. A few cars were parked close to the hotel wall, which fell away beneath him. There was one car directly below. It was some kind of jeep, with a square flat roof. Its presence reduced the drop, but it was still a long way down.

Lucas looked around the room for something he could use as a rope. There was no cord for the curtain or for any of the lights. But there was the dressing gown which Lucas had tossed on to the table the night before. As he went to pick it up, he heard the footsteps outside. They stamped down the corridor past his door to number 17. Someone shouted and immediately he could hear a key rattling in the lock. They had gone to the wrong room, but it would only be a minute before they were at his door.

Lucas pulled the belt out of the towelling bathrobe and held it up. It was about five feet long. He went back to the window and looked out. Driven into the wall on either side were metal catches which rotated to hold the open casements in place. To the nearest one he attached the end of the belt in a slip knot and pulled it tight. The knot was too big for the catch, but it held when Lucas tugged.

There was a furious hammering on his door. Lucas could see his key vibrating in the lock. It would only be a matter of seconds before it was forced out. If he was to leave, it had to be now. He raced to the bed and grabbed his wallet and passport, abandoning everything else. He couldn't carry more and make the drop to the car. Back at the window, he wrapped the cord round his arm and stretched out with one hand to hold the metal catch. He pulled his body out of the window, letting the metal take his weight for as long as possible until he had to commit. With a loud grunt, he let go of the catch, grabbing the cord with both hands.

For a moment, the knot held, but he could see it slipping. He slithered down the cord, and as he reached the end, the knot gave way. He dropped with the cord still in his hand.

He fell feet first on to the roof of the car. The force of his impact dented the roof and buckled his knees. He lost his balance, fell sideways, down over the windscreen. As he went, he grabbed a wiper blade and held on as it bent and then snapped in his hand, but it was enough to bring his feet round, so that when he cascaded off the bonnet, he landed in the road feet first.

He stood shakily and looked up. There was a face at the window above. Lucas needed no further encouragement. He ran quickly towards the road at the back of the hotel.

The street was busy with vendors and traffic. He ran along the cracked pavement, wincing from bruises on his legs and torso, trying to put as much distance as possible between him and whoever might follow. Ahead was a car parked in the gutter and he rushed over to the driver who was sitting on the bonnet smoking a cigarette. With a mixture of gesticulations and repetition of the word 'Petionville', Lucas made it clear he needed a lift. The man's repeated refusal suddenly changed to a 'yes' when Lucas produced a thick wad of gourdes from his wallet. It took nearly all his money, but the man agreed to drive him to the top of the hill, near to Marie's house.

Lucas told him to stop well short of the turning he needed and watched as the car headed back towards the city. He then walked the remaining distance down the little road to the iron gates that led to the garden.

He found Marie talking to Pierre; she was sitting on the sofa, he was on the chair next to her, both deep in conversation. Pierre stood quickly as he heard the door open behind him. He looked ready to deal with an intruder, but when he saw it was Lucas, he stepped forward in greeting.

"Lucas!" Marie intervened, joining Pierre. "Where have you been? I thought you would have called by now."

"I've had some problems. I have so much to tell you and I don't have much time. Listen," he said, short of breath. "I have to ask a great favour of you. If you don't agree, I'm going to have to call the BBC and tell them not to broadcast the piece I've just filed."

"What do you mean?"

"I've sent a report and when it's broadcast, they're going to come after you." And as he said these words, the image of his bed and everything he had left behind, including the bank print outs, flashed into his mind. "Oh God!" He buried his head in his hands as the realisation hit home. "I've left it all at the hotel! I'm so sorry Marie." Lucas moved to a side chair and sat down heavily.

"What's going on Lucas?" Marie sounded stern and Pierre joined in.

"You said we didn't have much time. What's happened?" They both stood over Lucas as he tried to pull himself together and explain. He quickly recounted the events since he had last seen them: his betrayal by Henri, the meeting with Lazarre and the others, the threats against Marie, the box at the post office, the disc left by Headley. Finally, he told Marie what his report contained and how in a few hours' time the BBC was going to broadcast the very accusation which he had been warned not to make. Martinez was waiting at the airport to get them on a plane.

Pierre and Marie looked stunned. "Dear God." said Pierre. "Do they know you came here?"

"No. A stranger gave me a lift, and I stopped well short of the house, so even if he talks, he doesn't know where I went."

"But your notes, the recording, the print outs. If they know you're exposing them. They'll be coming for Marie anyway. They'll be coming now."

"I know, I know," said Lucas. "They can't have heard the report yet, but they'll see the evidence. They're already looking for me and they're bound to come for you, Marie. That's why you must come with me to the airport. You must leave now." Lucas looked at his watch. It was now one hour before the plane was due to take off and half an hour before Martinez had said they had to be there. Pierre turned to Marie.

"You have to get out. You can't stay here. This is the first place they'll look for you. I have my car outside. I can take you both."

"But I'm not leaving Haiti," said Marie quickly. "I made up my mind ages ago I wasn't going to leave. I didn't go with my mother and I'm not going now. This is where I belong. I'm not going to be driven out."

"It doesn't have to be forever, Marie," said Lucas. "Just until this has died down."

Pierre gripped her arm. "Marie, whatever happens you have to leave this house."

"But the demonstration tomorrow…" said Marie, sounding exasperated. "How can I leave? I won't be the coward who runs and leaves others to face up to these thugs."

"If you don't go, I'm not going," said Lucas. "I'm not leaving you here to face all this alone when it's me who's putting you in danger. If you stay, I stay too."

"Oh Lucas…" Marie sounded hurt. "You can't do this. You can't make these decisions for me."

Pierre stood up, pulling Marie by the hand. He suddenly looked much taller and more commanding. "You must get your passport and some clothes," he said. "We must be quick. Come." He started to guide her to the door that led to Michel's study and the rest of the house. Lucas's hopes rose.

"You can't bring much," Lucas said, "just a carry-on bag. There's no time. Bring money and a passport – that's all that matters."

Pierre had his arm firmly round Marie as he ushered her through the door. "Come on. I'll help you," he said.

For the first time, Lucas saw Marie give Pierre a look that fell short of admiration and trust. Disappointment was written across her face, but she reluctantly let herself be led through the door, leaving Lucas alone.

After a few moments, he heard Marie begin to argue. He could hear her indistinct protests as they moved around. But Pierre seemed to counter her every complaint. Gradually the rhythm of his speech, low and even, eroded her opposition and she became quiet, listening to reason. Whatever he said, it worked, for when Marie reappeared, she looked more compliant.

"It's not fair." She was carrying a small woven basket. "You're blackmailing me by saying you'll stay if I stay." She took out her passport. "But I couldn't bear it if something happened to you."

"Good," said Pierre. "That's decided. We must move quickly." He took her by the arm. "Come – my car's by the gate."

They all stepped into the garden, Marie locking the door tightly shut. A light was still on inside.

"Don't worry about that," said Marie. "The maid will be in tomorrow."

CHAPTER 35

Pierre drove at speed to the airport, slowing only when he saw the terminal building in the distance. He pulled the car over on to the scratchy verge by the long perimeter fence.

"There's an army checkpoint at the entrance. We'd better walk from here." They all got out of the car and Pierre led the way. "This fence has been here forever," he said. "There'll be a way through somewhere." And soon he was tugging away at some jagged wiring that was already bent up and away from the ground. "Here," he said. "Be my guest." On all fours, they scrambled on to the dusty grass beyond. The checkpoint was a few hundred yards away and Lucas could see one of the soldiers bent low at a driver's window, checking paperwork. The three of them ran across the rough ground and followed a track which led towards the car park by the terminal. Once there, Pierre led them round the edge, hopping from one piece of broken concrete to another, until they got to the far end of the terminal. Looking over rows of dusty cars, Lucas could see the sign for the VIP lounge by a door on the far side.

Pierre took them through the entrance, down a short corridor to doors which opened inwards to reveal a small hangar. It had comfortable sofas on either side, each one sitting on its own square of carpet, and separated by tall pot plants. As they entered, a black suited figure appeared from behind the opening door and confronted Pierre, who stopped, surprised by the sudden presence.

"You with him?" he asked, pointing at Lucas, who recognised the security man from the Embassy car.

"He's a friend of Marie's," said Lucas. "He's driven us here."

"Okay. Wait," came the curt reply, and the man walked to a side office, returning with Martinez.

"Jeez, you cut it fine – I need your passports," said Martinez quickly. Lucas and Marie handed them over. "You can wait in there, out of sight." Pierre followed Martinez as he retreated with the passports. Lucas and Marie were shown into the little office from which Martinez had emerged.

Suddenly alone with Marie, Lucas sat down next to her and tried to put his arm round her, but she leant away.

"I'm sorry. I didn't mean for this. I know you want to stay. It all happened so fast this morning. We knew that Headley was working on something important, but I had no idea it was going to be this big or would involve you like this."

"This is where I belong," said Marie fiercely. "You can't just hijack me like this." Her eyes flashed at Lucas.

"I'm sorry," he said again, wincing at the force of her reaction. "I just can't see what choice we have. I can't tell this story and leave you here to face the consequences."

"I know, I know," said Marie, welling up, her hands raised to stop him from saying more. "If Michel was here, he would say you have to go with the story." She covered her mouth, stifling her grief. "I still hear his voice. I still see him. Feel him. And I know he'd understand what you're doing."

By the time Pierre reappeared, she had her head on Lucas's shoulder, letting him comfort her.

"Marie, Martinez wants a word with you. Something about your student visa."

Marie stood slowly and left.

"She's a very brave woman," said Pierre, taking a seat across from Lucas. "She could be in the States or Europe. She has the contacts and the brains to go anywhere, but always comes back to us. It's people like her that mean we can carry on our work and one day we'll make the change that must come. Père Baptiste is an inspiration and a good man, but without the likes of Marie, he would be a voice in the wilderness." Lucas nodded, wondering who was more important to Pierre; Baptiste or Marie. "Rome and his bishop have deserted him. The Church wants him out of Haiti and away from politics. He's really isolated now, but with the people behind him, I believe he can lead a revolution."

"What about you, Pierre? Will you be alright?" asked Lucas.

"Don't worry about me. BP's always under pressure. If he can take it, we all can. There have been many times when I thought they were going to kill him in the street or in his own church, but God seems to look after his own." Pierre smiled at Lucas, seeming to imply his comment applied as much to him as to anyone else.

Martinez appeared at the door. He looked stressed. For a moment, Lucas thought he was angry.

"Gotta go," Martinez barked. Marie was standing behind him and he half turned to include her in what he was saying.

"We've got one shot at this. From here on, we just walk and keep going. You don't look back. You don't talk to anyone. You don't show your papers. We go straight across the tarmac to the plane. Stay silent. No questions. I want you invisible, whatever happens, okay?"

"Okay," said Lucas and the four of them walked through the hangar out into the night, with the security man at their backs. Martinez handed back the passports as he went.

The big American Airlines plane sat at an angle on the tarmac, engines running, with two sets of stairs front and rear. Lucas could see attendants at both doors. Passengers' heads were clearly visible through the little portals along the fuselage. Martinez walked between Lucas and Marie, keeping them close so he could be heard above the engines.

"The plane's full. I couldn't get you tickets together. You're at the front, Lucas. Marie, you're at the back." Martinez motioned to the security man, who stepped up and led Marie towards the back set of stairs, and Pierre followed them. Martinez accompanied Lucas to the front. When they reached the stairs, he turned and put his hands on Lucas's shoulders.

"Good job, Lucas. You get out of here before the shit hits the fan." He laughed. "I seem to have picked up a few choice phrases from Headley. I think that's one of his!" They shook hands. "I wish you luck my friend. Now you'd better go." He produced a small, padded envelope from his inner pocket. "When the plane has taken off and you have a quiet moment, open this will you?"

"Sure," said Lucas.

"Not before, mind. We've had enough trouble getting you this far. Just make sure you're well on your way before you read it, okay?"

Lucas nodded and, caught by a wave of gratitude, he embraced Martinez before going up the steps.

"Mr Gould?" The steward gave him a taut smile. "Just in time. I'm told you're our special guest tonight. Welcome aboard. Follow me please," and he showed him to an aisle seat in row two. The window seat was empty.

"I thought the flight was full?" said Lucas, taking his seat.

"Not in business class, sir." A second attendant was already closing the door.

"Well – I have a friend in the back. Can she join me?"

"We don't normally allow economy passengers up here, but when we're in the air, you can invite her up for a while. Wait until we've been round with the trolley service." Lucas felt the plane move. On came the safety announcement, and the steward took his position at the front of the cabin.

Lucas looked out of the window. There was no sign of Martinez.

It was not until the trolley came with the drinks that he remembered the envelope. He ordered a glass of rum with ice and put it on a little napkin on the table, which came up from his seat. Lucas took a sip and decided it was far inferior to the rum at the hotel. He slid his finger under the seal of the envelope and pealed back the flap. Marie's necklace tumbled on to the table, its fine chain lacing round the complex pendant. He looked inside the envelope and there was a folded piece of paper. Lucas opened it up. It was from Martinez.

"Lucas, my friend, I am sorry. Marie refused to travel. She was adamant but said to give you this. At least I got one of you out. Forgive me. I'll do what I can. Martinez."

He read it twice, not believing what lay in front of him. The third time he looked, the words blurred, and his hand crumpled the paper, shaking. Something touched his shoulder, and he looked up.

"Are you alright, sir? Is there anything I can do?" The steward was there, picking his drink off the table. Lucas stuffed the note in his pocket, sat up, unaware that he had caused a disturbance.

"I'm alright," he mumbled. He just needed a moment.

As the steward moved away, a wave of hope ran through him. Marie could still be on the plane. He had seen her walking to the steps. Martinez must have written the note in the hangar; there was a chance Marie had changed her mind. He leapt from his seat and strode down the aisle to the Economy section, the necklace tightly wound round his hand. He worked his way systematically past the packed rows of seats. Faces peered up, seeing the distress on his face, but none belonged to Marie. He reached the end by the rear door and sank into the corner, hands pressed against his eyes, lights exploding in his head and the words no, no, no quietly falling from him.

Unaware that attendants came and went, afraid to touch him unless he erupted, Lucas rocked on his haunches berating himself for leaving Marie in such danger, but he was helpless. There was nothing he could do. By the time he arrived in Miami it would be too late. The one thing he could be sure of was that Lazarre would be hunting for her. Lucas's absence would only serve to make him more determined.

353

He pushed his body against the door. 'What have I done?' he asked himself over and over, appalled by the disaster unfolding before him. Michel was dead and now Marie would be the butt of all the fury his report would unleash. He moaned aloud.

"I'm sorry Mr Gould," it was the steward from business class. "I must ask you to return to your seat. Can I help? Do you need anyone or anything?"

Lucas looked up in despair. "No. No. Nothing. Thank you. There's nothing you can do."

He walked slowly back to the front of the plane, dreading what awaited him back in London.

CHAPTER 36

It was raining as Lucas walked round the Aldwych from the tube station, heading straight in to work. Yesterday's headlines hung limply from the news-stand on the corner: *'PM's Advisor Sacked'*. *'Keller Out after BBC investigation.'*

"Ah! Here comes the wrecker of worlds." Carla was standing outside the main entrance of Bush House, laced in smoke, wearing a face thick with make-up, watching the comings and goings of another busy day at World Service. "They've banished me, the bastards," she said as Lucas paused under the portico with its torch-bearing statues. Carla continued as he brushed the rain from his shoulders: "It turns out that some new pescatarian producer is allergic to smoke as well as pollen and every other damn organism known to man…including women, it would appear. Anyway, I now can't smoke at all – not even in the stationery cupboard. So, I'm condemned to the elements and you, Lucas." She looked at him carefully. "I take it I'm your welcoming party? You just off the flight?"

Lucas nodded.

"Thought so. You look like death if you don't mind me saying so. Your bombshell ran last night. I suppose while you were in mid-air?"

Again, Lucas nodded, muted by lack of sleep and anxiety.

"Well, all hell will break loose today," Carla continued casually. "Drug lords don't like having their finances exposed – I should think your president elect will be dead by dusk." She gave Lucas a sceptical look. "You did well to get a flight back or you might be in a box with him."

"I'm just checking in with Flo," Lucas managed. Carla's antennae continued to assess the evidence before her.

"You need sleep, Lucas. Go to bed. No point in killing yourself. There'll be plenty of others who'll do that for you." Lucas recognised sympathy when he heard it and mustered a smile.

"Thanks Carla," he said. "Are those your headlines?" He nodded at the news-stand.

"You bet. Got the bastard. Our little foray with the Freedom of Information Act came up trumps, plus a little wizardry on my part. The programme went out Wednesday. Keller went Thursday. Thank God it's Friday. I'm off on holiday."

"Holiday? But next week's programme. What happens to that?"

"Got one on the shelf, so I've told them to play it. They couldn't say no really – not after this scoop. And I say 'we' Lucas – you did some of the legwork on this one. So, you get some of the credit. I mentioned you in despatches. Seems you can do no wrong at the mo. Enjoy it while it lasts." Lucas looked so exhausted Carla gave him a push. "You'd better get on. The Queen Bee awaits."

Sheila nodded at him as he appeared and pointed towards Flo's open door. His attendance was clearly top of her to-do list.

"Ah Lucas. Good! I got your text saying you were on your way. Thanks for that." Flo swivelled round in her chair as he came in. "Great story. It's still the lead and News are chasing up to get some reaction. It's only morning in Port au Prince of course, so still a bit early..." Flo paused. "Are you alright?"

Lucas slumped down on the sofa, head down, staring at the floor, face ashen. He didn't respond. Putting thoughts into words was almost beyond him.

"Lucas?"

"Sorry," he mumbled.

"Are you alright? Tell me."

"No, I'm not alright. It all went wrong..." He looked up at Flo: "I've done something terrible." And this confession unleashed a torrent so great that Flo had to stop him. She rose, placing a hand on his shoulder to calm him. She told him to stay where he was and breathe. Just breathe; She ordered tea, closed the door, calmed him down, told him to start from the beginning and take it slowly. She couldn't help unless he took it slowly.

So, Lucas – mug of tea in hand – told her about Headley's key and the disc and the interrogation and the threat to Marie. Finally, he described the plan to break the story and keep Marie safe.

"But it all went wrong. The plane had already taken off before I realised Marie wasn't on it. I'd never have left if I'd known. Martinez knew that. And now Lazarre and his thugs will be after her. They'll kill her, or worse, and it's my fault. All my fault…" Flo had her arm on his, trying to console him, now only too aware of the dreadful consequences of the story that was currently top of the news bulletin.

"Lucas," she said. "This isn't your fault. You tried to get her out. Refusing to get on the plane was her call. You can't blame yourself. But why didn't she fly?"

"She's so proud," explained Lucas, "so determined, so independent." His hand came up to touch Marie's necklace beneath his shirt. "She's so sure they can face the army down…"

"Yes, I see," said Flo, "and you love her…"

She said it in such a matter-of-fact way that it brought Lucas up short, shocked that it was so obvious.

"Yes. Yes," he said. "I love her. I think I loved her from the moment I saw her."

Flo stood up. "Then we have a lot to do," she said. "You must call. Call her now. Call her, call Martinez, call anyone who might know where she is, who might be able to help. It's early there, but now this story's out. I doubt if anyone will be asleep."

"I don't have the numbers. I lost my contact book," said Lucas. "I left everything at the hotel, my notes, phones everything. I had to run. They were coming for me. All my kit, everything's gone. It's all still there."

"My God Lucas. You really have been through the mill." Flo picked up the phone. "Sheila, get me the US Embassy in Port au Prince, will you?" She replaced the receiver and pushed the phone towards Lucas. "You can use this. I'll get Sheila to dig out what numbers we have, and we'll put them through." The phone immediately rang, and Flo picked it up. "Right," she said, holding out the receiver, "it's the Embassy. Talk to them, and I'll brief Sheila." And with that, she left Lucas to it.

The woman on the line said she'd check, but she thought Martinez was out of the office. She told him to hang on. Lucas sat there listening to a silence that spoke of long corridors and empty offices until she returned slightly breathless and when she spoke, she seemed to understand why Lucas was calling.

"I'm sorry he's not there, but look, I know Martinez has been up all night. It looks like he left the Embassy a couple of hours ago – before the curfew lifted." Lucas started to question her about Marie, but she interrupted. "Lucas, I know your departure last night didn't go to plan, but Martinez is on the case. Really, that's all I can say...I'll get him to call you when he returns. Don't worry. He will call – I'll see to it personally. Give me all your numbers."

And Lucas did before she hung up.

Sheila came in to report that she was getting no answer from Michel's home phone, and she'd called the hotel, but nobody there had seen Marie. Lucas asked her to try Radio Rèv and within a matter of minutes JP was on the line.

"She'll be okay Lucas," said JP, trying to sound reassuring. "She can look after herself. But she'll be keeping her head down. Since the story broke the army's been on the streets again. There's been shooting around the palace. It's been a scary night, but the curfew's ending now and there's no sign of it being extended." JP's voice was rising, unable to contain his excitement. "They must know how angry everyone is about Chambert being on the take. The city's a powder keg and it'll

359

blow today at some point. I'm heading to the square. We're going to do this morning's broadcast live from outside the palace. I'm not missing this one." Alarmed at this news, Lucas begged JP to be careful. "Sure – but if the bastards are going to kill me, they can do it while I'm on air. Be bloody great radio!"

"You're mad!" laughed Lucas, JP's bravado piercing the cloud of anxiety that had hung over him. "But if you see Marie get her to call me." And Lucas relayed his London numbers again.

Flo put her head round the door and signalled that he should hang up.

"It's the Embassy. Sheila's putting them through." The phone buzzed as soon as he put it down.

"Martinez?"

"Yeah buddy. It's me. I just got your message. Look I owe you an apology. I'm sorry I cheated you. I really didn't have a choice. Marie cut me down like a tree when she got me alone at the airport. She said she'd scream her head off if I tried to put her on the plane. Made me promise not to tell you. She really put me in an impossible position. I figured having one lunatic staying behind was bad enough. I didn't want you on my conscience as well. So, I made out she was going with you and wrote that note – sorry!"

"But is she okay? Have you seen her?"

"No – not since the airport. She left with that Pierre guy. He said something about getting Baptiste's people to hide her – although she doesn't strike me as the kind of person to lie low very long. But listen, your report's really set things off here. There's some kind of stand-off going on outside the barracks next to the palace. We've had to go out and pick up

360

some of our guys who were in trouble. But the curfew's over now and there are thousands of people on the move, all heading for the city centre and the square. Either Chambert's going or there's going to be a bloodbath."

"But you can't let Marie walk in to all that."

"No, no. I'm heading back now with a couple of my team. We're setting up base at the Etoile and I'll put a spotter up high. If she's there, we'll see her and we'll get her out – assuming, of course, that Lazarre hasn't got to her already." Martinez fell silent and for a moment Lucas thought the line had been cut. "I'm sorry, Lucas. I kinda feel responsible, so I'll do my best but look – this was her call. You shouldn't beat yourself up over it and I did all I could to get her out. We'll do our best, but I can't promise anything. You understand?" Lucas understood.

"I appreciate all you're doing," said Lucas. "I really do. But for the record, when Marie insisted on staying, then I should have stayed too."

"No way. After what happened to Headley, I couldn't let you stay. You were getting on that plane whatever happened as far as I was concerned. As for Marie…well she had me over a barrel."

"Okay," said Lucas reluctantly, seeing Martinez's point. "You did what you thought was right," and he finally gave voice to a thought that had been nagging him all the way back on the plane: "I should have known she wouldn't leave. I suppose I wanted to believe she'd go with me…but look, thanks for going to the square and looking out for her. I'm grateful. Really."

"Well, she's a tiger. I'll say that for her. And if I find her, you'll be the first to know. Hey, I've got to go."

There was a click and then only the dial tone. What was it that one of his trainers had said? 'No story is worth dying for.' Try saying that to Marie, he thought.

"Time to go." Flo was standing at the door. "We've called everyone we can think of. Now we just have to wait." She pulled Lucas up from his seat and went back to her desk. "Go home and get some sleep. If we hear anything, we'll call you, but you'll be no good to anyone like this. Go and get some rest."

So, with a wave of thanks to Sheila, Lucas left. He descended the marble staircase and then out to the portico, the grey skies and a red London bus that took him back to the shelter of his flat, where he tumbled into bed, head throbbing, thinking sleep impossible.

He lay there trying to picture Marie. For what seemed an age he couldn't conjure her face but suddenly there she was standing in the palace square, next to Michel, proud, defiant, holding her head up. He pushed towards her, straining against the crowd, but progress was impossible. Hands clung to him; bodies gave no ground. Every time he looked, Marie was further away and, as she receded, Lucas lost consciousness.

CHAPTER 37

It was dark when the phone rang, hauling Lucas back from oblivion. For a moment, he didn't know where he was. The darkness was so complete. He groped for his watch and saw it was five am. He had slept for nearly twelve hours. He scrambled from his bed, flipped on the light and made it to the kitchen counter where the phone was still ringing. It was Martinez.

"Sorry to call at this hour Lucas, but I'm back at the Embassy and I've got some news. It's been mad here…"

"Marie, is she okay?" Lucas couldn't listen to any more without knowing. "Have you seen her?" He stopped himself from asking more questions, afraid that Martinez wouldn't know where to begin.

"I'm sorry buddy. I haven't, but I do have other news. I've just come from the airport where I put Colonel Chambert on one of our planes."

"Chambert's leaving?"

"Yeah. He thought I was doing him a favour, but there's a reception committee waiting for him in Miami. He'll be facing multiple charges for money laundering."

"So, you've got him. How on earth did you pull that off? He didn't just give himself up?"

"Well, it's been a hell of a night. And this morning there were huge demonstrations across the city. Everyone's been clamouring for him to go. It seems the Presidential Guard moved against him and in the end, he had no choice but to get out. They had him bottled up in the barracks. And when the crowd outside the palace realised the Guard had turned on him, it just became a massive celebration. It's like a carnival here. Anyway, at some point in all this, Chambert calls the Embassy, asking if we could get him safe passage. My guys scooped him up."

"He doesn't know about the charges against him?"

"I thought best not to mention them." Martinez chuckled. "Thought he might change his mind if he knew. He seems to think he'll be heading off to some safe haven – don't know what gave him that impression – but he'll find out soon enough. Oh, and I made it a condition that Lazarre and Toussaint left with him. We've got charges against them too. They'll all be picked up in Miami.

"Did you see Lazarre? Talk to him? Did he say anything about Marie?"

"Yeah, I got him on his own before we took him to the airport." Lucas heard a weary sigh down the line. "I did my best, Lucas, but I wanted them on that plane and didn't have much time. I really pushed him about Marie, tried to find out whether he'd got to her. But he just sat there. The bastard gave me nothing. He just looked at me with that grin on his face – clearly enjoying it. He's a real psycho." Martinez hesitated for a moment. "I couldn't be sure. I mean he'd never admit anything, but it was like he wanted me to think he'd got her. He looked so damned pleased with himself. I just wanted to murder him. And then time ran out, and I had to get him on the plane… I'm so sorry Lucas."

Lucas was struggling. All his worst fears crowded in on him, but eventually he managed a question – already knowing the answer:

"And there was no sign of Marie at the demonstration this morning?"

"No, we looked everywhere. My guys were scanning the crowd for ages, but they couldn't see her. Nothing."

"He didn't actually say he got her, though?" asked Lucas, grasping at hope. "I just can't imagine Marie missing the celebrations."

The lengthy silence from Martinez was more revealing than anything he could have said, but he did manage one last comment before the call ended.

"I really am sorry Lucas. But look, we'll keep searching. We're not giving up. And if I hear anything I'll be sure to let you know. Okay?"

Lucas dropped on to the sofa. A cold grey dawn revealed the houses across the road. He sat there alone trying to persuade himself that she might still be alive but all he could think of was Lazarre with that fixed sneer and the livid scar.

CHAPTER 38

"In real life, stories don't have endings." Carrick was having one of his more philosophical turns, staring at Lucas intently across the piles of paper on his desk, which seemed to have grown even higher since Lucas was last there.

"I suppose so," replied Lucas. "But at the time Headley's death felt like an ending. And Chambert's departure feels like a conclusion. But you're right. It doesn't end. There are too many unanswered questions: too many people missing or dead. I suppose they're kind of cadences not conclusions."

"Chambert's departure doesn't resolve anything. The army, thugs and traffickers aren't finished with Haiti yet. It's just another moment in time." Carrick leant back in his chair, hands behind his head, elbows wide. "But look, you caught it. That's what journalists do – live in moments. The narrative comes later – but conclusions? We don't do conclusions." Carrick slumped forward and picked up the airline tickets that were on his desk and tossed them across at Lucas who took them up and studied them, checking the details.

It was two days since he had heard from Martinez and he had spent all that time in his flat, gradually coming to terms with the fact that Marie was gone. The time had passed in a fog of regret, recrimination, and helplessness. Martinez had not called again, and Lucas understood only too well what that meant.

Two hours ago, Carrick had phoned asking him to go to Miami, and he had thrown himself at the opportunity, appalled at the idea of being alone any longer with his loss. Carrick had told him to come in, and here he was.

"So, how long do you want me there?"

"Well, a couple of months initially," said Carrick. You're still formally based in London, but we need someone covering the Miami beat until we can replace Headley. You've worked in the region so if you can fill in until we manage to make a full-time appointment…" Carrick fidgeted in his chair. It was unusual for him to sit this long. He needed the bustle of the newsroom. "And yeah – before you ask – you can apply, but it'll depend on the field. Don't go getting your hopes up. You've only been in this job for a few days…" Lucas was staring at the tickets in his hand. "Look, you don't have to go. You can take time off – as much as you need. I know you've been hit hard by this Marie thing."

Lucas sat up sharply at the mention of her name.

"No, no. I want to go. I need to keep busy. I can't sit in my flat any longer. It's the silence…" Carrick nodded.

"I know – it's hard. It's horrible to say it but if there's a body there's a chance of some sort of closure but the ones who just disappear…well they just leave us all in limbo. It's haunting – hard to deal with." Carrick leant forward, his chair complaining. "Don't underestimate how tough this'll be. I'll have the HR people check in with you while you're away, make sure you're alright. And if you need time off, you can have it."

Carrick stood. His need for action overcoming his brief display of concern.

"Sure," said Lucas, rising to his feet, grateful that the conversation was being curtailed. "I'll be on my way tomorrow." Carrick placed his hand on Lucas's back, simultaneously indicating both support and a desire to clear him out of his office so he could get back to work.

Lucas picked up the large kit bag from the floor, which Junior had pulled together earlier. It had all the equipment he would need. At Carrick's instruction, it had been delivered to his office. With the heavy bag over his shoulder, Lucas made his way across the newsroom. A sub editor wished him luck as he passed her desk. Word had already spread about his posting. He pushed through the swing door on to the landing and took the lift to the ground floor, the portico, and the street.

It was dusk. The sun had already set behind the tall buildings to the west of the Aldwych. The rain had stopped, but the dark clouds scudding overhead threatened much more to come. Lucas crossed the road into the gathering gloom and walked through the narrow streets of Covent Garden half-thinking he would find a bar to postpone his return to the flat.

The wind whistled into him, and he bent forward against its force: a man outwardly determined, but inside he was hollowed out. From the moment he had set foot on the plane in Port au Prince, he had been a casualty – powerless and in pain. Was this the price he had to pay for doing the job he had wanted so much?

He slackened his pace, staring down at the cobbled street that led him away from the Aldwych, oblivious to the office workers and tourists who pushed past him. The old cobbles beneath his feet looked back at him. They spoke to him of past lives and forgotten ways, all now invisible but still present, propping up the city, touching the soles of innumerable passers-by, telling anyone who would listen that everything that is stands on everything that ever was – inseparable.

He drifted on, pushing up the incline, past narrow alleys that ran behind the shops weaving away to other parts of the city – endlessly intricate, ready to confuse and disorientate the unwary visitor. Ahead on the corner, a wooden barrow selling iced drinks sat askew on the pavement by a wall with nobody there to serve. He was here. He was in Haiti. He was nowhere – cut adrift.

Wretched and alone, he passed the barrow and twisted and turned his way through a maze of side alleys until he found himself on a long lane meandering along the back of Covent Garden tube station. Small shop windows framed his path. All were shuttered. Only the faintest glow revealed what lay within. He felt suddenly very tired. His shoulder ached from carrying the heavy bag and he swung it down. It hit the cobbles with the sound of a dead man dropping. But its removal made no difference. He stood, a terrible weight still on him, weary of what had brought him to this place. Without Marie what was the point? If he was never to see her again, he didn't want to continue. What was his life worth without her passion and her will and her presence?

And as he stood there, the rain returned. A squall whipped down the lane, forcing him upright, and it was then that he saw her. She was in front of him, in the wet, her arms outstretched: Marie, miraculously present.

She wrapped him round. He could smell her, her cheek against his, her hair on his face, her body curving in to his. She was breathing fast against him, his lips on her skin, her neck damp with rain.

"It can't be you. Lazarre took you. You can't be here." Yet even as he spoke, he felt her presence, unmistakable on the dark street and he pulled her closer. "I won't let you go," his words muffled against her. "Not again. I can't lose you, not like I lost Zoe. I couldn't stand it. Please be here. Please stay…"

She said nothing and Lucas looked half expecting her to have vanished, but there she was in front of him. And it was then he remembered what Zoe had said – in that dark room before Toussaint and Lazarre arrived – when fear had brought her to him.

*Tell her…Don't wait…Tell her…you may never get this chance again…*And the words tumbled out of him, urgent and confused, mumbled at first, then louder, stronger against the growing storm.

"I love you. I love you. I've loved you since we first met. I need you…" The wind whipped the words from his lips, carrying them off, inaudible to anyone but him.

Too late, he thought. *It's too little, too late. First Zoe and now Marie…* and for a moment, he wished the elements would carry him off. But then he heard her, so close he could feel her breath against his face.

"I love you too. I've always loved you. I just can't be with you."

And part of him knew that there was only the wind and the rain and the cold, but he hung on.

I won't let go, he thought. *You showed me. You showed me what really matters. It's the spirit that lasts. Spirits go on forever. I'll hold on to that. It was you who told me that without others we're not truly ourselves and, now I'm here alone you're here to keep me whole. But I miss you… miss you… miss you…*

The rain slashed down. A rumble of thunder rolled over the rooftops, but in spite of it all Lucas didn't feel the cold. Water had penetrated to his skin and his skin had warmed it. This, he thought, was what it meant to be alive. This was what mattered, no matter how painful: giving yourself completely, being present, facing facts. Even when the fact was that the person you loved was not here, that she was lying somewhere beaten and bloody. Even if this was all that was left of her – a spirit blown by the wind, wordless in the elements, whispering of love in a violent world. He spoke her name, pleading for her to stay, and he reached for the chain around his neck, pulling it up with his fingers until the pendant shone in his hand. He held it out from his neck for her to see. He had kept it safe. And for a moment he saw her eyes shine, fixed on him, still proud, still defiant. And then she was gone.

***

Lucas did not remember how he got back to the flat. He stood, shivering uncontrollably, staring at the wet kit bag on the floor. Next to it were his soaking clothes. He had a towel round him. The meagre gas fire burned to his right by the tatty sofa, the heat too feeble to spread much warmth. The single overhead bulb spread its white light onto the bare walls and threadbare curtains, confirming that nobody really lived here. This was a place you passed through on the way to somewhere else – maybe never to return.

It's been little more than another dormitory, he thought, a place of isolation and sleep. Better to get out. Better to try to be that person Marie had seen in him…but how could he do that without her? He wiped his wet face on the towel and only then became conscious that the phone was ringing. Maybe it had been ringing for some time. He was in no state to know.

"Lucas, is that you?" Martinez's voice sounded strained.

Lucas saw his hand shaking. This call was the one he had been dreading. The final one.

"Yes – it's me," said Lucas – not asking the question that would provoke an answer he couldn't bear to hear.

"Sorry buddy. Not sure what time it is with you. I didn't check. You sound knackered, but I thought you would want to know as soon as we did. We found Marie. But look, it's not good."

"Found her? Where? Is she alive?" Lucas screwed his eyes, shutting himself up, silently urging Martinez to get it over with.

"My guys found her in one of the houses the army uses. She's in a bad way. Lazarre clearly got to her."

"Tell me," said Lucas, his stomach knotting hard. "Just give it to me straight."

"Well, you remember Headley in the hospital. She looks a lot like that. There's hardly a mark on her, but she wasn't conscious or at least not responding when they found her. It's that voodoo thing and – well we know what that can do. But look, I've got her on a flight. The medivac people will get her to a specialist unit today. The closest one is in Miami. I was wondering – can you get there?"

Could he get there? Was he mad? Of course, he'd get there. He'd swim. He'd run. She's alive. That's what he had seen in the street – her spirit, that look in her face, that life still burning, and now he could really see her. Go to her. Do something. Move.

"I'm on my way," said Lucas. "I'll catch a flight. I've already got tickets. Give me the address…"

"How could you have tickets? Lucas, I've only just told you…"

"Never mind that…" said Lucas, and he took down the address, grabbed his bags and picked up a taxi at the end of the street.

CHAPTER 39

It was mid-afternoon the next day when Lucas arrived at the hospital in Miami. The receptionist made a call and within minutes, a white-coated doctor was by his side.

"Lucas Gould?" He was a slight man, crisply efficient, with straight black hair swept back from a high forehead and a large name tag on his lapel: '*Dr Chen, professor, Tampa General*'. "We've been expecting you. Look, you'd better come with me. Let's get somewhere with more privacy."

Dr Chen pressed the buzzer on the video entry to the Intensive Care Unit and the large door swung open. He led the way past a reception desk where nurses bent over charts and busied themselves at computer screens. Lucas followed the professor to a small consultation room, taking in the long line of ICU cubicles running down an adjacent corridor. Each one was packed to head height with electronic equipment, and the air hummed with the bleeping of monitors.

"I'll be brief," Dr Chen said, directing Lucas to one of half a dozen plastic chairs, the only furniture in the room. "You'll be wanting to see Marie. I think you already know, the embassy in Port au Prince arranged for her to come here. She was admitted late yesterday afternoon. They told us you were coming."

"Yes," said Lucas, sitting down. "I've flown in from London. I got here as fast as I could. How is she?"

"Well, when she arrived, she was unconscious, very dehydrated. The paramedic notes said she may have been poisoned. And the doctors here called me in from Tampa." He pointed to his badge. "I'm a professor of toxicology at the Tampa poisons unit. I've done some work in Haiti, analysing some of the potions used in voodoo ceremonies. We think something like that is involved in this case."

"Marie was an expert on voodoo," said Lucas. "She studied it. And she made some enemies who might well have forced her to take something."

The doctor nodded. "Yeah, I talked to Martinez at the embassy. He filled me in on what she might have gone through. He told me about you." He leant forward, the concern clear on his face. "Look, our tests show that she's got a cocktail of toxins in her blood. I think that's what's causing the paralysis. The brain scan initially showed significantly reduced function, but she has been making progress this morning. It's a difficult case. She's essentially young and healthy. Her vitals are looking better and an hour ago she regained consciousness. She's been asking for you." Relief welled up in Lucas. He was going to see her, talk to her. This was so much better than he'd expected.

"Thank you doctor, that's good news…" he said, his optimism shining through.

"Well, yes," Dr Chen picked up quickly. "She's made progress. Frankly, much better than I expected. But I don't want to mislead you. She's very ill and I'm still concerned. I don't like what we've found. The lab analysed that mix of toxins and found traces of tetrodotoxin, for which there is no known antidote." Lucas's smile dissipated. The look on the professor's face gave Lucas that awful sense again of time running out on him.

"And what is it exactly – this poison?" he asked.

"Well, it's very rare. It can paralyse. And it can kill – quickly in the right quantity. The problem is we don't know how much she was originally given. But no amount is good. So, we're not out of the woods yet. I'm certainly not releasing her from the ICU." Lucas nodded grimly and Chen seemed to approve of the effect his words were having on him. "Look, I need to be straight with you. Above a certain level – in my experience – people don't survive a significant dose of tetrodotoxin. But look, whoever found her did well. No silly early interventions that might have made things worse. I know she wants to see you, so we'll take her off the oxygen for a short while and she may be able to talk. But don't stay too long and you need to know…well, the outcome's still very uncertain." Dr Chen stood. "I'll take you to her now."

Lucas stopped, suddenly remembering. "Her mother? She has a mother. Has she been told?"

"Yes," replied Chen. "I think we finally tracked her down this morning, but she's been travelling, and I don't think she'll be able to get here until tonight."

The professor took Lucas down the line of cubicles. Marie was in the last one. Two nurses obscured the scene, busily pushing monitors as far back from the bed as possible, making more room. One was bending over the bed, concentrating on the maze of tubes and wires that connected Marie to the equipment, and then she rolled up a plastic oxygen tent which had been covering Marie's head and shoulders. The nurses bustled, tested the alarms, and then stood back so Lucas could see Marie clearly for the first time.

Her face was pale on the pillow, eyes closed, arms straight out beside her on the bedspread, her slender form clearly visible under the tightly tucked sheet. She looked so fragile and there was a bruise on her upper lip which was slightly swollen. The two nurses hovered until – at a sign from the professor – they withdrew.

Lucas was not sure what to do. He hesitated to touch her. He still couldn't quite believe this ghostly figure was really Marie lying in front of him. The long silence before Martinez's phone call had convinced him he had lost her. And then the news and the hope and now this. Was this really the beautiful woman who had been his guide, helped him at every turn, opened her world to him, stood defiant in the square against all odds?

As Lucas watched, he saw a little tear in the corner of her eye, and he could no longer hold back. His face was against hers. He could feel her breathing, and her hand touched his back, holding him to her, and they lay there listening to the life in each other until Lucas pulled himself upright to look at her afresh. With his fingers, he gently dried her cheek, and her eyes flickered open. There was the same striking blue – like a pure, sun-struck sea with his shadow at its centre. Slowly, her hand reached up to his neck, and she felt for the chain, pulling it up gently to reveal the pendant.

"So, you've brought it back to me…"

"I wear it all the time," and there was the same light in her eyes from the night before.

"I know," said Marie, "I saw it last night. You showed me…"

"You can't have seen it last night, Marie," said Dr Chen. "You were here, unconscious. Lucas was in London." The doctor was looking troubled. "Lucas has only just got …"

"It's okay," said Lucas, a note of exasperation in his voice. "I know what she means." And they both looked across at the professor, who stared from one to the other before getting the message. He withdrew – taking his disbelief with him.

"I thought I'd lost you," Lucas said, holding Marie's hand, careful not to disturb the lines running to the monitors.

"You won't lose me." Marie's voice was little more than a whisper. "I'm not going anywhere."

She gave a slight cough, struggling to speak. He reached for some water, and she drank a little.

"What did he do to you?" Lucas bristled, thinking of Lazarre.

"Lazarre? He found me. I was in the crypt at St Mark. Someone must have told him, and they came for me. I don't remember much but they took me away, and I remember him forcing me to drink something and then I don't remember…"

"But you know what's happened, don't you?" said Lucas, realising that Marie wouldn't have heard about Chambert's flight. "Martinez flew them all out, Chambert, Lazarre, Toussaint. They've fled the country. They're under arrest here. They're going to be prosecuted. You can testify, we both can. Port au Prince is celebrating. You should be there." A smile spread across Marie's face.

"So, it was all worth it?" she whispered, and Lucas nodded and smiled back at her, drinking in the relief apparent on her face.

"We should go there," he said. "We can go together." And Marie's eyes widened as Lucas had seen before when she was urging him on, trying to understand him. "I'm going to be based in Miami. I've got a posting here – at least for a few months. So, I'll be close by. When you're well, we can go together." Marie's hand found his and squeezed. He thrilled at her touch, so happy to be with her again, just to look at her. But all the time the professor's warning was playing on his mind. He mustn't let this moment pass.

"Since you left me on that plane, I've thought about you all the time – about everything." He leaned in, speaking softly, needing to tell her. "I was so miserable when you left me. I just spiralled down. And it wasn't just about being apart – I know that in some ways that's inevitable. It was not knowing, not being able to talk to you, not sharing, feeling helpless, fearing the worst for you…" He came up short, suddenly daunted by all the things he wanted to say and not sure in what order to say them, not sure of the effect it would have. But he gathered himself and set to work, like a cane cutter, clearing away everything that stood between him and some respite.

"Look, I've thought about how impossible we are. How hard it would be for us to be together. You love Haiti. You're so committed to its future. We come from worlds apart. I want to work, to report, to go where I'm needed, but I've come to realise that we *could* be together, couldn't we? I mean, if we chose." Marie's eyes were locked on his, a faint smile still on her lips. "I know it's hard. I know so many things separate us –

culture, language, geography, I know how insanely difficult it would be. I mean look at your parents. They loved each other but couldn't be together, but I think we could – even if we had to spend long periods apart. I always thought such a relationship would be impossible, ridiculous. God knows, I've run away from the idea often enough." He took a deep breath, cutting through the honesty to the essence of what he needed to say: "But with you – anything's possible. So, one way or another I want to be with you. Marry you even, if you'll have me. I don't care what kind of ceremony: secular, Hindu, Christian, Voodoo – whatever you want, as long as it's forever."

Marie put her hand up and gently pressed her finger against his lips. He stopped talking. He stared down at her, not sure what she was thinking. Was this all too much? Too much to ask when she was so ill, so exhausted.

She turned her head to look at the water glass. Again, Lucas helped her, and she drank carefully. He put his hand behind her head to steady her. She was hot to the touch – too hot – and Lucas took a tissue and soaked it in water. He smoothed it across her brow, and she closed her eyes at his touch. Then she spoke – still a whisper, but she was clear and firm.

"If that's what you really want Lucas. We can be together. We can be apart too – but always together. Being in the same place isn't all that matters, is it? We think the same. We want the same things. We both believe in a world of ideas because we know ideas shape the world." Then her eyes looked in to his, he her sole focus. "When we stood together in the palace square, that's all any of us had; an idea about freedom and a desire to express it." She paused, suppressing a cough, and Lucas could see that talking was exhausting her.

"We can do this later," he said, but she gently shook her head and took his hand.

"It's okay. No time like the present. I want to talk." Lucas felt her fingers lace between his. "In the end, it's what we think that matters most, and you and I are kindred spirits. Different, but with so much in common." Lucas slowly moved their joined hands to rest on the pillow next to Marie's cascading hair and he leaned down gently to kiss her, but she moved her head, determined to have her say. "I'm difficult Lucas. You know that. I'm independent, impulsive, unreasonable ..." He managed to kiss her cheek and then he hovered over her, face to face, so close he could feel the waft of her words. "I want to rip things up by the roots, challenge lies, corruption. But you're different. You're cool. You stand back. You're an observer." She smiled. "So detached – I love you for that." His lips brushed hers briefly before she continued. "It's not action that changes the world. Ideas are the thing, and you love ideas, you let them flourish, watch them grow, take them out into the world." And then she kissed him, her lips fluttering briefly on his, every caress a punctuation for what she had to say. "So, we don't have to be together Lucas...we're together wherever we are... And the answer to your question is ...voodoo...if it's a voodoo wedding...Yes, of course...Yes."

And then there were no more words.

Lucas traced the contours of her face, feeling her beneath him, her breath quickening as he moved from cheek to chin to neck, returning to look at her again, eye to eye, all sense of loss and pain left behind in London. And for a moment, he felt this was a conclusion, a place of release, but he knew it was so much more than that. It was a beginning, a future opening up ahead of him, like the paths leading to Michel's house, complex, twisting but all leading to a place he wanted to be.

An alarm sounded above the bed. First one, then another.

The professor was behind him, shaking his head.

"That's it. You must leave now. We need to get her back on oxygen."

The nurses reappeared, checking the monitors, reaching for the plastic hood above her head.

Lucas rose reluctantly, feeling her weakly squeeze his hand before letting him go. The nurses brought down the tent. Oxygen hissed, sealing Marie away, an alarm still sounding.

"You can wait outside," said the professor. "Just for a moment. We'll do our best." And Lucas went back to the little consulting room on his own. He sat down, staring at the wall.

***

Many years later, looking back on his life from his old apartment high up on the corniche in Beirut, surrounded by artifacts from Haiti, he spent evenings reminiscing about his long and distinguished career as a foreign correspondent. He remembered in great detail the many uprisings and conflicts he had covered across three continents. He remembered the places: the dangers; the people; the horror; the self-sacrifice; and above all, the hope that people cling to when their world falls apart. The details never left him. They were contained in half a dozen books that bore his name and sold well at airports and railway terminuses. But whenever he thought of that day with Marie, the only woman he ever wanted to marry, he couldn't remember how he got from that small consulting room back to the entrance of the hospital. He could remember the professor. He remembered his warning, how he seemed to think that Marie's death was inevitable. But above everything that was said, and all that happened, what he remembered most clearly – and never wrote about – was walking out through the huge glass doors into the brilliant Florida sunshine. He remembered the loud swish as the doors slid shut behind him. He remembered looking up at the sun, which struck his face and warmed him through. And that extraordinary noise. It was the sound of a million rustling leaves, more leaves than there were in the world except they weren't leaves. They were birds. A huge number rising from every tree and every bush along the paths leading away from the hospital, flying high into the air, all separate, all together, moving as one and making the same sound he'd heard so vividly at the ceremony below Michel's house. Every soul in the world whispering, whispering in recognition of one of their own, the one who even now remained beside him watching the sun set over Beirut.

ACKNOWLEDGEMENTS

This book owes a lot to many fine international journalists at BBC World Service. Their influence permeates its pages. It's also intended as a small tribute to the BBC's Caribbean Service which essentially had two incarnations from 1939 - 1958 and 1988 to 2011 and showcased many great writers and journalists over the years.

My thanks to all of them and to my editors Amanda Horan and Jane Hammett, BJ for proof reading, Sheila and Charles, whose conversation in our garden led me to put pen to paper, to Nick for his endless encouragement, Adam and Clare for their brilliance and my wife Sue, whose support and feedback always spurred me on.

ABOUT THE AUTHOR

Jeremy Maxwell-Timmins was a producer and reporter at the BBC, covering major stories in the UK, the Americas and beyond. In 1994 he joined the Board of BBC World Service, where he was responsible for all media across the Americas Region and then Africa and Middle East. On leaving in 2010, he spent a decade working as a consultant with governments and media owners in countries emerging from conflict.

Before working in the media, he was a professional drummer, and now plays regularly with jazz and rock bands in Surrey where he lives with his wife and two children. He was educated at Kingswood School, Bath and has an English degree from Oxford University.

Printed in Great Britain
by Amazon

56723707R00219